DATE DUE

DEC 2 1 2003	
MAR - 8 2004	
JUL 2 4 2006	

GAYLORD   PRINTED IN U.S.A.

ON GLORIOUS WINGS

Forge Books edited by Stephen Coonts

Combat

Victory

On Glorious Wings

ON GLORIOUS WINGS

THE BEST FLYING STORIES OF THE CENTURY

EDITED AND INTRODUCED BY

STEPHEN COONTS

A TOM DOHERTY ASSOCIATES BOOK

NEW YORK

ON GLORIOUS WINGS: THE BEST FLYING STORIES OF THE CENTURY

Copyright © 2003 by Stephen Coonts

A Forge Book
Published by Tom Doherty Associates, LLC
175 Fifth Avenue
New York, NY 10010

www.tor.com

Forge® is a registered trademark of Tom Doherty Associates, LLC.

Library of Congress Cataloging-in-Publication Data

On glorious wings : the best flying stories of the century / [compiled by] Stephen Coonts.—
1st ed.
      p. cm.
   "A Tom Doherty Associates book."
   ISBN 0-312-87724-2 (acid-free paper)
    1. Aeronautics—Fiction. 2. Air pilots—Fiction. 3. Air pilots, Military—Fiction. 4. Air warfare—Fiction. 5. Air travel—Fiction. 6. Flight—Fiction. 7. Short stories, American.
I. Coonts, Stephen, 1946–   813
                                                                        on
PS648.A365O5 2003   11.03
813'.5080356—dc21

                                                              2003046853

First Edition: October 2003

Printed in the United States of America

0   9   8   7   6   5   4   3   2   1

COPYRIGHT ACKNOWLEDGMENTS

Contents

INTRODUCTION

If any one tangible item could be the symbol of the twentieth century, that item would be the airplane. No invention in the history of our species has had a greater impact on human life than the contraption born in a Dayton, Ohio, bicycle shop at the dawn of the twentieth century.

For hundreds of years people could see how flying machines would revolutionize life on earth. Some of the very best brains of the past speculated on how a machine might be made to fly, and some of those ideas were very good. Still, numerous attempts that ended in failure caused early experimenters to be the butt of crude humor. The Wright brothers worked in secret for business reasons, but also because they didn't want to be laughed at. When they actually achieved powered flight on December 17, 1903, few believed it. The reality of heavier-than-air flight had to be proven over and over again.

Imagine yourself standing in a Dayton, Ohio, bicycle shop, about 1902, trying to explain Boeing 747s and stealth fighters to two bicycle mechanics busy tinkering with wood and canvas and piano wire on something they call the "Flyer." Do you think they would believe much of what you said?

Yet once a person saw a flying machine noisily soaring on canvas wings, swooping and gliding, moving at the will of the pilot through the great open spaces of the sky, his imagination was set free. *Oh, to fly, to fly . . . like a bird on the wing . . . to fly free. . . .*

Man had conquered the land and the sea, and now the sky. It was heady stuff. An ancient dream had been fulfilled, and the world was never the same again.

After a hundred years of flight, many people still feel a twinge of awe when they see an airplane accelerate down a runway or watch it move across the sky under a deck of clouds . . . at least I do.

Engineers and scientists can talk until they are blue, but to me there is something a bit . . . magical . . . about the whole thing. An airplane is really just a magic carpet with wings, isn't it? You get on in New York; two meals and a snack later you get off in Europe. And just what did you see in the interim? Some clouds, a movie?

Even today, after a century of aviation, most people still feel some tiny sense of wonder when they see an airplane. Imagine the delight our grandparents and great-grandparents felt when *they* saw an airplane in the sky for the very first time.

Early in the century the airplane came to symbolize danger and adventure. Danger sold well, so the first pilots posed as daredevils to raise money to finance their aviation adventures. Every crash—and there were many—only added to the delicious aura of courage and romance that surrounded those daring few who flew.

Aviation as an industry could not live with the "dangerous" label. Emphasizing safety, the government stepped in, licensing the machines and regulating the companies that manufactured and flew them and setting standards for and licensing the men and women who sat in the cockpits.

Flying became glamorous. The airplane was transformed into a magic carpet to whisk people to far-away places and extraordinary adventures. One has only to look at photos of the early years of air travel to see how well that image sold: The passengers are uniformly dressed to the nines, the men in suits and ties, the women in the latest fashions. Flying was the realm of successful, adventurous people living life to the hilt.

In the 1950s the jet engine was married to the airliner. The number of people who could be quickly and safely carried across oceans expanded exponentially, which led to the most extraordinary exchange of people, technology, culture, thought, and philosophy between continents that the world has ever seen. For good or ill, the exchange stimulated quantum changes in the way people live worldwide, changes that occurred at an ever-accelerating pace: changes in mores and ways of thinking about problems which used to take centuries now happened in decades. The airplane transformed the world from a huge, far-flung place of curious people living different ways of life that they learned from their ancestors into a single, interdependent global village with a single, interdependent economy. And, alas, a single culture, a technology-intense westernized one that many people resent.

Love it or hate it, the revolution caused by the airplane has just begun. The free flow of people, products, and ideas made possible by the airplane will continue to accelerate the rate of change in the twenty-first century. By the end of the next century, one suspects that nations as we know them will become obsolete, that mankind will live under some type of world government, with a world police force to maintain public order, which we now know to be an essential precondition to ever more sophisticated technology and a growing world economy.

The warplane produced more complex emotions than barnstormers or airliners. As we look back at early military aviation, we must see it against the background of the nearly universal military experience of the age, which was mass armies of draftees, millions of them, slogging to the slaughter through mud, artillery barrages, machine-gun bursts, and deadly clouds of poison gas. The aviator aloft in the clean, blue sky, betting his life on his skill, honoring the valor of his foe, was almost a throw-back to ages long past. The fliers weren't called the knights of the sky for nothing. Their courage and honor seemed the only bright spots in an age of universal, total war.

Unfortunately the image was mostly propaganda. By definition, fighter pilots are assassins. Throughout the century the most successful fighter pilots have been men who slipped up on their unaware opponents, quickly shot them in the back and made their escape before the victims' friends could successfully retaliate.

Today, in the age of push-button aerial warfare, not the faintest whiff of chivalry survives. The winner of a battle in the skies is the man, or woman, who electronically detects his opponent first and launches a missile that the opponent cannot avoid. Aerial battles today are usually won by the pilot flying the most technically advanced fighter. Still, the vision of a hero or heroine playing a high-tech game with their life on the line fascinates us.

Bomber crews—we could write ten volumes about the vast gulf between the romance and the reality of aerial bombardment. Fortunately we don't have to. Some really great novelists have explored that field for us; excerpts of their work are included in this volume.

The airplane's ability to deliver an atomic weapon revolutionized human life: This capability led to the Cold War, which led to political and national alliances that touched the life of every human on the planet. It is not overstating the case to say that the world looks the way it does today because of the airplane.

At the end of the century we have come full circle. Once again the airplane is a symbol of danger and vulnerability. At the dawn of the twenty-first century the airliner is both a flying bus for the routine carriage of extraordinary numbers of people and stupendous tonnages of cargo . . . and a tempting target for lunatics and terrorists, a flying sardine can packed with innocent people just waiting to be spectacularly murdered. As we learned on September 11, 2001, the airliner can also serve as a kamikaze missile to destroy large buildings, murder thousands, and crack the foundations of western civilization.

The idea that civilization today is so vulnerable is troubling. That there are so many who wish to destroy it in the name of religion, or to right imagined wrongs, or simply because their piece of the pie isn't big enough, troubles us profoundly. Once again we long for "the good old days," for the noon of the British empire when civilized people could travel anywhere on earth, free from murder and mayhem by the great unwashed.

Since the airplane had such an extraordinary impact in the twentieth century, it was inevitable that stories about flying became an integral part of the literature of that century. Some of the very best writers wrote them. Some of the very best still do.

I am always irritated by people who tell me that they only read nonfiction. They are missing a great deal. Fiction is art, and as such is far more eloquent than the dry language of the scientist or historian. Only in fiction can the true reality of our humanity, our mortality, be thoroughly explored. Only in fiction can we examine the vast gulf that usually separates perception and reality. Only in fiction can we marvel at the depth and breadth of the chasm between the world as it is and the world as we wish it to be. Only in fiction can the real truth of the human condition be told in words.

Fiction is, by definition, written to entertain, but the fiction we find most satisfying is usually grounded in universal truths that speak to humans of every time and culture. Many of the stories contained in this book are of this type.

One of the greatest advantages of fiction, to my mind, is the storyteller's freedom to tell as much or as little of everyone's story as he chooses. Only in fiction can we see the world and all its creatures as God sees it. We can hear the doomed aviator's prayers as the night fighter stalks him, we can see the bombs rushing down, we can huddle fearfully with the people in the trenches awaiting random death. In fiction we can see everyone and everything and we can know the length and breadth and depth of the human reality. And fiction allows us to see the wonder of this great mystery we call flight.

Buckle your seat belt and open your mind. In this collection you will find excerpts from some of the best flying stories of the first century of flight. Enjoy.

Stephen Coonts

THE BALLOON HOAX

by EDGAR ALLAN POE

We begin this volume with two tales written before the dawn of the age of powered flight—one by the great American writer Edgar Allan Poe, the other by the Frenchman Jules Verne.

Like the legions of scribblers who would follow him, Poe was usually desperate for money. In 1844 he wrote and submitted to the *New York Sun* a story he assured them was absolute fact, and in their haste to be the first to break the story, they paid him and ran the tale as news. Two days later they sheepishly published a retraction. In the interim, of course, they sold a lot of newspapers.

Poe wisely played on the public's fascination with balloons and the widespread sense that someday, perhaps soon, man would conquer the air in the same way he had conquered the sea. If it wasn't true . . . well, it ought to be!

To everyone who ever looked up
when they heard an airplane

Astounding News by Express, *via* Norfolk!—The Atlantic crossed in Three Days! Signal Triumph of Mr. Monck Mason's Flying Machine!—Arrival at Sullivan's Island, near Charleston, S.C., of Mr. Mason, Mr. Robert Holland, Mr. Henson, Mr. Harrison Ainsworth, and four others, in the Steering Balloon, *Victoria,* after a passage of Seventy-five Hours from Land to Land! Full Particulars of the Voyage!

The great problem is at length solved! The air, as well as the earth and the ocean, has been subdued by science, and will become a common and convenient highway for mankind. *The Atlantic has been actually crossed in a Balloon!* and this too without difficulty—without any great apparent danger—with thorough control of the machine—and in the inconceivably brief period of seventy-five hours from shore to shore! By the energy of an agent at Charleston, S.C., we are enabled to be the first to furnish the public with a detailed account of this most extraordinary voyage, which was performed between Saturday, the 6th instant, at 11 A.M., and 2 P.M., on Tuesday, the 9th instant, by Sir Everard Bringhurst; Mr. Osborne, a nephew of Lord Bentinck's; Mr. Monck Mason and Mr. Robert Holland, the well-known aeronauts; Mr. Harrison Ainsworth, author of *Jack Sheppard,* &c.; and Mr. Henson, the projector of the late unsuccessful flying machine—with two seamen from Woolwich—in all, eight persons. The particulars furnished below may be relied on as authentic and accurate in every respect, as, with a slight exception, they are copied *verbatim* from the joint diaries of Mr. Monck Mason and Mr. Harrison Ainsworth, to whose politeness our agent is also indebted for much verbal information respecting the balloon itself, its construction, and other matters of interest. The only alteration in the MS. received, has been made for the purpose of throwing the hurried account of our agent, Mr. Forsyth, in a connected and intelligible form.

THE BALLOON

Two very decided failures, of late—those of Mr. Henson and Sir George Cayley—had much weakened the public interest in the subject of aerial navigation. Mr. Henson's scheme (which at first was considered very feasible even by men of science), was founded upon the principle of an inclined plane, started from an eminence by an extrinsic force, applied and continued by the revolution of impinging vanes, in form and number resembling the vanes of a windmill. But, in all the experiments made with models at the Adelaide Gallery, it was found that the operation of these fans not only did not propel the machine, but actually impeded its flight. The only propelling force it ever exhibited, was the mere *impetus* acquired from the descent of the inclined plane; and this *impetus* carried the machine farther when the vanes were at rest than when they were in motion— a fact which sufficiently demonstrates their inutility; and in the absence of the propelling, which was also the *sustaining* power, the whole fabric would necessarily descend. This consideration led Sir George Cayley to think only of adapting a propeller to some machine having of itself an independent power of support—in a word, to a balloon; the idea, however, being novel, or original, with Sir George, only so far as regards the mode of its application to practice. He exhibited a model of his invention at the Polytechnic Institution. The propelling principle, or power, was here, also, applied to interrupted surfaces, or vanes, put in revolution. These vanes were four in number, but were found entirely ineffectual in moving the balloon, or in aiding its ascending power. The whole project was thus a complete failure.

It was at this juncture that Mr. Monck Mason (whose voyage from Dover to Weilburg in the balloon, *Nassau,* occasioned so much excitement in 1837) conceived the idea of employing the principle of the Archimedean screw for the purpose of propulsion through the air—rightly attributing the failure of Mr. Henson's scheme, and of Sir George Cayley's, to the interruption of surface in the independent vanes. He made the first public experiment at Willis's Rooms, but afterwards removed his model to the Adelaide Gallery.

Like Sir George Cayley's balloon, his own was an ellipsoid. Its length was thirteen feet six inches—height, six feet eight inches. It contained about three hundred and twenty cubic feet of gas, which, if pure hydrogen, would support twenty-one pounds upon its first inflation, before the gas has time to deteriorate or escape. The weight of the whole machine and apparatus was seventeen pounds—leaving about four pounds to spare. Beneath the center of the balloon, was a frame of light wood, about nine feet long, and rigged on to the balloon itself with a network in the customary manner. From this framework was suspended a wicker basket or car.

The screw consists of an axis of hollow brass tube, eighteen inches in length, through which, upon a semi-spiral inclined at fifteen degrees, pass a series of steel wire radii, two feet long, and thus projecting a foot on either side. These radii are connected at the outer extremities by two bands of flattened wire—the whole in this manner forming the framework of the screw, which is completed by a covering of oiled silk cut into gores, and tightened so as to present a tolerably uniform surface. At each end of its axis this screw is supported by pillars of hollow brass tube descending from the hoop. In the lower ends of these tubes are holes in which the pivots of the axis revolve. From the end of the axis which is next the car, proceeds a shaft of steel, connecting the screw with the pinion of a piece of spring machinery fixed in the car. By the operation of this spring, the screw is made to revolve with great rapidity, communicating a progressive motion to the whole. By means of the rudder, the machine was readily turned in any direction. The spring was of great power, compared with its dimensions, being capable of raising forty-five pounds upon a barrel of four inches diameter, after the first turn, and gradually increasing as it was wound up. It weighed, altogether, eight pounds six ounces. The rudder was a light frame of cane covered with silk, shaped somewhat like a battledoor, and was about three feet long, and at the widest, one foot. Its weight was about two ounces. It could be turned *flat*, and directed upwards or downwards, as well as to the right or left; and thus enabled the aeronaut to transfer the resistance of the air which in an inclined position it must generate in its passage, to any side upon which he might desire to act; thus determining the balloon in the opposite direction.

This model (which, through want of time, we have necessarily described in an imperfect manner) was put in action at the Adelaide Gallery, where it accomplished a velocity of five miles per hour; although, strange to say, it excited very little interest in comparison with the previous complex machine of Mr. Henson—so resolute is the world to despise anything which carries with it an air of simplicity. To accomplish the great desideratum of aerial navigation, it was very generally supposed that some exceedingly complicated application must be made of some unusually profound principle in dynamics.

So well satisfied, however, was Mr. Mason of the ultimate success of his invention, that he determined to construct immediately, if possible, a balloon of sufficient capacity to test the question by a voyage of some extent—the original design being to cross the British Channel, as before, in the *Nassau* balloon. To carry out his views, he solicited and obtained the patronage of Sir Everard Bringhurst and Mr. Osborne, two gentlemen well known for scientific acquirement, and especially for the interest they have exhibited in the progress of aerostation. The project, at the desire of Mr. Osborne, was kept a profound secret from the public—the only persons entrusted with the design being those actually engaged in the construction of the machine, which was built (under the superintendence of Mr. Mason, Mr. Holland, Sir Everard Bringhurst, and Mr. Osborne) at the seat of the latter gentleman near Penstruthal, in Wales. Mr. Henson, accompanied by his friend Mr. Ainsworth, was admitted to a private view of the balloon, on Saturday last— when the two gentlemen made final arrangements to be included in the adventure. We are not informed for what reason the two seamen were also included in the party—but, in the course of a day or two, we shall put our readers in possession of the minutest particulars respecting this extraordinary voyage.

The balloon is composed of silk, varnished with the liquid gum caoutchouc. It is of vast dimensions, containing more than 40,000 cubic feet of gas; but as coal gas was employed in place of the more expensive and inconvenient hydrogen, the supporting power of the machine, when fully inflated, and immediately after inflation, is not more than about 2500 pounds. The coal gas is not only much less costly, but is easily procured and managed.

For its introduction into common use for purposes of aerostation, we are indebted to Mr. Charles Green. Up to his discovery, the process of inflation was not only exceedingly expensive, but uncertain. Two, and even three days, have frequently been wasted in futile attempts to procure a sufficiency of hydrogen to fill a balloon, from which it had great tendency to escape owing to its extreme subtlety, and its affinity for the surrounding atmosphere. In a balloon sufficiently perfect to retain its contents of coal gas unaltered, in quality or amount, for six months, an equal quantity of hydrogen could not be maintained in equal purity for six weeks.

The supporting power being estimated at 2500 pounds, and the united weights of the party amounting only to about 1200, there was left a surplus of 1300, of which again 1200 was exhausted by ballast, arranged in bags of different sizes, with their respective weights marked upon them—by cordage, barometers, telescopes, barrels containing provision for a fortnight, water casks, cloaks, carpetbags, and various other indispensable matters, including a coffee-warmer, contrived for warming coffee by means of slacklime, so as to dispense altogether with fire, if it should be judged prudent to do so. All these articles, with the exception of the ballast, and a few trifles, were suspended from the hoop over head. The car is much smaller and lighter, in proportion, than the one appended to the model. It is formed of a light wicker, and is wonderfully strong for so frail-looking a machine. Its rim is about four feet deep. The rudder is also very much larger, in proportion, than that of the model; and the screw is considerably smaller. The balloon is furnished, besides, with a grapnel and a guide-rope; which latter is of the most indispensable importance. A few words, in explanation, will here be necessary for such of our readers as are not conversant with the details of aerostation.

As soon as the balloon quits the earth, it is subjected to the influence of many circumstances tending to create a difference in its weight; augmenting or diminishing its ascending power. For example, there may be a disposition of dew upon the silk, to the extent, even, of several hundred pounds; ballast has then to be thrown out, or the machine may descend. This ballast being discarded, and a clear sunshine evaporating the dew, and at the same time expanding the gas in the silk, the whole will again

24

rapidly ascend. To check this ascent, the only resource is (or rather was, until Mr. Green's invention of the guide rope) the permission of the escape of gas from the valve; but in the loss of gas is a proportionate general loss of ascending power; so that, in a comparatively brief period, the best constructed balloon must necessarily exhaust all its resources, and come to the earth. This was the great obstacle to voyages of length.

The guide rope remedies the difficulty in the simplest manner conceivable. It is merely a very long rope which is suffered to trail from the car, and the effect of which is to prevent the balloon from changing its level in any material degree. If, for example, there should be a deposition of moisture upon the silk, and the machine begins to descend in consequence, there will be no necessity for discharging ballast to remedy the increase of weight, for it is remedied, or counteracted, in an exactly just proportion, by the deposit on the ground of just so much of the end of the rope as is necessary. If, on the other hand, any circumstances should cause undue levity, and consequent ascent, this levity is immediately counteracted by the additional weight of rope upraised from the earth. Thus, the balloon can neither ascend nor descend, except within very narrow limits, and its resources, either in gas or ballast, remain comparatively unimpaired. When passing over an expanse of water, it becomes necessary to employ small kegs of copper or wood, filled with liquid ballast of a lighter nature than water. These float, and serve all the purposes of a mere rope on land. Another most important office of the guide rope, is to point out the *direction* of the balloon. The rope *drags,* either on land or sea, while the balloon is free; the latter, consequently, is always in advance, when any progress whatever is made: a comparison, therefore, by means of the compass, of the relative positions of the two objects, will always indicate the course. In the same way, the angle formed by the rope with the vertical axis of the machine, indicates the *velocity*. When there is *no* angle—in other words, when the rope hangs perpendicularly, the whole apparatus is stationary; but the larger the angle, that is to say, the farther the balloon precedes the end of the rope, the greater the velocity; and the converse.

As the original design was to cross the British Channel, and alight as near Paris as possible, the voyagers had taken the precaution to prepare themselves with passports directed to all parts of the Continent, specifying the nature of the expedition, as in the case of the *Nassau* voyage, and entitling the adventurers to exemption from the usual formalities of office: unexpected events, however, rendered these passports superfluous.

The inflation was commenced very quietly at daybreak, on Saturday morning, the 6th instant, in the Court-Yard of Weal-Vor House, Mr. Osborne's seat, about a mile from Penstruthal, in North Wales; and at 7 minutes past 11, everything being ready for departure, the balloon was set free, rising gently but steadily, in a direction nearly south; no use being made, for the first half hour, of either the screw or the rudder. We proceed now with the journal, as transcribed by Mr. Forsyth from the joint MSS. of Mr. Monck Mason and Mr. Ainsworth. The body of the journal, as given, is in the handwriting of Mr. Mason, and a P.S. is appended, each day, by Mr. Ainsworth, who has in preparation, and will shortly give the public, a more minute and, no doubt, a thrillingly interesting account of the voyage.

THE JOURNAL

Saturday, April the 6th.—Every preparation likely to embarrass us, having been made overnight, we commenced the inflation this morning at daybreak; but owing to a thick fog, which encumbered the folds of the silk and rendered it unmanageable, we did not get through before nearly eleven o'clock. Cut loose, then, in high spirits, and rose gently but steadily, with a light breeze at north, which bore us in the direction of the

British Channel. Found the ascending force greater than we had expected; and as we arose higher and so got clear of the cliffs, and more in the sun's rays, our ascent became very rapid. I did not wish, however, to lose gas at so early a period of the adventure, and so concluded to ascend for the present. We soon ran out our guide rope; but even when we had raised it clear of the earth, we still went up very rapidly. The balloon was unusually steady, and looked beautifully. In about ten minutes after starting, the barometer indicated an altitude of 15,000 feet. The weather was remarkably fine, and the view of the subjacent country—a most romantic one when seen from any point—was now especially sublime. The numerous deep gorges presented the appearance of lakes, on account of the dense vapors with which they were filled, and the pinnacles and crags to the southeast, piled in inextricable confusion, resembled nothing so much as the giant cities of Eastern fable. We were rapidly approaching the mountains in the south; but our elevation was more than sufficient to enable us to pass them in safety. In a few minutes we soared over them in fine style; and Mr. Ainsworth, with the seamen, were surprised at their apparent want of altitude when viewed from the car, the tendency of great elevation in a balloon being to reduce inequalities of the surface below, to nearly a dead level. At half-past eleven, still proceeding nearly south, we obtained our first view of the Bristol Channel; and, in fifteen minutes afterwards, the line of breakers on the coast appeared immediately beneath us, and we were fairly out at sea. We now resolved to let off enough gas to bring our guide rope, with the buoys affixed, into the water. This was immediately done, and we commenced a gradual descent. In about twenty minutes our first buoy dipped, and at the touch of the second soon afterwards, we remained stationary as to elevation. We were all now anxious to test the efficiency of the rudder and screw, and we put them both into requisition forthwith, for the purpose of altering our direction more to the eastward, and in a line for Paris. By means of the rudder we instantly effected the necessary change of direction, and our course was brought nearly at right angles to that of the wind; when we set in motion the spring of the screw, and were rejoiced to find it propel us readily as desired. Upon this we gave nine hearty cheers, and dropped in the sea a bottle, enclosing a slip of parchment with a brief account of the principle of the invention. Hardly, however, had we done with our rejoicings, when an unforeseen accident occurred which discouraged us in no little degree. The steel rod connecting the spring with the propeller was suddenly jerked out of place, at the car end (by a swaying of the car through some movement of one of the two seamen we had taken up), and in an instant hung dangling out of reach, from the pivot of the axis of the screw. While we were endeavoring to regain it, our attention being completely absorbed, we became involved in a strong current of wind from the east, which bore us, with rapidly increasing force, towards the Atlantic. We soon found ourselves driving out to sea at the rate of not less, certainly, than fifty or sixty miles an hour, so that we came up with Cape Clear, at some forty miles to our north, before we had secured the rod, and had time to think what we were about. It was now that Mr. Ainsworth made an extraordinary, but to my fancy, a by no means unreasonable or chimerical proposition, in which he was instantly seconded by Mr. Holland—viz.: that we should take advantage of the strong gale which bore us on, and in place of beating back to Paris, make an attempt to reach the coast of North America. After slight reflection I gave a willing assent to this bold proposition, which (strange to say) met with objection from the two seamen only. As the stronger party, however, we overruled their fears, and kept resolutely upon our course. We steered due west; but as the trailing of the buoys materially impeded our progress, and we had the balloon abundantly at command, either for ascent or descent, we first threw out fifty pounds of ballast, and then wound up (by means of a windlass) so much of a rope as brought it quite clear of the sea. We perceived the effect of this maneuver immediately, in a vastly increased rate of progress; and, as the gale freshened, we flew with a velocity nearly inconceivable; the guide rope flying out behind the car like a streamer from a vessel. It is needless to say that a very short time sufficed us to lose sight of the coast. We passed over innumerable vessels of all kinds, a few of which were endeavoring to beat up, but the most of them lying to. We occasioned the greatest excitement on board all—an excitement greatly relished by ourselves, and especially by our two men, who, now under the influence of a dram of Geneva, seemed resolved to give all scruple, or fear, to the wind. Many of the vessels fired signal guns; and in all we were saluted with loud cheers (which we heard with surprising distinctness) and the waving of caps and handkerchiefs. We kept on in this manner throughout the day, with no material incident, and, as the shades of night closed around us, we made a rough estimate of the distance traversed. It could not have been less than five hundred miles, and was probably much more. The propeller was kept in constant operation, and, no doubt, aided our progress materially. As the sun went down, the gale freshened into an absolute hurricane, and the ocean beneath was clearly visible on account of its phosphorescence. The wind was from the east all night, and gave us the brightest omen of success. We suffered no little from cold, and the dampness of the atmosphere was most unpleasant; but the ample space in the car enabled us to lie down, and by means of cloaks and a few blankets, we did sufficiently well.

P.S. [by Mr. Ainsworth]. The last nine hours have been unquestionably the most exciting of my life. I can conceive nothing more sublimating than the strange peril and novelty of an adventure such as this. May God grant that we succeed! I ask not success for mere safety to my insignificant person, but for the sake of human knowledge and—for the vastness of the triumph. And yet the feat is only so evidently feasible that the sole wonder is why men have scrupled to attempt it before. One single gale such as now befriends us—let such a tempest whirl forward a balloon for four or five days (these gales often last longer) and the voyager will be easily borne, in that period, from coast to coast. In view of such a gale the broad Atlantic becomes a mere lake. I am more struck, just now, with the supreme silence which reigns in the sea beneath us, notwithstanding its agitation, than with any other phenomenon presenting itself. The waters give up no voice to the heavens. The immense flaming ocean writhes and is tortured uncomplainingly. The mountainous surges suggest the idea of innumerable dumb gigantic fiends struggling in impotent agony. In a night such as is this to me, a man *lives*—lives a whole century of ordinary life—nor would I forego this rapturous delight for that of a whole century of ordinary existence.

Sunday, the 7th [Mr. Mason's MS.]. This morning the gale, by 10, had subsided to an eight or nine knot breeze (for a vessel at sea), and bears us, perhaps, thirty miles per hour, or more. It has veered, however, very considerably to the north; and now, at sundown we are holding our course due west, principally by the screw and rudder, which answer their purposes to admiration. I regard the project as thoroughly successful, and the easy navigation of the air in any direction (not exactly in the teeth of a gale) as no longer problematical. We could not have made head against the strong wind of yesterday; but, by ascending, we might have got out of its influence, if requisite. Against a pretty stiff breeze, I feel convinced, we can make our way with the propeller. At noon today, ascended to an elevation of nearly 25,000 feet, by discharging ballast. Did this to search for a more direct current, but found none so favorable as the one we are now in. We have an abundance of gas to take us across this small pond, even should the voyage last three weeks. I have not the slightest fear for the result. The difficulty has been strangely exaggerated and misapprehended. I can choose my current, and should I find *all* currents against me, I can make very tolerable headway with the propeller. We have had no incidents worth recording. The night promises fair.

P.S. [by Mr. Ainsworth]. I have little to record, except the fact (to me quite a surprising one) that, at an elevation equal to that of Cotopaxi, I experienced neither very intense cold, nor headache, nor difficulty of breathing; neither, I find, did Mr. Mason, nor Mr. Holland, nor Sir Everard. Mr. Osborne complained of constriction of the chest—but this soon wore off. We have flown at a great rate during the day, and we must be more than halfway across the Atlantic. We have passed over some twenty or thirty vessels of various kinds, and all seem to be delightfully astonished. Crossing the ocean in a balloon is not so difficult a feat after all. *Omne ignotum pro magnifico. Mem:* at 25,000 feet elevation the sky appears nearly black, and the stars are distinctly visible; while the sea does not seem convex (as one might suppose), but absolutely and most unequivocally concave.*

Monday, the 8th [Mr. Mason's MS.]. This morning we had again some little trouble with the rod of the propeller, which must be entirely remodeled, for fear of serious accident—I mean the

---

*Note.—Mr. Ainsworth has not attempted to account for this phenomenon, which, however, is quite susceptible of explanation. A line dropped from an elevation of 25,000 feet, perpendicularly to the surface of the earth (or sea), would form the perpendicular of a right-angled triangle, of which the base would extend from the right angle to the horizon, and the hypothenuse from the horizon to the balloon. But the 25,000 feet of altitude is little or nothing, in comparison with the extent of the prospect. In other words, the base and hypothenuse of the supposed triangle would be so long when compared with the perpendicular, that the two former may be regarded as nearly parallel. In this manner the horizon of the aeronaut would appear to be *on a level* with the car. But, as the point immediately beneath him seems, and is, at a great distance below him, it seems, of course, also, at a great distance below the horizon. Hence the impression of *concavity;* and this impression must remain, until the elevation shall bear so great a proportion to the extent of prospect, that the apparent parallelism of the base and hypothenuse disappears—when the earth's real convexity must become apparent.

steel rod, not the vanes. The latter could not be improved. The wind has been blowing steadily and strongly from the northeast all day; and so far fortune seems bent upon favoring us. Just before day, we were all somewhat alarmed at some odd noises and concussions in the balloon, accompanied with the apparent rapid subsidence of the whole machine. These phenomena were occasioned by the expansion of the gas, through increase of heat in the atmosphere, and the consequent disruption of the minute particles of ice with which the network had become encrusted during the night. Threw down several bottles to the vessels below. See one of them picked up by a large ship— seemingly one of the New York line packets. Endeavored to make out her name, but could not be sure of it. Mr. Osborne's telescope made it out something like "Atalanta." It is now 12 at night, and we are still going nearly west at a rapid pace. The sea is peculiarly phosphorescent.

P.S. [by Mr. Ainsworth]. It is now 2 A.M., and nearly calm, as well as I can judge—but it is very difficult to determine this point, since we move with the air so completely. I have not slept since quitting Wheal-Vor, but can stand it no longer, and must take a nap. We cannot be far from the American coast.

Tuesday, the 9th [Mr. Ainsworth's MS.]. *One P.M. We are in full view of the low coast of South Carolina.* The great problem is accomplished. We have crossed the Atlantic—fairly and easily crossed it in a balloon! God be praised! Who shall say that any- thing is impossible hereafter?

The Journal here ceases. Some particulars of the descent were communicated, however, by Mr. Ainsworth to Mr. Forsyth. It was nearly dead calm when the voyagers first came in view of the coast, which was immediately recognized by both the sea- men, and by Mr. Osborne. The latter gentleman having acquaintances at Fort Moultrie, it was immediately resolved to descend in its vicinity. The balloon was brought over the beach (the tide being out and the sand hard, smooth, and admirably adapted for a descent), and the grapnel let go, which took firm hold at once. The inhabitants of the island, and of the fort, thronged out, of course, to see the balloon; but it was with the greatest difficulty that anyone could be made to credit the actual voyage—*the crossing of the Atlantic.* The grapnel caught at 2 P.M., precisely; and thus the whole voyage was completed in seventy-five hours; or rather less, counting from shore to shore. No serious accident occurred. No real danger was at any time apprehended. The balloon was exhausted and secured without trouble; and when the MS. from which this narrative is compiled was despatched from Charleston; the party were still at Fort Moultrie. Their farther intentions were not ascertained; but we can safely promise our readers some additional information either on Monday or in the course of the next day, at farthest.

This is unquestionably the most stupendous, the most interesting, and the most important undertaking, ever accomplished or even attempted by man. What magnificent events may ensue, it would be useless now to think of determining.

FIVE WEEKS IN A BALLOON

by JULES VERNE

Published in 1869, "Five Weeks in a Balloon" is pure adventure from the man who gave us *20,000 Leagues Under the Sea* and *Around the World in 80 Days*. Air travel captured Verne's rich imagination, and he in turn captured the imagination of the reading public.

Verne's explanations of things mechanical is high art, rivaling anything you can find in a modern techno-thriller, but it is dubious pseudo-science, quackery. Heating hydrogen under pressure would be an excellent way to speed your departure from this life—please don't try this at home.

The *Resolute* plunged along rapidly toward the Cape of Good Hope, the weather continuing fine, although the sea ran heavier.

On the 30th of March, twenty-seven days after the departure from London, the Table Mountain loomed up on the horizon. Cape City lying at the foot of an amphitheatre of hills, could be distinguished through the ship's glasses, and soon the *Resolute* cast anchor in the port. But the captain touched there only to replenish his coal bunkers, and that was but a day's job. On the morrow, he steered away to the south'ard, so as to double the southernmost point of Africa, and enter the Mozambique Channel.

This was not Joe's first sea-voyage, and so, for his part, he soon found himself at home on board; every body liked him for his frankness and good-humor. A considerable share of his master's renown was reflected upon him. He was listened to as an oracle, and he made no more mistakes than the next one.

So, while the doctor was pursuing his descriptive course of lecturing in the officers' mess, Joe reigned supreme on the forecastle, holding forth in his own peculiar manner, and making history to suit himself—a style of procedure pursued, by the way, by the greatest historians of all ages and nations.

The topic of discourse was, naturally, the aërial voyage. Joe had experienced some trouble in getting the rebellious spirits to believe in it; but, once accepted by them, nothing connected

with it was any longer an impossibility to the imaginations of
the seamen stimulated by Joe's harangues.

Our dazzling narrator persuaded his hearers that, after this
trip, many others still more wonderful would be undertaken. In
fact, it was to be but the first of a long series of superhuman
expeditions.

"You see, my friends, when a man has had a taste of that
kind of travelling, he can't get along afterward with any other;
so, on our next expedition, instead of going off to one side, we'll
go right ahead, going up, too, all the time."

"Humph! then you'll go to the moon!" said one of the
crowd, with a stare of amazement.

"To the moon!" exclaimed Joe, "To the moon! pooh! that's
too common. Every body might go to the moon, that way.
Besides, there's no water there, and you have to carry such a lot
of it along with you. Then you have to take air along in bottles,
so as to breathe."

"Ay! ay! that's all right! But can a man get a drop of the real
stuff there?" said a sailor who liked his toddy.

"Not a drop!" was Joe's answer. "No! old fellow, not in the
moon. But we're going to skip round among those little twin-
klers up there—the stars—and the splendid planets that my old
man so often talks about. For instance, we'll commence with
Saturn—"

"That one with the ring?" asked the boatswain.

"Yes! the wedding-ring—only no one knows what's become
of his wife!"

"What? will you go so high up as that?" said one of the
ship-boys, gaping with wonder. "Why, your master must be Old
Nick himself."

"Oh! no, he's too good for that."

"But, after Saturn—what then?" was the next inquiry of his
impatient audience.

"After Saturn? Well, we'll visit Jupiter. A funny place that is, too, where the days are only nine hours and a half long—a good thing for the lazy fellows—and the years, would you believe it—last twelve of ours, which is fine for folks who have only six months to live. They get off a little longer by that."

"Twelve years!" ejaculated the boy.

"Yes, my youngster; so that in that country you'd be toddling after your mammy yet, and that old chap yonder, who looks about fifty, would only be a little shaver of four and a half."

"Blazes! that's a good 'un!" shouted the whole forecastle together.

"Solemn truth!" said Joe, stoutly.

"But what can you expect? When people will stay in this world, they learn nothing and keep as ignorant as bears. But just come along to Jupiter and you'll see. But they have to look out up there, for he's got satellites that are not just the easiest things to pass."

All the men laughed, but they more than half believed him. Then he went on to talk about Neptune, where seafaring men get a jovial reception, and Mars, where the military get the best of the sidewalk to such an extent that folks can hardly stand it. Finally, he drew them a heavenly picture of the delights of Venus.

"And when we get back from that expedition," said the indefatigable narrator, "they'll decorate us with the Southern Cross that shines up there in the Creator's button-hole."

"Ay, and you'd have well earned it!" said the sailors.

Thus passed the long evenings on the forecastle in merry chat, and during the same time the doctor went on with his instructive discourses.

One day the conversation turned upon the means of directing balloons, and the doctor was asked his opinion about it.

"I don't think," said he, "that we shall succeed in finding

out a system of directing them. I am familiar with all the plans attempted and proposed, and not one has succeeded, not one is practicable. You may readily understand that I have occupied my mind with this subject, which was, necessarily, so interesting to me, but I have not been able to solve the problem with the appliances now known to mechanical science. We would have to discover a motive power of extraordinary force, and almost impossible lightness of machinery. And, even then, we could not resist atmospheric currents of any considerable strength. Until now, the effort has been rather to direct the car than the balloon, and that has been one great error."

"Still there are many points of resemblance between a balloon and a ship which is directed at will."

"Not at all," retorted the doctor, "there is little or no similarity between the two cases. Air is infinitely less dense than water, in which the ship is only half submerged, while the whole bulk of a balloon is plunged in the atmosphere, and remains motionless with reference to the element that surrounds it."

"You think, then, that aërostatic science has said its last word?"

"Not at all! not at all! But we must look for another point in the case, and if we cannot manage to guide our balloon, we must, at least, try to keep it in favorable aërial currents. In proportion as we ascend, the latter become much more uniform and flow more constantly in one direction. They are no longer disturbed by the mountains and valleys that traverse the surface of the globe, and these, you know, are the chief cause of the variations of the wind and the inequality of their force. Therefore, these zones having been once determined, the balloon will merely have to be placed in the currents best adapted to its destination."

"But then," continued Captain Bennet, "in order to reach

them, you must keep constantly ascending or descending. That is the real difficulty, doctor."

"And why, my dear captain?"

"Let us understand one another. It would be a difficulty and an obstacle only for long journeys, and not for short aërial excursions."

"And why so, if you please?"

"Because you can ascend only by throwing out ballast; you can descend only after letting off gas, and by these processes your ballast and your gas are soon exhausted."

"My dear sir, that's the whole question. There is the only difficulty that science need now seek to overcome. The problem is not how to guide the balloon, but how to take it up and down without expending the gas which is its strength, its life-blood, its soul, if I may use the expression."

"You are right, my dear doctor; but this problem is not yet solved; this means has not yet been discovered."

"I beg your pardon, it *has* been discovered."

"By whom?"

"By me!"

"By you?"

"You may readily believe that otherwise I should not have risked this expedition across Africa in a balloon. In twenty-four hours I should have been without gas!"

"But you said nothing about that in England?"

"No! I did not want to have myself overhauled in public. I saw no use in that. I made my preparatory experiments in secret and was satisfied. I have no occasion, then, to learn any thing more from them."

"Well! doctor, would it be proper to ask what is your secret?"

"Here it is, gentlemen—the simplest thing in the world!"

The attention of his auditory was now directed to the doctor in the utmost degree as he quietly proceeded with his explanation.

———

"The attempt has often been made, gentlemen," said the doctor, "to rise and descend at will, without losing ballast or gas from the balloon. A French aëronaut, M. Meunier, tried to accomplish this by compressing air in an inner receptacle. A Belgian, Dr. Van Hecke, by means of wings and paddles, obtained a vertical power that would have sufficed in most cases, but the practical results secured from these experiments have been insignificant.

"I therefore resolved to go about the thing more directly; so, at the start, I dispensed with ballast altogether, excepting as a provision for cases of special emergency, such as the breakage of my apparatus, or the necessity of ascending very suddenly, so as to avoid unforeseen obstacles.

"My means of ascent and descent consist simply in dilating or contracting the gas that is in the balloon by the application of different temperatures, and here is the method of obtaining that result.

"You saw me bring on board with the car several cases or receptacles, the use of which you may not have understood. They are five in number.

"The first contains about twenty-five gallons of water, to which I add a few drops of sulphuric acid, so as to augment its capacity as a conductor of electricity, and then I decompose it by means of a powerful Buntzen battery. Water, as you know, consists of two parts of hydrogen to one of oxygen gas.

"The latter, through the action of the battery, passes at its positive pole into the second receptacle. A third receptacle, placed above the second one, and of double its capacity, receives the hydrogen passing into it by the negative pole.

"Stopcocks, of which one has an orifice twice the size of the other, communicate between these receptacles and a fourth one, which is called the *mixture reservoir*, since in it the two gases obtained by the decomposition of the water do really commingle. The capacity of this fourth tank is about forty-one cubic feet.

"On the upper part of this tank is a platinum tube provided with a stopcock.

"You will now readily understand, gentlemen, the apparatus that I have described to you is really a gas cylinder and blow-pipe for oxygen and hydrogen, the heat of which exceeds that of a forge fire.

"This much established, I proceed to the second part of my apparatus. From the lowest part of my balloon, which is hermetically closed, issue two tubes a little distance apart. The one starts among the upper layers of the hydrogen gas, the other amid the lower layers.

"These two pipes are provided at intervals with strong jointings of India-rubber, which enable them to move in harmony with the oscillations of the balloon.

"Both of them run down as far as the car, and lose themselves in an iron receptacle of cylindrical form, which is called the *heat-tank*. The latter is closed at its two ends by two strong plates of the same metal.

"The pipe running from the lower part of the balloon runs into this cylindrical receptacle through the lower plate; it penetrates the latter and then takes the form of a helicoidal or screw-shaped spiral, the rings of which, rising one over the other, occupy nearly the whole of the height of the tank. Before again issuing from it, this spiral runs into a small cone with a concave base, that is turned downward in the shape of a spherical cap.

"It is from the top of this cone that the second pipe issues, and it runs, as I have said, into the upper beds of the balloon.

43

"The spherical cap of the small cone is of platinum, so as not to melt by the action of the cylinder and blow-pipe, for the latter are placed upon the bottom of the iron tank in the midst of the helicoidal spiral, and the extremity of their flame will slightly touch the cap in question.

"You all know, gentlemen, what a calorifere, to heat apartments, is. You know how it acts. The air of the apartments is forced to pass through its pipes, and is then released with a heightened temperature. Well, what I have just described to you is nothing more nor less than a calorifer.

"In fact, what is it that takes place? The cylinder once lighted, the hydrogen in the spiral and in the concave cone becomes heated, and rapidly ascends through the pipe that leads to the upper part of the balloon. A vacuum is created below, and it attracts the gas in the lower parts; this becomes heated in its turn, and is continually replaced; thus, an extremely rapid current of gas is established in the pipes and in the spiral, which issues from the balloon and then returns to it, and is heated over again, incessantly.

"Now, the gases increase $\frac{1}{480}$ of their volume for each degree of heat applied. If, then, I force the temperature 18 degrees, the hydrogen of the balloon will dilate $\frac{18}{480}$ or 1614 cubic feet, and will, therefore, displace 1614 more cubic feet of air, which will increase its ascensional power by 160 pounds. This is equivalent to throwing out that weight of ballast. If I augment the temperature by 180 degrees, the gas will dilate $\frac{180}{480}$ and will displace 16,740 cubic feet more, and its ascensional force will be augmented by 1,600 pounds.

"Thus, you see, gentlemen, that I can easily effect very considerable changes of equilibrium. The volume of the balloon has been calculated in such manner that, when half inflated, it displaces a weight of air exactly equal to that of the envelope containing the hydrogen gas, and of the car occupied by the passengers, and all its apparatus and accessories. At this point of inflation, it is in exact equilibrium with the air, and neither mounts nor descends.

"In order, then, to effect an ascent, I give the gas a temperature superior to the temperature of the surrounding air by means of my cylinder. By this excess of heat it obtains a larger distention, and inflates the balloon more. The latter, then, ascends in proportion as I heat the hydrogen.

"The descent, of course, is effected by lowering the heat of the cylinder, and letting the temperature abate. The ascent would be, usually, more rapid than the descent; but that is a fortunate circumstance, since it is of no importance to me to descend rapidly, while, on the other hand, it is by a very rapid ascent that I avoid obstacles. The real danger lurks below, and not above.

"Besides, as I have said, I have a certain quantity of ballast, which will enable me to ascend more rapidly still, when necessary. My valve, at the top of the balloon, is nothing more nor less than a safety-valve. The balloon always retains the same quantity of hydrogen, and the variations of temperature that I produce in the midst of this shut-up gas are, of themselves, sufficient to provide for all these ascending and descending movements.

"Now, gentlemen, as a practical detail, let me add this:

"The combustion of the hydrogen and of the oxygen at the point of the cylinder produces solely the vapor or steam of water. I have, therefore, provided the lower part of the cylindrical iron box with a scape-pipe, with a valve operating by means of a pressure of two atmospheres; consequently, so soon as this amount of pressure is attained, the steam escapes of itself.

"Here are the exact figures: 25 gallons of water, separated into its constituent elements, yield 200 pounds of oxygen and 25 pounds of hydrogen. This represents, at atmospheric tension, 1,890 cubic feet of the former and 3,780 cubic feet of the latter, or 5,670 cubic feet, in all, of the mixture. Hence, the stopcock of my cylinder, when fully open, expends 27 cubic feet per hour, with a flame at least six times as strong as that of the large lamps used for lighting streets. On an average, then, and in order to keep myself at a very moderate elevation, I should not burn more than nine cubic feet per hour, so that my twenty-five gallons of water represent six hundred and thirty-six hours of aërial navigation, or a little more than twenty-six days.

"Well, as I can descend when I please, to replenish my stock of water on the way, my trip might be indefinitely prolonged.

"Such, gentlemen, is my secret. It is simple, and, like most simple things, it cannot fail to succeed. The dilation and contraction of the gas in the balloon is my means of locomotion, which calls for neither cumbersome wings, nor any other mechanical motor. A calorifere to produce the changes of temperature, and a cylinder to generate the heat, are neither inconvenient nor heavy. I think, therefore, that I have combined all the elements of success."

Dr. Ferguson here terminated his discourse, and was most heartily applauded. There was not an objection to make to it; all had been foreseen and decided.

"However," said the captain, "the thing may prove dangerous."

"What matters that," replied the doctor, "provided that it be practicable?"

An invariably favorable wind had accelerated the progress of the *Resolute* toward the place of her destination. The navigation of the Mozambique Channel was especially calm and pleasant. The agreeable character of the trip by sea was regarded as a good omen of the probable issue of the trip through the air.

46

Every one looked forward to the hour of arrival, and sought to give the last touch to the doctor's preparations.

At length the vessel hove in sight of the town of Zanzibar, upon the island of the same name, and, on the 15th of April, at 11 o'clock in the morning, she anchored in the port.

The island of Zanzibar belongs to the Imaum of Muscat, an ally of France and England, and is, undoubtedly, his finest settlement. The port is frequented by a great many vessels from the neighboring countries.

The island is separated from the African coast only by a channel, the greatest width of which is but thirty miles.

It has a large trade in gums, ivory, and, above all, in "ebony," for Zanzibar is the great slave-market. Thither converges all the booty captured in the battles which the chiefs of the interior are continually fighting. This traffic extends along the whole eastern coast, and as far as the Nile latitudes. Mr. G. Lejean even reports that he has seen it carried on, openly, under the French flag.

Upon the arrival of the *Resolute*, the English consul at Zanzibar came on board to offer his services to the doctor, of whose projects the European newspapers had made him aware for a month past. But, up to that moment, he had remained with the numerous phalanx of the incredulous.

"I doubted," said he, holding out his hand to Dr. Ferguson, "but now I doubt no longer."

He invited the doctor, Kennedy, and the faithful Joe, of course, to his own dwelling. Through his courtesy, the doctor was enabled to have knowledge of the various letters that he had received from Captain Speke. The captain and his companions had suffered dreadfully from hunger and bad weather before reaching the Ugogo country. They could advance only with extreme difficulty, and did not expect to be able to communicate again for a long time.

"Those are perils and privations which we shall manage to avoid," said the doctor.

The baggage of the three travellers was conveyed to the consul's residence. Arrangements were made for disembarking the balloon upon the beach at Zanzibar. There was a convenient spot, near the signal-mast, close by an immense building, that would serve to shelter it from the east winds. This huge tower, resembling a tun standing on one end, beside which the famous Heidelberg tun would have seemed but a very ordinary barrel, served as a fortification, and on its platform were stationed Belootchees, armed with lances. These Belootchees are a kind of brawling, good-for-nothing Janizaries.

But, when about to land the balloon, the consul was informed that the population of the island would oppose their doing so by force. Nothing is so blind as fanatical passion. The news of the arrival of a Christian, who was to ascend into the air, was received with rage. The negroes, more exasperated than the Arabs, saw in this project an attack upon their religion. They took it into their heads that some mischief was meant to the sun and the moon. Now, these two luminaries are objects of veneration to the African tribes, and they determined to oppose so sacrilegious an enterprise.

The consul, informed of their intentions, conferred with Dr. Ferguson and Captain Bennet on the subject. The latter was unwilling to yield to threats, but his friend dissuaded him from any idea of violent retaliation.

"We shall certainly come out winners," he said. "Even the imam's soldiers will lend us a hand, if we need it. But, my dear captain, an accident may happen in a moment, and it would require but one unlucky blow to do the balloon an irreparable injury, so that the trip would be totally defeated; therefore we must act with the greatest caution."

"But what are we to do? If we land on the coast of Africa, we shall encounter the same difficulties. What are we to do?"

"Nothing is more simple," replied the consul. "You observe those small islands outside of the port; land your balloon on one of them; surround it with a guard of sailors, and you will have no risk to run."

"Just the thing!" said the doctor, "and we shall be entirely at our ease in completing our preparations."

The captain yielded to these suggestions, and the *Resolute* was headed for the island of Koumbeni. During the morning of the 16th April, the balloon was placed in safety in the middle of a clearing in the great woods, with which the soil is studded.

Two masts, eighty feet in height, were raised at the same distance from each other. Blocks and tackle, placed at their extremities, afforded the means of elevating the balloon, by the aid of a transverse rope. It was then entirely uninflated. The interior balloon was fastened to the exterior one, in such manner as to be lifted up in the same way. To the lower end of each balloon were fixed the pipes that served to introduce the hydrogen gas.

The whole day, on the 17th, was spent in arranging the apparatus destined to produce the gas; it consisted of some thirty casks, in which the decomposition of water was effected by means of iron-filings and sulphuric acid placed together in a large quantity of the first-named fluid. The hydrogen passed into a huge central cask, after having been washed on the way, and thence into each balloon by the conduit-pipes. In this manner each of them received a certain accurately-ascertained quantity of gas. For this purpose, there had to be employed eighteen hundred and sixty-six pounds of sulphuric acid, sixteen thousand and fifty pounds of iron, and nine thousand one hundred and sixty-six gallons of water. This operation commenced on the following night, about three A.M., and lasted nearly eight hours. The next day, the balloon, covered with its network, undulated gracefully above its car, which was held to the ground by numerous sacks of earth. The inflating apparatus was put together with extreme care, and the pipes issuing from the balloon were securely fitted to the cylindrical case.

The anchors, the cordage, the instruments, the travelling-wraps, the awning, the provisions, and the arms, were put in the place assigned to them in the car. The supply of water was procured at Zanzibar. The two hundred pounds of ballast were distributed in fifty bags placed at the bottom of the car, but within arm's-reach.

These preparations were concluded about five o'clock in the evening, while sentinels kept close watch around the island, and the boats of the *Resolute* patrolled the channel.

The blacks continued to show their displeasure by grimaces and contortions. Their *obi-men*, or wizards, went up and down among the angry throngs, pouring fuel on the flame of their fanaticism; and some of the excited wretches, more furious and daring than the rest, attempted to get to the island by swimming, but they were easily driven off.

Thereupon the sorceries and incantations commenced; the "rain-makers," who pretend to have control over the clouds, invoked the storms and the "stone-showers," as the blacks call hail, to their aid. To compel them to do so, they plucked leaves of all the different trees that grow in that country, and boiled them over a slow fire, while, at the same time, a sheep was killed by thrusting a long needle into its heart. But, in spite of all their ceremonies, the sky remained clear and beautiful, and they profited nothing by their slaughtered sheep and their ugly grimaces.

The blacks then abandoned themselves to the most furious orgies, and got fearfully drunk on "tembo," a kind of ardent spirits drawn from the cocoa-nut tree, and an extremely heady sort of beer called "togwa." Their chants, which were destitute of all melody, but were sung in excellent time, continued until far into the night.

About six o'clock in the evening, the captain assembled the travellers and the officers of the ship at a farewell repast in his cabin. Kennedy, whom nobody ventured to question now, sat with his eyes riveted on Dr. Ferguson, murmuring indistinguishable words. In other respects, the dinner was a gloomy one. The approach of the final moment filled everybody with the most serious reflections. What had fate in store for these daring adventurers? Should they ever again find themselves in the midst of their friends, or seated at the domestic hearth? Were their travelling apparatus to fail, what would become of them, among those ferocious savage tribes, in regions that had never been explored, and in the midst of boundless deserts?

Such thoughts as these, which had been dim and vague until then, or but slightly regarded when they came up, returned upon their excited fancies with intense force at this parting moment. Dr. Ferguson, still cold and impassible, talked of this, that, and the other; but he strove in vain to overcome this infectious gloominess. He utterly failed.

As some demonstration against the personal safety of the doctor and his companions was feared, all three slept that night on board the *Resolute*. At six o'clock in the morning they left their cabin, and landed on the island of Koumbeni.

The balloon was swaying gently to and fro in the morning breeze; the sand-bags that had held it down were now replaced by some twenty strong-armed sailors, and Captain Bennet and his officers were present to witness the solemn departure of their friends.

At this moment Kennedy went right up to the doctor, grasped his hand, and said:

"Samuel, have you absolutely determined to go?"

"Solemnly determined, my dear Dick."

"I have done every thing that I could to prevent this expedition, have I not?"

"Every thing!"

"Well, then, my conscience is clear on that score, and I will go with you."

"I was sure you would!" said the doctor, betraying in his features swift traces of emotion.

At last the moment of final leave-taking arrived. The captain and his officers embraced their dauntless friends with great feeling, not excepting even Joe, who, worthy fellow, was as proud and happy as a prince. Every one in the party insisted upon having a final shake of the doctor's hand.

At nine o'clock the three travellers got into their car. The doctor lit the combustible in his cylinder and turned the flame so as to produce a rapid heat, and the balloon, which had rested on the ground in perfect equipoise, began to rise in a few minutes, so that the seamen had to slacken the ropes they held it by. The car then rose about twenty feet above their heads.

"My friends!" exclaimed the doctor, standing up between his two companions, and taking off his hat, "let us give our aërial ship a name that will bring her good luck! let us christen her *Victoria!*"

This speech was answered with stentorian cheers of "Huzza for the Queen! Huzza for Old England!"

At this moment the ascensional force of the balloon increased prodigiously, and Ferguson, Kennedy, and Joe, waved a last good-by to their friends.

"Let go all!" shouted the doctor, and at the word the *Victoria* shot rapidly up into the sky, while the four carronades on board the *Resolute* thundered forth a parting salute in her honor.

THE HORROR OF THE HEIGHTS

OF THE

HEIGHTS

by SIR ARTHUR CONAN DOYLE

The dawn of the age of flight was an event that shook the world. The established writers of the day were as stirred as their audiences, and many cranked out stories for their loyal fans.

You will enjoy this short story by the creator of Sherlock Holmes, despite its obvious technical shortcomings. In fact, the nonsense of the tale is its charm—rain lashing the pilot's face, turning tail to hail, a mechanical wind-speed gauge, an unreliable compass above a certain height, breathing without oxygen at 30,000 feet, meteors zipping past, and so on. . . . But in those innocent days the reading public knew no more than the author. Oh, if only that were still true!

The idea that the extraordinary narrative which has been called the Joyce-Armstrong Fragment is an elaborate practical joke, evolved by some unknown person cursed by a perverted and sinister sense of humor, has now been abandoned by all who have examined the facts. The most macabre and imaginative of plotters would hesitate before linking his morbid fancies with the unquestioned and tragic facts which reinforce the statement. Though the assertions contained in it are amazing and even monstrous, it is none the less forcing itself upon the general intelligence that they are true, and that we must readjust our ideas to the new situation.

This world of ours appears to be separated by a slight and precarious margin of safety from a most singular and unexpected danger. I will endeavor in this narrative, which reproduces the original document in its necessarily somewhat fragmentary form, to lay before the reader the whole of the facts up to date, prefacing my statement by saying that if there be any who doubt the narrative of Joyce-Armstrong there can be no question at all as to the facts concerning Lieutenant Myrtle, R.N., and Mr. Hay Connor, who undoubtedly met their end in the manner described.

The Joyce-Armstrong Fragment was found in the field which is called Lower Haycock, lying one mile to the westward of the village of Withyham, upon the Kent and Sussex border. It was on the fifteenth of September last that an agricultural laborer, James Flynn, in the employment of Matthew Dodd, farmer of the Chauntry Farm, Withyham, perceived a briar pipe lying near the footpath which skirts the hedge in Lower Haycock. A few paces farther on he picked up a pair of broken binocular glasses. Finally, among some nettle in the ditch, he caught sight of a flat canvas-backed book which proved to be a notebook with detachable leaves, some of which had come loose and were fluttering along the base of the hedge. These he collected, but some, including the first, were never recovered and leave a deplorable hiatus in this all-important statement.

The notebook was taken by the laborer to his master, who in turn showed it to Dr. J. H. Atherton of Hartfield. This gentleman at once recognized the need for an expert examination, and the manuscript was forwarded to the Obro Club in London, where it now lies.

The first two pages of the manuscript are missing. There is also one torn away at the end of the narrative, though none of these affects the general coherence of the story. It is conjectured that the missing opening is concerned with the record of Mr. Joyce-Armstrong's qualifications as an aeronaut, which can be gathered from other sources and are admitted to be unsurpassed among the air pilots of England. For many years he has been looked upon as among the most daring and the most intellectual of flying men, a combination which has enabled him both to invent and to test several new devices, including the common gyroscopic attachment which is known by his name.

The main body of the manuscript is written neatly in ink, but the last few lines are in pencil and are so ragged as to be hardly legible—exactly, in fact, as they might be expected to appear if they were scribbled off hurriedly from the seat of a moving aeroplane.

There are, it may be added, several stains both on the last page and on the outside cover which have been pronounced by the Home Office experts to be blood—probably human and certainly mammalian. The fact that something closely resembling the organism of malaria was discovered in this blood, and that Joyce-Armstrong is known to have suffered from intermittent fever, is a remarkable example of the new weapons which modern science has placed in the hands of our detectives.

And now a word as to the personality of the author of this epoch-making statement. Joyce-Armstrong, according to the few friends who really knew something of the man, was a poet and a dreamer as well as a mechanic and an inventor. He was a man of considerable wealth, much of which he had spent in the pursuit of his aeronautical hobby. He had four private aeroplanes in his hangars near Devizes, and is said to have made no less than one hundred and seventy ascents in the course of last year.

He was a retiring man, with dark moods in which he would avoid the society of his fellows. Captain Dangerfield, who knew him better than anyone else, says that there were times when his eccentricity threatened to develop into something more serious. His habit of carrying a shotgun with him in his aeroplane was one manifestation of it. Another was the morbid effect which the fall of Lieutenant Myrtle had upon his mind.

Myrtle, who was attempting the height record, fell from an altitude of something over thirty thousand feet. Horrible to narrate, his head was entirely obliterated, though his body and limbs preserved their configuration. At every gathering of airmen, Joyce-Armstrong, according to Dangerfield, would ask with an enigmatic smile: "And where, pray, is Myrtle's head?" This dreadful question and the strange fashion in which it was asked froze the blood of men who were callous to the dangers of their perilous calling.

On another occasion, after dinner at the mess of the Flying School on Salisbury Plain, he started a debate as to what will be the most permanent danger which airmen will have to encounter. Having listened to successive opinions as to air pockets, faulty engines and over-banking, he ended by shrugging his shoulders and refusing to put forward his own views, though he gave the impression that they differed from any advanced by his companions. It is worth remarking that after his own complete disappearance it was found that his private affairs were arranged with a precision which may show that he had a strong premonition of disaster.

With these essential explanations I will now give the narrative exactly as it stands, beginning at page 3 of the blood-soaked notebook.

Nevertheless, when I dined at Rheims with Coselli and Gustav Raymond I found that neither of them was aware of any particular danger in the higher layers of the atmosphere. I did not actually say what was in my thoughts, but I got so near to it that if they had had any corresponding idea they could not have failed to express it. But then they are two empty, vainglorious fellows with no thought beyond seeing their silly names in the newspaper. It is interesting to note that neither of them had ever been much beyond the twenty-thousand-foot level. Of course, men have been higher than this both in balloons and in the ascent of mountains. It must be well above that point that the aeroplane enters the danger zone—always presuming that my premonitions are correct.

Aeroplaning has been with us now for more than twenty years, and one might well ask, why should this peril be only revealing itself in our day? The answer is obvious. In the old days of weak engines, when a hundred-horsepower Gnome was considered ample for every need, the flights were very restricted. Now that three hundred horsepower is the rule rather than the exception, visits to the upper layers have become easier and more common. Some of us can remember how in our youth Garros made a world-wide reputation by attaining 19,000 feet, and it was considered a remarkable achievement to fly over the Alps.

Our standard now has been immeasurably raised, and there are twenty high flights for one in former years. Many of them have been undertaken with impunity. The thirty-thousand-foot level has been reached time after time with no discomfort beyond cold and asthma.

What does this prove? A visitor might descend upon this planet a thousand times and never see a tiger. Yet tigers exist, and if he chanced to come down into a jungle he might be devoured. There are jungles of the upper air, and there are worse things than tigers which inhabit them. I believe in time these jungles will be accurately mapped out. Even at the present moment I could name two of them. One of them lies over the Pau-Biarritz district of France. Another is just over my head as I write here in my house at Wiltshire. I rather think there is a third in the Homburg-Wiesbaden district.

It was the disappearance of the airmen that first set me thinking. Of course, everyone said that they had fallen into the sea, but that did not satisfy me at all. First, there was Verrier in France; his machine was found near Bayonne, but they never got his body.

There was the case of Baxter also, who vanished, though his engine and some of the iron fixings were found in a wood in Leicestershire. In that case, Dr. Middleton of Amesbury, who was watching the flight with a telescope, declares that just before the clouds obscured the view he saw the machine, which was at an enormous height, suddenly rise perpendicularly upward in a succession of jerks, in a manner which he would have thought to be impossible. That was the last seen of Baxter. There was a correspondence in the papers, but it never led to anything.

There were several other similar cases, and then there was the death of Hay Connor. What a cackle there was about an unsolved mystery of the air, and what columns in the halfpenny papers, and yet how little was ever done to get at the bottom of the business! He came down in a tremendous volplane from an unknown height. He never got off his machine, and died in his pilot's seat.

Died of what? "Heart disease," said the doctors. Rubbish! Hay Connor's heart was as sound as mine is. What did Venables say? Venables was the only man who was at his side when he died. He said that he was shivering and looked like a man who had been badly scared. "Died of fright," said Venables, but could not imagine what he was frightened about. Only said one word to Venables, which sounded like "Monstrous." They could make nothing of that at the inquest. But I could make something of it.

Monsters! That was the last word of poor Harry Hay Connor. And he did die of fright, just as Venables thought.

And then there was Myrtle's head. Do you really believe—does anyone really believe—that a man's head could be driven clean into his body by the force of a fall? Well, perhaps it may be possible, but I for one have never believed that it was so with Myrtle. And the grease upon his clothes—"all slimy with grease," said somebody at the inquest. Queer that nobody got thinking after that! I did—but then I had been thinking for a good long time.

I've made three ascents—how Dangerfield used to chaff me about my shotgun!—but I've never been high enough! Now, with this new, light Paul Veroner machine and its 175 Robur, I should easily touch the 30,000 tomorrow. I'll have a shot at the record. Maybe I shall have a shot at something else as well. Of course, it's dangerous. If a fellow wants to avoid danger he had best keep out of flying altogether and subside finally into flannel slippers and a dressing gown. But I'll visit the air jungle tomorrow—and if there's anything there I shall know it.

If I return, I'll find myself a bit of a celebrity. If I don't, this notebook may explain what I am trying to do, and how I lost my life in doing it. But no drivel about accidents or mysteries, if you please.

I chose my Paul Veroner monoplane for the job. There's nothing like a monoplane when real work is to be done. Beaumont found that out in very early days. For one thing, it doesn't mind damp and the weather looks as if we should be in the clouds all the time. It's a bonny little model, and answers my hand like a tender-mouthed horse. The engine is a ten-cylinder rotary Robur, working up to 175. It has all the modern improvements, enclosed fuselage, high-curved landing-skids, brakes, gyroscopic steadiers, and three speeds worked by an alteration of the angle of the planes, upon the Venetian-blind principle.

I took a shotgun with me, with a dozen cartridges filled with buckshot. You should have seen the face of Perkins, my new mechanic, when I directed him to put them in. I was dressed like an Arctic explorer, with two jerseys under my overalls, thick socks inside my padded boots, a storm cap with flaps, and my talc goggles. It was stifling outside the hangars, but I was going for the summit of the Himalayas, and had to dress for the part.

Of course, I took an oxygen bag; the man who goes for the altitude record without one will either be frozen or smothered—or both.

I had a good look at the planes, the rudder bar and the elevating lever before I got in. Everything was in order so far as I could see. Then I switched on my engine and found that she was running sweetly. When they let her go she rose almost at once, upon the lowest speed. I circled my home field once or twice just to warm her up, and then with a wave to the others I flattened out my planes and put her on her highest. She skimmed like a swallow downwind for eight or ten miles until I turned her nose up a little and she began to climb in a great spiral for the cloud bank above me. It's all-important to rise slowly and adapt yourself to the pressure as you go.

It was a close, warm day for an English September, and there was the hush and heaviness of impending rain. Now and then there came sudden puffs of wind from the southwest—one of them so gusty and unexpected that it caught me napping and turned me half-round for an instant. I remember the time when gusts and whirls and air pockets used to be things of danger— before we learned to put an over-mastering power into our engines. Just as I reached the cloud banks, with the altimeter marking 3,000, down came the rain.

My word, how it poured! It drummed upon my wings, and lashed against my face, blurring my glasses so that I could hardly see. I got down on to a low speed, for it was painful to travel against it. As I got higher it became hail, and I had to turn tail to it. One of my cylinders was out of action—a dirty plug, I should imagine; but still I was rising steadily with plenty of power.

After a bit the trouble passed, whatever it was, and I heard the full, deep-throated purr—the ten singing as one. That's where the beauty of our modern silencers comes in. We can at last control our engines by ear. How they squeal and squeak and sob when they are in trouble! All those cries for help were wasted in the old days when every sound was swallowed up by the monstrous racket of the machine. If only the early aviators could come back to see the beauty and perfection of the mechanism which has been bought at the cost of their lives!

About 9:30 I was nearing the clouds. Down below me, all blurred and shadowed with rain, lay the vast expanse of Salisbury Plain. Half a dozen flying machines were doing hack work at the thousand-foot level, looking like little black swallows against the green background. I dare say they were wondering what I was doing up in Cloudland.

Suddenly a gray curtain drew across beneath me, and the wet folds of vapor were swirling round my face. It was clammily cold and miserable. But I was above the hail storm and that was something gained. The cloud was as dark and thick as a London fog. In my anxiety to get clear, I cocked her nose up until the automatic alarm bell rang and I actually began to slide backward. My sopped and dripping wings had made me heavier than I thought, but presently I was in lighter cloud and soon had cleared the first layer.

There was a second—opal-colored and fleecy—at a great height above my head: a white, unbroken ceiling above, and a dark, unbroken floor below, with the monoplane laboring upward upon a vast spiral between them. It is deadly lonely in these cloud spaces. Once a great flight of some small water bird went past me, flying very fast to the westward. The quick whir of their wings and their musical cry were cheery to my ear. I fancy that they were teal, but I am a wretched zoologist. Now that we humans have become birds we must really learn to know our brethren by sight.

The wind down beneath me whirled and swayed the broad cloud-plain. Once a great eddy formed in it, a whirlpool of vapor, and through it, as down a funnel, I caught sight of the distant world. A large white biplane was passing at a vast depth beneath me. I fancy it was the morning-mail service between Bristol and London. Then the drift swirled inward again and the great solitude was unbroken.

Just after ten I touched the lower edge of the upper-cloud stratum. It consisted of fine, diaphanous vapor drifting swiftly from the westward. The wind had been steadily rising all this time, and it was now blowing a sharp breeze—twenty-eight an hour by my gage. Already it was very cold, though my altimeter marked only nine thousand. The engines were working beautifully and we went droning steadily upward. The cloud bank was thicker than I had expected, but at last it thinned out into a golden mist before me, and then in an instant I had shot out from it, and there was an unclouded sky and a brilliant sun over my head—all blue and gold above, all shining silver below, one vast, glimmering plain as far as my eyes could reach.

It was quarter-past ten o'clock, and the barograph needle pointed to twelve thousand eight hundred. Up I went and up, my ears concentrated upon the deep purring of my motor, my eyes busy always with the watch, the revolution indicator, the petrol lever, and the oil pump. No wonder aviators are said to be a fearless race. With so many things to think of there is no time to trouble about oneself. About this time I noted how unreliable is the compass when above a certain height from earth. At fifteen thousand feet mine was pointing east and a point south. The sun and the wind gave me my true bearings.

I rose steadily, reflecting the sun like a great, smooth river across these empty solitudes of air. I had hoped to reach an eternal stillness in these high altitudes, but with every thousand feet of ascent the gale grew stronger. My machine groaned and trembled in every joint and rivet as she faced it, and swept away like a sheet of paper when I banked her on the turn, skimming down wind at a greater pace, perhaps, than ever mortal man has moved. Yet I had always to turn again and tack up in the wind's eye, for it was not merely a height record that I was after. By all my calculations it was above Wiltshire that my air jungle lay, and all my labor might be lost if I struck the outer layers at some farther point.

When I reached the nineteen-thousand-foot level, which was about midday, the wind was so severe that I looked with some anxiety to the stays of my wings, expecting momentarily to see them snap or slacken. I even cast loose the parachute behind me, and fastened its hook into the ring of my leathern belt so as to be ready for the worst. This is the time when a bit of skimped work by the mechanic is paid for by the life of the aeronaut. But she held together bravely. Every cord and strut was humming and vibrating like a harp string; but it was glorious to see how, for all the beating and the buffeting, she was still the mistress of the sky.

There is surely something divine in man himself that he should rise so superior to the limitations which Creation seems to impose—rise, too, by such unselfish, heroic devotion as this air conquest has shown. Talk of human degeneration! When has such a story as this been written in the annals of our race!

These were the thoughts in my head as I climbed that monstrous inclined plane, with the wind sometimes beating in my face and sometimes whistling behind my ears, while the cloud-land beneath me fell away to such a distance that the folds and hummocks of silver had all smoothed out into one flat, shining plain.

But suddenly I had a horrible and unprecedented experience. I have known before what it is to be in what our neighbors called a "tour-billon," but never on such a scale as this. That huge, sweeping river of wind of which I have spoken had, as it appears, whirlpools within it which were as monstrous as itself. Without a moment's warning I was dragged suddenly into the heart of one. I spun around for a minute or two with such velocity that I almost lost my senses, and then fell suddenly, left wing foremost, down the vacuum funnel in the center. I dropped like a stone, and lost nearly a thousand feet in about twenty seconds. It was only my belt that kept me in my seat, and the shock and breathlessness left me hanging half-sensible over the side of the fuselage.

But I am always capable of a supreme effort—it is my one great merit as an aviator. I was conscious that the descent was slower. The whirlpool was a cone rather than a funnel, and I had come to the apex. With a terrific wrench, throwing my weight all to one side, I leveled my planes and brought her head away from the wind. In an instant I had shot out of the eddies and was skimming down the sky.

Then, shaken but victorious, I turned her nose up and began once more my steady grind on the upward spiral. I took a large sweep to avoid the danger spot of the whirlpool, and soon I was safely above it. Just after one o'clock I was 21,000 feet above the sea level. To my great joy I had topped the gale, and with every hundred feet of ascent the air grew stiller. On the other hand, it was very cold, and I was conscious of that peculiar nausea which goes with rarefication of the air. For the first time I unscrewed the mouth of my oxygen bag and took an occasional whiff of the glorious gas. I could feel it running like a cordial through my veins, and I was exhilarated almost to the point of drunkenness. I shouted and sang as I soared upward into the cold, still outer world.

It was very clear to me that the insensibility which came upon Glaisher, and in a lesser degree upon Coxwell, when in 1862 they ascended in a balloon to the height of 30,000 feet, was due to the extreme speed with which a perpendicular ascent is made. Doing it at an easy gradient and accustoming oneself to the lessened barometric pressure by slow degrees, there are no such dreadful symptoms. At the same great height I found that even without my oxygen inhaler I could breathe without undue distress.

It was bitterly cold, however, and my thermometer was at zero Fahrenheit. At 1:30, I was nearly seven miles above the surface of the earth, and still ascending steadily. I found, however, that the rarefied air was giving markedly less support to my planes, and that my angle of ascent had to be considerably lowered in consequence. It was already clear that even with my light weight and strong engine power there was a point in front of me where I should be held. To make matters worse, one of my sparking plugs was in trouble again and there was intermittent misfiring in the engine. My heart was heavy with the fear of failure.

It was about that time that I had a most extraordinary experience. Something whizzed past me in a trail of smoke and exploded with a loud hissing sound, sending forth a cloud of steam. For the instant I could not imagine what had happened. Then I remembered that the earth is forever being bombarded with meteor stones and would be hardly inhabitable were they not in nearly every case turned to vapor in the outer layers of the atmosphere. Here is a new danger for the high-altitude man, for two others passed me when I was nearing the forty-thousand-foot mark. I can not doubt that at the edge of the earth's envelope the risk would be a very real one.

My barograph needle marked 41,300 when I became aware that I could go no further. Physically, the strain was not as yet greater than I could bear, but my machine had reached its limit. The attenuated air gave no firm support to the wings, and the least tilt developed into side-slip, while she seemed sluggish on her controls. Possibly, had the engine been at its best, another thousand feet might have been within our capacity; but it was still misfiring, and two out of the ten cylinders appeared to be out of action. If I had not already reached the zone for which I was searching, then I should never see it upon this journey.

But was it not possible that I had attained it? Soaring in circles like a monstrous hawk upon the forty-thousand-foot level, I let the monoplane guide herself, and with my Mannheim glass I made a careful observation of my surroundings. The heavens were perfectly clear; there was no indication of those dangers which I had imagined.

I have said that I was soaring in circles. It struck me suddenly that I should do well to take a wider sweep and open up a new air tract. If the hunter entered an earth jungle he would drive through it if he wished to find his game. My reasoning had led me to believe that the air jungle lay somewhere over Wiltshire. This should be to the south and west of me. I took my bearings from the sun, for the compass was hopeless and no trace of earth was to be seen—nothing but the distant silver cloud plain. However, I got my direction as best I might and kept her head straight to the mark. I reckoned that my petrol supply would not last for more than an hour or so, but I could afford to use it to the last drop, since a single magnificent volplane would at any time take me to the earth.

Suddenly I was aware of something new. The air in front of me had lost its crystal clearness. It was full of long, ragged wisps of something which I can only compare to very fine cigarette smoke. It hung about in wreaths and coils, turning and twisting slowly in the sunlight. As the monoplane shot through it, I was aware of a faint taste of oil upon my lips, and there was a greasy scum upon the woodwork of the machine. Some infinitely fine organic matter appeared to be suspended in the atmosphere.

There was no life there. It was inchoate and diffuse, extending for many square acres and then fringing off into the void. No, it was not life. But might it not be the remains of life? Above all, might it not be the food of life, of monstrous life, even as the humble grease of the ocean is the food for the mighty whale? The thought was in my mind when my eyes looked upward and I saw the most wonderful vision that ever man has seen. Can I hope to convey it to you, even as I saw it myself last Thursday!

Conceive a jellyfish such as sails in our summer seas, bell-shaped and of enormous size—far larger, I should judge, than the dome of Saint Paul's. It was of a light pink color veined with a delicate green, but the whole huge fabric so tenuous that it was but a fairy outline against the dark blue sky. It pulsated with a delicate and regular rhythm. From it there depended two long, drooping green tentacles which swayed slowly backward and forward. This gorgeous vision passed gently with noiseless dignity over my head, as light and fragile as a soap bubble, and drifted upon its stately way.

I had half-turned my monoplane that I might look after this beautiful creature, when in a moment I found myself amidst a perfect fleet of them, of all sizes, but none so large as the first. Some were quite small, but the majority about as big as an average balloon, and with much the same curvature at the top. There was in them a delicacy of texture and coloring which reminded me of the finest Venetian glass. Pale shades of pink and green were the prevailing tints, but all had a lovely iridescence where the sun shimmered through their dainty forms. Some hundreds of them drifted past me, a wonderful fairy squadron of strange, unknown argosies of the sky—creatures whose forms and substance were so attuned to these pure heights that one could not conceive anything so delicate within actual sight or sound of earth.

But soon my attention was drawn to a new phenomenon— the serpents of the outer air. These were long, thin, fantastic coils of vapor-like material, which turned and twisted with great speed, flying round and round so fast that the eyes could hardly follow them. Some of these ghost-like creatures were twenty or thirty feet long; but it was difficult to tell their girth, for their outline was so hazy that it seemed to fade away into the air around them. These air snakes were of a very light gray or smoke color, with some darker lines within which gave the impression of a definite organism. One of them whisked past my very face, and I was conscious of a cold, clammy contact; but their composition was so unsubstantial that I could not connect them with any thought of physical danger, any more than the beautiful bell-like creatures which had preceded them. There was no more solidity in their frames than in the floating spume from a broken wave.

But a more terrible experience was in store for me. Floating downward from a great height, there came a purplish patch of vapor, small as I first saw it, but rapidly enlarging as it approached me, until it appeared to be hundreds of square feet

in size. Though fashioned of some transparent jelly-like substance, it was none the less of much more definite outline and
solid consistence than anything which I had seen before.

There were more traces, too, of a physical organization,
especially two vast, shadowy, circular plates upon either side,
which may have been eyes, and a perfectly solid white projec-
tion between them which was as curved and cruel as the beak
of a vulture. The whole aspect of this monster was formidable
and threatening, and it kept changing its color from a very light
mauve to a dark, angry purple so thick that it cast a shadow as
it drifted between my monoplane and the sun. On the upper
curve of its huge body there were three great projections which
I can only describe as enormous bubbles, and I was convinced
as I looked at them that they were charged with some
extremely light gas which served to buoy up the misshapen and
semi-solid mass in the rarefied air.

The creature moved swiftly along, keeping pace easily with
the monoplane, and for twenty miles or more it formed my horrible escort, hovering over me like a bird of prey which is waiting to pounce. Its method of progression—done so swiftly that
it was not easy to follow—was to throw out a long, glutinous
streamer in front of it, which in turn seemed to draw forward
the rest of its writhing body. So elastic and gelatinous was it
that never for two successive minutes was it the same shape,
and yet each change made it more threatening and loathsome
than the last.

I knew that it meant mischief. Every purple flush of its
hideous body told me so. The vague, goggling eyes, which were
turned always upon me, were cold and merciless in their viscid
hatred. I dipped the nose of my monoplane downward to
escape it. As I did so, as quick as a flash, there shot out a long
tentacle from this mass of floating blubber, and it fell as light
and sinuous as a whiplash across the front of my machine.
There was a loud hiss as it lay for a moment against the hot

engine, and it whisked itself into the air again while the huge, flat body drew itself together as if in sudden pain.

I dipped to a vol-pique, but again a tentacle fell over the monoplane, and was shorn off by the propeller as easily as it might have cut through a smoke wreath. A long, gliding, sticky, serpent-like coil came from behind and caught me round the waist, dragging me out of the fuselage. I tore at it, my fingers sinking into the smooth, glue-like surface, and for an instant I disengaged myself, but only to be caught round the boot by another coil, which gave me a jerk that tilted me almost on to my back.

As I fell over I blazed off both barrels of my gun, though indeed it was like attacking an elephant with a peashooter to imagine that any human weapon could cripple that mighty bulk. And yet I aimed better than I knew, for with a loud report one of the great blisters upon the creature's back exploded with the puncture of the buckshot. It was very clear that my conjecture was right, and that these vast, clear bladders were distended with some lifting-gas, for in an instant the huge, cloud-like body turned sideways, writhing desperately to find its balance, while the white beak snapped and gaped in horrible fury.

But already I had shot away on the steepest glide that I dared to attempt, my engine still full on, the flying propeller and the force of gravity shooting me downward like an aerolite. Far behind me I saw a dull purplish smudge growing swiftly smaller and merging into the blue sky behind it.

I was safe out of the deadly jungle of the outer air.

Once out of danger I throttled my engine, for nothing tears a machine to pieces quicker than running on full power from a height. It was a glorious spiral volplane from nearly eight miles of altitude, first to the level of the silver cloud bank, then to that of the storm cloud beneath it, and finally in beating rain to the surface of the earth. I saw the Bristol Channel beneath me as I broke from the clouds; but having still some petrol in my tank I got twenty miles inland before I found myself stranded in a field near the village of Ashcombe.

There I got three tins of petrol from a passing motorcar, and at ten minutes past six that evening I alighted gently in my own home meadow at Devizes after such a journey as no mortal upon earth has ever yet taken and lived to tell the tale. I have seen the beauty and I have seen the horror of the heights—and greater beauty or horror than that is not within the ken of man.

And now it is my plan to go once again into the outer air before I give my results to the world.

My reason for this is that I must surely have something to show by way of proof before I lay such a tale before my fellow men. It is true that others will soon follow and will confirm what I have said, and yet I should wish to carry conviction from the first. Those lovely iridescent bubbles of the air should not be hard to capture. They drift slowly upon their way, and the swift monoplane could intercept their leisurely course. It is likely enough that they would dissolve in the heavier layers of the atmosphere, and that some small heap of amorphous jelly might be all that I should bring to earth with me. And yet something there would surely be, by which I could substantiate my story.

Yes, I will go, even if I run a risk by doing so. These purple horrors would not seem to be numerous. It is probable that I shall not see one. If I do I shall dive at once. At the worst there is always the shotgun and my knowledge of . . .

[Here a page of the manuscript is unfortunately missing. On the next page is written in large, straggling writing]:

Forty-three thousand feet. I shall never see earth again. They are beneath me, three of them. God help me, it is a dreadful death to die!

———

Such in its entirety is the Joyce-Armstrong Statement.

Of the man nothing has since been seen. Pieces of his shattered monoplane have been picked up in the preserves of Mr. Budd-Lushington upon the borders of Kent and Sussex, within a few miles of the spot where the notebook was discovered.

If the unfortunate aviator's theory is correct that this air jungle, as he called it, existed only over the southwest of England, then it would seem that he had fled from it at the full speed of his monoplane, only to be overtaken and devoured by these horrible creatures at some spot in the outer atmosphere above the place where the grim relics were found. The picture of that monoplane skimming down the sky, with the nameless terrors flying swiftly beneath it and cutting it off always from the earth, while they gradually closed in upon their victim, is one upon which a man who valued his sanity would prefer not to dwell.

There are many, as I am aware, who still jeer at the facts which I have here set down, but even they must admit that Joyce-Armstrong has disappeared, and I would commend to them his own words:

"This notebook may explain what I am trying to do, and how I lost my life in doing it. But no drivel about accidents or mysteries, if you please."

MARY POSTGATE

---

by RUDYARD KIPLING

Nobel Prize–winning author Rudyard Kipling (1865–1936) used his years of experience as assistant editor of the *Civil and Military Gazette* and assistant editor and overseas correspondent for the *Pioneer* to write dozens of books and hundreds of short stories and poems, many for children, including his celebrated tales *The Jungle Book, Kim*, and *Captains Courageous*. However, he was adept at writing just about any type of story for any audience. His war stories are particularly dark, and many, including "The Lost Legion," "Swept and Garnished," and "A Madonna of the Trenches," contain supernatural overtones.

The story included here, "Mary Postgate," deals with a pilot, but more directly concerns the aunt and governess he leaves behind to go fight in the Royal Air Force during World War I. With his keen eye for detailing the typical British unflappability, Kipling illustrates how civilians can be as cruel as soldiers during wartime.

Of Miss Mary Postgate, Lady McCausland wrote that she was "thoroughly conscientious, tidy, companionable, and ladylike. I am very sorry to part with her, and shall always be interested in her welfare."

Miss Fowler engaged her on this recommendation, and to her surprise, for she had had experience of companions, found that it was true. Miss Fowler was nearer sixty than fifty at the time, but though she needed care she did not exhaust her attendant's vitality. On the contrary, she gave out, stimulatingly and with reminiscences. Her father had been a minor Court official in the days when the Great Exhibition of 1851 had just set its seal on Civilisation made perfect. Some of Miss Fowler's tales, none the less, were not always for the young. Mary was not young, and though her speech was as colourless as her eyes or her hair, she was never shocked. She listened unflinchingly to every one; said at the end, "How interesting!" or "How shocking!" as the case might be, and never again referred to it, for she prided herself on a trained mind, which "did not dwell on these things." She was, too, a treasure at domestic accounts, for which the village tradesmen, with their weekly books, loved her not. Otherwise she had no enemies; provoked no jealousy even among the plainest; neither gossip nor slander had ever been traced to her; she supplied the odd place at the Rector's or the Doctor's table at half an hour's notice; she was a sort of public aunt to very many small children of the village street, whose parents, while accepting everything, would have been swift to resent what they called "patronage"; she served on the Village Nursing Committee as Miss Fowler's nominee when Miss Fowler was crippled by rheumatoid arthritis, and came out of six months' fort-nightly meetings equally respected by all the cliques.

And when Fate threw Miss Fowler's nephew, an unlovely orphan of eleven, on Miss Fowler's hands, Mary Postgate stood to her share of the business of education as practised in private and public schools. She checked printed clothes-lists, and unitemised bills of extras; wrote to Head and House masters, matrons, nurses and doctors; and grieved or rejoiced over half-term reports. Young Wyndham Fowler repaid her in his holidays by calling her "Gatepost," "Postey," or "Packthread," by thumping her between her narrow shoulders, or by chasing her bleating, round the garden, her large mouth open, her large nose high in air, at a stiff-necked shamble very like a camel's. Later on he filled the house with clamour, argument, and harangues as to his personal needs, likes and dislikes, and the limitations of "you women," reducing Mary to tears of physical fatigue, or, when he chose to be humorous, of helpless laughter. At crises, which multiplied as he grew older, she was his ambassadress and his interpretress to Miss Fowler, who had no large sympathy with the young; a vote in his interest at the councils on his future; his sewing-woman, strictly accountable for mislaid boots and garments; always his butt and his slave.

And when he decided to become a solicitor, and had entered an office in London; when his greeting had changed from "Hullo, Postey, you old beast," to "Mornin' Packthread," there came a war which, unlike all wars that Mary could remember, did not stay decently outside England and in the newspapers, but intruded on the lives of people whom she knew. As she said to Miss Fowler, it was "most vexatious." It took the Rector's son who was going into business with his elder brother; it took the Colonel's nephew on the eve of fruit-farming in Canada; it took Mrs. Grant's son who, his mother said, was devoted to the ministry; and, very early indeed, it took Wynn Fowler, who announced on a postcard that he had joined the Flying Corps and wanted a cardigan waistcoat.

"He must go, and he must have the waistcoat," said Miss Fowler. So Mary got the proper-sized needles and wool, while Miss Fowler told the men of her establishment—two gardeners and an odd man, aged sixty—that those who could join the Army had better do so. The gardeners left. Cheape, the odd man, stayed on, and was promoted to the gardener's cottage. The cook, scorning to be limited in luxuries, also left, after a spirited scene with Miss Fowler, and took the house-maid with her. Miss Fowler gazetted Nellie, Cheape's seventeen-year-old daughter, to the vacant post; Mrs. Cheape to the rank of cook with occasional cleaning bouts; and the reduced establishment moved forward smoothly.

Wynn demanded an increase in his allowance. Miss Fowler, who always looked facts in the face, said, "He must have it. The chances are he won't live long to draw it, and if three hundred makes him happy—"

Wynn was grateful, and came over, in his tight-buttoned uniform, to say so. His training centre was not thirty miles away, and his talk was so technical that it had to be explained by charts of the various types of machines. He gave Mary such a chart.

"And you'd better study it, Postey," he said. "You'll be seeing a lot of 'em soon." So Mary studied the chart, but when Wynn next arrived to swell and exalt himself before his womenfolk, she failed badly in cross-examination, and he rated her as in the old days.

"You *look* more or less like a human being," he said in his new Service voice. "You *must* have had a brain at some time in your past. What have you done with it? Where d'you keep it? A sheep would know more than you do, Postey. You're lamentable. You are less use than an empty tin can, you dowey old cassowary."

"I suppose that's how your superior officer talks to *you*?" said Miss Fowler from her chair.

"But Postey doesn't mind," Wynn replied. "Do you, Packthread?"

"Why? Was Wynn saying anything? I shall get this right next time you come," she muttered, and knitted her pale brows again over the diagrams of Taubes, Farmans, and Zeppelins.

In a few weeks the mere land and sea battles which she read to Miss Fowler after breakfast passed her like idle breath. Her heart and her interest were high in the air with Wynn, who had finished "rolling" (whatever that might be) and had gone on from a "taxi" to a machine more or less his own. One morning it circled over their very chimneys, alighted on Vegg's Heath, almost outside the garden gate, and Wynn came in, blue with cold, shouting for food. He and she drew Miss Fowler's bathchair, as they had often done, along the Heath foot-path to look at the biplane. Mary observed that "it smelt very badly."

"Postey, I believe you think with your nose," said Wynn. "I know you don't with your mind. Now, what type's that?"

"I'll go and get the chart," said Mary.

"You're hopeless! You haven't the mental capacity of a white mouse," he cried, and explained the dials and the sockets for bomb-dropping till it was time to mount and ride the wet clouds once more.

"Ah!" said Mary, as the stinking thing flared upward. "Wait till our Flying Corps gets to work! Wynn says it's much safer than in the trenches."

"I wonder," said Miss Fowler. "Tell Cheape to come and tow me home again."

"It's all downhill. I can do it," said Mary, "if you put the brake on." She laid her lean self against the pushing-bar and home they trundled.

"Now, be careful you aren't heated and catch a chill," said overdressed Miss Fowler.

"Nothing makes me perspire," said Mary. As she bumped the chair under the porch she straightened her long back. The exertion had given her a colour, and the wind had loosened a wisp of hair across her forehead. Miss Fowler glanced at her.

"What do you ever think of, Mary?" she demanded suddenly.

"Oh, Wynn says he wants another three pairs of stockings— as thick as we can make them."

"Yes. But I mean the things that women think about. Here you are, more than forty—"

"Forty-four," said truthful Mary.

"Well?"

"Well?" Mary offered Miss Fowler her shoulder as usual.

"And you've been with me ten years now."

"Let's see," said Mary. "Wynn was eleven when he came. He's twenty now, and I came two years before that. It must be eleven."

"Eleven! And you've never told me anything that matters in all that while. Looking back, it seems to me that I've done all the talking."

"I'm afraid I'm not much of a conversationalist. As Wynn says, I haven't the mind. Let me take your hat."

Miss Fowler, moving stiffly from the hip, stamped her rubber-tipped stick on the tiled hall floor. "Mary, aren't you *anything* except a companion? Would you *ever* have been anything except a companion?"

Mary hung up the garden hat on its proper peg. "No," she said after consideration. "I don't imagine I ever should. But I've no imagination, I'm afraid."

She fetched Miss Fowler her eleven-o'clock glass of Contrexeville.

That was the wet December when it rained six inches to the month, and the women went abroad as little as might be. Wynn's flying chariot visited them several times, and for two mornings (he had warned her by postcard) Mary heard the thresh of his propellers at dawn. The second time she ran to the window, and stared at the whitening sky. A little blur passed overhead. She lifted her lean arms towards it.

That evening at six o'clock there came an announcement in an official envelope that Second Lieutenant W. Fowler had been killed during a trial flight. Death was instantaneous. She read it and carried it to Miss Fowler.

"I never expected anything else," said Miss Fowler; "but I'm sorry it happened before he had done anything."

The room was whirling round Mary Postgate, but she found herself quite steady in the midst of it.

"Yes," she said. "It's a great pity he didn't die in action after he had killed somebody."

"He was killed instantly. That's one comfort," Miss Fowler went on.

"But Wynn says the shock of a fall kills a man at once—whatever happens to the tanks," quoted Mary.

The room was coming to rest now. She heard Miss Fowler say impatiently, "But why can't we cry, Mary?" and herself replying, "There's nothing to cry for. He has done his duty as much as Mrs. Grant's son did."

"And when he died, *she* came and cried all the morning," said Miss Fowler. "This only makes me feel tired—terribly tired. Will you help me to bed, please, Mary?—And I think I'd like the hot-water bottle."

So Mary helped her and sat beside, talking of Wynn in his riotous youth.

"I believe," said Miss Fowler suddenly, "that old people and young people slip from under a stroke like this. The middle-aged feel it most."

"I expect that's true," said Mary, rising. "I'm going to put away the things in his room now. Shall we wear mourning?"

"Certainly not," said Miss Fowler. "Except, of course, at the funeral. I can't go. You will. I want you to arrange about his being buried here. What a blessing it didn't happen at Salisbury!"

Every one, from the Authorities of the Flying Corps to the Rector, was most kind and sympathetic. Mary found herself for the moment in a world where bodies were in the habit of being despatched by all sorts of conveyances to all sorts of places. And at the funeral two young men in buttoned-up uniforms stood beside the grave and spoke to her afterwards.

"You're Miss Postgate, aren't you?" said one. "Fowler told me about you. He was a good chap—a first-class fellow—a great loss."

"Great loss!" growled his companion. "We're all awfully sorry."

"How high did he fall from?" Mary whispered.

"Pretty nearly four thousand feet, I should think, didn't he? You were up that day, Monkey?"

"All of that," the other child replied. "My bar made three thousand, and I wasn't as high as him by a lot."

"Then *that's* all right," said Mary. "Thank you very much."

They moved away as Mrs. Grant flung herself weeping on Mary's flat chest, under the lych-gate, and cried, "*I* know how it feels! *I* know how it feels!"

"But both his parents are dead," Mary returned, as she fended her off. "Perhaps they've all met by now," she added vaguely as she escaped towards the coach.

"I've thought of that too," wailed Mrs. Grant; "but then he'll be practically a stranger to them. Quite embarrassing!"

Mary faithfully reported every detail of the ceremony to Miss Fowler, who, when she described Mrs. Grant's outburst, laughed aloud.

"Oh, how Wynn would have enjoyed it! He was always utterly unreliable at funerals. D'you remember—" And they talked of him again, each piecing out the other's gaps. "And now," said Miss Fowler, "we'll pull up the blinds and we'll have a general tidy. That always does us good. Have you seen to Wynn's things?"

"Everything—since he first came," said Mary. "He was never destructive—even with his toys."

They faced that neat room.

"It can't be natural not to cry," Mary said at last. "I'm *so* afraid you'll have a reaction."

"As I told you, we old people slip from under the stroke. It's you I'm afraid for. Have you cried yet?"

"I can't. It only makes me angry with the Germans."

"That's sheer waste of vitality," said Miss Fowler. "We must live till the war's finished." She opened a full wardrobe. "Now, I've been thinking things over. This is my plan. All his civilian clothes can be given away—Belgian refugees, and so on."

Mary nodded. "Boots, collars, and gloves?"

"Yes. We don't need to keep anything except his cap and belt."

"They came back yesterday with his Flying Corps clothes"—Mary pointed to a roll on the little iron bed.

"Ah, but keep his Service things. Some one may be glad of them later. Do you remember his sizes?"

"Five feet eight and a half; thirty-six inches round the chest. But he told me he's just put on an inch and a half. I'll mark it on a label and tie it on his sleeping-bag."

"So that disposes of *that*," said Miss Fowler, tapping the palm of one hand with the ringed third finger of the other.

"What waste it all is! We'll get his old school trunk tomorrow and pack his civilian clothes."

"And the rest?" said Mary. "His books and pictures and the games and the toys—and—and the rest?"

"My plan is to burn every single thing," said Miss Fowler. "Then we shall know where they are and no one can handle them afterwards. What do you think?"

"I think that would be much the best," said Mary. "But there's such a lot of them."

"We'll burn them in the destructor," said Miss Fowler.

This was an open-air furnace for the consumption of refuse; a little circular four-foot tower of pierced brick over an iron grating. Miss Fowler had noticed the design in a gardening journal years ago, and had had it built at the bottom of the garden. It suited her tidy soul, for it saved unsightly rubbish-heaps, and the ashes lightened the stiff clay soil.

Mary considered for a moment, saw her way clear, and nodded again. They spent the evening putting away well-remembered civilian suits, underclothes that Mary had marked, and the regiments of very gaudy socks and ties. A second trunk was needed, and, after that, a little packing-case, and it was late next day when Cheape and the local carrier lifted them to the cart. The Rector luckily knew of a friend's son, about five feet eight and a half inches high, to whom a complete Flying Corps outfit would be most acceptable, and sent his gardener's son down with a barrow to take delivery of it. The cap was hung up in Miss Fowler's bedroom, the belt in Miss Postgate's; for, as Miss Fowler said, they had no desire to make tea-party talk of them.

"That disposes of *that*," said Miss Fowler. "I'll leave the rest to you, Mary. I can't run up and down the garden. You'd better take the big clothes-basket and get Nellie to help you."

"I shall take the wheel-barrow and do it myself," said Mary, and for once in her life closed her mouth.

Miss Fowler, in moments of irritation, had called Mary deadly methodical. She put on her oldest water-proof and gardening-hat and her ever-slipping goloshes, for the weather was on the edge of more rain. She gathered fire-lighters from the kitchen, a half-scuttle of coals, and a faggot of brushwood. These she wheeled in the barrow down the mossed paths to the dank little laurel shrubbery where the destructor stood under the drip of three oaks. She climbed the wire fence into the Rector's glebe just behind, and from his tenant's rick pulled two large armfuls of good hay, which she spread neatly on the fire-bars. Next, journey by journey, passing Miss Fowler's white face at the morning-room window each time, she brought down in the towel-covered clothes-basket, on the wheel-barrow, thumbed and used Hentys, Marryats, Levers, Stevensons, Baroness Orczys, Garvices, schoolbooks, and atlases, unrelated piles of the *Motor Cyclist*, the *Light Car*, and catalogues of Olympia Exhibitions; the remnants of a fleet of sailing-ships from nine-penny cutters to a three-guinea yacht; a prep-school dressing-gown; bats from three-and-sixpence to twenty-four shillings; cricket and tennis balls; disintegrated steam and clockwork locomotives with their twisted rails; a grey and red tin model of a submarine; a dumb gramophone and cracked records; golf-clubs that had to be broken across the knee, like his walking-sticks, and an assegai; photographs of private and public school cricket and football elevens, and his O.T.C. on the line of march; kodaks, and film-rolls; some pewters, and one real silver cup, for boxing competitions and Junior Hurdles; sheaves of school photographs; Miss Fowler's photograph, her own which he had borne off in fun and (good care she took not to ask!) had never returned; a playbox with a secret drawer; a load of flannels, belts, and jerseys, and a pair of spiked shoes unearthed in the attic; a packet of all the letters that Miss Fowler and she had ever written to him, kept for some absurd reason through all these years; a five-day attempt at a diary;

framed pictures of racing motors in full Brooklands career, and load upon load of undistinguishable wreckage of tool-boxes, rabbit-hutches, electric batteries, tin soldiers, fret-saw outfits, and jig-saw puzzles.

Miss Fowler at the window watched her come and go, and said to herself, "Mary's an old woman. I never realised it before."

After lunch she recommended her to rest.

"I'm not in the least tired," said Mary. "I've got it all arranged. I'm going to the village at two o'clock for some paraffin. Nellie hasn't enough, and the walk will do me good."

She made one last quest round the house before she started, and found that she had overlooked nothing. It began to mist as soon as she had skirted Vegg's Heath, where Wynn used to descend—it seemed to her that she could almost hear the beat of his propellers overhead, but there was nothing to see. She hoisted her umbrella and lunged into the blind wet till she had reached the shelter of the empty village. As she came out of Mr. Kidd's shop with a bottle full of paraffin in her string shopping-bag, she met Nurse Eden, the village nurse, and fell into talk with her, as usual, about the village children. They were just parting opposite the "Royal Oak," when a gun, they fancied, was fired immediately behind the house. It was followed by a child's shriek dying into a wail.

"Accident!" said Nurse Eden promptly, and dashed through the empty bar, followed by Mary. They found Mrs. Gerritt, the publican's wife, who could only gasp and point to the yard, where a little cart-lodge was sliding sideways amid a clatter of tiles. Nurse Eden snatched up a sheet drying before the fire, ran out, lifted something from the ground, and flung the sheet round it. The sheet turned scarlet and half her uniform too, as she bore the load into the kitchen. It was little Edna Gerritt, aged nine, whom Mary had known since her perambulator days.

"Am I hurted bad?" Edna asked, and died between Nurse Eden's dripping hands. The sheet fell aside and for an instant, before she could shut her eyes, Mary saw the ripped and shredded body.

"It's a wonder she spoke at all" said Nurse Eden. "What in God's name was it?"

"A bomb," said Mary.

"One o' the Zeppelins?"

"No. An aeroplane. I thought I heard it on the Heath but I fancied it was one of ours. It must have shut off its engines as it came down. That's why we didn't notice it."

"The filthy pigs!" said Nurse Eden, all white and shaken. "See the pickle I'm in! Go and tell Dr. Hennis, Miss Postgate." Nurse looked at the mother, who had dropped face down on the floor. "She's only in a fit. Turn her over."

Mary heaved Mrs. Gerritt right side up, and hurried off for the doctor. When she told her tale, he asked her to sit down in the surgery till he got her something.

"But I don't need it, I assure you," said she. "I don't think it would be wise to tell Miss Fowler about it, do you? Her heart is so irritable in this weather."

Dr. Hennis looked at her admiringly as he packed up his bag.

"No. Don't tell anybody till we're sure," he said, and hastened to the "Royal Oak," while Mary went on with the paraffin. The village behind her was as quiet as usual, for the news had not yet spread. She frowned a little to herself, her large nostrils expanded uglily and from time to time she muttered a phrase which Wynn, who never restrained himself before his women-folk, had applied to the enemy. "Bloody pagans! They *are* bloody pagans. But," she continued, falling back on the teaching that had made her what she was, "one mustn't let one's mind dwell on these things."

Before she reached the house Dr. Hennis, who was also a special constable, overtook her in his car.

"Oh, Miss Postgate," he said, "I wanted to tell you that that accident at the 'Royal Oak' was due to Gerritt's stable tumbling down. It's been dangerous for a long time. It ought to have been condemned."

"I thought I heard an explosion too," said Mary.

"You might have been misled by the beams snapping. I've been looking at 'em. They were dry-rotted through and through. Of course, as they broke, they would make a noise just like a gun."

"Yes?" said Mary politely.

"Poor little Edna was playing underneath it," he went on, still holding her with his eyes, "and that and the tiles cut her to pieces, you see?"

"I saw it," said Mary, shaking her head. "I heard it too."

"Well, we cannot be sure." Dr. Hennis changed his tone completely. "I know both you and Nurse Eden (I've been speaking to her) are perfectly trustworthy, and I can rely on you not to say anything—yet at least. It is no good to stir up people unless—"

"Oh, I never do—anyhow," said Mary, and Dr. Hennis went on to the county town.

After all, she told herself, it might, just possibly, have been the collapse of the old stable that had done all those things to poor little Edna. She was sorry she had even hinted at other things, but Nurse Eden was discretion itself. By the time she reached home the affair seemed increasingly remote by its very monstrosity. As she came in, Miss Fowler told her that a couple of aeroplanes passed half an hour ago.

"I thought I heard them," she replied, "I'm going down to the garden now. I've got the paraffin."

"Yes, but—what *have* you got on your boots? They're soaking wet. Change them at once."

Not only did Mary obey but she wrapped the boots in a newspaper, and put them into the string bag with the bottle. So, armed with the longest kitchen poker, she left.

"It's raining again," was Miss Fowler's last word, "but—I know you won't be happy till that's disposed of."

"It won't take long. I've got everything down there, and I've put the lid on the destructor to keep the wet out."

The shrubbery was filling with twilight by the time she had completed her arrangements and sprinkled the sacrificial oil. As she lit the match that would burn her heart to ashes, she heard a groan or a grunt behind the dense Portugal laurels.

"Cheape?" she called impatiently, but Cheape, with his ancient lumbago, in his comfortable cottage would be the last man to profane the sanctuary. "Sheep," she concluded, and threw in the fusee. The pyre went up in a roar, and the immediate flame hastened night around her.

"How Wynn would have loved this!" she thought, stepping back from the blaze.

By its light she saw, half hidden behind a laurel not five paces away, a bareheaded man sitting very stiffly at the foot of one of the oaks. A broken branch lay across his lap—one booted leg protruding from beneath it. His head moved ceaselessly from side to side, but his body was as still as the tree's trunk. He was dressed—she moved sideways to look more closely—in a uniform something like Wynn's, with a flap buttoned across the chest. For an instant she had some idea that it might be one of the young flying men she had met at the funeral. But their heads were dark and glossy. This man's was as pale as a baby's, and so closely cropped that she could see the disgusting pinky skin beneath. His lips moved.

"What do you say?" Mary moved towards him and stooped.

"Laty! Laty! Laty!" he muttered, while his hands picked at the dead wet leaves. There was no doubt as to his nationality. It made her so angry that she strode back to the destructor, though it was still too hot to use the poker there. Wynn's books seemed to be catching well. She looked up at the oak behind the man; several of the light upper and two or three rotten lower branches had broken and scattered their rubbish on the shrubbery path. On the lowest fork a helmet with dependent strings showed like a bird's-nest in the light of a long-tongued flame. Evidently this person had fallen through the tree. Wynn had told her that it was quite possible for people to fall out of aeroplanes. Wynn told her too, that trees were useful things to break an aviator's fall, but in this case the aviator must have been broken or he would have moved from his queer position. He seemed helpless except for his horrible rolling head. On the other hand, she could see a pistol case at his belt—and Mary loathed pistols. Months ago, after reading certain Belgian reports together, she and Miss Fowler had had dealings with one—a huge revolver with flat-nosed bullets, which latter, Wynn said, were forbidden by the rules of war to be used against civilised enemies. "They're good enough for us," Miss Fowler had replied. "Show Mary how it works." And Wynn, laughing at the mere possibility of any such need, had led the craven winking Mary into the Rector's disused quarry, and had shown her how to fire the terrible machine. It lay now in the top-left-hand drawer of her toilet-table—a memento not included in the burning. Wynn would be pleased to see how she was not afraid.

She slipped up to the house to get it. When she came through the rain, the eyes in the head were alive with expectation. The mouth even tried to smile. But at sight of the revolver its corners went down just like Edna Gerritt's. A tear trickled from one eye, and the head rolled from shoulder to shoulder as though trying to point out something.

"Cassée. Tout cassée," it whimpered.

"What do you say?" said Mary disgustedly, keeping well to one side, though only the head moved.

"Cassée," it repeated. "Che me rends. Le médicin! Toctor!"

"Nein!" said she, bringing all her small German to bear with the big pistol. "Ich haben der todt Kinder gesehn."

The head was still. Mary's hand dropped. She had been careful to keep her finger off the trigger for fear of accidents. After a few moments' waiting, she returned to the destructor, where the flames were falling, and churned up Wynn's charring books with the poker. Again the head groaned for the doctor.

"Stop that!" said Mary, and stamped her foot. "Stop that, you bloody pagan!"

The words came quite smoothly and naturally. They were Wynn's own words, and Wynn was a gentleman who for no consideration on earth would have torn little Edna into those vividly coloured strips and strings. But this thing hunched under the oak-tree had done that thing. It was no question of reading horrors out of newspapers to Miss Fowler. Mary had seen it with her own eyes on the "Royal Oak" kitchen table. She must not allow her mind to dwell upon it. Now Wynn was dead, and everything connected with him was lumping and rustling and tinkling under her busy poker into red black dust and grey leaves of ash. The thing beneath the oak would die too. Mary had seen death more than once. She came of a family that had a knack of dying under, as she told Miss Fowler, "most distressing circumstances." She would stay where she was till she was entirely satisfied that It was dead—dead as dear papa in the late 'eighties; aunt Mary in 'eighty-nine; mamma in 'ninety-one; cousin Dick in 'ninety-five; Lady McCausland's housemaid in 'ninety-nine; Lady McCausland's sister in nineteen hundred and one; Wynn buried five days ago; and Edna Gerritt still waiting for decent earth to hide her. As she thought—her underlip caught up by one faded canine, brows knit and nostrils wide—she wielded the poker with lunges that jarred the grating at the bottom, and careful scrapes round the brick-work above. She looked at her wrist-watch. It was getting on to half-past four, and the rain was coming down in earnest. Tea would be at five. If It did not die before that time, she would be soaked and would have to change. Meantime, and this occupied her, Wynn's things were burning well in spite of the hissing wet though now and again a book-back with a quite distinguishable title would be heaved up out of the mass. The exercise of stoking had given her a glow which seemed to reach to the marrow of her bones. She hummed—Mary never had a voice—to herself. She had never believed in all those advanced views—though Miss Fowler herself leaned a little that way—of woman's work in the world; but now she saw there was much to be said for them. This, for instance, was *her* work—work which no man, least of all Dr. Hennis, would ever have done. A man, at such a crisis, would be what Wynn called a "sportsman;" would leave everything to fetch help, and would certainly bring It into the house. Now a woman's business was to make a happy home for—for a husband and children. Failing these—it was not a thing one should allow one's mind to dwell upon—but—

"Stop it!" Mary cried once more across the shadows. "Nein, I tell you! Ich haben der todt Kinder gesehn."

But it was a fact. A woman who had missed these things could still be useful—more useful than a man in certain respects. She thumped like a pavior through the settling ashes at the secret thrill of it. The rain was damping the fire, but she could feel—it was too dark to see—that her work was done. There was a dull red glow at the bottom of the destructor, not enough to char the wooden lid if she slipped it half over against the driving wet. This arranged, she leaned on the poker and waited, while an increasing rapture laid hold on her. She ceased to think. She gave herself up to feel. Her long pleasure was broken by a sound that she had waited for in agony several times in her life. She leaned forward and listened, smiling. There could be no mistake. She closed her eyes and drank it in. Once it ceased abruptly.

"Go on," she murmured, half aloud. "That isn't the end."

Then the end came very distinctly in a lull between two rain-gusts. Mary Postgate drew her breath short between her teeth and shivered from head to foot. "*That's* all right," said she contentedly, and went up to the house, where she scandalised the whole routine by taking a luxurious hot bath before tea, and came down looking, as Miss Fowler said when she saw her lying all relaxed on the other sofa, "quite handsome!"

BILL'S FIRST AIRPLANE RIDE

FROM *BILL BRUCE AND THE PIONEER AVIATORS*

---

by MAJOR HENRY H. ARNOLD

The giants of aviation history rarely wrote fiction. One of the few who did, perhaps the only one, was Henry H. "Hap" Arnold, who penned a series of novels for youngsters in the 1920s to supplement his income as an Army officer. A 1907 graduate of the U.S. Military Academy, Arnold learned to fly with the Wright brothers in 1911, earning Pilot's license #29 and becoming one of only two active Army aviators. A disciple of Billy Mitchell, Arnold was named Chief of the Air Corps in 1938. In March 1942, he was named Commanding General of the U.S. Army Air Forces. From the seat of a Wright Model B Flyer to command of the largest air force the world will ever know . . . that was Hap Arnold.

In the following excerpt from a book published in 1928, the hero of Arnold's tales, Bill Bruce, is a youngster of thirteen years getting his first airplane ride with Arch Hoxey, a real historical figure who was one of the Wrights' pilots and a man Arnold undoubtedly knew well. The setting is the International Aviation Meet held at New York's Belmont Park in the fall of 1910.

If only . . . if only I could be thirteen again . . . have Wilbur Wright slap me on the shoulder and send me off for my very first airplane ride with all the world watching, scramble aboard the Flyer as Arch shouts over the noise of the engine to turn my cap around backwards and hang on tight. To see the earth fall away and ride those magic wings . . . To feel so fully, completely *alive*!

Bill did not take any chances of missing out on his first trip in an airplane. He hurried to a nearby lunch stand and bought a "hot dog" which he consumed as he raced back to the Wright hangars. Jim Taylor, the only one there, was sitting on a box eating his lunch.

"Why didn't you get your lunch?" asked Jim. "You had better take some of mine."

"I wanted to be sure and get here in time for that airplane ride, so I bought a 'hot dog' for lunch," answered Bill. "Aren't the others back yet?"

"You must be in a hurry to get that ride," said Jim. "They haven't been gone more than fifteen minutes."

"How will Hoxey carry two passengers in that plane?" asked Bill.

"One passenger will have to kneel in back of the seats and hold on as best he can. I don't know which of you it will be. This is the plane that he is going to use for the flight. We have been working on the engine all morning. It's running like a watch now."

"I don't see much there to hold on to," said Bill as he carefully inspected the frame work of the plane. "The backs of the seats are nothing but wood, and thin wood at that."

"I wouldn't worry about that now," said Jim. "When you are up on a flight, you won't have any trouble hanging on. I venture to say that we will find the imprints of your fingers in the wood if Hoxey does any of his famous stunts."

Jim got up from the box, gathered together the scraps from his lunch and went out of the tent to throw them in the trash can.

"Did you know that Hoxey took President Roosevelt for a ride in an airplane in St. Louis?" he asked when he returned.

"No, I didn't," said Bill.

"Well he did, and President Roosevelt enjoyed the trip, too. That being the case, you shouldn't worry about your trip. When an ex-president of the United States is willing to risk his life with Hoxey, you should have confidence enough to take a flight with him."

"I am not worrying about the risk," said Bill. "I just didn't see anything to hold on to. How long will we have to stay up in order to break the record?"

"The present record is a little less than two hours, so if you stay up for two hours a new record will be made."

"Will that little engine take three of us off the ground?" anxiously inquired Bill.

"You'd be surprised at what one of these little engines will do," replied Jim. "Why, one of these engines took a plane and a nine-hundred-pound load in the plane off the ground. It seems like a big load to put on a thirty horsepower engine, but the plane not only left the ground but also stayed in the air for some time. Frank Coffyn was piloting the plane at the time. The airplane ran quite a distance before it took off, but Coffyn made a beautiful getaway. The load that Hoxey is going to carry this afternoon will not be anywhere near as heavy as that."

Hoxey joined them during the conversation.

"Are you getting squeamish about going up?" he asked when Jim had finished speaking.

"I should say not," emphatically responded the boy.

"If you are," said Hoxey, "there are plenty of others who would be only too glad to take your place."

"I particularly desired to take you on this trip for two reasons," continued Hoxey. "First, Wilbur Wright promised you a ride. Second, you are light in weight. Naturally the lighter my passengers, the more gasoline I can carry and the longer I can stay in the air."

"Who will the third passenger be?" asked Bill.

"Another chap about your weight by the name of Ned Erickson."

While they were talking the plane was being rolled out onto the flying field and the engine was warmed up. Bill stood gazing at the plane, but his thoughts were far away. He was trying to anticipate how he was going to feel while flying. His thoughts were interrupted by Jim, who touched his arm and pointed toward the hangar. There Bill noticed Hoxey, who was motioning for him to come into the tent. Bill entered the tent and was given a sweater and a pair of goggles.

"Take off your coat and put this sweater on," said Hoxey. "You will be riding in the wind and you may get cold. After I once leave the ground, I don't want to come down until I have broken the record. You had better turn your cap backwards before you put your goggles on. Here comes Ned now."

After a few words of introduction, the three who were to be fellow passengers on an epoch-making flight went out to the plane together. They had but reached it when word was received from the starter that the plane must leave the ground in ten minutes. Ten minutes may be a long time in some cases, but with Bill it passed rapidly. He rather doubted his ability to enjoy the ride in spite of the bold front that he had put up.

Hoxey motioned for Bill to get into the plane first. Bill climbed up onto the seats, over their backs and knelt down as close to the backs of the seats as he could. Then Hoxey and Ned climbed into the seats in front of him. Bill had but little to hold on to as the backs of the seats were hard to grasp. However, by kneeling very low, he could run his arms through the braces which held up the back of one of the seats. His was a cramped position at best, but he made up his mind that if they had to come down before the two hours were up, it would be through no fault of his, even if he were paralyzed when they landed.

Hoxey gave a signal, the men released their hold on the wings and the plane rolled slowly over the ground. For a while Bill did not think that they were making any headway at all, but he looked ahead and saw that the distance to the trees which lined the field was rapidly diminishing. He looked at Hoxey and was confident that there was no cause for worry, for he sat there as unconcerned as if they were sitting around in the tent.

Bill looked ahead again. The trees were very much closer. It was not till then that Bill realized they had left the ground. There had been no bumps, no change of speed, in fact nothing to tell when the plane had left the ground and was flying through the air.

The smooth grass-covered flying field seemed to drop farther and farther beneath them as they approached the trees. Bill was sure that the plane would hit them, for it was still well below the highest branches. Just when he expected to hit, he closed his eyes and waited for the shock, but it never came. He opened his eyes and saw that they were high above a long open field. The trees were no longer in sight.

The air was rough and every once in a while the plane would drop several yards and then suddenly rise with a bump. He had a strong tendency to get air sick, the flying was so rough. He looked at Ned, who at that moment had turned and was smiling. That made Bill feel better, but the bumps still bothered him. They came with too much frequency for him to enjoy the ride.

By this time the plane was about two hundred feet in the air. Bill could see far across country and saw several small villages. The roads stretched out beneath in all directions. He picked up the road leading to Flower City and tried to follow it, but lost it in a clump of trees. He saw a stream that wound around through the meadow lands and woods like a silver ribbon. He began to take note of other details which unfolded themselves below as the plane traveled along. Automobiles moved along the roads, here and there people were walking, and off to the right was a farmer working in a field. How small they all looked! Near the farmer was a small dark object which moved rapidly across the ground. Could it be a dog? Bill looked closer. It was a dog; he could see it playing around its master.

The plane circled and came back over the aviation field. Bill picked out the different tents. He wondered if Cap Baldwin and Charlie Hamilton were watching the plane. He suddenly realized that he had recovered from his feeling of sickness. He was actually enjoying the ride. It was such a clean way to travel, no dust or dirt and no cinders like there were when riding on a railroad train.

The whole country stretched out beneath him like a large map. He picked out the different roads over which he had ridden on his motorcycle. As they made another large circle, he saw Garden City and at last Flower City, but he was too far away to recognize his own house. He longed to ask Hoxey to fly closer to Flower City so that he could get a good look at it from the air and perhaps wave to Bob, who might be out, but there was no way of making himself heard above the roar of the engine.

Hoxey pointed to a watch hanging from a strut, and Bill saw that they had been in the air for a half hour. For the first time he felt cramped in his knees. He changed his position as much as he could in order to get relief. It was only when he thought about his cramped position that he realized how tired his legs were. When he looked over the wide expanse of country beneath him, he forgot his physical discomforts.

They passed over the Hempstead aviation field and Bill

tried to find the place where the model race had started. He followed the line of hangars with his eyes and was astonished at the ease with which he could identify the spot. Then he looked for the place where his model had landed when it had won the distance race and was more astonished at the comparatively short distance that it had covered.

In the meantime the bumps were getting steadily worse. It seemed sometimes as if the bottom had dropped out of the air and the plane must surely crash to the ground, but each time the plane would catch some solid air and come back upward with a thump. Bill thought that those terrific jolts must surely break the wings off the plane, but there was no indication of any such dire results. A look at Hoxey, who was sitting calmly piloting the plane, restored his confidence.

Once the plane jumped upward so fast that he was sure that his knees would be forced through the wing. He had no more than recovered from that bump before the plane dropped from under him and his knees left the wing. Hanging on only with his hands, he found himself struggling to keep from hitting the top wing. The plane hit solid air again and he took a new grip on the seat brace.

Hoxey turned the plane and headed back toward the aviation field. Either the bumps were not now so bad or he was becoming accustomed to them. Hoxey turned in his seat and said something, but Bill could not hear a sound. He judged by the movement of Hoxey's lips that he was asking if it was too rough and whether or not he should land the plane. Bill, remembering that Hoxey had said that under no circumstances did he want to land until they had been in the air for at least two hours, shook his head "No." Hoxey smiled. "Evidently," thought Bill. "I made the proper answer."

Hoxey was still looking to the rear when the plane made a violent jump and Bill started to slide toward the rear of the plane. The seat brace of Ned's seat had given way. Bill grabbed for anything that he could reach to save himself. In back of him were a few wires to stop him from sliding off the wing, but there were also many large open spaces where there was nothing but the air between him and the ground.

His hand came into contact with Ned's sweater and he held on like grim death. Ned himself, however, held a position none too secure, for he had fallen to the rear when the back of his seat had given way. Hoxey turned the controls loose and gave Bill a jerk that brought him forward on the wing. Once again they were safe for a time at least, but an even more violent uncontrolled movement of the plane was yet to give them the crowning thrill of the day.

When Hoxey turned and caught Bill to keep him from slipping off the lower wing, the airplane made a vertical dive toward the ground. The sudden change in direction of the plane brought Ned back to a sitting position and Bill back to a kneeling position in back of Hoxey's seat. Ned braced his feet against the foot rest and wrapped his arms around one of the wires crossing in front of his seat. Bill grabbed the brace in back of Hoxey's seat and hoped that it was stronger than the one which had given way so unexpectedly a few seconds before.

Hoxey caught the controls almost as soon as the plane went into the dive, but not before it had plunged vertically downward for almost a hundred feet. He worked frantically with the controls to level it out again. Bill looked down and the plane was headed directly toward a clump of very high trees. It seemed ages before Hoxey regained control and brought the plane out of the dive. When they were flying on a level keel again, Hoxey turned and smiled encouragingly at his passengers. He then gazed intently at Bill to ascertain how he was holding on. Then, after seeing that Ned had a firm hold onto the brace wires, he motioned for Bill to grasp Ned's belt with his free hand. Once again the conditions were such that the flight could be continued, provided that the passengers were willing.

Bill was scared, but hoped that he did not show it. He smiled at Ned, but had a feeling that it had been a sickly smile. Finally he had sufficient courage to look down at the ground again and there saw groups of people who had evidently been running toward the place where it was thought that the plane would crash. Automobiles were speeding along the roads toward the clump of trees from all directions. When the plane had been brought out of its dive, the men running on the ground stopped where they were and now looked up at it. Bill could see their upturned faces.

It occurred to Bill that theirs must have been a miraculous escape, for obviously the people on the ground had rushed toward the plane believing that there was no possible chance of the occupants of the plane surviving the fall. The near accident must have furnished a far greater thrill to the people on the ground than it did to the passengers in the plane. Hoxey knew at all times what was happening, Bill and Ned thought that they knew, but the observers on the ground could only conjecture what had taken place.

Hoxey turned and Bill, seeing that his lips were moving, knew that Hoxey was talking, but what was he saying? The roar of the engine drowned all sounds save its own. Bill shook his head, he could not hear. Hoxey made motions with his hand. First he pointed to the watch hanging on the strut, then down to the ground, and finally, after a pause, made a circle with his hand upward. Bill surmised that he was being asked if he wanted to land or to continue the flight. He looked at the watch. They had been up almost an hour. Hoxey would undoubtedly keep on flying if the passengers were willing. Bill wondered if he could hang on for another hour. If he could they would probably break the record.

Bill glanced at Ned, who was pointing up into the air and shaking his head "Yes." That decided Bill. If Ned could last the flight out with his arms wrapped around the wires, there was no reason why he couldn't hang on to Ned's belt and stick it out, too. It seemed to Bill that it had taken hours for him to make his decision, whereas actually it had taken but a very few seconds. He cautiously released one hand, made a circular motion upward and nodded his head "Yes." Hoxey said something which Bill understood to be "That's the stuff."

The air became smoother after that last violent bump which had come so near to wrecking them. It was a little rough, but not uncomfortably so. Bill was glad of this, for his position in the plane was somewhat precarious to say the least. He was holding on with one hand through Ned's belt and the other through the brace in back of Hoxey's seat. It was a most uncomfortable position, but he had made up his mind to stick it out and his decision was final. No one was ever going to have the opportunity of saying that he was a quitter.

After they had made another wide circle around the field, Bill looked at the watch. It had been but ten minutes since the mishap. Time was dragging terribly. However, he had recovered from his fright and was taking an interest again in the ever changing scenes which were passing beneath them.

The sun was sinking in the sky and the shadows were getting longer. Areas under trees and bushes on the eastward side of buildings had grown much darker, so dark in fact that it was difficult to penetrate them with the eye. He found it harder to pick up individual people on the ground. Here and there the wind shield of an automobile was set at just the right angle to reflect the sun into their faces. Although blinding while they lasted, these reflections were gone in an instant. The water in creeks, ponds and lakes took on a golden hue as it lay between them and the sun, but changed in color to a deep dark blue as it passed beneath the plane. The bumps in the air grew less as the sun sank toward the tree tops and finally disappeared altogether.

Bill was thoroughly enjoying the flight now in spite of the fact that his legs were almost numb from being in the same position so long. He wanted to move them, but did not dare for fear that he would start slipping again. When he thought of the pain in his legs, he had a desire to look at the watch and see if it wasn't time to land, but when he thought of this being his first and possibly his only airplane ride, he wished that they still had the full two hours to remain in the air.

Hoxey held up his hand and opened it twice. Bill then looked at the watch and saw that they had to stay up only ten minutes more to complete the two hours. There seemed to be no reason why they shouldn't stay up even longer, for the engine was running perfectly and, as far as he was concerned, all danger of his sliding off the plane was gone. He hoped that they would stay up for three hours.

They flew across the aviation field and Bill saw the upturned faces of the mechanics as they stood in front of the tents. During the first part of their flight other planes had been in the air. Now and again a plane would come close to theirs and the occupants would wave to them, but now it was getting late and the other planes had landed. Some had already been taken into their tents, others he could see being rolled in. How small they all looked! He could hardly realize that the miniature planes on the ground were in reality as large as the one in which he was riding and the mechanics handling them were truly life-sized men.

Bill figured that with two more turns of the field they would have broken the record. He wondered if Hoxey would land at once or stay up longer. This was by far the most pleasant method of traveling that he had ever experienced. It was better than motorcycling in every way. In the air they were not tied down to roads. They could follow any route which their fancy dictated. No wonder that the birds seemed to enjoy themselves so much when soaring overhead. Hills, trees, villages, fences and rivers were all alike when flying. It was possible to go over them or pass around them, whichever the pilot preferred. How different it was from earthbound travel!

Bill again looked at the watch. Two more minutes and they would probably make a landing. One more turn and they would be headed toward the landing field. Just then the engine sputtered, gave a cough and stopped running. What had happened? Most certainly their flight was now over and they must land, but where and how? Bill did not know whether a plane could be safely landed with a dead engine or not, so he looked at Hoxey. Hoxey was smiling. Everything must be all right.

"Don't worry," shouted Hoxey, and they could hear his voice above the whir of the propellers. "We are out of gasoline, but we will make the field all right."

Bill looked for the landing field and it seemed to be miles away. As the ground came closer, he knew that they were losing altitude rapidly. The field was getting closer, too, but there were many high trees between them and that level stretch of ground. Another glance at the watch and Bill saw that they had been up for two hours and one minute. No matter where they landed now, the record had been broken.

The plane was not losing altitude so fast now, but they were not moving forward so swiftly either. The plane seemed to be gliding down a long hill, but it was a smooth hill, for there were none of the rough spots which threw him about so when coasting on his motorcycle. More than anything else, it was like one of the ethereal trips that he had made in the dreams of his early childhood.

The trees at the edge of the aviation field came closer, but the plane was still above them. As they passed over the top branches, Bill was sure that he could reach out and touch the leaves. They dropped closer to the ground and then the plane leveled off and sailed along just a few feet above the grass. Just when the wheels touched, Bill never knew, for there had been no bump or jar to mark the time or place when the plane ceased to be supported by the air and was running on its own wheels on the ground.

The plane rolled a few yards and then stopped. Ned jumped out with a shout. Hoxey climbed out more slowly, but Bill, when he tried to get out, became aware of the fact that his legs would not move. They had lost all feeling. He rubbed them with his hands to try and restore the circulation.

"Here," called Hoxey, "give me a hand and help me lift out from the plane one of the gamest youngsters that I have ever seen."

By that time Jim and Mart, with several of the other mechanics, had arrived. They lifted Bill from the plane and rubbed his legs.

"You must have had some flight," said Jim after he had examined the plane. "You broke the record, but I'll be darned if I see how you did it. What did you hold on to, Bill?"

"Part of the time nothing, and the rest of the time Ned's belt," answered Bill.

"But what did you hold on to, Ned?" asked Jim Taylor.

"It was up to me to get a grip on something that would hold us both in the plane, so I wrapped my arms around those front brace wires," said Ned.

By that time Bill's legs were behaving almost normally and he stood up. He saw Hoxey talking to Wilbur Wright and Johnstone and knew that he was telling them the details of the flight. Bill staggered over to the group.

"I want to congratulate you upon the way that you kept

your head," said Wilbur Wright to Bill. "There are a lot of people who would have done just the wrong thing and then not one of you would be here now. The old record is no more, for you stayed up in the air for two hours and two minutes, official time."

He then went over to the plane and took the watch from the strut.

"Bill," he said, "I want you to take this as a souvenir of the flight. If it had not been for your courage, the record would never have been broken. You are the one who made the decision to stay up after the seat back gave way. The others had comfortable positions during the flight, but it took a lot of nerve for you to stick to it in that cramped position. How do you feel now?"

"I'm all right now," said Bill. "For a while up there in the air I thought that, if any record was broken, it would have been a two-man instead of a three-man record. One thing sure, I'll never forget this flight."

"You had better come over tomorrow and do your flying on the ground while you watch someone else give the crowd the thrills," remarked Hoxey. "You have done your share today."

"Tomorrow's events are all of a spectacular nature and you will enjoy them," said Johnstone.

"I'll be here all right tomorrow, but the next time that I go up as an added passenger, I am going to have a backstop put in along the rear edge of the wings," called Bill as he started for home.

LEARNING TO FLY

FROM *WINGED VICTORY*

---

by V. M. YEATES

In my opinion, the best novel, bar none, about World War I aviation is *Winged Victory*. Victor Yeates flew Sopwith Camels, was shot down twice, and crashed several more times, all in 248 hours of flying without a parachute on the Western Front. The RAF discharged him in the summer of 1918 after he contracted tuberculosis.

The flying is central to *Winged Victory*—no one ever wrote it better—but it was only a part of Yeates' tale. Unlike the typical ex-pilot scribbling for the pulps, Yeates wanted to tell us of the savagery of war, tell us of the grim, bitter reality of young pilots who had found a new way to butcher each other. What he achieved was one of the great war novels of all time. It was his only book; he died of TB in 1934, the year it was published.

On the twenty-first of March, the batman called Tom and Allen for C flight's dawn job, and for once Tom did not go to sleep again. There was a tremendous racket going on; every kind of artillery seemed to be in action. It was certainly the prelude to the big German push. Thank God he was away from that rain of high explosives. Even to hear the distant tumult made his belly unhappy. Allen sat up.

"What a row! I suppose it's started."

Seddon awoke. Williamson awoke. They sat up in their camp beds, listening.

"Good Lord! It must be on a fifty mile front," said Williamson.

"Anyhow, it brings the end nearer."

Outside the sky must be bubbling with flame, but the light of the lamps prevented their seeing more of it than small alterations in the tone of the windows' blankness as the tree-filtered glare varied.

"I expect we shall find it quite interesting watching the big push from above, and I dare say we shan't get machine-gunned so much as in peace-time. They'll be busier with other targets."

"You're a great optimist, Bill," Tom replied. "All the same, I wouldn't mind an armour plated seat."

"Why not a seat at the War Office while you're wishing? All among the patriots. Haven't you any influence?" Seddon inquired.

"If you only disliked Germans as much as you dislike patriots, in two months you would be known to the press as Captain Seddon, Terror of the Huns."

"Put in a V.C. if you can spare me one."

"V.C., R.I.P., Defender of the Faith."

"Against Tom Cundall."

"Stop it, you back-chat comedians," Williamson demanded. "You're painful. I'm going to sleep again."

"Sleep no more, Macbill. The push has started." Tom got out of bed. "What about it, Allen? Shall we try to capture our eggs before they're hard boiled?"

"Right. I'm with you." Allen sprang out of bed.

"It's the greatest achievement of the Huns so far, getting Cundall up twenty minutes earlier than necessary," declared Seddon.

The eggs, nevertheless, were boiled hard; but they had time for a comfortable smoke before going up, and Allen fortified himself by re-reading a letter from his girl.

It was a fine morning, but misty. To the west the mist lay in dense patches, but it was clearer towards the lines. There the ground was thickly dotted with appearing and dissolving smoke of shell bursts. Tom's engine started to miss, and would not pick up, so he gave the "dud engine" signal and turned back to the aerodrome. As it was only a matter of a plug, the trouble was soon put right. Then Tom wondered whether he should stop at home or go out again and try to find the flight, which was not due back for an hour. He wasn't particularly likely to run across them, but perhaps the attempt should be made. He need not go far over the lines alone if it looked dangerous, and it seemed out of proportion to miss nearly a whole job just for a dirty plug. So he took off again and made for the lines. The ground mist was increasing, better not stay out long. He turned south when he reached the lines, watching the eastern sky carefully for Huns; but he seemed quite alone in the sky. Looking westwards, there was little to be seen but the white carpet of mist. He made a quick dash over Hunland, dropped his bombs from six thousand feet, and dived away westwards. It seemed to take an hour to get down to a thousand feet, with the mist all the time increasing until it covered everything except for here and there breaks. Soon he was flying over an apparently limitless sea of shining white cloud; and his engine started missing again. He flew north to where Arras had been a few minutes ago, but Arras was quite obliterated. All he could see through occasional rifts was the infinite desolation of an old battlefield; water-filled shell-holes and disused trench-systems.

He must remember that the wind was from the west, and would drift him towards Hunland. He turned west to look for a gap in the fog where he could land: the sooner he found one the better, or there might not be any gaps left to find. He soon came to a dark patch in the whiteness, and went down to investigate it. Circling, he made out a road with all sorts of motor traffic passing along it. He was on the right side of the lines, but there were too many shell-holes about for him to attempt landing there, and he wandered farther west.

Gaps were very scarce. He had been a fool to set out again. In consequence of an exaggerated sense of duty, seemingly brought on by the big push, he ran a considerable risk of being wiped out in a stupid crash trying to land in a fog. But if he got away with it this time, he would always listen to the still, small voice of discretion.

He made calculations. Probably he could keep on another forty minutes. There was no chance of the mist clearing in that time. He had to find a gap or crash.

He flew and flew. A dark line showed ahead. As he approached, it broadened into a long gap in which lay part of a village and a strip of fields. He circled and glided down into the nearest field; but he found when he tried to land that it was impossible; he was floating down the side of a hill, and he had to open out and climb through the mist. Probably the gap was along a ridge of high ground. He flew over the end of the village and went down to have a look at a field visible there. This seemed flat enough, but it was ploughed land. He zoomed out of the mist, but quickly decided he must take the chance of trying to land on furrows. He might not find another gap. He circled to get in position. He had never come down on furrows before, but he knew that the correct thing was to land with them and not across them. Luckily they seemed to run more or less with the direction in which the wind would be blowing, if there still was any wind; there had been a little when he took off. Landing, you had to hold off as long as possible so as to pancake, and touch ground with as little forward motion as might be.

Having got the theory of it clear in his mind, Tom glided down, side-slipping to lose speed. Then he straightened out and floated along the furrows into the mist. He got his tail well down and pancaked a little way in good style, but the ground was so soft that the wheels dug in dead, and up went the tail till the Camel was standing on its nose; then gently over on its back, with Tom hanging upside down in the cockpit.

He put one hand on the ground and undid the belt with the other and wriggled out of the wreck, a little muddy and feeling foolish. There was nothing to be seen but a small area of ploughland in the enclosing mist; but he could hear again, and the dominant sound was the thunder of unceasing bombardment: it was very distant.

He lighted a cigarette and inspected the aeroplane. It had settled down gently and did not seem damaged beyond the broken prop and crumpled rudder upon which the tail was resting. It would have to be stripped to be taken away, and that would be a muddy job for somebody. Well, he must do something, and the correct thing was to find a guard for the aeroplane and then telephone the squadron. The village was probably half a kilometre away, but where was the road to it? He certainly could not explore in the mud and fog with nothing to guide him. So he sat down on the tail plane and listened for any approaching sounds that might indicate the direction of the nearest road. For a long ten minutes nothing happened. Then he heard a motor. He got off his perch and went forwards a few yards and came to the edge of a bank which had lain just beyond the range of vision and would have caused a more interesting crash if the aeroplane had drifted a very little farther. A few feet below him lay a road. He scrambled down the bank, and the motor, an A.S.C. lorry, loomed through the mist.

The driver said that the next village (they were almost there) was "Arkeeves," but he didn't think there was anything there; he was bound for the railhead about two miles beyond. There would be a telephone at the railhead. There were two men beside the driver on the lorry. They both wanted to see the crash.

"I shall want one of you to guard the aeroplane while I go along to the railhead and telephone. The lorry can pick up the guard on its return."

"It's a mercy you weren't killed, sir," said the guard, when he saw with wonder the upside-down wreck.

"I could do that a dozen times without getting hurt. Now your job is to see that nobody so much as lays a finger on it, and that no matches are struck near it."

Tom returned to the lorry and they set out for the railhead. They soon ran out of the mist and through the village of Arquèves and down a hill into the mist again, but it was beginning to clear. In ten minutes they reached the railhead, and Tom went to the telephone room and asked the operator to get the squadron for him; but the operator said he couldn't get

Arras area, the line had been broken somewhere by shell fire. Perhaps if he tried again in an hour or two it might have been repaired. The operator was a difficult man to talk to, being permanently engaged, apparently, in six different but simultaneous conversations. So Tom went out of the telephone room with the immediate idea of looking for food. It was half past nine. A tender emerged from the fog, and he was pleased to see that the driver was in R.F.C. uniform. He waved a beckoning arm, and the tender pulled up by him. The driver, who was alone, got out and saluted.

He was from a local Aircraft Park, about ten miles away. Tom told him what had happened, and he said he thought his people would send over and collect the crash right away. He would get them on the telephone. He was an elderly man, and inclined to father Tom.

"I'll get you some breakfast, sir, if you like. I dare say you could do with it. If you wouldn't mind eating it in the tender. I'll get it a lot quicker than if you went to the R.T.O. I know my way about here, sir."

"Thanks," said Tom, "I wish you would. But we'd better ring through to your people first and make arrangements."

So they went to the telephone room and talked to the A.P. which said it would send along transport to deal with the crash at once, and the Ak Emma[1] went off in search of food. He returned in a few minutes with a tray containing plenty of bacon and eggs, bread, butter, marmalade, and coffee.

"That's fine," said Tom; "you're a friend in need."

"That's all right, sir. If you'll excuse me, I'll go and have a snack myself."

Tom ate his breakfast with appetite. It was these wallahs with stationary jobs away in the rear who did themselves well, he reflected. They had means of tapping supplies before they

---

[1] Air Mechanic.

got through to the mere cannon fodder in the trenches. A rail-head must be a particularly good spot. Who would be a hero? "Not me," said Tom to himself. The distant gunfire rumbled and rattled: heroes were being blown to pieces while other people ate bacon and eggs in comfort. Who would belong to the death or glory group if he could join the bacon-and-eggs party? There was no point in being blown to pieces, and as for glory, it might some day help to keep a first offender out of jail, and that was about all that could be said for it. And anyhow, what was it all about, this fighting? It certainly wasn't Tom Cundall's affair. Let the property owners fight their own battles. He would have bacon and eggs if he could get them.

The Ak Emma returned later with an air of serenity. "Had enough, sir?"

"Yes, thanks. Good feed. I gather you manage to do your-selves pretty well in these parts."

"Grub's none too good at the A.P., sir. But there's usually plenty doing 'ere if you know the cook."

"Well, have you anything more to do here? We'd better be getting along to the crash in case your people turn up."

"I've got a few things to pick up. Won't take me long, sir."

"Right. Will you tell the driver of the A.S.C. lorry I don't want him to do anything else except pick up his man."

Before he left the railhead Tom inquired again at the tele-phone room. The line to Arras was still out of order.

The mist had cleared at the scene of the crash, and the news of it had spread. A dozen people of various races were looking at the aeroplane, and the guard appeared to be having an argu-ment with some of the khaki element who possibly did not take his authority very seriously. However, the argument ceased at Tom's approach, and some saluting was done.

"Anything to report?"

"No, sir. All correct."

"Your lorry will be along soon. You are relieved now."

The guard saluted and dismissed himself for a smoke. Tom had nothing to do but wait. He leaned against the fuselage and listened while his new friend the Ak Emma told him about his wife and family at Camberwell. He had a girl of seventeen and a boy of fifteen, besides smaller children. But it was the two eldest that were troubling him. The boy swore he would join up the day he was sixteen. And as for the girl, the missis said there was no holding her.

By half past ten the Ak Emma had become restless, and suggested he had better go and find out why help had not come. Tom was bored with him and agreed. He was in no hurry. Doubtless he would be able to get lunch in Arquèves. He sat on the fuselage and waited.

The number of sightseers remained fairly constant, but the individuals kept coming and going. No officer, however, appeared among them for some time after the Ak Emma's departure, and then Tom saw the approach of a captain's badges and a clerical collar. He slid to earth.

"Good morning, padre."

"Good morning. Are you all right?"

"Quite, thanks."

"That's good. I heard there had been a crash here, and I came over to see if anyone was hurt. Is your machine damaged?"

"Not a great deal. But I shan't be able to fly it away."

"Won't you? Oh, it's upside down. I see now." The padre laughed with remarkable heartiness, and then checked himself. "You're lucky to be alive, I suppose."

"Not on account of this little crash. I only turned over landing on this soft ground. I might do it a dozen times without hurting myself."

"Indeed. And what are you going to do now?"

Tom gave him an account of the then state of affairs, and the conversation became discursive. After a time Dulwich for some reason entered into it, and they discovered that they had both been born there. That two natives of so sequestered a hamlet as nineteenth-century Dulwich should meet for the first time beside an overturned aeroplane in a field near Arquèves was too queer an event to be disregarded. There must be some Purpose in it, if only to secure Tom a luncheon. It appeared that the padre lived at a Corps School, which had its locus in a valley some fifteen minutes walk away.

"School?" inquired Tom. "What do you teach?"

"Oh, gas and bombs and such things."

Tom glanced at the padre, but saw no doubt in his face. The man of God and the men of gas; by a supreme act of tolerance, was it, that they fraternized? Not so. Neither of them really meant what they taught. Their real selves were compartmented from their professions; they were all good fellows together steering by Current Usage. Not exactly hypocrites, Tom thought, for *fingent simul credunique*, they believed in their own simulations.

The padre was a charming man to talk to. The time passed quickly, and it was half past twelve.

"Come back with me and have some lunch. We can send a guard for your aeroplane, and you can telephone your squadron from there, and wait in some comfort."

"Thanks very much. I'd like to. But I must get one of these men to do guard until you can send a proper guard."

That done, they set off. A little way along the road they met an R.F.C. tender, which stopped when the driver saw Tom.

"Do you know where an aeroplane has landed near here, sir?"

"I landed a little way along the road."

"Oh well, sir, we're from 72 Squadron. The Aircraft Park rang up and asked us to send someone along to start you up."

"They're crazy. I turned over. I told them it was a crash. You can wash out."

Tom held on his way lunchwards indignantly. These noncombatant R.F.C. people must be quite mad.

"Never mind," said the padre, "whose things happen in wartime."

The immense reverberations of gunfire supported his statement.

———————

The Corps School was a restful place, undisturbed by hurly-burlies and war, except for noises incidental to courses in bombing. And the staff mess was the most peaceful spot in the happy valley. The C.O. was a colonel and his adjutant a major. Besides the padre, there were two captains and two lieutenants in charge of courses of instruction. The actual instructing was done by sergeant-instructors, so that they had little to do but put in an occasional modest appearance in the background of a class, and fill in a few daily returns. The adjutant also prepared daily returns, or supervised their preparation by the orderly sergeant, and the colonel signed them. The colonel also took part occasionally in instructing a class, probably with the object of infusing the right atmosphere of kindliness. He was very well seconded in the kindliness department by the padre, who was in himself a tower of good will. It was impossible to be in his presence and not receive the illusion of the fundamental goodness of things, let the guns rumble in the distance how they might. Such, Tom thought, was the triumphant power of professional training allied with good natural ability.

Being introduced into this mess was, to one used to the R.F.C. atmosphere, something like finding oneself in the holy calm of a Pall Mall club miraculously endowed with faint but persistent Moral Purpose, after a New Year hullaballo in a Regent Street bar. Conversation was leisurely, prolonged, and decorous, and alcohol was used only in such small quantities as stimulated the larynx to this sort of talk. No one swore or discussed women. The profound purity of the mature English gentleman away from his womenfolk reigned.

They were pleased to have a flying man to talk to, being all quite ignorant of flying and having the impression that there was something specially daring and heroic about it. At luncheon, Tom, being plied with questions, yarned away about the war in the air; how whacked (the word was tolerated) the Huns were, and how the R.F.C. was keeping them whacked. Then he was taken to the office to telephone, and was able to get through to the squadron and had a rather indistinct conversation with James. If he was comfortable he might as well stay where he was, and transport would be sent for him as soon as possible, but it would not be till to-morrow. The rest of the flight had got back before the mist covered the aerodrome. Glad he was all right. . . .

Tom felt very foolish; if only someone else as well as he had been caught by the fog so would he have been kept in countenance. But to be caught by the fog foolishly and unnecessarily, and then to crash his bus forty miles from home just at the time when it was most needed, that was not the sort of thing to do whether the war was his concern or not. It was a failure, and it hurt his pride to fail ridiculously. He had taken on a job that officially assumed that he possessed all sorts of fine qualities of head and heart, and even if it was pure bluff, he hated his bluff to be seen through. Nothing hurts pride, he reflected, like being found out. But was he "found out?" Suppose someone else, Williamson for instance, had done what he had done, what would he have thought of him? None the worse; he would have congratulated him on getting away with it unharmed. There was nothing extraordinary in turning over landing on soft ploughed stuff, rather it was to be expected; Camels were notorious for that sort of thing. And he would probably have congratulated him for having got a day's rest from the war by the crash.

While this debate was going on inside him, he had reported the substance of his conversation to the adjutant, who at once placed a cubicle at his disposal for the night and put him in charge of his own batman. The batman borrowed pyjamas and toilet apparatus for him and told him the history of everyone in the mess; they were all gentlemen, if ever there were gentlemen, he said. The batman also talked about himself. He was by trade a dental mechanic, and he strongly advised Tom to have all his teeth out at the earliest opportunity, as it would save him a lot of bother in the long run, and false teeth were far easier to keep properly clean. Tom thanked him and went to sleep for two hours and the batman brought him a cup of tea and some cake. The colonel thought he might prefer tea in his room, as he must be tired after his adventures. Dinner would be at seven, and would he care to borrow a pair of slacks? Tom would, and some note-paper too. He had found the right spot for a forced landing.

At dinner the subject of conversation was flying. The usual questions were asked: why had he taken it up? what did he feel like the first time he went up? had he ever looped the loop? had he shot down any Huns? did he know McCudden or Micky Mannock or the Mad Major?

Tom told them that he had transferred to the R.F.C. because he needed a change from the infantry. He had been assured at the time that the average life of a pilot was six weeks. That was ten months ago. He was very glad he had made the change, for it meant a great deal to live in comfort and cleanliness all the time. And in winter the life was not so very trying, days being short and the weather often too bad for flying. Sometimes it was impossible to leave the ground for three or four days at a time. No doubt with summer coming on life would be a great deal harder, but the war might be over quite soon now, didn't they think?

This suggestion split the conversation up. The balance of opinion was against the probability of an early finish. The summer campaigns would have to work themselves out, and if nothing decisive happened, such as the capture of Paris and the Channel Ports, or on the other hand a German reverse ending in demoralization, then the war might be prolonged into next year. The colonel did not think the war would be won in the field at all, as a real break through had been proved impossible. It was a matter of which population was starved to breaking point first. One of the junior officers suggested that the American invasion must lead eventually to victory on the western front, but the colonel smiled. For him there were only two real nations on earth, English and French. And even the French had their faults, being pig-headed and rather too French.

Then they got back to flying, and Tom told them the first time he went up was in a Rumpty, that was to say, a Maurice Farman Shorthorn, a queer sort of bus like an assemblage of birdcages. You climbed with great difficulty through a network of wires into the nacelle, and sat perked up there, adorned with a crash helmet, very much exposed to the wondering gaze of men. There did not seem to be any *a priori* reason why this structure should leave the ground, but after dashing across the aerodrome at forty miles an hour for some time the thing did imperceptibly and gradually climb into the air. It was very like a ride on top of an omnibus. A Rumpty was no aeroplane for stunting. The flight was a quiet trip up to three hundred feet and down again. A few daring spirits who had tried stunting were dead. The C.O. of that squadron, a pompous and bossy penguin, Major Beak, maintained that Rumpties were good buses when you knew how to fly them. He had been on active service on them, in Mesopotamia, where he had contended valiantly with the heat bumps engendered by the fierce sun until the heat made him so bad tempered that he was invalided home to get rid of him. On the home front he was sufficiently senior to be able to avoid flying, and work off his bad temper on junior people who did fly. According to him Rumpties were fine, and it was only damned junior stupidity that jeered at them. They had to be used, for hundreds of them existed, a big order having been placed; and as they were of no use for any practical purpose, the only thing to do with them was to use them for training. The trainees would have to unlearn later all that they learnt then, but young pilots must begin at the beginning, and a Rumpty certainly was only just beginning to be an aeroplane. Flying with their antiquated controls was a mixture of playing a harmonium, working the village pump, and sculling a boat.

However, Tom became habituated to staggering through the atmosphere in these soaring cat's-cradles, and in the fullness of time he took one up by himself, and stayed up for an hour and a half, reaching in this time the eagle-baffling height of three thousand feet, whence he gazed down on the still sleeping western suburbs of London and felt himself to be a pilot. This flight was so successful that after breakfast he was sent up again in another machine.

By this time a fairly strong breeze was blowing from the southwest, and there was a ceiling of cloud at about seven hundred feet; not the weather in which a novice in a Rumpty was likely to enjoy himself. He flew round and round the aerodrome at five hundred feet, being bumped about irksomely by the choppy air. It was a great change from the still clear atmosphere of dawn . . . but an hour passed, and he might soon land. Then the engine spluttered and stopped. Tom knew one thing, that he must not stall, and immediately put the nose down into gliding position to maintain speed. The engine did not pick up. This was a forced landing, and by the time he realized the alarming truth he did not seem to have enough height to glide on to the aerodrome so as to land into the wind. There was a field in front that he must make for. The engine gave a splutter but subsided again. The field was rushing up at him. He was going down much too steeply. He was almost in the field. He was doing seventy; he would never get in. Trees were in front. The engine spluttered again. He had left the throttle open. He looked down and pulled it off, and then there was a shock and he was out of the aeroplane, lying on the ground a dozen yards from the remains of it. He had been thrown on his head, but the crash helmet had saved him. He must have flown into the ground; he didn't really know exactly what had happened; he found himself on the ground and the Rumpty smashed. He might have been unconscious for a little while. The nacelle was upside down on the ground with a pile of wreckage on it. He had been strapped in, but the safety belt had given; otherwise his neck must have been broken. But what a mess the old Rumpty was! One more write off. It was an achievement to smash up a Rumpty like that and not be hurt. He shook himself. Yes, he was quite uninjured; one shoe was missing, and the ankle felt a little bit wrenched. He walked over to the wreck and found his shoe wedged upside down under the nacelle with the toe projecting. He pulled at it, but it was fixed firmly. He got both hands to it and tugged and wriggled it, and suddenly it came away and he rolled over on his back.

Someone flew overhead as he was putting on his shoe, leaning over to look at him. He walked round the wreck, his own wreck. It was a good one. He ought to be dead. Was he, by the way? He couldn't see his dead body about, but it might be under the nacelle. The motor ambulance came jolting over the field towards him, and it was a relief when the orderly spoke to him, and he knew he was not a spirit. The matter ended with a fortnight's sick leave and a few words with Major Beak about his incompetence.

Since then he had had a number of minor crashes, mere landing accidents, but nothing to compare with that destruction of the Rumpty. Probably he had done the right thing in keeping straight on when his engine had conked. It was very easy for an inexperienced pilot to stall when he was doing turns with his engine off to try to reach a landing place, and that meant a dive or spin into the ground, which killed in nine cases out of ten. On a Rumpty, with the engine behind you, there was no hope at all. It would pulp you. How many fellows, some that could fly too, had been killed through trying to turn back to the aerodrome when their engine had cut out after taking off! Engines had a way of cutting out just then, and the instinct was to turn back, when really there wasn't room to do it, and the pilot inevitably held the nose up too much in trying to keep height and in a jiffy he was spinning with no chance whatever of getting out of it, and that was the end of him. Tom had only seen one case where the fellow got away with it. He had spun a Camel from a hundred and fifty feet right into the arms of a sturdy oak which caught him. He climbed down to earth none the worse and went into a pub across the road and celebrated his escape with an admiring audience which stood him so much whisky that he had to go back on the ambulance after all.

Tom yarned away. After Rumpties he had gone on to Avros which really were aeroplanes, and quite different to fly. A number of people were killed on their first solos through doing a flat turn after taking off, and getting into a spin near the ground; but there was no hope for flat turn merchants. They just hadn't flying sense, and might as well kill themselves quickly.

Apart from flat turns an Avro would do anything you wanted, and when it had got used to you would even do a flat turn just for fun if you kicked the rudder with decision. Touch was the thing in flying; though not so much in war flying, in which the heavy-handed pilot was more likely to survive, because he yanked his bus about and sideslipped so much that he was a difficult target. On the other hand, the fine pilot gained more height on turns, and perhaps turned in less radius.

But Tom put his faith in sideslipping for getting out of trouble. No sights could allow for movement sideways.

You soon got used to doing steep turns and spins on Avros. To do a vertical turn you just pushed the stick hard over and then pulled it back and held it like that for as long as you wanted to go on turning. There was not much sensation about it unless you hung over the side and watched the earth. You were sitting parallel to, as it were, an earth that was swinging round like a huge wheel that was painted as a large scale map. A spin was much better, and more difficult to get used to. Some Avros were so stable that it was difficult to make them spin. You shut off the engine and pulled her nose up until she stalled. As she fell into a vertical dive you kicked on full rudder and held the stick as far back as it would come on the same side, and you should spin. But sometimes, especially if you tried to spin to the left, you fell into a steep spiral, which gave a very different sensation. In a spiral you were on the inside of the turn, with centrifugal force pressing you into your seat, whereas, with the machine rotating about its longitudinal axis in a spin, its tendency was rather to throw you out. A spinning machine was really out of control, but you could quickly regain control by pushing the joystick forwards, when the spin changed into a dive. Once he had been spun when doing dual with Baker, before he was used to aerobatics. Instructors as a rule had no time for anything but circuits and landings and a few turns; everything else the pupil had to find out for himself. But once Baker had wanted to get down from three thousand feet in a hurry. The engine stopped, the nose went nearly vertically upwards and the Avro hung like that for a second and then fell over to the right. He clung to the sides of the cockpit as he was thrown out of the seat on to the loose safety belt. The earth vanished and there was nothing but dizzying sky until the sheer catastrophic flop brought the world leaping at him, rushing to swallow up the sky, and there was no heaven but only the titubating earth. He had never been able to recapture the breath-less horror of that first spin, when he had clung terrified to a bucking aeroplane that seemed trying to throw him, and the world had jerked past as though a giant were spinning it with a whip. It was always the first time that was memorable: more-over it was more shocking to be stunted than to stunt, just as one couldn't tickle one's own ribs effectively.

But he had never been looped and didn't know quite what to expect when he made his first attempt. It was on a day of westerly wind and patches of nimbus clouds between fifteen hundred and two thousand feet that he took off with his mind made up that he was going to loop. He had had to screw his courage to the sticking place before he had been able to make the resolution. It was always an effort for him to do a new stunt; he was nervous. He flew steadily up through a space in the clouds into the bright upper air, from where, looking down, the patches and rifts between the clouds were dark and sombre, and it was difficult to distinguish features of the dun world of shadowed fields and pale roads against the brilliant cloud-floor.

He flew until he was some five hundred feet above the clouds and had a definite horizon to steer by. He was invigor-ated by the pure sparkling air above the cloud belt, and happy enough to try anything. He held the joystick forwards to put his nose down for speed. There was nothing dangerous about loop-ing at that height, but there was a certain blind physical repug-nance and timidity of earth-bound habit to be overcome. The pilot soon showed a speed of eighty miles an hour, then eighty-five, and as soon as it touched ninety he brought the joystick slightly back. The cloud-horizon dropped away at once, and he was heading into blank space. He felt himself pressed tightly and more tightly into his seat as he shot upwards, till it seemed he would be forced through it. He was doing a bad loop. He had jerked the stick ever so slightly and pulled the aeroplane upwards too abruptly, creating excessive centrifugal pressure.

For perhaps two seconds he felt crushed against the seat and then the pressure suddenly ceased and he was hanging uncomfortably in the belt. Petrol spurted in his face from the pressure gauge, the engine spluttered, and the whole aeroplane shook. The controls were limp. He pulled the stick further back with the intention of getting over the top of the loop, but the machine would not respond, and fell out of its stall with a great lurch. The clouds leapt from beyond the limits of vision and occupied the whole of space. He realized that he was diving vertically, and quickly shut off petrol from the spluttering engine and let the stick go forwards until he could ease out of the dive; and when he was in a normal glide, he pumped up pressure in the petrol tank vigorously and relieved his feelings by shouting. He had stalled on top of the loop because friction against the air had caused loss of speed, had hung upside down, and fallen out sideways; a thoroughly unsatisfactory attempt. He must do better than that.

He flew steadily for a minute to regain lost height, and then got up speed again. This time he let the stick come back as it were of its own accord. The horizon dropped away, and he continued upwards drawing the stick towards him with only the minimum of pressure that would make it continue to come back. There was no unpleasant feeling either of pressure or falling and he was sitting quite comfortably when the opposite horizon appeared from behind him, and he knew he was successfully over the top. He shut off the petrol and let the stick go slowly forwards while the cloud-floor swung past and the horizon he had originally been facing reappeared. A perfect loop ending in a normal glide.

Tom went on talking until he thought they might have heard enough of his voice for one evening, and then he forbore. The air was still shaking with the unceasing gunfire. They played bridge. Tom was out of luck; kings were in the wrong place, distribution upset his attempts to establish: but what did it matter at a franc a hundred? He was like a generalissimo sending his forces to do battle; if they were slaughtered it mattered very little to him. The game, the battle was the thing. How ever many more clubs had the fellow got? Where ever did they get all the explosives from to keep up this interminable tattoo? It was very trying when an opponent established a long suit and you had to throw away a lot of good cards; but it was all in the game. Re-deal and play a fresh hand. He wondered how the new American troops were liking the war. A useful hand this time if his partner could support him a little better than last time. The Americans would be more effective allies than the Russians. . . .

In the morning, after family breakfast at eight o'clock, all the staff except the padre went off to attend to duties. The padre was good company and the morning passed pleasantly enough. The battle still raged and there were rumours of a big German break-through. The padre said that the death-roll was not terrible to a believer in personal immortality; how could it be? It had never occurred to Tom before that this queer belief could be practically efficacious; and could it, indeed, to a combatant? To old-style Mohammedans and such, yes; but to civilized Christians? If it could, here was another pernicious effect of religion, to encourage war by removing dislike of death. At every turn, it seemed to him, the religious, with their preposterous insistence on the unimportance of the world (except as a snare, the barbarians!) hindered mankind from making the world comfortable. They did not believe their own doctrine after they were thirty, but it was part of their mental habit then, and so very useful for keeping young people in order and swindling them into fighting their elders' wars. God, what a wicked crew!

"Apart, for the moment, from revelation," he said to the padre, "do you think there is any logical reason for believing that one is immortal?"

The padre thought it was one of those subjects where the reasons pro and contra balanced, and it was impossible to know anything about it except by revelation. The Christian Revelation established the fact but left the mode quite uncertain, as he read the scriptures. That did not matter; the fact was sufficient.

How the deuce could an otherwise reasonable man of the twentieth century talk comfortably about the Christian revelation? It was one of those extraordinary failures of human intelligence that Tom could see no accounting for.

After lunch he telephoned to the squadron to inquire about his transport. It would be there that day some time. The squadron was busy.

ALL THE DEAD PILOTS

by WILLIAM FAULKNER

One of the true giants of American literature, William Faulkner (1897–1962), along with many of the other authors in this volume, had a passion for writing and a burning desire to fly. After being passed over for the U.S. Army Air Corps because of his height, Faulkner lied about his personal history and passed himself off as British to get into the Royal Air Force in Canada during World War I. He was accepted and trained in Toronto, but the war ended before he could be certified.

"All the Dead Pilots" is Faulkner's take on flying during the crazy World War I years, when the airplanes were barely safer than their original counterparts invented scarcely fifteen years before. The first part of the story is a brief prologue about pilots after their tour of duty is over, and how the "pilot" dies, leaving only the man behind, grounded for the rest of his life. But then, Faulkner turns ninety degrees and recounts the tale of an American, one of the notorious Snopes family, and his rivalry with a British officer. Love, war, death, and airplanes—all come together in a masterful short tale by one of the twentieth century's greatest authors.

I

In the pictures, the snapshots hurriedly made, a little faded, a little dog-eared with the thirteen years, they swagger a little. Lean, hard, in their brass-and-leather martial harness, posed standing beside or leaning upon the esoteric shapes of wire and wood and canvas in which they flew without parachutes, they too have an esoteric look; a look not exactly human, like that of some dim and threatful apotheosis of the race seen for an instant in the glare of a thunderclap and then forever gone.

Because they are dead, all the old pilots, dead on the eleventh of November, 1918. When you see modern photographs of them, the recent pictures made beside the recent shapes of steel and canvas with the new cowlings and engines and slotted wings, they look a little outlandish: the lean young men who once swaggered. They look lost, baffled. In this saxophone age of flying they look as out of place as, a little thick about the waist, in the sober business suits of thirty and thirty-five and perhaps more than that, they would look among the saxophones and miniature brass bowlers of a night club orchestra. Because they are dead too, who had learned to respect that whose respect in turn their hardness had commanded before there were welded center sections and parachutes and ships that would not spin. That's why they watch the saxophone girls and boys with slipstream-proof lipstick and aeronautical flasks piling up the saxophone crates in private driveways and on golf greens, with the quick sympathy and the bafflement too. "My gad," one of them—ack emma, warrant officer pilot, captain and M.C. in turn—said to me once; "if you can treat a crate that way, why do you want to fly at all?"

But they are all dead now. They are thick men now, a little thick about the waist from sitting behind desks, and maybe not so good at it, with wives and children in suburban homes almost paid out, with gardens in which they putter in the long evenings after the 5:15 is in, and perhaps not so good at that either: the hard, lean men who swaggered hard and drank hard because they had found that being dead was not as quiet as they had heard it would be. That's why this story is composite: a series of brief glares in which, instantaneous and without depth or perspective, there stood into sight the portent and the threat of what the race could bear and become, in an instant between dark and dark.

II

In 1918 I was at Wing Headquarters, trying to get used to a mechanical leg, where, among other things, I had the censoring of mail from all squadrons in the Wing. The job itself wasn't bad, since it gave me spare time to experiment with a synchronized camera on which I was working. But the opening and reading of the letters, the scrawled, brief pages of transparent and honorable lies to mothers and sweethearts, in the script and spelling of schoolboys. But a war is such a big thing, and it takes so long. I suppose they who run them (I don't mean the staffs, but whoever or whatever it is that controls events) do get bored now and then. And it's when you get bored that you turn petty, play horse.

So now and then I would go up to a Camel squadron behind Amiens and talk with the gunnery sergeant about the synchronization of the machine guns. This was Spoomer's squadron. His uncle was the corps commander, the K.G., and so Spoomer, with his Guards' Captaincy, had also got in turn a Mons Star, a D.S.O., and now a pursuit squadron of single seaters, though the third barnacle on his tunic was still the single wing of an observer.

In 1914 he was in Sandhurst: a big, ruddy-colored chap with china eyes, and I like to think of his uncle sending for him when the news got out, the good news. Probably at the uncle's club (the uncle was a brigadier then, just recalled hurriedly from Indian service) and the two of them opposite one another across the mahogany, with the newsboys crying in the street, and the general saying, "By gad, it will be the making of the Army. Pass the wine, sir."

I daresay the general was put out, not to say outraged, when he finally realized that neither the Hun nor the Home Office intended running this war like the Army wanted it run. Anyway, Spoomer had already gone out to Mons and come back with his Star (though Ffollansbye said that the general sent Spoomer out to get the Star, since it was going to be one decoration you had to be on hand to get) before the uncle got him transferred to his staff, where Spoomer could get his D.S.O. Then perhaps the uncle sent him out again to tap the stream where it came to surface. Or maybe Spoomer went on his own this time. I like to think so. I like to think that he did it through pro patria, even though I know that no man deserves praise for courage or opprobrium for cowardice, since there are situations in which any man will show either of them. But he went out, and came back a year later with his observer's wing and a dog almost as large as a calf.

That was in 1917, when he and Sartoris first came together, collided. Sartoris was an American from a plantation at Mississippi, where they grew grain and Negroes, or the Negroes grew the grain—something. Sartoris had a working vocabulary of perhaps two hundred words, and I daresay to tell where and how and why he lived was beyond him, save that he lived in the plantation with his great-aunt and his grandfather. He came through Canada in 1916, and he was at Pool. Ffollansbye told me about it. It seems that Sartoris had a girl in London, one of those three-day wives and three-year widows. That's the bad thing about war. They—the Sartorises and such—didn't die until 1918, some of them. But the girls, the women, they died on the fourth of August, 1914.

So Sartoris had a girl. Ffollansbye said they called her Kitchener, "because she had such a mob of soldiers." He said they didn't know if Sartoris knew this or not, but that anyway for a while Kitchener—Kit—appeared to have ditched them all for Sartoris. They would be seen anywhere and any time together, then Ffollansbye told me how he found Sartoris alone and quite drunk one evening in a restaurant. Ffollansbye told how he had already heard that Kit and Spoomer had gone off somewhere together about two days ago. He said that Sartoris was sitting there, drinking himself blind, waiting for Spoomer to come in. He said he finally got Sartoris into a cab and sent him to the aerodrome. It was about dawn then, and Sartoris got a captain's tunic from someone's kit, and a woman's garter from someone else's kit, perhaps his own, and pinned the garter on the tunic like a barnacle ribbon. Then he went and waked a corporal who was an ex-professional boxer and with whom Sartoris would put on the gloves now and then, and made the corporal put on the tunic over his underclothes. "Namesh Spoomer," Sartoris told the corporal. "Cap'm Spoomer;" swaying and prodding at the garter with his finger. "Distinguishing Sheries Thighs," Sartoris said. Then he and the corporal in the borrowed tunic, with his woolen underwear showing beneath, stood there in the dawn, swinging at one another with their naked fists.

III

You'd think that when a war had got you into it, it would let you be. That it wouldn't play horse with you. But maybe it wasn't that. Maybe it was because the three of them, Spoomer and Sartoris and the dog, were so humorless about it. Maybe a humorless person is an unflagging challenge to them above the thunder and the alarms. Anyway, one afternoon—it was in the spring, just before Cambrai fell—I went up to the Camel aerodrome to see the gunnery sergeant, and I saw Sartoris for the first time. They had given the squadron to Spoomer and the dog the year before, and the first thing they did was to send Sartoris out to it.

The afternoon patrol was out, and the rest of the people were gone too, to Amiens I suppose, and the aerodrome was deserted. The sergeant and I were sitting on two empty petrol tins in the hangar door when I saw a man thrust his head out the door of the officers' mess and look both ways along the line, his air a little furtive and very alert. It was Sartoris, and he was looking for the dog.

"The dog?" I said. Then the sergeant told me, this too composite, out of his own observation and the observation of the entire enlisted personnel exchanged and compared over the mess tables or over pipes at night: that terrible and omniscient inquisition of those in an inferior station.

When Spoomer left the aerodrome, he would lock the dog up somewhere. He would have to lock it up in a different place each time, because Sartoris would hunt until he found it, and let it out. It appeared to be a dog of intelligence, because if Spoomer had only gone down to Wing or somewhere on business, the dog would stay at home, spending the interval grubbing in the refuse bin behind the men's mess, to which it was addicted in preference to that of the officers. But if Spoomer had gone to Amiens, the dog would depart up the Amiens road immediately on being freed, to return later with Spoomer in the squadron car.

"Why does Mr. Sartoris let it out?" I said. "Do you mean that Captain Spoomer objects to the dog eating kitchen refuse?"

But the sergeant was not listening. His head was craned around the door, and we watched Sartoris. He had emerged from the mess and he now approached the hangar at the end of the line, his air still alert, still purposeful. He entered the hangar. "That seems a rather childish business for a grown man," I said.

The sergeant looked at me. Then he quit looking at me. "He wants to know if Captain Spoomer went to Amiens or not."

After a while I said, "Oh. A young lady. Is that it?"

He didn't look at me. "You might call her a young lady. I suppose they have young ladies in this country."

I thought about that for a while. Sartoris emerged from the first hangar and entered the second one. "I wonder if there are any young ladies any more anywhere," I said.

"Perhaps you are right, sir. War is hard on women."

"What about this one?" I said. "Who is she?"

He told me. They ran an estaminet, a "bit of a pub" he called it—an old harridan of a woman, and the girl. A little place on a back street, where officers did not go. Perhaps that was why Sartoris and Spoomer created such a furor in that circle. I gathered from the sergeant that the contest between the squadron commander and one of his greenest cubs was the object of general interest and the subject of the warmest conversation and even betting among the enlisted element of the whole sector of French and British troops. "Being officers and all," he said.

"They frightened the soldiers off, did they?" I said. "Is that it?" The sergeant did not look at me. "Were there many soldiers to frighten off?"

"I suppose you know these young women," the sergeant said. "This war and all."

And that's who the girl was. What the girl was. The sergeant said that the girl and the old woman were not even related. He told me how Sartoris bought her things—clothes, and jewelry; the sort of jewelry you might buy in Amiens, probably. Or maybe in a canteen, because Sartoris was not much more than twenty. I saw some of the letters which he wrote to his great-aunt back home, letters that a third-form lad in Harrow could have written, perhaps bettered. It seemed that Spoomer did not make the girl any presents. "Maybe because he is a captain," the sergeant said. "Or maybe because of them ribbons he don't have to."

"Maybe so," I said.

And that was the girl, the girl who, in the centime jewelry which Sartoris gave her, dispensed beer and wine to British and French privates in an Amiens back street, and because of whom Spoomer used his rank to betray Sartoris with her by keeping Sartoris at the aerodrome on special duties, locking up the dog to hide from Sartoris what he had done. And Sartoris taking what revenge he could by letting out the dog in order that it might grub in the refuse of plebeian food.

He entered the hangar in which the sergeant and I were: a tall lad with pale eyes in a face that could be either merry or surly, and quite humorless. He looked at me. "Hello," he said.

"Hello," I said. The sergeant made to get up.

"Carry on," Sartoris said. "I don't want anything." He went on to the rear of the hangar. It was cluttered with petrol drums and empty packing cases and such. He was utterly without self-consciousness, utterly without shame of his childish business.

The dog was in one of the packing cases. It emerged, huge, of a napped, tawny color; Ffollansbye had told me that, save for Spoomer's wing and his Mons Star and his D.S.O., he and the dog looked alike. It quitted the hangar without haste, giving me a brief, sidelong glance. We watched it go on and disappear around the corner of the men's mess. Then Sartoris turned and went back to the officers' mess and also disappeared.

Shortly afterward, the afternoon patrol came in. While the

machines were coming up to the line, the squadron car turned onto the aerodrome and stopped at the officers' mess and Spoomer got out. "Watch him," the sergeant said. "He'll try to do it like he wasn't watching himself, noticing himself."

He came along the hangars, big, hulking, in green golf stockings. He did not see me until he was turning into the hangar. He paused; it was almost imperceptible, then he entered, giving me a brief, sidelong glance. "How do," he said in a high, fretful, level voice. The sergeant had risen. I had never seen Spoomer even glance toward the rear, toward the overturned packing case, yet he had stopped. "Sergeant," he said.

"Sir," the sergeant said.

"Sergeant," Spoomer said. "Have those timers come up yet?"

"Yes, sir. They came up two weeks ago. They're all in use now, sir."

"Quite so. Quite so." He turned; again he gave me a brief, sidelong glance, and went on down the hangar line, not fast. He disappeared. "Watch him, now," the sergeant said. "He won't go over there until he thinks we have quit watching him."

We watched. Then he came into sight again, crossing toward the men's mess, walking briskly now. He disappeared beyond the corner. A moment later he emerged, dragging the huge, inert beast by the scruff of its neck. "You mustn't eat that stuff," he said. "That's for soldiers."

IV

I didn't know at the time what happened next. Sartoris didn't tell me until later, afterward. Perhaps up to that time he had not anything more than instinct and circumstantial evidence to tell him that he was being betrayed: evidence such as being given by Spoomer some duty not in his province at all and which would keep him on the aerodrome for the afternoon, then finding and freeing the hidden dog and watching it vanish up the Amiens road at its clumsy hand gallop.

But something happened. All I could learn at the time was, that one afternoon Sartoris found the dog and watched it depart for Amiens. Then he violated his orders, borrowed a motor bike and went to Amiens too. Two hours later the dog returned and repaired to the kitchen door of the men's mess, and a short time after that, Sartoris himself returned on a lorry (they were already evacuating Amiens) laden with household effects and driven by a French soldier in a peasant's smock. The motor bike was on the lorry too, pretty well beyond repair. The soldier told how Sartoris had driven the bike full speed into a ditch, trying to run down the dog.

But nobody knew just what had happened, at the time. But I had imagined the scene, before he told me. I imagined him there, in that bit of a room full of French soldiers, and the old woman (she could read pips, no doubt; ribbons, anyway) barring him from the door to the living quarters. I can imagine him, furious, baffled, inarticulate (he knew no French), standing head and shoulders above the French people whom he could not understand and that he believed were laughing at him. "That was it," he told me. "Laughing at me behind their faces, about a woman. Me knowing that he was up there, and them knowing I knew that if I busted in and dragged him out and bashed his head off, I'd not only be cashiered, I'd be clinked for life for having infringed the articles of alliance by invading foreign property without warrant or something."

Then he returned to the aerodrome and met the dog on the road and tried to run it down. The dog came on home, and Spoomer returned, and he was just dragging it by the scruff of the neck from the refuse bin behind the men's mess, when the afternoon patrol came in. They had gone out six and come back five, and the leader jumped down from his machine before it had stopped rolling. He had a bloody rag about his right hand and he ran toward Spoomer stooped above the passive and stiff-legged dog. "By gad," he said, "they have got Cambrai!"

Spoomer did not look up. "Who have?"

"Jerry has, by gad!"

"Well, by gad," Spoomer said. "Come along, now. I have told you about that muck."

A man like that is invulnerable. When Sartoris and I talked for the first time, I started to tell him that. But then I learned that Sartoris was invincible too. We talked, that first time. "I tried to get him to let me teach him to fly a Camel," Sartoris said. "I will teach him for nothing. I will tear out the cockpit and rig the duals myself, for nothing."

"Why?" I said. "What for?"

"Or anything. I will let him choose it. He can take an S.E. if he wants to, and I will take an Ak.W. or even a Fee and I will run him clean out of the sky in four minutes. I will run him so far into the ground he will have to stand on his head to swallow."

We talked twice: that first time, and the last time. "Well, you did better than that," I said the last time we talked.

He had hardly any teeth left then, and he couldn't talk very well, who had never been able to talk much, who lived and died with maybe two hundred words. "Better than what?" he said.

"You said before that you would run him clean out of the sky. You didn't do that; you did better: you have run him clean off the continent of Europe."

V

I think I said that he was invulnerable too. November 11, 1918, couldn't kill him, couldn't leave him growing a little thicker each year behind an office desk, with what had once been hard and lean and immediate grown a little dim, a little baffled, and betrayed, because by that day he had been dead almost six months.

He was killed in July, but we talked that second time, that other time before that. This last time was a week after the patrol had come in and told that Cambrai had fallen, a week after we heard the shells falling in Amiens. He told me about it himself, through his missing teeth. The whole squadron went out together. He left his flight as soon as they reached the broken front, and flew back to Amiens with a bottle of brandy in his overall leg. Amiens was being evacuated, the roads full of lorries and carts of household goods, and ambulances from the Base hospital, and the city and its immediate territory was now interdict.

He landed in a short meadow. He said there was an old woman working in a field beyond the canal (he said she was still there when he returned an hour later, stooping stubbornly among the green rows, beneath the moist spring air shaken at slow and monstrous intervals by the sound of shells falling in the city) and a light ambulance stopped halfway in the roadside ditch.

He went to the ambulance. The engine was still running. The driver was a young man in spectacles. He looked like a student, and he was dead drunk, half sprawled out of the cab. Sartoris had a drink from his own bottle and tried to rouse the driver, in vain. Then he had another drink (I imagine that he was pretty well along himself by then; he told me how only that morning, when Spoomer had gone off in the car and he had found the dog and watched it take the Amiens road, how he had tried to get the operations officer to let him off patrol and how the operations officer had told him that La Fayette awaited him on the Santerre plateau) and tumbled the driver back into the ambulance and drove on to Amiens himself.

He said the French corporal was drinking from a bottle in a

doorway when he passed and stopped the ambulance before the estaminet. The door was locked. He finished his brandy bottle and he broke the estaminet door in by diving at it as they do in American football. Then he was inside. The place was empty, the benches and tables overturned and the shelves empty of bottles, and he said that at first he could not remember what it was he had come for, so he thought it must be a drink. He found a bottle of wine under the bar and broke the neck off against the edge of the bar, and he told how he stood there, looking at himself in the mirror behind the bar, trying to think what it was he had come to do. "I looked pretty wild," he said.

Then the first shell fell. I can imagine it: he standing there in that quiet, peaceful, redolent, devastated room, with the bashed-in door and the musing and waiting city beyond it, and then that slow, unhurried, reverberant sound coming down upon the thick air of spring like a hand laid without haste on the damp silence; he told how dust or sand or plaster, something, sifted somewhere, whispering down in a faint hiss, and how a big, lean cat came up over the bar without a sound and flowed down to the floor and vanished like dirty quick-silver.

Then he saw the closed door behind the bar and he remembered what he had come for. He went around the bar. He expected this door to be locked too, and he grasped the knob and heaved back with all his might. It wasn't locked. He said it came back into the shelves with a sound like a pistol, jerking him off his feet. "My head hit the bar," he said. "Maybe I was a little groggy after that."

Anyway, he was holding himself up in the door, looking down at the old woman. She was sitting on the bottom stair, her apron over her head, rocking back and forth. He said that the apron was quite clean, moving back and forth like a piston, and he standing in the door, drooling a little at the mouth. "Madame," he said. The old woman rocked back and forth. He propped himself carefully and leaned and touched her shoul-

148

der. " 'Toinette," he said. "Où est-elle, 'Toinette?" That was probably all the French he knew; that, with *vin* added to his 196 English words, composed his vocabulary.

Again the old woman did not answer. She rocked back and forth like a wound-up toy. He stepped carefully over her and mounted the stair. There was a second door at the head of the stair. He stopped before it, listening. His throat filled with a hot, salty liquid. He spat it, drooling; his throat filled again. This door was unlocked also. He entered the room quietly. It contained a table, on which lay a khaki cap with the bronze crest of the Flying Corps, and as he stood drooling in the door, the dog heaved up from the corner furthest from the window, and while he and the dog looked at one another above the cap, the sound of the second shell came dull and monstrous into the room, stirring the limp curtains before the window.

As he circled the table the dog moved too, keeping the table between them, watching him. He was trying to move quietly, yet he struck the table in passing (perhaps while watching the dog) and he told how, when he reached the opposite door and stood beside it, holding his breath, drooling, he could hear the silence in the next room. Then a voice said:

"Maman?"

He kicked the locked door, then he dived at it, again like the American football, and through it, door and all. The girl screamed. But he said he never saw her, never saw anyone. He just heard her scream as he went into the room on all-fours. It was a bedroom; one corner was filled by a huge wardrobe with double doors. The wardrobe was closed, and the room appeared to be empty. He didn't go to the wardrobe. He said he just stood there on his hands and knees, drooling, like a cow, listening to the dying reverberation of the third shell, watching the curtains on the window blow once into the room as though to a breath.

He got up. "I was still groggy," he said. "And I guess that

brandy and the wine had kind of got joggled up inside me." I daresay they had. There was a chair. Upon it lay a pair of slacks, neatly folded, a tunic with an observer's wing and two ribbons, an ordnance belt. While he stood looking down at the chair, the fourth shell came.

He gathered up the garments. The chair toppled over and he kicked it aside and lurched along the wall to the broken door and entered the first room, taking the cap from the table as he passed. The dog was gone.

He entered the passage. The old woman still sat on the bottom step, her apron over her head, rocking back and forth. He stood at the top of the stair, holding himself up, waiting to spit. Then beneath him a voice said: "Que faites-vous en haut?"

He looked down upon the raised moustached face of the French corporal whom he had passed in the street drinking from the bottle. For a time they looked at one another. Then the corporal said, "Descendez," making a peremptory gesture with his arm. Clasping the garments in one hand, Sartoris put the other hand on the stair rail and vaulted over it.

The corporal jumped aside. Sartoris plunged past him and into the wall, banging his head hollowly again. As he got to his feet and turned, the corporal kicked at him, striking for his pelvis. The corporal kicked him again. Sartoris knocked the corporal down, where he lay on his back in his clumsy overcoat, tugging at his pocket and snapping his boot at Sartoris' groin. Then the corporal freed his hand and shot point-blank at Sartoris with a short-barreled pistol.

Sartoris sprang upon him before he could shoot again, trampling the pistol hand. He said he could feel the man's bones through his boot, and that the corporal began to scream like a woman behind his brigand's moustaches. That was what made it funny, Sartoris said: that noise coming out of a pair of moustaches like a Gilbert and Sullivan pirate. So he said he stopped it by holding the corporal up with one hand and hitting him on the chin with the other until the noise stopped. He said that the old woman had not ceased to rock back and forth under her starched apron. "Like she might have dressed up to get ready to be sacked and ravaged," he said.

He gathered up the garments. In the bar he had another pull at the bottle, looking at himself in the mirror. Then he saw that he was bleeding at the mouth. He said he didn't know if he had bitten his tongue when he jumped over the stair rail or if he had cut his mouth with the broken bottle neck. He emptied the bottle and flung it to the floor.

He said he didn't know then what he intended to do. He said he didn't realize it even when he had dragged the unconscious driver out of the ambulance and was dressing him in Captain Spoomer's slacks and cap and ribboned tunic, and tumbled him back into the ambulance.

He remembered seeing a dusty inkstand behind the bar. He sought and found in his overalls a bit of paper, a bill rendered him eight months ago by a London tailor, and, leaning on the bar, drooling and spitting, he printed on the back of the bill Captain Spoomer's name and squadron number and aerodrome, and put the paper into the tunic pocket beneath the ribbons and the wing, and drove back to where he had left his aeroplane.

There was an Anzac battalion resting in the ditch beside the road. He left the ambulance and the sleeping passenger with them, and four of them helped him to start his engine, and held the wings for his tight take-off.

Then he was back at the front. He said he did not remember getting there at all; he said the last thing he remembered was the old woman in the field beneath him, then suddenly he was in a barrage, low enough to feel the concussed air between the ground and his wings, and to distinguish the faces of troops. He said he didn't know what troops they were, theirs or ours, but that he strafed them anyway. "Because I never heard of a man on the ground getting hurt by an aeroplane," he said. "Yes, I did; I'll take that back. There was a farmer back in Canada plowing in the middle of a thousand-acre field, and a cadet crashed on top of him."

Then he returned home. They told at the aerodrome that he flew between two hangars in a slow roll, so that they could see the valve sterns in both wheels, and that he ran his wheels across the aerodrome and took off again. The gunnery sergeant told me that he climbed vertically until he stalled, and that he held the Camel mushing on its back. "He was watching the dog," the sergeant said. "It had been home about an hour and it was behind the men's mess, grubbing in the refuse bin." He said that Sartoris dived at the dog and then looped, making two turns of an upward spin, coming off on one wing and still upside down. Then the sergeant said that he probably did not set back the air valve, because at a hundred feet the engine conked, and upside down Sartoris cut the tops out of the only two poplar trees they had left.

The sergeant said they ran then, toward the gout of dust and the mess of wire and wood. Before they reached it, he said the dog came trotting out from behind the men's mess. He said the dog got there first and that they saw Sartoris on his hands and knees, vomiting, while the dog watched him. Then the dog approached and sniffed tentatively at the vomit and Sartoris got up and balanced himself and kicked it, weakly but with savage and earnest purpose.

VI

The ambulance driver, in Spoomer's uniform, was sent back to the aerodrome by the Anzac major. They put him to bed, where he was still sleeping when the brigadier and the Wing Commander came up that afternoon. They were still there when an ox cart turned onto the aerodrome and stopped, with, sitting on a wire cage containing chickens, Spoomer in a woman's skirt and a knitted shawl. The next day Spoomer returned to England. We learned that he was to be a temporary colonel at ground school.

"The dog will like that, anyway," I said.

"The dog?" Sartoris said.

"The food will be better there," I said.

"Oh," Sartoris said. They had reduced him to second lieutenant, for dereliction of duty by entering a forbidden zone with government property and leaving it unguarded, and he had been transferred to another squadron, to the one which even the B.E. people called the Laundry.

This was the day before he left. He had no front teeth at all now, and he apologized for the way he talked, who had never really talked with an intact mouth. "The joke is," he said, "it's another Camel squadron. I have to laugh."

"Laugh?" I said.

"Oh, I can ride them. I can sit there with the gun out and keep the wings level now and then. But I can't fly Camels. You have to land a Camel by setting the air valve and flying it into the ground. Then you count ten, and if you have not crashed, you level off. And if you can get up and walk away, you have made a good landing. And if they can use the crate again, you are an ace. But that's not the joke."

"What's not?"

"The Camels. The joke is, this is a night-flying squadron. I suppose they are all in town and they don't get back until after dark to fly them. They're sending me to a night-flying squadron. That's why I have to laugh."

"I would laugh," I said. "Isn't there something you can do about it?"

"Sure. Just keep that air valve set right and not crash. Not wash out and have those wing flares explode. I've got that beat. I'll just stay up all night, pop the flares and sit down after sunrise. That's why I have to laugh, see. I can't fly Camels in the daytime, even. And they don't know it."

"Well, anyway, you did better than you promised," I said. "You have run him off the continent of Europe."

"Yes," he said. "I sure have to laugh. He's got to go back to England, where all the men are gone. All those women, and not a man between fourteen and eighty to help him. I have to laugh."

VII

When July came, I was still in the Wing office, still trying to get used to my mechanical leg by sitting at a table equipped with a paper cutter, a pot of glue and one of red ink, and laden with the meager, thin, here soiled and here clean envelopes that came down in periodical batches—envelopes addressed to cities and hamlets and sometimes less than hamlets, about England—when one day I came upon two addressed to the same person in America: a letter and a parcel. I took the letter first. It had neither location nor date:

Dear Aunt Jenny

Yes I got the socks Elnora knitted. They fit all right because I gave them to my batman he said they fit all right. Yes I like it here better than where I was these are good guys here except these damn Camels. I am all right about going to church we dont always have church. Sometimes they have it for the ak emmas because I

*reckon a ak emma needs it but usually I am pretty busy
Sunday but I go enough I reckon. Tell Elnora much
oblige for the socks they fit all right but maybe you
better not tell her I gave them away. Tell Isom and the
other niggers hello and Grandfather tell him I got the
money all right but war is expensive as hell.*

Johnny.

But then, the Malbroucks don't make the wars, anyway. I suppose it takes too many words to make a war. Maybe that's why.

The package was addressed like the letter, to Mrs Virginia Sartoris, Jefferson, Mississippi, U.S.A., and I thought, What in the world would it ever occur to him to send to her? I could not imagine him choosing a gift for a woman in a foreign country; choosing one of those trifles which some men can choose with a kind of infallible tact. His would be, if he thought to send anything at all, a section of crank shaft or maybe a handful of wrist pins salvaged from a Hun crash. So I opened the package. Then I sat there, looking at the contents.

It contained an addressed envelope, a few dog-eared papers, a wrist watch whose strap was stiff with some dark dried liquid, a pair of goggles without any glass in one lens, a silver belt buckle with a monogram. That was all.

So I didn't need to read the letter. I didn't have to look at the contents of the package, but I wanted to. I didn't want to read the letter, but I had to.

*—Squadron, R.A.F., France.
5th July, 1918.*

Dear Madam,
I have to tell you that your son was killed on yesterday morning. He was shot down while in pursuit of duty over the enemy lines. Not due to carelessness or lack of

155

skill. He was a good man. The E.A. outnumbered your son and had more height and speed which is our misfortune but no fault of the Government which would give us better machines if they had them which is no satisfaction to you. Another of ours, Mr R. Kyerling 1000 feet below could not get up there since your son spent much time in the hangar and had a new engine in his machine last week. Your son took fire in ten seconds Mr Kyerling said and jumped from your son's machine since he was side slipping safely until the E.A. shot away his stabiliser and controls and he began to spin. I am very sad to send you these sad tidings though it may be a comfort to you that he was buried by a minister. His other effects sent you later.

I am, madam, and etc.
C. Kaye Major

He was buried in the cemetary just north of Saint Vaast since we hope it will not be shelled again since we hope it will be over soon by our padre since there were just two Camels and seven E.A. and so it was on our side by that time.

C. K. Mjr.

The other papers were letters, from his great-aunt, not many and not long. I dont know why he had kept them. But he had. Maybe he just forgot them, like he had the bill from the London tailor he had found in his overalls in Amiens that day in the spring.

. . . let those foreign women alone. I lived through a war myself and I know how women act in war, even with Yankees. And a good-for-nothing bellion like you . . .

And this:

. . . we think it's about time you came home. Your grandfather is getting old, and it don't look like they will ever get done fighting over there. So you come on home. The Yankees are in it now. Let them fight if they want to. It's their war. It's not ours.

And that's all. That's it. The courage, the recklessness, call it what you will, is the flash, the instant of sublimation; then flick! the old darkness again. That's why. It's too strong for steady diet. And if it were a steady diet, it would not be a flash, a glare. And so, being momentary, it can be preserved and prolonged only on paper: a picture, a few written words that any match, a minute and harmless flame that any child can engender, can obliterate in an instant. A one-inch sliver of sulphur-tipped wood is longer than memory or grief; a flame no larger than a sixpence is fiercer than courage or despair.

THE WHITE FEATHER ACE

FROM *G-8 AND HIS BATTLE ACES*

———

by ANONYMOUS

Before the dawn of the television age popular entertainment consisted of black-and-white movies, radio, and the pulps, which were magazines and paperbacks printed on cheap, high-acid content paper that turned yellow almost as quickly as you could turn the pages. Pulp fiction used an over-the-top, exclamation-point formula heavy with adjectives and action, a style that survives today in comic books, which matured during the pulp era. This wasn't literature or even good writing; still, the tremendous amount of fiction the pulps published made them an excellent market for struggling writers. Many of the great novelists of the twentieth century got their start writing for the pulps, which paid by the word—not much, but enough to eat on.

We felt this anthology would be incomplete without a rock-'em, sock-'em flying tale from the pulps. The one we have selected is from one of the premier pulp flying-adventure magazines of the 1930s, *G-8 and His Battle Aces.* The magazine was published monthly, or twice a month, from 1933 until the early 1940s. Every issue featured a novella about G-8, always referred to as "Master Spy," and his sidekicks, and one or two complete short stories. All the stories were World War I flying tales in which the good guys gave the Germans hell on the Western Front. Like most pulp fiction, these tales wore pseudonym by-lines or were published without one. G-8 also starred in his own comic book, which simplified the problem of illustrating the magazine.

"The White Feather Ace" was a short story published in the February 1939 magazine without a byline. The teaser in the table of contents proclaimed: "Jimmy Putnam rode into the flaming inferno of the skies and let his hot guns speak the words he wanted them all to hear."

A man does not wear his courage on his sleeve, but keeps it stored within himself. It stands side by side with fear in any pilot's breast, and to deny this is a lie! Jimmy Putnam discovered the difference between valour and panic, but only after he had dipped his wings in blood!

Second Lieutenant Jimmy Putnam was scared silly as he arrived at the field of the 101st Pursuits. He knew the front lines weren't very far away, and he knew that death lurked over those lines. But his fear was not particularly unusual, for Jimmy Putnam had never been known to be an outstanding hero.

He was a small, retiring youngster of nineteen. He had wavy blond hair, a rather angelic face, and clear blue eyes that must, he thought as he stood before his new commanding officer, have a very startled look in them.

Captain Warren, commander of the 101st, was a tall, angular fellow with glasses riding his sharp nose. He had a rather cocksure air about him. He was one of those exceptions to the rule in the World War, for through some fluke of mismanagement or by dint of political pull, Captain Warren was not a flying man. Nevertheless he commanded the 101st Squadron.

The captain surveyed young Jimmy Putnam in an annoying manner as if he were studying an experimental guinea pig in a laboratory.

Jimmy stood as straight and quiet as he could before his commander's desk as the latter asked, "Have you ever had any experience on the Front?"

Young Putnam shook his head.

"No, sir," he said.

As he said that, he felt almost as though he were pronouncing his own death sentence. Captain Warren squinted harder at him, then he leaned back in his chair and tapped the top of his desk with his finger tips.

"There are certain things, Lieutenant Putnam, that a man must understand before he goes over."

He waited for that to sink in.

"Yes, sir," Jimmy agreed meekly.

"You've heard about our great aces, Lufberry, Rickenbacker, Frank Luke. Those men stand for true bravery and courage." He leaned forward and took a closer look at Jimmy Putnam, and Jimmy jumped inwardly. Then the captain shook his finger in Jimmy's face and charged in a loud voice, "You're scared! You're scared silly even before you've made your first flight over the lines!"

Captain Warren's acts angered Jimmy Putnam a little, but he remained meek and admitted, "I do feel a little nervous, sir."

"Bah!" Captain Warren ranted. "You've got to get over that. You must remember one thing. If you're frightened going over the lines, you're licked before you start. You've got to get hold of yourself, Putnam. Remember what the boys said in the Battle of the Marne? Do you want to live forever?"

Jimmy gulped. He wasn't sure just what made him say what he did next.

"Yes, sir," he answered automatically. "I want to live as long as I can."

"Then, by thunder," Captain Warren roared, "your death warrant is sealed! You must acquire a devil-may-care attitude. We all have to die sometime, my boy." He glanced at his wrist watch. "Go to your quarters and steel yourself for the ordeal to come. You're going out on patrol with the others in one hour."

To say that Jimmy Putnam was more nervous and scared than when he had entered the C.O.'s office would be putting it mildly. He tried to hang up some of his clothing, but his hands were trembling so that he could hardly hold the clothes long enough to get them on the nails that were driven in the wooden wall of the barracks.

Someone was coming down the barracks corridor, and he jumped as the footsteps turned into his room. A big, amiable pilot with first lieutenant's bars on his shoulders entered, smiling. Jimmy snapped to attention and brought up a salute. The big fellow knocked it down good-naturedly.

"Forget that stuff around me," he said with a grin. "I'm Wingy Corbett, senior flight leader. I suppose the skipper has been talking to you about bravery and all that stuff."

Jimmy nodded.

"Pay no attention to him," Corbett advised. "That guy's a phony."

"What do you mean?" Jimmy asked, staring at him. "Isn't he the commanding officer here?"

"Sure," Corbett nodded, "but maybe you didn't notice that he doesn't wear any wings on his chest."

"Gee!" Jimmy said. "Do you mean he's a kiwi?"

"You said it, brother," Corbett said sourly.

"But," Jimmy Putnam ventured, "I thought that they always had flying officers to command squadrons."

"Listen, fellow," Corbett boomed, "when Washington politics enters into a war, anything is liable to happen. None of us here are quite sure how this guy Warren got his appointment, when he's never piloted a plane himself and doesn't know anything about it, but the chances are he was worked in because his mother's aunt's brother by marriage knew a lobbyist who knew a Congressman, or something like that.

"As if it wasn't enough for this guy to know nothing about flying, he has to have some crazy idea that he's a psychologist and knows how to handle men. The crazy fool scares all the replacements stiff as soon as they get up here, then he gives me the devil because the new men are killed off faster in this squadron than they are in any other. The War Department would have done a lot better by the 101st if they'd sent up a smallpox epidemic instead of Warren."

Wingy Corbett paced up and down the little room that was to be Jimmy Putnam's quarters with an angry expression on his face.

"I'd give a lot," he snorted, "if I could figure out some way to get rid of that kiwi."

Jimmy gulped and said, "Captain Warren told me we're going out on patrol in less than an hour."

"Yeah," Corbett nodded. "We'll go out for evening patrol at four o'clock." He looked at his wrist watch. "It's almost a quarter past three now. Would you like to have a drink or two before you go?"

Jimmy Putnam shook his head.

"No, thanks," he said. He hadn't learned to drink hard liquor and he felt that he wanted a clear head when he went over. "There is one thing I would like to do if it's possible," he said. "I would like to spend some time down in the gun pits at target practice."

Wingy Corbett stared at him, then began to grin.

"Say, kid, you're all right," he said. "You're not going to let anything slip, are you? Well, you go right ahead. Go down to the gun pits and shoot all you want, and if that no-good kiwi skipper says anything to you, tell him I sent you down."

"Thanks," Jimmy said.

He felt much better when he reached the gun pits and began slamming slugs into the bullseye. When he heard Hissos warming, he came out of the pits and walked toward the newest Spad that stood on the tarmac. He saw a group of pilots standing beside one of the hangars. Wingy Corbett called to him from the center of that group and Jimmy went over. Corbett

introduced him to Bert Holbert, his flight leader; to Ted Gleason, the pilot who led C flight, and to eleven other young pilots.
Corbett cursed under his breath as he saw Captain Warren
striding down the tarmac.

"Here comes our brave and courageous hero to give us
another one of his pep talks," he groaned.

Then Captain Warren was there, shouting an order for them
to line up and stand at attention. The pilots stood in two ragged
lines while Warren bellowed at them.

"You are all here for a purpose!" he barked. "We've got to
win this war. But fear isn't going to win it. Remember Lufberry,
and Luke, and Rickenbacker. They are brave men who do not
fear anything. If you're going to live long, you've got to be fearless like them. As the boys cried in the Marne—Do you want to
live forever?"

No one spoke. Many of the pilots shifted nervously, at which
Captain Warren bellowed, "Attention! Now hold out your right
arms straight in front of you and extend the fingers. I'm going to
look you men over and see who's got the jitters and who hasn't."

He moved on down the lines of men, barking at this one,
condemning that one because of his shaky fingers:

"You'll never win that way!" he roared. "There's nothing to
be afraid of. Now get in your planes and go out there and fight!"

There was hatred in some of the glances that the pilots gave
him. For the most part the men walked to their ships on rub-
bery legs and with quaking hearts.

Jimmy Putnam was moving through a maze of apprehension, as if he were walking to the gallows. Somehow he got into
his cockpit. Automatically he tested his controls as he had
learned to do at the advanced flying school.

Then Wingy Corbett was giving the signal for the take-off.
Jimmy pushed forward his throttle with a feeling of a doomed
man sitting in the electric chair and throwing the switch for his

own electrocution. His knees wobbled and he had hard work keeping his feet on the rudder bar as his Spad swept across the field and gathered speed.

Then, somehow, he was in the air and he felt a little better. He was following Bert Holbert in the left flight. Opposite them at the head of C flight was Ted Gleason, and leading the center forward flight was Wingy Corbett.

Jimmy saw the front lines, with their winding trenches, coming at him. The planes of the 101st were five thousand feet above them and still climbing. He was thinking of the heroes down there, the men in the trenches who faced death with smiles on their faces.

He recalled the words of Captain Warren. Rickenbacker, Lufberry, Luke. Those brave men didn't have any fear. Putnam was suddenly convinced that he was the most scared man in the entire war. Yet he was determined to go on to what he felt was his almost certain death. A million dollars wouldn't make him turn back and show the rest of the boys that he was yellow.

As they crossed the German lines, the Archie guns began grunting up at them, but all fifteen Spads were too high for them to have any effect. A half mile back of the enemy lines they made a ninety degree turn and began flying parallel with those lines.

Suddenly Jimmy saw Wingy Corbett's plane, wobbling in a signal. He was pointing high in the air, off to the north. Instinctively, Jimmy looked up in the sky and his heart began pounding twice as fast as it had before. At first he couldn't see enemy planes up there, but he was sure Wingy Corbett had spotted them.

The other pilots were staring, too. There was a sudden flurry of excitement among those three close-flying formations. Abruptly, Jimmy Putnam spotted the German planes. They were tearing down from a white cloud, coming straight for them. He tried to count them, for he knew there was a great number. He counted fifteen, and still there were more. He felt a little faint, and his heart was pounding like a great drum. Jimmy's fingers tightened over his triggers and he felt a little more confident.

The approaching planes grew larger with astounding speed, and suddenly the terrific dog fight was on. All semblance of formation was abandoned; it was every man for himself, now.

A Fokker was coming at Jimmy from the side. In desperation he thrashed the stick about and kicked rudder. He heard Spandau slugs pounding on the back of his fuselage just as a Fokker was crossing his sights. Like a flash Jimmy aimed his gun with a movement of stick and rudder and clamped down on the triggers. His Vickers guns lashed out. He watched the tracers crash into the center section of the Fokker, and down went his stick. The tracer ribbons slashed into the cockpit and riddled across it.

He saw the pilot jerk backward as bullets stabbed through his body. The Fokker leaped up, stalled, and began spinning down out of control.

The roar of the Spandau and Vickers guns was deafening. Jimmy found himself flying through a haze of yellow and white tracer smoke. He heard the pounding of Spandau slugs on his tail section, eating up toward his cockpit.

He sent his crate into a wild, gyrating movement. Jimmy was too busy saving his neck, too busy knocking down Fokkers before they knocked him down, to be scared.

Two Jerry ships came in, one from either side, to catch him in their crossfire. Somehow he managed to send his Spad whirling over in a lightning maneuver.

Another Fokker that was pulling up into a stall under the belly of a Spad was about to cross his sights. Down went Jimmy Putnam's triggers again and his guns yammered out. The Fokker dove for the ground, a dead pilot at the stick.

———

In the maelstrom of tangled planes, Jimmy recognized Wingy Corbett's Spad, and he saw that a Fokker with a black fuselage was riding his tail. Instantly Jimmy Putnam snarled after the Fokker. Split seconds meant the difference between life and death, and he fought to get his sights on that Jerry ship. Wingy Corbett was flying like the devil himself to shake the Fokkers from his tail, but the black-fuselaged crate was hanging on like a leech.

Suddenly Jimmy had his sights trained on the Fokker cockpit. He jammed on his triggers and his Vickers guns stuttered. At that same instant, yellow tracers ribboned out from the Fokker and crashed into the cockpit, gas tank, and engine of Wingy's Spad. His ship burst into flames and black smoke belched out, covering the cockpit completely.

Jimmy Putnam was frozen to his stick and triggers. He compensated slightly, and suddenly his tracers were slamming into the Fokker cockpit. The Fokker was suddenly a ball of fire. The two ships, Wingy Corbett's Spad and the Fokker of the man who had sent him to his hellish death, streaked down side by side to eternity.

The firing had ceased. The Fokkers that remained were streaking toward home, and Jimmy Putnam was trailing along behind Bert Holbert's lead. He stared about the sky in a daze and began counting the Spads. There had been fifteen of them when they started out; there were eleven now. He spotted Ted Gleason's ship. That meant Gleason and Bert Holbert, two pilots whose names he could remember, were alive.

Jimmy was still pretty much in a daze when he landed back at the field. Captain Warren was out to meet them. He stared at the eleven planes.

"Where's the rest?" he demanded of Holbert and Gleason.

"Down," Holbert told him. "About twenty Heinies hopped on us. Wingy Corbett went down in flames. Besides that, each flight lost a man apiece."

He mentioned their names.

"That's too bad," Captain Warren said, with about as much feeling in his voice as though he were talking of lost sales at a business conference. "Confound it, you men have got to do better than that."

"You should have been there," Ted Gleason said savagely.

"What do you mean by that?" Captain Warren demanded.

Gleason didn't back down.

"Just what I said," he snorted. "All you do is stay on the ground and tell us how to win a war. What do you know about air fighting?"

"I know men," Warren snapped, glaring through his glasses. "I know what makes them fight and win battles, and that's enough for any commander to know. And if there's any more cracks from you, Gleason, I'll bust you all the way down to a private."

"That," Gleason snapped, "would be a pleasure if I could get out of this outfit."

"Silence!" Warren yelled. He glared at the other pilots. "What's the matter with you? Why couldn't you beat those Fokkers?"

Bert Holbert spoke up, then, angrily.

"We did beat them." he said. "Twenty of them attacked us. They shot down four of our ships and we shot down five of theirs. The newest man here, Putnam, got three of them."

Captain Warren stared at Jimmy.

"Is that true, Jimmy?" he demanded.

Jimmy nodded.

"I think so, sir," he nodded.

"Fine, excellent!" Warren barked. "What's the matter with the rest of you men? Here a new man comes to the field, and although he's never been over the lines before, yet he brings down three enemy planes on his first trip. That's the kind of fighting I want to see in this squadron. That takes bravery. Now

I want you all to rest up for the dawn patrol tomorrow morning. If you'll follow Lieutenant Putnam's lead, we'll get somewhere. We can show the Germans how we Americans can fight."

With that, Captain Warren strode down the field and Jimmy Putnam stared after him.

He scarcely realized the others were standing around him as he said half to himself, "Holy Gee, does he expect me to do that every time?"

Bert Holbert, his flight leader, laid a comforting hand on his shoulder.

"Don't worry, kid," he said. "Pay no attention to him. If you ask me, he's crazy."

The others chimed in to offer their congratulations.

That night at evening mess, Jimmy learned much about the squadron's history. Except for Bert Holbert and Ted Gleason, who had been with the 101st for a little over a month and were considered veterans; the oldest man in the outfit had been there only ten days. He was Bill Farley. As he himself put it, he was mighty lucky to have stayed alive that long.

"There will be four replacements up tomorrow," Bert Holbert told Jimmy. "They'll get the same line that you got. Lufberry, Rickenbacker, and Luke. They don't fear death, they're not afraid of anything, and all that stuff. If they're already scared when they reach the field, they'll be twice as scared when Warren gets through working on them."

The glory of shooting down three enemy planes didn't mean much to Jimmy Putnam. He slept little that night, and when it was time for the dawn patrol, he was as jittery as he had been before his first trip the day before. Lufberry, Rickenbacker, and Luke. He dreamed of those names; they became a nightmare to him. They were fearless men, afraid of nothing.

And what was he? He was as scared as a rabbit on the run. Afraid that the next morning would be his last.

There were eleven planes on the line at dawn. Captain Warren was there to give them the same old pep talk. Courage. Don't be afraid of anything.

Jimmy Putnam tried to steel himself against his fear. He talked to himself as he held his position in the one big formation in which the 101st planes flew this time. He tried to tell himself that he must not be afraid, but strong and courageous. Again and again he talked to himself, and at the end of each talk, he held out his free hand with fingers extended. Each time his fingers shook like aspen leaves in a stiff wind. He was no good—just a scared kid. Spandau slugs would surely pick him off.

As they reached the lines, a flight of sixteen Fokkers came storming at them. Hissos and Mercedes screamed at each other and Spandau and Vickers tracers tangled their yellow and white ribbons. When the fighting was over, Jimmy Putnam was still alive, even though his Spad was sieved full of holes, and he had two more Fokkers to his credit.

Bert Holbert had gone down out of control and Jimmy had seen him crash horribly in No Man's Land. Four of the newer men had gone the same way, two of them in flames.

Six Spads came back to the field of the 101st. Captain Warren said it was too bad that five of the men had been lost, but whatever grief he felt was completely drowned by his pleasure in finding out that Jimmy Putnam had become an ace in his first two trips over the lines.

"Excellent work, Putnam," he praised. "Commendable. Why don't the rest of you fight like Putnam instead of lying down?"

Jimmy Putnam stood up against him.

"Nobody laid down, Captain Warren," he said. "Everyone did his best. I just happened to be lucky."

"Nonsense," the C. O. snorted. "You couldn't be lucky twice in succession like that. It was sheer courage and bravery that brought you through. I'll send for more replacements at once."

Late that afternoon, two groups of replacements arrived. There were nine all together. That brought the squadron up to a full fifteen pilots. At four o'clock, Captain Warren assembled the men on the tarmac.

"Putnam," he said, "you will be the leader of your flight from now on. Gleason, you will lead C flight and be senior flight leader as well. Farley, you will head A flight."

Then came the usual harangue on bravery. Jimmy Putnam, only twenty-four hours with the squadron, watched and pitied the replacements. He saw their knees wobble as they walked to their planes, saw their hands tremble as they climbed in. He was still pretty scared himself, but he forgot part of his fear in his sympathy for these nine new men. It made him a little proud to lead B flight, but he felt deeply the loss of Holbert who had gone down that morning and Wingy Corbett, who had gone the day before.

They encountered no enemy planes that afternoon. Ted Gleason saw to it that they patrolled quiet areas. As he explained at mess afterward, he wanted to give the new men a chance to catch their breath before he plunged them into action.

They got their first taste of real air combat on the next patrol, when they ran into a group of enemy planes. Jimmy Putnam accounted for two German ships. Three of the replacements were left behind as the 101st flew home.

The third day after that, Ted Gleason went down in flames. By that time Jimmy had chalked up nine victories for himself, but he felt no glory in that fact; he had killed only to keep the Germans from killing him or some of his squadron mates. After evening mess, Captain Warren called him into headquarters office.

"I'm appointing you as senior flight leader, Putnam," he said. "That's all."

Jimmy did a great deal of thinking from then on, for he felt his new responsibility keenly. The lives of the present personnel of the 101st Squadron and those of the replacements who filled the gaps left by the scared kids who had gone west depended upon him. He realized where his own strength lay. At every opportunity, all during his training, he had practised in the gun pits, on the rifle ranges, and at trap shooting to quicken his eye.

He got one more Fokker on the dawn patrol, making his score ten, but the outfit lost three men. It was getting to be a regular thing. Young replacements arrived at the field, feeling that their appointment to the 101st was as good as a death sentence.

But Jimmy Putnam was working on a new tack. Whenever the men were free from patrol, he had them down in the gun pits, shooting at moving targets. He taught them all he knew about marksmanship, about quick firing, and about the coordination of aim and trigger fingers.

By now Jimmy Putnam had twelve Fokkers to his credit. There had apparently been a change in the personnel of the opposing German *staffel*. Baron von Yessel had been moved up with his squadron of crack German pilots to stem the phenomenal record that Jimmy was running up.

One day, after Jimmy's record had mounted to thirteen Fokkers, an enemy ship came screaming over the field. It was painted black from tip to tip. As it roared by, a message streamer ribboned out from the cockpit and fluttered to the ground.

In the pocket of the streamer was a challenge from Baron von Yessel to Jimmy Putnam to meet him over No Man's Land, at dawn, for a fight to the finish. Every pilot at the field knew about that challenge before Captain Warren heard of it. When the news reached him, he called Jimmy into his office.

"Putnam," he said, "you're not going to accept that challenge."

Jimmy stared at him.

"What do you mean?" he demanded.

"I mean," Warren continued, "that we are not going to chance losing you on a fool mission like that. This Baron von Yessel has you marked for the kill. It may be a trap. I won't let you go. The 101st can't afford to lose you. You're too valuable."

"You've done a great deal of talking about my courage," Jimmy reminded him. "I'm not going to let the boys think I'm afraid this time."

"You'll follow my orders," Captain Warren snapped. "Tomorrow morning you will go out on the regular patrol with the men. That's all."

But Jimmy Putnam had his own ideas on courage. At dawn he prepared for the regular patrol. As flight leader of the 101st, he led his men from the field, then he motioned them to a safe area, cut out of formation, and headed for the point over No Man's Land that the Baron Von Yessel had designated.

Jimmy was tense and nervous, but he calmed down a little as he saw the Baron's black ship circling high over No Man's Land. The two screamed at each other in open attack. They were the only two planes in the sky at that point.

They maneuvered carefully, each trying to gain an advantage. Spandau and Vickers bullets ripped wing covering to ribbons. For almost a half hour they fought in plain sight of the German and American lines, neither being able to down the other.

Jimmy's ammunition was getting low, and he knew he must save his last ten slugs for a final burst. Suddenly, the baron held up his hands in a signal, waved, and turned north. He had run out of ammunition, too. Jimmy Putnam answered the signal in similar fashion and the two parted.

If Captain Warren received news of the forbidden battle, he said nothing about it to Jimmy. He continued to give his pep talks and hold Jimmy up as the shining example of courage, and Jimmy went on training the men at target practise. Each day thousands of rounds of ammunition were poured into bullseyes. Even the greenest replacements were becoming almost as accurate with their machine guns as Jimmy himself.

One evening at mess, Captain Warren got up importantly to make a speech.

"Men," he said, "within an hour or so, two very important things are going to happen here. First, Colonel Stanford, our Wing commander, is going to visit the field for inspection. Immediately afterward, you will all take off and fly to the Front. The Yank forces are beginning a drive and they will need your cooperation. You will drive back every German plane in sight."

In a half hour, Colonel Stanford arrived at the field. Pilots and planes were lined up for inspection.

While the colonel stood there before the men, Captain Warren began his usual pep talk.

"Men," he said, "there are too many of you here who are cowards. But we have one notable exception, of whom we are very proud. That man is Lieutenant Putnam. He has become an ace almost three times over, and it is because of his unfailing courage. I want you all to look at him as he stands there. He isn't afraid of anything; he's brave and fearless—the way all of you men should be."

Something snapped inside Jimmy Putnam. He marched out of the line and stood before Captain Warren, and while the colonel listened, he said, "Captain Warren, you're wrong. I'm not brave. I'm not a great hero. I'm going to talk to the men in my own way, and I'm going to make them understand."

Captain Warren roared angrily, "I forbid you to speak of anything but courage!"

At that point, Colonel Stanford stepped up.

"Just a moment, Captain Warren," he said. "Let the lieutenant talk to the men."

Jimmy turned to his squadron mates.

"Fellows," he said, "as long as you have been at the field, you've heard Captain Warren tell you how brave I am. He's been holding me up as an example of a superman. I think I know the feelings that you've all had, because I've been through the same thing myself. Ever since I came to the 101st, Captain Warren has made me feel that all the big aces were supermen who possessed a type of courage that I could never hope to have.

"But I've had one advantage. I've done target practise constantly and I've improved my aim as much as possible. I've been trying to train you fellows the same way, until now practically every man among you can drill a bullseye as well as I can. We're going out now to try and drive enemy planes back while this push of ours is going on. Remember, as you go out there with me, that I'm just as scared as you are—and that you can shoot just as well as I can. It takes only one bullet to kill a German, you know."

He turned to his plane.

He didn't look once at Captain Warren. All fifteen planes swept off the field and roared toward the Front. The Yanks had already started the push against the German lines, and Fokkers roared out of the northeast to straff the advancing Yanks.

But the men of the 101st were imbued with a new confidence by the knowledge that the great and the small were pretty much alike. Not once, since Captain Warren had taken command, had the men of the 101st fought as they did on this morning. In spite of the fact that they were outnumbered by the Fokkers, they drove them back. There were losses on both sides, but when the Yank advance had stopped after pushing the Germans back for a considerable distance, Jimmy Putnam found that his outfit was much better off than the German squadron.

Colonel Stanford was waiting at the field for them when they landed. The wise old Wing commander smiled and spoke to them.

"You won't see Captain Warren around here again very soon. I had no idea this sort of thing was going on. He's been relieved of his post and we're looking for a new commander for this outfit." He was looking at Jimmy. "Lieutenant Putnam, from now on, you'll be in charge of the 101st."

A loud cheer went up from the pilots clustered about Jimmy, the youngster who had given them a new lease on life and a chance to continue living in spite of the fact that they were attached to the suicide 101st.

FOR WANT OF A FOKKER

FROM *THE BLUE MAX*

MAX

———

by JACK D. HUNTER

During World War I, the Imperial German Army's highest decoration for valor was the *Pour Le Merité* or Blue Max. In 1964, Jack D. Hunter launched an enviable writing career with an impressive first novel about a group of German airmen striving to win these bits of tin and blue enamel, a novel that led to a great flying movie of the same name starring George Peppard.

Let's go flying now with the twisted hero of Hunter's tale, Bruno Stachel, who is about to sell his soul for a chance at a Blue Max, and glory.

The Spads had come out of nowhere, fat, stub-winged, and fast. It was the first time Stachel had directly encountered the Spad, a French machine that the British seemed to favor on occasion. He had been horribly sick that morning, and had barely been able to pull himself from his cot, even after a heavy dose of brandy. He had thrown up twice, a rare event for him, and he had avoided the mess hall, heading directly to his machine at the end of the line so as to escape the *Jastaführer*'s questioning eyes. Throughout the uneventful low-level *Jasta* run he had remained queasy and shaky, cursing himself for failing to bring along a bottle. Behind the physical upset, the anxiety and remorse had been the most severe he had ever experienced. Upon landing he had virtually run to his billet and had gulped a great quantity of white wine, pausing only to fill his flat flask with the good cognac. It had helped considerably, and, after completing his combat report and checking on the refueling of the Pfalz, he had felt somewhat human again. He and Von Klugermann had climbed away from the field on their extra at five minutes to eleven—ten minutes late.

The five Spads had jumped them above the clouds when they had completed the southeasterly leg of their swing and were preparing to turn northeast toward Cambrai. One minute the sky had been empty; the next, the Englishmen were all around them, snapping like terriers.

It did not take Stachel long to sense that the Tommies weren't of the most experienced breed. They scattered their attacks, they wheeled widely on recoveries, they tended to get in the way of one another. He selected one Spad and gave it his full attention.

The Englishman was a great one for acrobatics. As Stachel rolled the Pfalz into a *Kurvensturz,* eying the Spad over his top wing, the Tommy did a slow roll for no apparent reason. This enabled Stachel to close the gap with gratifying speed, and his first burst for range startled the other pilot into a ridiculous snap-roll. His second burst for effect needled through the Spad's lower wing just abeam of the cockpit. He could see the Englishman's white face looking backward at him. The Spad, incredibly, attempted a loop, and as it hung high on its back, Stachel fired again. This time the tracers danced around the center section and he could see pieces flying. The enemy machine never recovered from its inverted attitude, but mushed down the sky, upside down and spinning wildly, a fire flaring brightly from its engine louvers.

Stachel took inventory.

Von Klugermann was just putting the finishing touches to one of the Englishmen, whose machine collapsed and tumbled end-over-end toward the cloud floor. A third Spad had preceded it, a huge blob of flame whose only resemblance to an airplane came from the stubs of wings that jutted from its core. So the fat Prussian had scored twice, Stachel once. A good bit of shooting all around.

Stachel reached into the seat cushion, assembled his siphoning gear, and drank deeply of the cognac. The remaining Spads were scurrying west, tails high.

As they headed home, Stachel was sullenly pensive.

The new Fokkers would arrive tomorrow. Once again he reviewed the list; Heidemann, of course, would keep one for himself, leaving four others to be distributed. Mueller would get one because, next to Heidemann, he was the *Jasta*'s high scorer. Braun, Mueller's eternal chess partner, no doubt would get one because of his exceptional skill at *Kette* tactics—he was even contributing to a manual on the subject; a fourth would go to Huemmel, now well recovered from his illness, who was simply a good, all-round pilot with a comfortable score. The fifth— that was the puzzle. Ulrich, Fritzinger, and Schneider could be considered out of the race, as could the two new replacements, Hochschild and Nagel. That left Von Klugermann and himself. Willi's score as of this morning stood exactly even with his own. Counting the two Spads he'd just nailed, the Prussian was now ahead by one.

Stachel thought about this for long minutes. Then, nodding once to himself, he eased back on the throttle.

He pulled on the machine gun charge handles, threw in the clutch, then fired a brief, stuttering burst.

Von Klugermann turned in his seat and let the Albatros fall back alongside. Stachel reached out and thumped the side of his fuselage, then pointed ahead to his engine. He repeated the gestures, but this time motioned to Von Klugermann to go on without him. The Prussian stared across at him questioningly, the wind distorting his cheeks. Stachel repeated the signals for a third time, then dropped away. He noted with satisfaction that Von Klugermann made no attempt to follow.

When the Pfalz had sunk into the cloud blanket, Stachel pulled up and restored power. He retained his altitude just below the surface of the mist and headed toward the airdrome at full throttle. Once or twice he permitted the Pfalz to rise to the cloud surface, stalking, he smiled to himself, like a U-boat. In these fleeting intervals he could see Von Klugermann's Albatros continuing its lonely course.

As the Prussian's dirty brown machine began a wide spiral, Stachel went into a fast power-glide, the sunlight surrendering to the solid gray vapor that formed beads of water on his face and rivulets on the surfaces of the Pfalz. The blind descent seemed interminable.

He broke free eventually, but noted in sodden satisfaction that the ground mists had all but obscured the field, just as he'd hoped they would. He took another long pull from the hose, waiting, his cheeks tight with brandied numbness.

The Albatros appeared finally, and as Stachel hung at the fringe of the overcast, he watched Von Klugermann make a tentative, exploratory circle above the lower haze. The Prussian arced around again and began a long power-glide. He had obviously elected to avoid the poplars and make his approach from the opposite end of the field. Stachel, feverishly alert, made rapid revisions to his calculations. Satisfied then, he gave the Mercedes full throttle and slanted down the sky toward the pocket of mist. When he saw Von Klugermann's propeller slow from a hardly visible blur into a windmilling of blades, he also cut power. The Pfalz's wires moaned with the speed of its otherwise silent plunge.

The Albatros sank out of sight into the fog, and the Pfalz was close behind.

Straining, Stachel could make out the shadowy outline of Von Klugermann's machine ahead. As the haze grew thinner and ground detail appeared to float by in enlarged and wispy procession, the Albatros began to correct and ease away from the long finger of the factory chimney that reached upward through the mist to the right front. It was then, hovering directly above and to the left rear, that Stachel fed full power to the Mercedes.

To Von Klugermann, whose open-mouthed, wild stare was clear even from the Pfalz, the sound must have been like that of an express train.

The Albatros went into a frantic turn with full power on, its nose high. As Stachel's machine screamed for altitude, he saw the Albatros' wings slam into the chimney, dissolving in a ghastly tangle and sending a shower of bricks cascading through the air. Then there was a muffled explosion below, and the mist brightened with an unearthly glow.

"Now go over this again for me, Stachel. Just what happened?" Heidemann leaned across the desk, his face stony.

"We were jumped by five Spads above Bernes. In the fight, the enemy lost three. We—"

"Who knocked down the Spads?"

"I got all three of them."

"What was Von Klugermann doing all this time?"

"Well, we were up to our hips in Spads. He gave a good account of himself, of course, but I was luckier in the shooting department."

"Then what happened?" Heidemann demanded.

"We returned here, but on the way my machine acted up. A vapor lock, I think. I signaled Willi to go on, since there was nothing he could do and I didn't want to risk him in the nearby air while I made a forced landing through that deep overcast."

"Yes?"

"Well, I straightened out the trouble, then came on back here. I decided to avoid the usual approach over the trees because of the mist. As I made my final glide, Willi's machine suddenly appeared right in front of me. I turned on full power and he did likewise. However, I guess he didn't see the chimney and flew right into it. . . ."

Kettering came into the office.

"Well?"

"Sir, the *Flugmeldedienst* confirms three Spads. They fell in a triangle near an antiaircraft battery at L-Twenty. But because of the overcast they couldn't trace the action." He looked at Stachel. "I suppose you'll have to console yourself with another moral victory."

Heidemann said in a warning tone: "Do you doubt Stachel's claim, Kettering?"

The big man's face reddened. "Why, no, sir. But the rules—"

"The wreckage of three Spads has been found. *Leutnant* Stachel claims the victories. Do you doubt his word?" His voice was flat.

"Well, of course not, sir, but—"

"Credit Stachel with the three Spads and send the claim forms, with my endorsement, to *Kofl*. At once."

Kettering swallowed hard. "Yes, sir."

"And arrange a full military burial ceremony for *Leutnant* von Klugermann."

After Kettering had left, Stachel sat in tense silence while Heidemann studied some papers on his desk. The *Jasta* leader signed his name twice, then looked up, a smile in his eyes.

"No doubt you've heard that the first five Fokkers arrive tonight."

"I admit I've heard the rumor."

"It's no rumor. And one of them will be yours, of course."

Stachel barely restrained a smile. "That's fine, sir. I wasn't certain you'd consider me eligible. . . ."

"Why?"

"Well, on those tryouts I was next to last, and knowing your habit of assigning all such things in descending order of merit—"

Heidemann laughed easily, shaking his head. "Stachel, you amuse and baffle me. You are so infernally sensitive, so wont to evaluate events in terms of your own egoism. If you had just used a little sense instead of emotion you'd have seen that I established the Fokker tryout sequence on a purely alphabetical basis."

Stachel was conscious of a roaring in his head.

"And, Stachel, let me point out that, next to me, you are the best pilot in this *Jasta*. It would have been asinine not to assign a Fokker to you after that spectacular exhibition you gave with it. Now—you've had a busy day. Take a rest. But first, I suggest you go by Von Klugermann's quarters and pull together his personal gear. I want you to compose a note to go with it when it's sent to the family. After all, you were Willi's friend."

CLEVELAND AIRPORT AUGUST 1933

FROM *TROPHY FOR EAGLES*

---

by WALTER J. BOYNE

Walter J. Boyne is a retired Air Force colonel, a former director of the National Air and Space Museum, an aviation historian, and a superb writer. He is the author of *The Smithsonian Book of Flight* and an excellent history of the United States Air Force, among many other works.

In *Trophy for Eagles*, the first of several historical novels set in the world of aviation between and into World War II, we meet young Frank Bandfield, born too late for World War I but determined to be the best pilot alive. The villain is German ace Bruno Hafner, who burned down Bandfield's hangar to prevent him from beating Lindbergh to Paris. In addition to Lindbergh, Boyne's characters hobnob with many of the legendary figures of aviation, including Howard Hughes, Jimmy Doolittle, Roscoe Turner, and Amelia Earhart.

In the excerpt that follows, Frank Bandfield is flying in one of the lesser events of the Cleveland Air Races of 1933, trying desperately to win $15,000 to finance an aircraft factory.

A mood as dark and gelatinous as sea-urchin soup hung over the Cleveland Institute of Aviation hangar that Stephan Dompnier had rented. His mood had been foul for the last two days. The aircraft's engine was still acting up, and his ground crew was no help. The two surly Frenchmen spent their time yammering about the inexcusable quality of American food and the lack of drinkable wine. The magnificent cigarettes, smoked end to end, compensated somewhat, but both longed to go back to Paris.

They were the only two sent from France with Dompnier. Pierre Nicolau was from the Caudron factory, and he knew the racer inside out. He looked like Jean Gabin, knew it, and mimicked him as much as possible in word and gesture. René Coty was from the Renault engine works, but had not yet been able to get the engine working right. A brooding Parisian with curly blue-black hair separated from his eyebrows by a slim gash of pockmarked flesh, he kept a cigarette dangling from his lips at all times. Something in his manner suggested that taking advice was not his strong suit.

It was their glowering presence that had inhibited Stephan from asking for help earlier. Now he had no choice—he had to qualify tomorrow, and race the following day. He had asked Hadley Roget to drop by and look at the engine.

Promptly at nine, Roget walked in, followed by Bandfield. Both men walked around the racer, admiring it, oblivious to the obvious dislike of the two mechanics.

Hadley listened to Stephan describe the problem, and what they had done to correct it. The engine would run perfectly well on the ground; as soon as he was airborne it would backfire, sometimes so badly that he wasn't sure he'd get it around the pattern to land.

Roget nosed around. The engine was installed so that the crankshaft lay on top, with the cylinders pointing toward the ground.

"Inverted engine, huh? What attitude do you run it up in on the ground?"

Stephan was annoyed by Bandfield's presence and was trying not to show it. He said, "Ah, three-point, of course. Nicolau holds down the tail, and I check it at full power. On the ground it is fine—in the air, pouf!"

Roget had Dompnier go through the drill; the engine sounded perfect.

"Stephan, this time let's run it up in a level attitude. Put a sawhorse under the tail and we'll see what happens."

Bandy placed a canvas cover on the stabilizer, then piled sandbags on it, while Roget and the two mechanics tethered the Caudron to tie-downs set in the concrete.

Dompnier started the engine. The airplane twitched and trembled, straining at the ropes. In less than sixty seconds, the engine song changed from a fluid roar and began backfiring, belching smoke and flame from the exhausts, the vibration shaking it as a terrier shakes a rat. Dompnier shut it down.

A quiet look of triumph crossed Roget's face, and he began pulling the cowling off. An hour later, he turned to Dompnier.

"There's your trouble. The oil return line is too small. When the oil pressure goes up, it can't handle it, and back pressure from the pump dumps oil down the rocker arms. Did you notice a rise in oil pressure after you took off?"

"*Oui*—from about one hundred to one-eighty. It seemed to me that high oil pressure is good, not bad."

"Not this time, my friend. I think we can fix this, but it will be risky. We have to run a new oil line, and bore out the inlet. If we don't tap into anything we'll be okay. Will you risk it?"

Stephan shrugged. "I have no choice."

"Lemme take a look at the pistons, too. You might have scuffed them during the backfires."

In another thirty minutes they had the pistons laid out. Two were clearly marred, one so badly that it couldn't be used again. Dompnier had spares, and the five men fell to work. By midnight, the engine was back together and Dompnier had run it up in a level position, the air-cooled Renault engine breaking the night-dampened silence of the airport.

Dompnier jumped down from the wing and embraced Hadley.

"Thank you, and thank you, too, Bandy."

"You're welcome, Stephan. We'd all better get some sleep. It's going to be an early morning."

The slanting rays of the late-afternoon sun had turned the haze into an incandescent ball. The crowds were streaming away in long lines, and a weary Frank Bandfield sat with Roget, their backs braced against the Chevy's bumper, watching a red-and-white Gee Bee Sportster practicing aerobatics across the northeast edge of the field.

"Whose airplane is that, Hadley?"

Roget, never idle, was cleaning spark plugs as they sat, pressing their ends into a cone-shaped tin and letting high-pressure air sandblast them clean. Squinting, he said, "Looks like Charlotte Hafner's bird."

"She's damn good. I don't think she's moved a yard out of the field boundaries, and she's done everything from snap rolls to spins."

The tiny Gee Bee landed out of a loop, touching down just inside the field boundary. It taxied to a stop inside the wire fence surrounding the hangars Hafner had rented. The pilot got out with the log book in her hand and ran inside, while mechanics pushed the airplane into the hangar. Without apology, they brushed past Bandfield and set up a protective restraining ring of wire, threaded through steel stanchions, designed to keep onlookers out. He was a little annoyed, but stood there, grasping the wire with both hands and jingling the little red "Team Members Only" signs.

Bandfield was waiting outside for Charlotte to emerge, but it was Patty who walked out, short hair glistening in the sun.

"Hello, Bandy. Thanks for helping Stephan with his engine last night."

"Aw, you're welcome, we were glad to do it. But I have to say you surprised me just now. I thought your mother was flying. You were really great." He suddenly felt awkward, all hands and feet uncomfortable, that she might think he was somehow following up on their dance of two nights before.

She turned and nodded in the direction of the hangar. Then she pivoted and said, "Don't go just yet."

The words "Well, how about a cup of coffee . . ." turned into an uncontrollable scream as pain coursed through his arms. Patty slumped to the ground laughing, and inside two mechanics fell into each other's arms, hysterical from the oldest joke in aviation—the electric fence hot-wired to a Model T magneto. Four turns sent a harmless jolt of electricity through anyone dumb enough to grab the wire.

"I'm sorry, Bandy, I couldn't resist. We don't often get people over here, and the guys get bored."

Feeling was returning to his arms, and he smiled weakly.

"Yeah, that's a good joke. We used to pull it back in Salinas. Ha ha."

Concerned but still smiling, she took his arm and rubbed it, and he realized the electricity wasn't all in the wires.

"I have to act a little rowdy once in a while just to make sure they know I'm one of the guys."

"You sure don't look like one of the guys in that outfit."

She glanced down, and buttoned the upper button of her blouse.

"Bandy, maybe you can help me. Stephan has been in a blue funk ever since that ridiculous incident at the dance. I'm worried that Dickens—or Stephan, for that matter—will do something stupid during their race."

Bandfield nodded. She was smart. It was just something like the fight that might cause either one of them to try to do a little more than was safe during the race.

She continued, "I'd like to get them at least to be civil to each other. I talked to Dickens earlier, and he offered me a ride in a friend's airplane he's making a test flight on."

"He shouldn't take you on a test flight—might be risky."

"No, he says it's just routine. He was apologetic, and I don't want him to be angry with Stephan."

Bandfield shuffled, uneasy at the prospect. "He won't be too happy to see me."

"Well, I'm worried about you too. Why not apologize for slugging him? What will it cost you?"

"Seeing as your little trick with the wire keeps me from moving my arms, it might cost me a black eye."

"You can move them, all right. I've seen that hot-wire trick played often enough to know how much sympathy you deserve, and you've already had your quota."

She kept her arm linked in his as they strolled across the dry grass, spotted here and there with empty Coca-Cola and Quaker State Oil bottles. He liked being close to her.

"When I talked to Dickens earlier, he apologized. He said he was just drunk. He promised to apologize to Stephan, too, if I'd take a hop with him. Just be nice and we'll get this all fixed up."

They talked about the dance and the Caudron's engine, and her mother's chances in the women's unlimited race the following morning.

"Dickens said he was test-flying the airplane to pay back a favor to an old friend of his who has entered in the Cleveland-Dayton-Toledo round-robin race."

"I didn't think Dickens had any friends," Bandfield scoffed.

As they approached the hangar Bandfield could see Dickens's head sticking up on the other side of an ancient Bach biplane. The patched and tattered airplane had obviously spent too many winters parked outside in the weather, and Dickens was checking everything with extra care. Bandy watched with distaste, unable to understand why Dickens would ask Patty to fly in such a wreck. When he glanced into the cabin, he saw that there was a bench fitted instead of the usual two separate seats. In the air, she'd have a hell of a time getting away from him if he decided to make a pass.

"Hello there, Bandfield. I guess I owe you one for that sucker punch the other night."

"No hard feelings, Roy. Have one on me, as a gift."

Dickens gave his usual nasty smile. "No, I've got hard feelings all over my ribs. I'll pay you back someday, you can count on it."

After the walk-around inspection, Dickens slid over to the left side, and Patty climbed up into the right. After propping the engine for them, Bandfield trotted alongside as they taxied slowly to the edge of the grassy field. The landing gear was splayed out like an old washerwoman's legs, the paint on the struts cracked like varicose veins.

Dickens leered at him as he went through the engine run-up, the tired engine coughing and backfiring. Bandfield could tell that the spark plugs were fouled with oil. Dickens stood on the brakes as he put the throttle forward to full power, deafening the onlookers with the sharp staccato exhaust noise. The plane strained forward like a sprinter against the chocks, slack fabric quivering, landing gear bending forward.

Bandfield made the classic "cut the engine" sign and bounded up on the wing. Dickens brought the power back and Patty opened her door.

With his left hand, Bandfield unbuckled her safety belt; he shot his right hand under her rump and scooped her out of the cabin, backing off the wing and falling with her on top of him.

Dickens sneered at them as he reached over and closed the door. Then he put on full power and the Bach began its takeoff roll.

Bandfield struggled to his feet, pulling Patty up with him. She was furious, but he held her to him and pointed at the airplane, now struggling a hundred yards down the runway.

Dickens had the power fully on, and as the Bach slowly accelerated, its landing gear began to spread, the wheels drifting farther and farther apart.

They stood stock still, his arms still around her, as with a mime's precision the airplane struggled toward its pratfall. There was a grinding roar as the gear snapped parallel to the wings and the Bach's propeller snubbed itself into a stub and the plane slammed on its belly.

Bandfield whispered, "Dear God, don't let it burn."

The airplane, wheels spread out as if it had stepped on a giant banana, slid to a stop, and Dickens sprang out the side like a runner stealing home, racing away from the inevitable explosion.

The Bach sat for a moment, white vapor showing where the fuel from the ruptured tanks was reaching the red-hot exhaust manifold. A hurricane of flame preceded the sound of the

explosion that tossed the airframe fifty feet in the air. It hesitated at the top of the arc, then dove down to impact vertically,
wings flying up parallel to the cabin, the tail driving down the
collapsing fuselage like a retracting spring.

For a frozen moment, there was no sound anywhere, and
Bandy could hear Patty's frantic breathing. Then the strident
sirens of the emergency wagons wailed.

The comic crash had diverted his mind but not his body
from the excitement of holding Patty Dompnier tightly. She
had ceased to struggle, and he was now aware that he was
pressing a giant erection against this lovely woman, the wife of
a friend.

She had noticed, at first annoyed, then amused.

"Thank you for saving me." She looked back over her
shoulder, hesitating for a moment, Then, Charlotte's daughter,
she paraphrased Mae West's line from a New York play. "Is that
a wrench in your pocket, or are you just glad to see me?"

Blushing, he let her go as Dickens wandered back in a state
of shock.

Embarrassed by her own joke, but not wanting to leave, she
asked, "How did you know it was going to happen?"

"I didn't. If I'd been sure it was, I wouldn't have let Dickens
go either, I'd have kicked a hole in the rudder or something.
But I knew I didn't want you to take a chance."

She nodded. "Thanks." Then, unable to resist, she added,
"For everything."

An hour later, he was still trying to think of something clever to
say as he polished the last of the Simonize compound off the
Rascal's fuselage. The line about the wrench had been funny;
she must have inherited her mother's bawdy sense of humor.
He wondered if she'd inherited her free and easy ways.

Cleveland and Patty inevitably reminded him of Oakland
and Millie. Patty Dompnier was totally different in appearance

and manner, but he felt the same stirrings of fundamental hunger for her. Might as well forget about it—she's married, he told himself.

Bandy knew there was a point in preparing an airplane when it was better just to button everything up and wait for the race. He tossed his polishing rag down and stretched out in the warm Ohio sun to watch the women's unlimited. Charlotte was competing against some of the best women flyers in the country, with the single exception of Amelia Earhart, who didn't fly closed-course races.

Most of the men pilots resented having women compete. The prizes were small enough without having to share them with women, many of whom were wealthy in their own right. Some rash talk about letting them race against the men had been buried in an avalanche of curses and catcalls.

The women's unlimited race results would depend almost entirely upon the pilots' skills, since two of the women were flying Gee Bee Sportsters identical to Charlotte's except for color. He could see them lined up for the racehorse start, quivering under power, dust swirling behind them.

All three bore the Granville Brothers trademark paint scheme of gleaming white fuselage and wings edged with a scallop of contrasting colors. Charlotte's plane was trimmed in red, with the racing number seventeen on the side and the wingtips. Gladys Traden was number nine, and her scallops were green. Gloria Engles bore a black eight-ball for a number, with matching black trim.

The fourth airplane, flown by young Nancy Alderman, was a taper-wing Laird biplane, clearly outclassed.

Roget joined him leaning down to yell in his ear, "Hey, Bandy—do you know why women can't fly upside down?"

It was the tenth time he'd heard the joke in the last four days. "No idea. Why not?"

"Cause they would have a crack-up!"

Hadley had gotten a laugh with this one from everybody but the French mechanics.

The decibel level of the engines went up and the starter's flag went down. Gladys Traden got off first, forcing Charlotte to fly high and outside. All the airplanes disappeared momentarily around the far turn, then came back in a blur as they whipped in front of them, hungry hornets racing wide open.

He wondered about Charlotte's mental set. A closed-course race was the most dangerous flying short of actual combat, and apparently she loved it.

The three Gee Bees looked as if they were tied in formation as they bored around the course, never changing position as they whipped around the pylons. They lapped the Laird the fourth time around, and Molly Alderman graciously pulled up high and wide, giving way. She continued to fly the course, waiting for someone to drop out.

Gloria Engles had attached herself to Traden's wing, flying in the number-two position all the way around, the turbulence from their prop wash combining to keep Charlotte well back and out of position. On the next lap Engles abruptly pulled deeply into the course in a tight turn that increased the force of gravity on her body four times, pressing her into her seat. She kept the elliptical wings of her racer hanging vertically as she rerounded the pylon.

Must have missed the turn, Bandfield thought.

He glanced at Charlotte, now flying number two to Traden, then back to Engles. She was gone. A billowing black cloud of smoke summoned the crash trucks, roaring out with sirens blaring.

"High-speed stall. I saw her snap. Goddam women shouldn't be racing anyway." Roget's expression was grim.

An involuntary response to the tragedy gripped the throttles of the two remaining Gee Bees, and their lap speeds slowed slightly. The Laird drifted down to reenter the pattern, lonely, watchful, waiting to finish third.

Charlotte had drifted a little farther back in her number-two spot, a thin streak of white smoke pouring from her exhausts streaking the white fuselage sides with an oil smear. The two Gee Bees roared past on the final lap, dead level, thirty feet separating them. Traden's right wing's fabric suddenly bellowed out to burst like a balloon, sending her aircraft snap-rolling to the right before burying itself inverted in the ground.

"Holy Christ, that's two down."

Charlotte, in a nervous fog, blasted past the checkered flag, then pulled up and headed off the course, gaining altitude slowly, trying to compose herself. The Laird circled again, Alderman delighted to have an unexpected second place.

Bandy had a box lunch from the airfield café, but he couldn't touch a bite. The vision of the two women going in wouldn't leave him.

"You'd better eat, Bandy. Twenty laps is one hell of a race, especially around this itty-bitty course." Hughes pushed a waxed-paper-wrapped sandwich at him.

"At least the legs are all the same length. But at two hundred and forty miles an hour, you'll be turning every fifty seconds or so, pulling lots of Gs. Lemme in the cockpit there."

Hughes had a roll of adhesive tape and a pair of scissors. He cut and pasted twenty small strips of tape along the bottom of the instrument panel.

"Its easy to lose track of where you are. Pull one piece of tape off after each lap, so you know how far you have to go."

A haunted-looking Stephan Dompnier limped by, glancing neither right nor left.

Eight airplanes were manhandled to the starting line.

Hadley stood towering beside the little airplane, polishing the windscreen with a chamois for the hundredth time, ready for any last-minute emergency. Bandy sat in the Rascal, shivering in spite of the sultry Cleveland weather and the heat roaring back from the 485-horsepower Curtiss engine. He glanced at the panel; the oil and cylinder head temperature gauges were up, the coolant temperature was up, the oil pressure was down. Goddam, another five minutes on the ground and the damn thing would cook itself to death. He eased the throttle forward to clear the engine, burning the plugs clean and keeping air flowing through the radiator, and Hadley turned his back to the blast, squinting to keep the dust out of his eyes.

Bandfield's qualifying time had been good enough to get him the third position in the line. It was a good break, because of the hazards of the racehorse start. The planes were lined up wingtip to wingtip; when the flag came down, they would be off and heading for the first pylon like wasps flying down a funnel. Number-two spot had gone to Roy Dickens, sitting comfortably in the Cessna racer he had flown for years, an airplane as pretty as he was ugly. He stuck out of it like a witch on a broomstick. The Cessna looked nose-heavy because of the disproportionately large Wasp engine that powered it.

A universe of people milled in close proximity, pressing down upon the racers in an inverted pyramid of flesh. A quarter of a million watched from the bleachers, and as many more were spread out around the field. Another three of four thousand—insiders, the cognoscenti—were in the pit area, past the wire that restrained the crowds. A covey of ten or twelve people gathered around each airplane, and each racer had a senior mechanic stationed like Hadley just outside the cockpit.

But as the minutes ground down toward the starting time, each solitary figure of a pilot became the tip of the inverted pyramid, carrying on his back the weight of the watchers as well as the job at hand. As the seconds ticked off, the pilots' vision narrowed to a tunnel which saw part of the cockpit and a little section of the windscreen. At the start he would become absolutely alone, launched like an arrow into a winding roar of confusion, a freewheeling gear in a Chaplinesque clock speeding to oblivion.

Dickens reached down and bottomed out his seat, pulling his head within the confines of the windscreen and doubling his legs up so that they almost reached his face. He'd had to make special cutouts in the instrument panel just to be able to squeeze into the airplane. He glanced to his left at the little Frog in the blue airplane and shook his head. It wasn't fair. The French government subsidized their racing team, paid Caudron and Renault to do their best. He'd put the Cessna together with hard work and an engine salvaged from one of last year's crashes. The Frog was rich and didn't need the prize money. Every cent Dickens had and all he could borrow was invested in the Cessna. He wanted to win, needed to win.

Looking to the right, he sneered at Bandfield's airplane, crude in comparison to his or the Frenchman's. All he had to do was get off first and take the first pylon, then let the rest of them catch up with him. If he got ahead of the Frenchman, he'd never let him pass.

Dompnier had won the pole position, and his head was now twitching in the cockpit, glancing from his instruments to the starter's flag and back again. The racehorse start worried him; his retractable gear might not be strong enough to hold up on the rough field surface. But if he could get off first and be first around the pylon, the race was won.

Bandy stared at the Caudron with admiration. It was the fastest plane on the field by ten miles an hour or so, capable of 260-mph laps when it was running right. It should be running right now, he thought, after all the care Roget had given it. God, after all their efforts, working double shifts to keep the bomber project going while they built the racer, they might have given the prize away to Stephan by rebuilding his engine.

Maybe they'd given the factory away! It had been crazy to help Dompnier.

On his right were five more airplanes—Roy Moore in a Keith Ryder Special, Bill Ong in Howard's Pete, and then a line of nondescript mechanic's specials, put together with cutting torch and spare parts.

Coveys of sweat-stained, grease-covered ground crews surrounded each airplane, blinking through the grit thrown back by the propellers, tugging on the wingtips and holding down on the tails to ease the strain on the brakes. The power would be full on when the starter's flag went down, and then they'd let go.

Bandy had finished a thermos of ice water and gone to the bathroom twenty minutes before, but his throat was parched and he needed to urinate badly.

Roget leaned down and yelled in his ear, "Dompnier's going to be first off, Bandy. I got a look at his prop. They pump it up with compressed air to fine pitch. When he takes off, a bleed valve opens, and it moves the prop to coarse pitch for the race. It's a hell of a gadget. I wish we had one."

"What's second prize? Seventy-five hundred?"

"There ain't no second prize for us. You got to win the fifteen grand or we'll lose the option on the plant. Don't go thinking second place.'

Bandy nodded agreement. He felt the nervous excitement building in his gut, a weird circular clawing that began in the pit of his stomach and forced bile up to his mouth like toothpaste squeezed from a tube. He spat into the slipstream, forgetting about the guys holding down the tail.

In the past, he'd trembled with the building tension until the starter's flag went down, and then everything was automatic. He hoped it would be the same today.

He tapped the clock. The second hand lurched toward start time, a long strand of temporal molasses that seemed never to disconnect. He brought the engine to full power just as the red-and-white-checkered flag came down. The outside world crystallized into silence as the rising pounding of his own engine totally deafened him. Bandy danced on the rudder to keep the Rascal straight in the wildly bouncing slipstream. One of the mechanic's specials veered left to run its prop right through its neighbor before they'd moved twenty feet.

Bandy saw the accident, knew no one was hurt. The goddam Caudron was already off the ground, gear coming up. He tugged at the stick and skidded toward the inside of the track behind Dickens, who was leading somehow, and Dompnier.

The Rascal was running perfectly, accelerating to top speed just before he reached the pylon marking the first turn. The race-course was tricky, with farmers' water tanks scattered around the perimeter looking just like pylons. It would be easy to make a mistake and fly off the course. The straightaways went by in less than a minute, then it was rudder, aileron, left wing down, pulling back on the stick to bend the airplane around the turn. G forces squashed him down in the seat, multiplying his weight to over six hundred pounds. Back to the straight with aileron, rudder, right wing down to level, release back pressure. It was brutal flying, a blacksmith's formula of pound, bend, pound, bend.

The grandstand had been a riot of color before he took off. In his turns he saw it as a variegated blur binding together two checkerboards that he knew were the parking lots. Rudder, aileron, wing down, back pressure. It became a horizontal dance, a ritual coercion of a gravity steamroller. Sweat sluiced down his face and arms. Once his hand slipped off the throttle. Better the throttle than the stick.

The pilot animal took over, the element within him that tuned itself to the machine, to the concept of winning. The other personality, the human element, sat back and watched, dispassionate save for fear.

205

Dickens was in the lead, with Dompnier half a length behind, twenty feet ahead of Bandfield. The rest of the pack were stretching out, waiting to be lapped by the faster leading trio.

He looked down at the twenty strips of tape.

"Christ, what lap is this?" He had already lost track, and determined to fly till everybody stopped.

His engine was running strong, broiling the cockpit with solid hot fumes untainted by telltale burned oil. The wind picked up. Straight down the field on the first stretch, it blew inward on the second, outward on the third.

On the second turn, the wind forced him toward the pylon. The outside world telescoped down to a narrow band of vision, his brain barely recovering from the blood-draining pull of one high-G turn before he was in another. In his turns he caught sight of the ground from the corner of his eye, two or three people, a man holding a square board with a number on it, automobile tracks in the dying grass, then it was level again with nothing in view but Dickens and Dompnier. A pylon loomed too close and he pumped the stick forward in the vertical turn, bucking the G forces to jump outward and losing another hundred feet on Dompnier.

He had no awareness of the passage of time, no ordered sense of motion. The racers became centrifugal extrusions of metal and man, spun out at random distances. The ground fifty feet below was a peripheral green-brown ribbon. He stared only at the two racers shimmering with speed ahead of him, no time to glance at his instruments. The sound and the feel told him the airplane was okay. When it wasn't he'd know it all too well.

Dickens knew he was flying perfectly, shaving the pylons, keeping down low in the smooth air. He could see Dompnier's airplane in the little rearview mirror mounted on his windscreen.

In the Caudron, Stephan Dompnier moved the wings as extensions of his shoulders, the engine as part of his heart and lungs. He watched the red airplane ahead. The pig Dickens was flying beautifully, but his Cessna was slower than the Caudron, and he knew he could pass him on the next lap.

Behind him, Bandy wished he'd counted the laps. It had to be ten at least. His arm muscles ached, the left from bending the throttle forward, trying to push it in the firewall, the right from controlling the maverick stick dancing in the turbulence of Dompnier's prop-wash. He was flying automatically now, grazing the pylon on each turn, pulling another half G to wrench the Rascal around a little quicker. He didn't hear the engine screaming, the wind whistling around the canopy, didn't feel the heat searing his shoes. He only saw Dompnier and Dickens, both now seeming to inch back, lap by lap, like heavy weights drawn on a string.

A juddering vibration forced Dompnier's eyes to the instrument panel. The tachometer was leaping in concert with the backfiring engine. Something was wrong, a valve going, a ring sticking. He saw the Cessna edge away, and then as he slowed, he watched Bandfield vault ahead of him.

Sweating, Dompnier played with the mixture control, easing it back and forth slightly to try to smooth his engine out. He racked the stick to his belly, squeezing speed from safety, clinging close to Bandfield by force of will and tighter turns. He clung to Bandfield's wing, matching gut-wrenching G for G.

A slight change in noise told Bandfield that he'd somehow picked up a few rpm. The engine was smoother, and he was gaining on Dickens foot by foot. The Cessna and the Rascal rocketed around the pylons, dumping the pilots into their seats with the G forces, airspeed reaching 250 mph on the straights with only a mile or two speed difference between them. He riveted his eyes on Dickens's airplane, watching the sharp movements of the controls as Dickens entered a turn—aileron in, wing up, aileron out, wing down—and on into the stretch. He was duplicating the movements exactly, unaware of it, unaware of anything except the blur of ground flashing by below, the jackhammer vibration that matched the airframe's groaning in the turns, and Dickens's red airplane creeping slowly back to him.

His thin body shuddering under the G forces, Dompnier forced his eyes down to the instrument panel. All the needles were off the scale, but the engine was running well again, no longer backfiring, and he began to gain on the leaders. Dickens was falling back, and he could see Bandfield ready to make his move, trying for the lead.

Bandfield's airplane had pulled just to the side of the little Cessna when Dickens rocked his ailerons and flicked a skidding turn out in front of him.

Dompnier watched, clinically detached. "*Merde*, he's bluffing, just as Turner said he would."

Bandfield saw the Cessna's control movements, ignored them. It was win or die, a high school game of chicken such as he'd once played in Model Ts on the country roads around Salinas.

Dickens flicked his controls again, saw the Rascal relentlessly boring in, the shimmering circle of its propeller aimed directly at his cockpit. Dickens wrenched his red racer down and outside as Bandfield slammed his plane over the top of the Cessna's cockpit with inches to spare, then dropped down to take advantage of the clear air of the lead.

Dompnier growled with delight. "He made it." The old 1918 ace's killer instinct stirred within him. Dickens's faked maneuver had cost him time, and he'd fallen a length behind Bandfield, and now was only half a length ahead. First Dickens, then Bandfield, then the trophy.

Dickens swore to himself, bending the throttle forward. He knew he didn't have the speed to catch Bandfield. He had to hold the Caudron off somehow and take at least second place. He needed the money, to live, to eat, to fly.

Dickens looked in his mirror again, saw the Caudron's prop between his wing and elevator. Dompnier was gaining—his engine must have cleared up. Dickens forgot about Bandfield, forgot about anything but the blue Caudron moving in to steal second place, steal his livelihood from him. He moved stick and rudder in short abrupt slamming movements, glancing back at Dompnier, who was gaining inch by inch. He had no choice; he had to fake this Frog out even if he hadn't fooled that fucking Bandfield.

Dickens viciously flicked his ailerons, kicked the rudder, jigged the Cessna right, then left.

Dompnier's face compressed to a tight smile. "No, my friend, not this time. You didn't fool Bandfield, you won't fool me."

Desperate, Dickens flicked his controls again, harder, jolting unseen molecules of air, scraping loose their grip on his tapered wings. The little Cessna shuddered in a high-speed stall, snapping directly into Dompnier's path.

The Cessna blotted out the sky before Dompnier, a bright red wall centered with the terrified white smear of Dickens's face. In the split second before the collision his hands automatically moved to jettison the canopy and unbuckle the safety harness. The two airplanes merged, disappearing in a thudding explosion that rocked the field. The French racer bored through the Cessna, propeller chewing Dickens and cockpit before lofting the engine away in a high arc as the Caudron disintegrated around Dompnier.

Thrown brutally from his shattered cockpit, Stephan was pain-gouged to a clear untrammeled consciousness by the midair splintering of his shredded body. Turning flat, arms and legs outstretched into a cross, he saw the ground spin beneath him. He did not scream. His last thought was that Patty would not bear his son after all, before he dropped to bounce like a skipped rock on the grassy stubble.

It was a second before the stricken crowd could compre-

hend what had happened, before the low, dolorous moan con-
cealing the shock of blood-bitten peasure rolled out.

Coming around for the last lap, Bandy took the checkered
flag wondering where Dompnier and Dickens had suddenly
gone. He pulled up to five hundred feet and brought the power
back, letting the Rascal coast down to 150 mph. His left hand
was trembling from the grip he had on the throttle, his muscles
sore from the strain and the G forces. But he had the $15,000.
They had the factory.

The other racers were spreading out to forge a landing pattern, Dompnier and Dickens not among them. He dropped
down to take a slow victory lap, fifty feet above the course. The
flame and smoke puzzled him until he saw Patty running
toward the wreckage.

WINGS OVER KHABAROVSK

---

by LOUIS L'AMOUR

Louis L'Amour began his writing career in the late 1930s, selling short stories to pulp fiction magazines, a medium that became extinct with the dawning of the television age. Volume was the key to making a living writing for the pulps—the magazines paid by the word and the rate was low: some pulp writers pounded out as many as 10,000 words a day, every day. They never rewrote. Those successful at the craft published under numerous pen names.

Pulp fiction was unoriginal and trite; it was written so fast it couldn't be anything else. The L'Amour story that follows contains this magnificent sentence: "He sat behind his table staring at Turk inscrutably." Takes your breath away, doesn't it?

Before he went on to fame and fortune writing formula westerns filled with stock characters who were wide at the shoulder, lean at the hip, and fast with a gun, Louis L'Amour wrote Turk Madden and his loyal sidekick, the Manchu Shin Bao. These two soldiers of fortune knocked about the world in a Grumman Goose and starred in numerous L'Amour pulp tales during World War II.

The plot of the following adventure is strikingly similar to the plots of many of the B-movie westerns Hollywood was cranking out about this time. Comrade Lutvin could have easily been a deputy sheriff shot in the back on the outskirts of town, Turk Madden, the hero, a ranch foreman who discovers the body and rides into town to tell the sheriff. One suspects this thought also occurred to Louis L'Amour.

L'Amour hot-rodded Madden's Goose for the pulps. The real Goose was a nice little amphibian transport from the 1930s with two 450-HP Pratt & Whitney Wasp Jr. radial engines. It carried six people or cargo, cruised at about 150 miles per hour, and was unarmed. Sporting eight fixed .50-caliber machine guns, the same as a P-51 Mustang, L'Amour's Goose routinely engages and shoots down fighter planes, including Zeros. Any attacking fighter pilot who gets behind Madden's Goose faces the fierce Shin Bao, who throws hot lead at the villain with a Thompson sub-machine gun. How Shin manages to shoot from a transport at trailing aircraft is never explained. L'Amour's airplanes do a lot of "streaking" around, and . . . read it yourself. Here's a pulp tale by a master of the genre.

The drone of the two radial motors broke the still white silence. As far as the eye could reach the snow-covered ridges of the Sihote Alin Mountains showed no sign of life. Turk Madden banked the Grumman and studied the broken terrain below. It was remote and lonely, this range along the Siberian coast.

He swung his ship in a slow circle. That was odd. A half dozen fir trees had no snow on their branches.

He leveled off and looked around, then saw what he wanted, a little park, open and snow-covered, among the trees. It was just the right size, by the look of it. He'd chance the landing. He slid down over the treetops, setting the ship down with just barely enough room. Madden turned the ship before he cut the motor.

Taking down a rifle, he kicked his feet into snowshoes and stepped out into the snow. It was almost spring in Siberia, but the air was crisp and cold. Far to the south, the roads were sodden with melting snow, and the rivers swollen with spring floods. War would be going full blast again soon.

He was an hour getting to the spot. Even before he reached it, his eyes caught the bright gleam of metal. The plane had plunged into the fir trees, burying its nose in the mountainside. In passing, it had knocked the snow from the surrounding trees, and there had been no snow for several days now. That was sheer luck. Ordinarily it would have snowed, and the plane would have been lost beyond discovery in these lonely peaks.

Not a dozen feet from the tangled wreckage of the ship he could see a dark bundle he knew instinctively was the flyer. Lutvin had been his friend. The boyish young Russian had been a great favorite at Khabarovsk Airport. Suddenly, Turk stopped.

Erratic footprints led from the crashed plane to the fallen body. Lutvin had been alive after the crash!

Madden rushed forward and turned the body over. His wild hope that the boy might still be alive died instantly. The snow under the body was stained with blood. Fyodor Lutvin had been machine-gunned as he ran from his fallen plane.

Machine-gunned! But that meant—

Turk Madden got up slowly, and his face was hard. He turned toward the wreckage of the plane, began a slow, painstaking examination. What he saw convinced him. Fyodor Lutvin had been shot down, then, after his plane had crashed, had been ruthlessly machine-gunned by his attacker.

But why? And by whom? It was miles from any known front. The closest fighting was around Murmansk, far to the west. Only Japan, lying beyond the narrow strip of sea at Sakhalin and Hokkaido. And Japan and Russia were playing a game of mutual hands off. But Lutvin had been shot down and then killed. His killers had wanted him dead beyond question.

There could be only one reason—because he knew something that must not be told. The fierce loyalty of the young flyer was too well known to be questioned, so he must have been slain by enemies of his country.

Turk Madden began a systematic search, first of the body, then of the wreckage. He found nothing.

Then he saw the camera. Something about it puzzled him. He studied it thoughtfully. It was smashed, yet—

Then he saw. The camera was smashed, but it had been smashed after it had been taken apart—*after the film had been removed.* Where then, was the film?

He found it a dozen feet away from the body, lying in the snow. The film was in a waterproof container. Studying the situation, Turk could picture the scene.

Lutvin had photographed something. He had been pursued, shot down, but had lived through the crash. Scrambling from the wrecked ship with the film, he had run for shelter in the rocks. Then, as he tumbled under the hail of machine-gun fire, he had thrown the film from him.

Turk Madden took the film and, picking up his rifle, started up the steep mountainside toward the park where he had left the Grumman. He was just stepping from a clump of fir when a shot rang out. The bullet smacked a tree trunk beside him and stung his face with bits of bark.

Turk dropped to his hands and knees and slid back into the trees. Ahead of him, and above him, was a bunch of boulders. Even as he looked a puff of smoke showed from the boulders, and another shot rang out. The bullet clipped a twig over his head. Madden fired instantly, coolly pinking every crevice and crack in the boulders. He did not hurry.

His final shot sounded, and instantly he was running through the soft snow. He made it to a huge fir a dozen feet away before the rifle above him spoke. He turned and fired again.

Indian-fashion, he circled the clump of boulders. But when he was within sight of them, there was no one about. For a half hour he waited, then slid down. On the snow in the center of the rocks, he found two old cartridge cases. He studied them.

"Well, I'll be blowed!" A Berdianka!" he muttered. "I didn't think there was one outside a museum!"

The man's trail was plain. He wore moccasins made of fur, called *unty.* One of them was wrapped in a bit of rawhide, apparently.

His rifle was ready, Turk fell in behind. But after a few minutes it became obvious that his attacker wanted no more of it. Outgunned, the man was making a quick retreat. After a few miles, Madden gave up and made his way slowly back to his own ship. The chances were the man had been sent to burn the plane, to be sure a clean job had been made of the killing. But that he was wearing *unty* proved him no white man, and no Jap either, but one of the native Siberian tribes.

It was after sundown when Turk Madden slid into a long glide for the port of Khabarovsk. In his coat pocket the film was heavy. He was confident that it held the secret of Lutvin's death.

There was a light in Commissar Chevski's office. Turk hesitated, then slipped off his helmet and walked across the field toward the shack. A dark figure rose up from the corner of the hangar, and a tall, stooped man stepped out.

"Shan Bao!" Madden said. "Take care of the ship, will you?"

The Manchu nodded, his dark eyes narrow.

"Yes, comrade." He hesitated. "The commissar asking for you. He seem angry."

"Yeah?" Madden shrugged. "Thanks. I'll see him." He walked on toward the shack without a backward glance. Shan Bao could be trusted with the plane. Where the tall Manchu had learned the trade, Turk could not guess, but the man was a superb plane mechanic. Since Madden's arrival from the East Indies, he had attached himself to Turk and his Grumman, and the ship was always serviced and ready.

Turk tapped lightly on Chevski's door, and at the word walked in.

Commissar Chevski was a man with a reputation for efficiency. He looked up now, his yellow face crisp and cold. The skin was drawn tightly over his cheekbones, his long eyes almost as yellow as his face. He sat behind his table staring at Turk inscrutably. Twice only had Turk talked with him. Around the port the man had a reputation for fierce loyalty and driving ambition. He worked hard and worked everyone else.

"Comrade Madden," he said sharply. "You were flying toward the coast today! Russia is at war with Germany, and planes along the coast invite trouble with Japan. I have given orders that there shall be no flying in that direction!"

"I was ordered to look for Comrade Lutvin," Madden said mildly, "so I flew over the Sihote Atlins."

"There was no need," Chevski's voice was sharp. "Lutvin did not fly in that direction."

"You're mistaken," Turk said quietly, "I found him."

Chevski's eyes narrowed slightly. He leaned forward intently.

"You found Lutvin? Where?"

"On a mountainside in the Sihote Atlins. His plane had crashed. He was dead. His ship had been shot down from behind, and Comrade Lutvin had been machine-gunned as he tried to escape the wreck."

Chevski stood up.

"What is this nonsense?" he demanded. "Who would machine-gun a Russian flyer on duty? We have no enemies here."

"What about Japan?" Madden suggested. "But that need make no difference. The facts are as I say. Lutvin was shot down—then killed."

"You *landed?*" Chevski demanded. He walked around from behind his desk. He shook his head impatiently. "I am sorry, comrade. I spoke hastily. This is serious business, very serious. It means sabotage, possibly war on a new front."

Chevski walked back behind the table. He looked up suddenly.

"Comrade Madden, I trust you will say nothing of this to anyone until I give the word. This is a task for the OGPU, you understand?"

Madden nodded, reaching toward his pocket. "But, com—"
The Russian lifted a hand.

"Enough. I am busy. You have done a good day's work. Report to me at ten tomorrow. Good night." He sat down abruptly and began writing vigorously.

Turk hesitated, thinking of the film. Then, shrugging, he went out and closed the door.

Hurrying to his own quarters, he gathered his materials and developed the film. Then he sat down and began studying the pictures. For hours, he sat over them, but could find nothing. The pictures were of a stretch of Siberian coast near the mouth of the Nahtohu River. They were that, and no more. Finally, almost at daylight, he gave up and fell into bed.

It was hours later when he awakened. For an instant he lay on his back staring upward, then glanced at his wristwatch. Nine-thirty. He would have barely time to shave and get to Chevski's office. He rolled over and sat up. Instantly, he froze. The pictures, left on the table, were gone!

Turk Madden sat very still. Slowly, he studied the room. Nothing had been taken except the pictures, the film, and the can in which it had been carried. He crossed the room and examined the door and window. The latter was still locked, bore no signs of having been opened. The door was as he had left it the night before. On the floor, just inside the door, was the fading print of a damp foot.

Madden dressed hurriedly and strapped on a gun. Then he went outside. The snow was packed hard, but when he stepped to the corner he saw a footprint. The snow was melting, and already there were three dark lines of earth showing across the track under his window, three lines that might have been made by an *unty* with a rawhide thong around it!

Suddenly, Turk glanced up. A squad of soldiers was coming toward him on the double. They halted before him, and their officer spoke sharply.

"Comrade Madden! You are under arrest!"

"Me?" Turk gasped, incredulous. "What for?"

"Come with us. You will know in good time."

They took him at once to Commissar Chevski's office. Turk was led in and stopped before Chevski's desk. There were five other men in the room. Colonel Granatman sat at the table beside Chevski. In a corner sat Arseniev of the Intelligence. He looked very boyish except for his eyes. They were hard and watchful. The other two men Madden did not know.

"Comrade Madden!" Granatman demanded. "You flew yesterday over the Sihote Atlin Mountains? You did this without orders?"

"Yes, but—"

"The prisoner," Chevski said coldly, "will confine himself to replies to questions."

"You reported that you found there the body of Comrade Fyodor Lutvin, is that right?"

"Yes." Turk was watching the proceedings with astonishment. What was this all about?

"What are the caliber of the guns on your ship?" Granatman asked. "Fifty caliber, are they not?"

"Yes."

"Comrade Olentiev," Granatman said, "tell us what you found when Commissar Chevski sent you to investigate."

Olentiev stepped forward, clinking his heels. He was a short, powerful man with a thick neck and big hands. He was, Madden knew, an agent of the OGPU, the all-powerful secret police.

"I found Fyodor Lutvin had been shot through the body with fifteen fifty-caliber bullets. His plane had been shot down. The gas tank was riddled, feedline broken, and instrument panel smashed. Most of the controls were shot away.

"I found the tracks of a man and where he had turned the

body over, and followed those tracks to where a plane had been landed in the mountains nearby.

"On return I reported to Commissar Chevski, then received the report of my assistant, Blavatski. He ascertained that on the night of Thursday last, Comrade Lutvin won three hundred rubles from Comrade Madden at dice."

"Commissar Chevski," Granatman asked slowly, "who in your belief could have attacked Lutvin in that area?"

"The colonel is well aware," Chevski said quietly, "that Russia is at war only with Germany. If we have a killing here, it is my belief it is murder!"

"Colonel Granatman," Turk protested, "there was evidence of another sort. I found near the body a can containing aerial photographs taken along the coast near the mouth of the Nahtohu River."

"Photographs?" Granatman frowned. "Did you report them to the commissar?"

"No, I—"

"You developed them yourself?" Granatman interrupted. "Where are they?"

"They were stolen from my quarters last night," Madden said.

"Ah!" Chevski said. "You had photographs but they were stolen. You did not report them last night. You flew over a forbidden area, and you, of all those who looked, knew where to find Fyodor Lutvin's body!"

Granatman frowned.

"I would like to believe you innocent, Comrade Madden. You have done good work for us, but there seems no alternative."

Turk Madden stared in consternation. Events had moved so rapidly he could scarcely adjust himself to the sudden and complete change in affairs. The matter of the three hundred rubles had been nothing, and he had promptly forgotten it. A mere sixty dollars or so was nothing. In Shanghai he had often lost that many hundreds, and won as much.

"Say, what is this?" Turk demanded. "I'm sent out to look for a lost plane, I find it, and then you railroad me! Whose toes have I been stepping on around here?"

"You will have a fair trial, comrade," Granatman assured him. "This is just a preliminary hearing. Until then you will be held."

Olentiev and Blavatski stepped up on either side of him, and he was marched off without another word. His face grim, he kept still. There was nothing he could do now. He had to admit there was a case, if a flimsy one. That he had gone right to the body, when it was where it wasn't expected to be—that there was no other known plane in the vicinity but his own—that the gun calibers were identical—that he had landed and examined the body—that money had been won from him by Lutvin—that he had told an unverified story of stolen photographs.

Through it all, Arseniev had said nothing. And Arseniev was supposed to be his friend! The thought was still puzzling him when he became conscious of the drumming of a motor. Looking to the runway, not sixty feet away, he saw a small pursuit ship. The motor was running, it had been running several minutes, and no one was anywhere near.

He glanced around quickly. There was no one in sight. His captors were at least a dozen feet away and appeared to be paying no attention. Their guns were buttoned under their tunics. It was the chance of a lifetime. He took another quick glance around, set himself for a dash to the plane. Then his muscles relaxed under a hammering suspicion.

It was too easy. The scene was too perfect. There wasn't a flaw in this picture anywhere. Deliberately, he stopped, waiting for his guards to catch up. As he half-turned, waiting, he saw a rifle muzzle projecting just beyond the corner of a building. Even as he looked, it was withdrawn.

He broke into a cold sweat. He would have been dead before he'd covered a dozen feet! Someone was out to get him. But who? And why?

The attitude of his captors changed suddenly, they dropped their careless manner, and came up alongside.

"Quick!" Olentiev snapped. "You loafer. You murderer. We'll show you. A firing squad you'll get for what you did to Lutvin!"

Turk Madden said nothing. He was taken to the prison and shoved into a cell. The room was of stone, damp and chilly. There was straw on the floor, and a dirty blanket. Above him, on the ground level, was a small, barred window.

He looked around bitterly.

"Looks like you're behind the eightball, pal!" he told himself. "Framed for a murder, and before they get through, you'll be stuck."

He walked swiftly across the cell, leaped, and seized the bars. They were strong, thicker than they looked. A glance at the way they were set into the concrete told him there was no chance there. He lay down on the straw and tried to think. Closing his eyes, he let his mind wander back over the pictures. Something. There had been something there. If he only knew!

But although the pictures were clear in his mind, he could remember nothing. Thinking of that lonely stretch of coast brought another picture to his mind. Before his trip to pick up Arseniev from the coast of Japan he had consulted charts of both coasts carefully. There was something wrong in his mind. Something about his memory of the chart of the coast and the picture of the coast near the Nahtohu River didn't click.

The day passed slowly. The prison sat near the edge of a wash or gully on the outskirts of town. The bank behind the prison, he had noticed, was crumbling. If he could loosen one of the floor-stones—it was only a chance, but that was all he asked.

Shadows lengthened in the cell, then it was dark, although the light through the window was still gray. Pulling back the straw, he found the outline of a stone block.

The prison was an old building, put together many years ago, still with a look of seasoned strength. Yet time and the elements had taken their toll. Water had run in through the ground-level window, and it had drained out through a hole on the low side. But in running off, it had found the line of least resistance along the crack in the floor. Using the broken spoon with which he was to eat, he began to work at the cement. It crumbled easily, but the stone of the floor was thick.

Four hours passed before he gave up. He had cut down over three inches all around, but still the block was firm, and the handle of his spoon would no longer reach far enough. For a long time he lay still, resting and thinking. Outside all was still, yet he felt restless. Someone about the airport wanted him dead. Someone here was communicating with the man who wore the *unty*, who had fired at him with the old Berdianka in the mountains. Whoever that person was would not rest until, he, Turk Madden, was killed.

That person would have access to this prison, and if he were killed, in the confusion of war, not too much attention would be paid. Arseniev had been his only real friend here, and Arseniev had sat quietly and said nothing. Chevski was efficiency personified. He was interested only in the successful functioning of the port.

But it was more than his own life that mattered. Here, at this key port, close to the line that carried supplies from Vladivostok to the western front, an enemy agent could do untold damage. Lutvin had discovered something, had become suspicious. Flying to the coast, he had photographed something the agent did not want known. Well, what?

At least, if he could not escape, he could think. What would there be on the coast that a man could photograph? A ship could be moved, so it must be some permanent construction. An airport? Turk sat up restlessly. Thinking was all right, but action was his line. He sat back against the wall and stared at the block of stone. The crack was wide. Suddenly, he forced both heels into the crack, and, bracing himself against the wall, pushed.

The veins swelled in his forehead, his palms pressed hard against the floor, but he shoved, and shoved hard. Something gave, but it was not the block against which he pushed. It was the wall behind him. He struggled to his feet, and turned. It was much too dark to see, but he could feel.

His fingers found the cracks in the stones, and his heart gave a great leap. The old wall was falling apart, the cheap cement crumbling. What looked so strong was obviously weak. The prison had been thrown together by convict labor eighty years before, or so he had been told. He seized his spoon and went to work.

In a moment, he had loosened a block. He lifted it out and placed it on the floor beside him. What lay beyond? Another cell? He shrugged. At least he was busy. He took down another block, another, and then a fourth. He crawled through the hole, then carefully, shielding it with his hands, struck a match.

His heart sank. He was in a cell, no different from his own. He rose to his feet and tiptoed across to the door. He took the iron ring in his hand and turned. It moved easily, and the door swung open!

A faint movement in the shadowy hall outside stopped him. Carefully, he moved himself into the doorway, and glanced along the wall.

He caught his breath. A dark figure crouched before his own door and, slowly, carefully, opened it!

Like a shadow, the man straightened, and his hand slipped into his shirt front, coming out with a long knife. Turk's eyes narrowed. In two quick steps he was behind the man. There must have been a sound, for the man turned, catlike. Turk Madden's fist exploded on the corner of the man's jaw like a six-inch shell, and the fellow crumpled. Madden stepped in, hooking viciously to the short ribs. He wet his lips. "That'll hold you, pal," he muttered.

Stooping, he retrieved the knife. Then he frisked the man carefully, grinned when he found a Luger automatic and several clips of cartridges. He pocketed them, then turned the man over. He was a stranger. Carefully, noticing signs of returning consciousness, he bound and gagged the man, then closed the cell door on him, and locked it. Returning to the cell from which he had escaped, he put the stones back into place, then put the key out of sight on a stone ledge above the door.

Turning, he walked down the hall. The back door was not locked, and he went out into the night. For an instant, he stood still. He was wondering about his own ship. He knew what there was to do. He had to fly to the coast and see for himself. He thought he knew what was wrong, but on the other hand—

Also, there was the business of Lutvin's killer. He had flown a plane. He might still be there, and if he saw the Grumman—

Turk Madden smiled grimly. He crossed the open spaces toward the hangars, walking swiftly. Subterfuge wouldn't help. If he tried slipping around he would surely be seen. The direct approach was best. A sleepy sentry stared at him, but said nothing. Turk opened the small door and walked in.

Instantly, he faded back into the shadows inside the door. Not ten feet away Commissar Chevski was staring at Shan Bao. The Manchu faced him, standing stiffly.

"This ship's motors are warm!" Chevski said sharply.

"Yes, Comrade," Shan Bao said politely. "The Colonel Granatman said to keep it warm, he might wish to use it for a flight."

"A flight?" Chevski said. He looked puzzled. From the

shadows, Turk could hear his heart pounding as he sensed what was coming. "What flight?"

"Along the coast," the Manchu said simply. "He said he might want to fly along the coast."

Chevski leaned forward tensely.

"The *coast?* Granatman said that?" He stared at Shan Bao. "If you're lyin—" He wheeled and strode from the hangar. As he stepped past Turk, his breath was coming hard, and his eyes were dilated.

The instant the door closed, Shan Bao's eyes turned to Turk.

"We must work fast, comrade. It was a lie."

Madden stepped out.

"A shrewd lie. He knows something, that one." Turk hesitated, then he looked at the Manchu. "You don't miss much. Have you seen a man with a Berdianka? You know, one of those old model rifles. You know, with a *soshki?* One of those wooden props to hold up the barrel?"

"I know," Shan Bao nodded. "There was one. A man named Batoul, a half-breed, has one. He meets frequently with Comrade Chevski in the woods. He threw it away this day. Now he has a new rifle."

"So," Turk smiled. "The ship is warmed up?"

Shan Bao nodded.

"I have started it every hour since you were taken and have run the motor for fifteen minutes. I thought you might need it. Did you have to kill many men getting away?"

"Not one." Turk smiled. "I'm getting in. When I give the word, start the motor that opens the doors. I'll be going out."

Shan Bao nodded.

"You did not kill even one? It is bad. But leave the door open in the cabin. I shall go with you. I was more fortunate—I killed one."

Turk sprang into the Grumman. The motors roared into

life. Killed one? Who? He waved his hand, and the doors started to move, then the Manchu left the motors running and dashed over. He crawled into the plane as it started to move. From outside there was a startled shout, then the plane was running down the icy runway. A shot, but the Grumman was beginning to lift. Another shot. Yells; they were in the air.

He banked the amphibian in a tight circle and headed for the mountains. They'd get him, but first he'd lead them to the coast, he'd let them see for themselves that something was wrong.

In the east, the skies grew gray with dawn. The short night was passing. Below him the first ridges of the mountains slid past, dark furrows in a field of snow.

Shan Bao was at his shoulder. Two planes showed against the sky where he pointed. Turk nodded. Two—one was bad enough when it was a fast pursuit job. One was far ahead of the other.

Madden's eyes picked out the gray of the sea, then he turned the plane north along the coast to the mouth of the Nahtohu. That was the place—and that long reeflike curving finger. That was it.

Ahead of him a dark plane shot up from the forest and climbed in tight spirals, reaching for altitude. Turk's jaws set. That was the plane that got Lutvin. He fired a trial burst from his guns and pulled back on the stick. The two planes rose together. Then the pursuit ship shot at him, guns blazing.

Turk's face was calm, but hard. He banked steeply, swinging the ship around the oncoming plane, opening fire with all his guns.

Suddenly the gray light of dawn was aflame with blasting guns as the two ships spun and spiraled in desperate combat. Teeth clenched, Turk spun the amphibian through a haze of maneuvers, side-slipping, diving, and squirming from position to position, his eight guns ripping the night apart with streaks of blasting fire. Tracers streamed by his nose, then ugly holes sprang into a wing, then he was out of range, and the streaking black ship was coming around at him again.

In desperation, Turk saw he had no chance. No man in an amphibian had a chance against a pursuit job unless the breaks were with him. Like an avenging fury, the black ship darted in and around him. Only Turk's great flying skill, his uncanny judgment of distance, and his knowledge of his ship enabled him to stay in the fight.

Suddenly, he saw the other two planes closing in. It was now or never. He spun the ship over in a half-roll, then shoved the stick all the way forward and went screaming for earth with the black ship hot on his tail. Fiery streams of tracer shot by him. His plane shot down faster and faster.

The black, ugly ridges of the mountains swept up at him. Off to one side he saw the black shoulder of a peak he remembered, saw the heavy circle of cloud around it and knew this was his chance. He pulled the Grumman out of the power-dive so quickly he expected her wings to tear loose, but she came out of it and lifted to an even keel.

Then, straight into that curtain of cloud around the mountain he went streaking, the black pursuit ship hot on his tail. He felt the ship wobble, saw his compass splash into splinters of glass as a bullet struck, then the white mist of the cloud was around him, and he pulled back on the stick. The Grumman shot up, and even as it zoomed, Turk saw the black, glistening shoulder of icy black mountain sweep below him. He had missed it by a fraction of an inch.

Below him as he glanced down he saw the streaking pursuit ship break through the cloud, saw the pilot grab frantically at his stick. Then the ship crashed full tilt into the mountain at three hundred miles an hour, blossomed into flame and fell, tangled, burning wreckage into the canyon below.

The Grumman lifted toward the sky, and Turk Madden's

eyes swept the horizon. Off to the south, not a half mile away, the two Russian ships were tangled in a desperate dogfight.

Opening the Grumman up, he roared down on them at full tilt. Shan Bao crouched in his seat, the straps tight about his body, his face stiff and cold. In his hands he clutched a Thompson machine gun. The nearer ship he recognized instantly. It was the specially built Havoc flown by Arseniev. The other—

The pilot of the strange ship sighted him, and, making a half roll, started for him. Madden banked the Grumman as though to escape, saw tracer streak by. Then, behind him, he heard an angry chatter. He made an Immelmann turn and swept back. The pursuit ship was falling in a sheet of flame, headed for the small bay at the mouth of the Nahtohu. The other ship swung alongside, and Turk saw Arseniev raise his clasped hands.

Shan Bao was smiling, cradling the Thompson in his arms like a baby.

"He thought he had us," he yelled. "Didn't know you had a behind gunner."

"A rear gunner, Shan," Turk said, grinning.

Hours later, the Grumman landed easily in the mouth of the Nahtohu.

"See?" Turk said, pointing. "A breakwater, and back there a stone pier, a perfect place for landing heavy armaments. It was ideal, a prepared bridgehead for invasion."

Arseniev nodded.

"Lutvin, he was a good man, but I wonder how he guessed?"

"As I did, I think," Turk told him. He sensed a difference in the coast line, a change. The chart showed no reef there, yet the breakwater was made to look like a reef. As it was, it would give the Japanese a secure anchorage, and a place to land tanks, trucks, and heavy artillery, land them securely."

"That Chevski," Arseniev said. "I knew there was something wrong, but I did not suspect him until he ran for a plane when you took off. But Granatman found the photographs in his belongings, and a code book. He was too sure of himself, that one. His mother, we found, was a Japanese."

Turk nodded.

"Lutvin suspected him, I think."

Arseniev shrugged.

"No doubt. But how could Chevski communicate with the Jap who flew the guarding pursuit ship? How could he communicate with Japan?"

Shan Bao cleared his throat.

"That, I think I can say," he said softly. "There was a man, named Batoul. A man who wore *unty*, the native moccasins, and one with thong wrappings about the foot. He came and went frequently from the airport."

"Was?" Arseniev looked sharply at the Manchu. "He got away?"

"But no, comrade," Shan Bao protested gently. "He had a queer gun, this man. An old-fashioned gun, a Berdianka with a *soshkin*. I, who am a collector of guns, wished this one above all. So you will forgive me, comrades? The man came prowling about this ship in the night. He"—Shan Bao coughed apologetically— "he suffered an accident, comrades. But I shall care well for his gun, an old Berdianka, with a *soshkin*. Nowhere else but in Siberia, comrades, would you find such a gun!"

THE RAID

FROM *THE WAR LOVER*

by JOHN HERSEY

A war correspondent during World War II, John Hersey became one of the towering literary figures of his generation. His first novel was *A Bell for Adano*, which won the 1945 Pulitzer Prize. His prodigious literary output included *The Wall*, *The Child Buyer*, *White Lotus*, *The Algiers Motel Incident*, *Hiroshima*, and, in 1959, *The War Lover*, a magnificent novel about the crew of a B-17, *The Body*, engaged in the strategic air war against Germany prior to D-Day.

The novel is narrated from the viewpoint of Boman, the copilot. He worships the pilot, Buzz Marrow, who is the war lover, the warrior who leads them and brings them home. And yet, on the last mission Boman finds that Buzz is human clay, a man who has kept his fear well-hidden, even from himself. The book was later made into a great movie starring Steve McQueen as Buzz and Robert Wagner as Boman. Restored B-17s were used to film the flying sequences.

No one ever captured the world of the bomber crews better than John Hersey, so we'll let him tell it. We will fly now with Boman and Buzz and *The Body*, which had survived repeated fighter attacks and was heavily damaged, flying on only three engines, when a large-caliber flak shell tore the nose off the airplane. She began to spin . . .

Marrow had one miraculous reflex left which pulled us out of that incipient spin, but I, still bellied down over my seat with my feet in the opening of the trapdoor, was so busy trying to put together in my mind what was happening that I think I lagged by several seconds in my realization that we were not, after all, falling. I was aware of a powerful, buffeting column of frozen air shooting up past my feet like a twister of prop wash forced through a funnel, and it seemed to me that we must have developed exactly that: a funnel, with the nose of the ship opened out as the outer cone, and the narrow passageway coming up between Marrow's seat and mine, the constriction of the trapdoor, serving as the spout; and out of the neck came this little directed hurricane at thirty-four degrees below zero. When my ears recovered from the crack of the first explosion, which like nearby thunder had been at a much higher pitch than one associated with its cause, I began to react to another unpleasant noise—a distinct sound of an engine running rough, if not altogether away. There seemed also to be sprinkles of air coming from my left, and I assumed there must be some holes in the instrument panel, but I was keeping my head down and holding on, and I had no desire to look. I was experiencing, within, a rush of feelings as swift and cold as the wind at my feet. I had been fearful before, when I had seen the Messerschmidts begin their dive at us, for it had seemed as if I *knew* that this pass, of all the enemy waves we had shouldered during the day, was the one that would cause us trouble, and I had been gripped by the paralyzing, numbing fear that had made my tussle with my flak suit so absurdly futile. The explosion had in an instant converted my terror to rage. It was not a noble anger at the Hun, but rather a fury of incredulity that this shame—yes, my first thought was of infamy—could be mine. I did not admit into my mind the possibility of being killed, but lying on my belly I had a picture of the boys in the hutment talking about the dope, Boman, getting himself shot down and having to spend the rest of the war in a prison camp, and I hammered with blind fury at the thought that this was happening to me. All this, of course, flickered through me in an instant, and was mixed together with my sensory reactions to our plight. It was only then that I realized, through a long habit of feeling with my body the relation of forces in flight, that we were more or less level; we were flying, not plummeting.

I pulled myself up in my seat, and before plugging myself in, I took one look at Marrow and saw that aside from a tiny cut in his right cheek he seemed not to have been wounded. Then, with a wonderful selective speed that was the fruit of experience, I turned my eyes to the manifold-pressure gauges, and I saw that the arrow for the number-two engine was jumping around like the needle of an oscilloscope, and, not wanting this time to cut an engine without Marrow's knowing, because on only two we would lose a lot of air speed and drop out of the formation, yet wanting to hurry because the unit was shaking enough to tear itself out of the wing, I tapped Marrow's shoulder, pointed at the number-two engine, beyond him, with a whole mitt, and then turned the glove in a flipping motion that simulated turning off a key. Marrow shrugged. How eloquent, in its indifference, that lift of the huge shoulders was! I killed the engine, and this time, in spite of all the vibration, the prop feathered in an orderly way. Our indicated air speed dropped at once to about a hundred and thirty, which was twenty-five miles per hour slower than the formation.

I looked out and saw that we were directly beneath our own squadron, perhaps three hundred feet down, and I had a vivid feeling of thankfulness that we had a good deal of formation, two whole task forces, in fact, to drift back through before we would be alone, straggling.

Vivid, I say. My senses, reactions, thoughts, and emotions had developed that remarkable post-critical fleetness and intensity which I had experienced once before, on the Kiel raid, the day the plane caught fire.

We were washing around, and Marrow, holding with bull-dog jaws till the last moment to the one skill that was the essence of his narrow genius, his marvelous reactive skill as the manipulator of an aircraft, was fiddling with trim-tab wheels and throttles, to steady our line of flight. Our yawing, and the wind through the trapdoor, and the holes in the instrument panel, and Marrow's having shrugged, and the fact that some of our instruments had gone dead—everything I could observe made me think it was inevitable that we would bail out. I refrained from buckling on my chute just out of a rather mor-bid curiosity, mixed with admiration, I admit, for Marrow's smooth, automatic response to what was happening. I believe that Marrow had already broken down in every way but the one that mattered. Like a frog's leg that will kick, or a lizard's tail that will lash, after amputation, the essential force in Marrow—the flying touch—was holding onto its vitality, when all the rest was gone, and was keeping us aloft. I assumed, though, that we would bail out soon, and I was planning the steps—hand Marrow his chute from under his seat, pass one back to Negrocus, strap my own to my chest and click it on, right and left, and then move—when something happened that made me realize we couldn't do that. We couldn't leave.

I looked down through the trapdoor, and I knew the front

end was blown out, and I knew I had just come back up from the front end, and my relief, my personal, self-interested relief at getting out of the greenhouse was so strong that I really had forgotten those other two up there, from the moment of the shock, and now I saw a hand. A left hand. It groped out, and then I saw the head, Max's, and he was dragging himself; the reaching hand and arm pulled him along, and the other arm was limp. I saw, as he moved rearward through my frame of vision, that his right leg was blown off right up to mid-thigh, pruned clean off, it appeared, though he was trailing tatters of flying clothes and was bleeding, and the furious wind made everything seem confused. He crawled into the lower level under the trapdoor. I knew we couldn't push Max out for a jump in his condition, and we couldn't leave him, so we couldn't bail out.

Right behind him came Clint, on his hands and knees, dragging his parachute, and he looked to be in one piece, and he crawled back, and slowly but methodically he took off his gloves and jettisoned the escape hatch, and he kneeled at the edge of the hole, perhaps praying, and he put his parachute on and then put his gloves back on and remained there, kneeling, looking down through the opening into the clear afternoon, with his hand on his rip cord.

Just when he was about to go out, as I supposed, I had a sudden idea, an impulse, "Well, now, I shouldn't let him do that." Since the lower compartment was confined and shallow, I could reach down and touch him easily from my seat, to dissuade him from what he planned, but then I thought, "The lucky bum, getting out of this thing before it goes to pieces," so I didn't reach out, for a moment. It seemed he would be blown out by the wind, or slide out, because of the fluid of poor Max that was spreading and freezing. And quickly I did reach down and touch him. That was all it took. Clint gave up the idea. He didn't even look up at me.

But I, as I leaned down, saw Max, lying on his back, writhing, and he was still conscious, that was the worst of it, and I saw that whatever had blown his leg off had also blown his oxygen mask off, and his goggles, and his helmet; his face wasn't the least bit scratched. Max was rational, and I saw him raise his left hand and, with a pathetic begging expression, point to his mouth, so there wasn't but one thing to do, the idea of which terrified me more than anything I'd ever known, and that was, recognizing that Max was going to die of anoxia and cold before he could get down to a hospital bed with white sheets— I had lost that wonderful clarity of thought—I hadn't listened to all those lectures you're supposed to listen to in training—I was going to have to go down there in the wind and give him my mask. Butcher Lamb, mild Butcher Lamb, the radio bug, who liked to read Westerns on missions, had pointed my way on that the day Jug Farr passed out.

As I started down Clint peeled *his* mask off, and I don't know whether Clint had any thought that he himself might not be conscious much longer without a mask at that altitude, and I doubt whether he had any feeling that he was performing an act of truly selfless love, which he was, even when, having slipped the mask over Max's face, he got his reward from Max—a deeply moving look of contentment, for Max, using his good hand to hold the rubber against his face, settled back like a baby with a bottle; you could see him ease down and relax.

The only trouble was, the tube of the mask wasn't plugged into anything. I reached a walk-around bottle down to Clint, and he hooked Max into it. Clint ripped a big piece of flying suit from what was left of Max's pants and wrapped it and tied it, bloody as it was, around Max's head for warmth.

I thought of the spare mask back on the bulkhead of the lower turret compartment, and I decided to tell Butcher Lamb to bring it forward for Clint. I realized then that I wasn't connected with the interphone system, and I pushed my headset wire into the jackbox and heard a man screaming.

It was Junior Sailen, in the ball turret, screaming, really screaming, and a man screaming makes a horrifying sound. He was trapped in his ball turret. Knowing that we had two engines out, for he could see them from his post, and not having a parachute with him, and not being able to get out even if he had it, unless he were exploded out, which he may have expected to be, Junior had reached a pitch of helplessness that a dependent man could not bear. At times distinct messages came through his screaming, "I'm trapped . . . Come help me . . . Get me out," with some of the words drawn out into held notes. Everybody who was on interphone was forced to hear him, as he had turned his jackbox to CALL, which cut through all other talk. A piece of shell had come through the plexiglass of his turret and had knocked out the electric motor that made the turret gyrate and revolve, but also another piece, or perhaps the same one, had sheared off the handle which would have enabled him to turn himself up and get out. Fortunately our ball turrets were supplied with a second, external crank for elevation, so that a man outside the turret could move it.

Urged by the need for the mask for Clint and by Junior's cries I skinned back, as fast as I could, through the empty bomb bay and the radio compartment, where Lamb was at his gun, to the lower turret compartment, and I found that Negrocus Handown had been way ahead of me; he had already cranked the turret into line, and he opened the hatch, and Junior almost squirted out, and the two men embraced like brothers in a myth who had been separated as children and were seeing each other again as men.

I ran forward with the spare mask and two walk-around bottles and handed them down to Clint, who was already looking blue around the lips.

When I was plugged in again, I asked Marrow if he was getting on all right. He didn't answer. I thought perhaps the interphone was knocked out, so I called Prien and he did respond, though his voice sounded farther away than the tail of *The Body*. Then I ran a check all around, and I got a sassy answer from Farr; an echo of it from Bragnani; an absent-minded response from Lamb, who sounded as if he weren't on this trip but were sashaying down to Florida by Eastern Air Lines; no word from Junior Sailen, who had been removed to the radio room; the usual stout and reassuring boom from Handown, who was back up in his turret; no answer, again, from Marrow; and of course I didn't even try Clint and Max.

For a second I wondered whether Marrow had lost the power of speech. I couldn't get anything out of him. He just flew along, and his control was still subtle and smooth, but otherwise he was a huge, leather-clad robot. I supposed that his jackbox might have been ruptured.

Some of our guns were firing.

A brief glance outside the plane showed me that we had fallen back underneath part of the lead group, but we still had an umbrella. The air battle was continuing. I saw two new German *Staffeln* coming up, and (no credit to myself; just the astonishing persistence of the human mind in its habitual patterns of association and rambling, even during a cataclysm) I began ruminating about the efficiency of the Germans, and the obvious co-ordination of their attacks. One could suppose that they must have assembled, to meet both the Regensburg strike and ours, fighter squadrons all the way down from Jever and Oldenburg—we knew those units from our battles with them over Wilhelmshaven, Hamburg, and Kiel—and up from airports we knew in France, such as Laon, Florennes, and Eyreux, and since the planes had limited range they must have set them down for refueling along the way to us, somewhere near our expected line of flight but far ahead of us, and then got them up not only in time to meet us but also just in time to replace other squadrons who were having to retire. Such ingenuity put to the service of killing!

These thoughts, in their dreamlike detachment from our real situation, and in their vividness that was also dreamlike, took only an instant or two.

Then it occurred to me that we would do well to climb, to hug as closely as we could the remainder of our group, so that *The Body* could take maximum advantage of the formation's firepower and not be singled out, yet, as a potential straggler, and I suggested this to Marrow on interphone. I shouted, thinking his headset might not be giving him but a shred of sound.

No answer.

Then I tapped his shoulder, to convey by gestures what his ears apparently could not hear, and he turned his face, and my heart froze at what I saw. Behind his goggles, which intensified the horror of the sight, I saw eyes that seemed to aim at me but that were unimaginably far away. It was like being looked at through the wrong end of binoculars, or no—because that's a game all children have played—it was like being viewed through two infinitely distant telescopes. I hovered off Saturn; I was somewhere out in the black eternity of the universe.

I went through with the gestures I had planned. The telescopes simply swiveled away.

I saw then that one of the instruments on the panel in front of us that had not been shot away was the rate-of-climb indicator. It showed that we were descending, almost imperceptibly, at the rate of fifty feet per minute. With my right hand lightly on the wheel, I could feel that Marrow was trying, with all his deep-driven skill, to hold altitude. Our loss of it was not serious yet, but climbing to attain shelter from the formation was out of the question.

I heard a faint call on the interphone, and it was for me. "Bo! Listen to me, Bo!" It was Junior Sailen's voice. It did not even occur to me at that moment that for a sergeant gunner, and of all sergeant gunners, formal Junior Sailen, to address his co-pilot by his nickname and not by his rank and surname was an act of unusual effrontery; I believe I may have felt faint relief and gratitude that Sailen had torn away a barrier between us. It was immediately evident why he had done so. Even though the interphone was fading, I could hear the pleading tone of his voice. "Can I get out? I want to jump. I have no gun, Bo. I'm no good any more."

I guess he was going batty sitting on a passenger seat in the radio room, doing nothing. Another guess about Junior: He had felt safe at his familiar post, locked into the ball turret, and he found rattling around in the radio room frightening.

A thought entered my mind which caused a leap of selfish joy in my chest: Junior Sailen had called me, not Marrow; he had asked my permission to bolt.

I looked at Marrow. He sat leaning forward, communing with the flight column.

Just at that moment, as it happened, Prien called in, with a hoarse shout, announcing an attack from the tail, and Marrow, though he had not responded to direct calls on the interphone in recent moments, automatically began to corkscrew *The Body* with the superb sinuous motions he had devised for self-defense at the height of his skill in the middle of our tour. He must have heard Prien.

I said on interphone, "Sailen! The answer is no. Repeat: No!" Because what if the others, Bragnani, for instance, heard an able-bodied man get permission to jump?

Junior could not (he did not want to) hear me. Far, far away I heard Junior shouting, "What? What, Lieutenant? What?" Yet perhaps he had understood me, after all, because now he called me Lieutenant, and, in any case, he stayed aboard, for whatever reason.

I called Butcher Lamb and tried to tell him the interphone was fading.

Butch heard me, I realized (some time later) when the interphone came in loud and clear; he must have left his gun and gone down into the radio room and—I can visualize him— begun checking out possible causes of trouble in the systematic, step-by-step way of the born radio ham, concentrating on his work so as to shut out all the rest of the world.

Right after calling Lamb—I suppose not more than four or five minutes, at most, had passed since our nose had been opened—I began to worry about Max Brindt. I leaned over and saw through the trapdoor that Haverstraw was not doing anything about Max. Clint was sitting by the big opening of the main hatchway, looking downward in a brooding way, and Max was still conscious, and for a moment the stump was exposed to sight there in that wind, the blood still spurting and coagulating and freezing on him and all over the deck, and I could see that I was going to have to do the most distasteful piece of work I had ever done in my life. I got up and unclipped the first-aid kit from the wiring-diagram box on the back of my seat and started down.

Going down through that small trapdoor was easier thought than done. We were making about a hundred and thirty miles an hour through the air, with the front end splayed out and wide open, funneling the air as if through a Venturi tube so that the blast in the trapdoor was tremendously powerful and concentrated, besides being thirty-four degrees below zero. It took all the strength I had, on top of all the courage I had, to force myself down through it. I had to ease myself past the revolting form of Max. The escape hatch on the left was open and looked very void and vacant, and a lot of the wind was being driven out through it, so the hatch opening was like the mouth of a vacuum-cleaner tube; once in a while something would pull loose and fly out through it, and you felt you might, too. The front end of the ship was pretty much as I had imagined it, with all the plexiglass gone and some of the metal bent outward, and Max's seat and Clint's desk and chair in a tangle, and wires flapping, and equipment all mashed and confused. And suddenly, like a blow in the chest, the thought hit me that I had no parachute.

Worst of all, there was Max, his eyes open, begging me to do something.

I tried to remember all those lectures on first aid, in large, warm auditoriums, often with a quite satisfactory and unhurt WAC modeling the slings or handing the bandage rolls to the fat, bald major who was demonstrating, on a stage, what one should do for every sort of imaginary injury. I had a moment's flash of anger at the image of one steak eater of a medical major, because I remembered his saying that the best thing you could do for a wounded man in a plane was to leave him alone.

"Cold conditions, flying clothing, harness, and limited fuselage space render the giving of effective first aid to such a man during flight a matter of extreme difficulty, and the less he is disturbed, generally, until the skilled assistance of a trained physician is available, the better." What did that fat slob know about kneeling in a murderous gale of cutting, boreal wind on a sheet of ice made of your crewmate's blood and seeing his eyes, looking out at you from a bundle of bloody trouser material, saying, "We've been through very much together, Bo, we took a walk together just the other day, so please, for the love of the God I didn't know till a minute ago I believed in, please, please, Bo, please, please, please." Suddenly there was a marked degree of love in the eyes, and though I had always, until this moment, considered that I despised Max and assumed that he despised me, here I was, struck to the very seat of my soul with horror and receiving messages of brotherly love from him. I believe this tender begging look increased my sense of terror by many fold, because I hated Max, I really did hate his deep aggressive drives, the love of dropping bombs that made him jump on his seat, after bombs-away, like a baby on a kiddy-car. I think he was one of them, one of the men with the taint Marrow had, a war lover—not so poisoned, maybe, as Marrow, but one of them. And his eyes were saying, "My dear Bo, my dear fellow man, my brother, sharer with me of life, do you understand what I am trying to say with my eyes?"

I began to attempt to order my thoughts. First aid. I took off one glove and crammed the glove between my knees and lifted the lid of the kit; my skin stuck to the metal, it was so cold. A small blue bandage box flew from the kit and out through the escape-hatch opening without even touching the floor. I turned with my back more to the wind and hunched way over and opened the lid again. I saw a morphine ampule. Morphine, pain, Max. Brother in life. I took the ampule out and crammed the first-aid box into a safe vee between an oxygen bottle and the

wall of the plane, and I banged Haverstraw on the arm, to bring
him out of a trance he seemed to be in, and he, without taking
his gloves off, bared some of the leg above the stump, and I held
the ampule in front of Max's eyes, and then he looked into
mine with more love than ever, and I stuck him, and Max
winced at that pin prick—goodness knows how Max felt it
through the torment of his leg—and I believe the pricking sensation itself gave Max relief, because he closed his eyes (which
gave me immeasurable relief) and looked contented; in spite of
the fact that I had not succeeded in getting much, if any, of the
morphine into him, because it had seemed thickened by the
cold, or, at any rate, had oozed out on his skin and had not gone
in him. I put my mitt back on.

Tourniquet. My thoughts, like the pain-relieving fluid, were
thickened and sluggish, on account of the very, very cold atmosphere of man's madness with which that cavern in the war
plane was invested, but at last two thoughts—bleeding, tourniquet—came slowly together, and I reached for the box, and
took out materials marked for a tourniquet and saw that a loop
had to be formed of the cord that was provided.

Kid Lynch came into my mind, and I guess that, at that, I had
had enough of war, really enough, because I simply had to leave.

I carefully stowed the first-aid kit by the oxygen bottle and
handed the tourniquet cord to Clint and made a circle with my
hands to show how big it should be, and I started to go up to
the flight deck. Unfortunately as I was going across above Max
he dreamily opened his eyes and a look of such gentle surprise
came into them, mixed still with that other look, of trusting
family love, that I did something I had least expected to do. I
straightened up my head, shoulders, and arms through the
trapdoor, turned my head to glimpse at Marrow, who was driving woodenly along as if mushing down Broadway with nothing but a few taxis to worry about, and then I reached for my
parachute, which was under my seat and on top of my flak suit,

and was not stuck, and I backed down again, pulling my chute pack after me.

Max's affectionate eyes took one look at the parachute and rolled to the left and saw Clint's chute on his chest, and the love fled from them, as he must have concluded that the whole crew was about to bail out. He began to flutter and roll from side to side. I've never seen a human being who affected me more with abject fright than Max reacting to the idea that we were going to leave him, in his condition, alone in a ship gliding down the sky on automatic pilot.

I pulled my mask loose and leaned over and yanked the bloody pants material aside and shouted in Max's ear, "Don't worry, chum, we're not going to leave you."

That worked better even than the prick of the ampule needle. It seemed to me that tears of joy came into Max's eyes.

Chum? Since when was Max Brindt my "chum"? The word was one of many commonplaces used around the base, expressive of a rough, sometimes sarcastic affection: chum, pal, friend, son, doc, bud, buddy, old man, brother. But not as between Boman and Brindt! I despised him with his *"Banzai!"* at the dropping of bombs. I really did not like him.

Clint had the loop made and handed it to me, and now came the job of getting it over the leg, and it was then, and only then—I'd been so shocked and braked by the whole deal, especially by the brotherly love in that man's eyes, that I hadn't realized it until then: that there was a shoe, with a foot in it, beating, or kicking, Max in the face, and it was his own right foot, and it was still attached to him.

I had a flash memory of Mrs. Krille, in something like seventh grade, telling us about Achilles, brave and generous warrior, slayer of Hector, who died when Paris struck with an arrow the Peleid's one vulnerable spot, the tendon above the heel, vulnerable because his mother, dipping him in the Styx as a baby to make him wound-proof, had held him by the heel, and Mrs. Krille (I could remember of her face only the sweet mouth, the warm eyes behind shell-rimmed glass, the astonishingly long black hairs in her nostrils) saying that this tendon had an extraordinary strength. "In animals," she said, "it is called the hamstring."

The bone was gone, flesh and pants were mostly gone, the flying boot had been blown off the shod foot, yet a ragged, tenacious length of tendon and muscle and back-of-the-knee sinews and more muscle, a living rope, in places an inch thick, had held firm, and in the terrible wind the foot had blown back and now was banging against Max.

I hadn't noticed it, and indeed I hoped it had just started blowing that way, and my idea was to try to keep him from realizing that his leg was cut mostly off and that his foot was striking him, so I grabbed the shoe and pulled it forward, and I forgot the knife in my boot with which I might have severed the tendon, and finally, being very heavy-handed, very slow, my fingers stiff, my heart and mind sick, I laboriously worked the tourniquet cord over the foot, and threaded it up the tendon.

While I was doing that, I noticed that Marrow was executing some exceedingly rough and even crude maneuvers. They seemed not like his.

I concentrated as best I could on getting the loop of the tourniquet in position, but we seemed to be bouncing as if in a front.

I felt a rage at Marrow. All this, Max's anguish, the insane work I was doing, *all* this was somehow Marrow's fault. He was the one whose natural climate was war.

Clint—having something to do was nourishing him wonderfully, and he was growing more and more alert—handed me the turning stick, and I inserted it and turned it, and the flow of blood stopped. I tucked the stick into the loop.

Then (I think because I saw a bundle of spare interphone wire stowed next to the oxygen bottles, back underneath the upper deck, beyond Max's head, and also because we were bouncing around in such a peculiar way) I got the brainy idea of trying to make Max more secure, so Clint and I dragged him back farther and we made the intercom wire fast to the back of Max's harness and lashed that to the foot of one of the top-turret stanchions. We had to stop and put our gloves on and whiff our oxygen every few seconds. We finally finished that absurd work. We gave Max another shot of morphine, and he seemed to be resting all right, and I was about to go back to my seat when he spoke again with his eyes—a piercing, questioning stare into mine.

I loosened my mask again and leaned down and shouted into the rags around his head, "Don't you worry, Maxie boy, we're going to get you back to England. England's in sight right now." How I wished that were true!

And the eyes, in the watery, bluish light of that recessed place, were flooded then with love, more and more of it, love of his friends, I guess, and of England, of home, of an uncertain, abstract, marvelous everything. Above the mask the eyes were so full of love that the emotion seemed intolerable, overwhelming, and then all that feeling drained out very quickly and the pupils rolled upward.

As I started, empty and numbed, up to my seat, I beckoned to Clint to follow me above to the flight deck, where he could be out of the worst of the wind and could be plugged into the permanent oxygen system. He climbed up after me and went back to the radio room.

Marrow was flying very badly. He was like a beginner, over-correcting, and jolting the controls.

I sat down and hooked myself up and looked at my watch. It was four thirty-nine. We must be past Eupen. We were supposed to get P-47s at Eupen.

The Body was now definitely a straggler. The last of the formation was three quarters of a mile ahead of us and six or seven hundred feet above us, in a sea-blue sky, and there were German fighters plunging into the squadrons of Forts, but for the moment they were leaving us alone. We were having some of what Marrow would have branded in the early days as *his* luck. They could have sent up a Fiesler Storch, a tiny single-engined scout plane like a Piper Cub, and armed it with a twelve-gauge shotgun, or maybe a slingshot, and they could have potted us with it.

I saw no P-47s, but I thought we might as well put up a straggler's signal just in case they were somewhere around but out of my sight, and besides, this would be something for Junior or Clint to do, and since there was a spare jackbox in the radio compartment, I called on interphone, "Haverstraw? You on there?"

The answer came back clear as a bell. Lamb must have shot the trouble, whatever it had been. Clint was on and asked what I wanted.

I told him there was a flare canister at the forward end of the ball-turret compartment; he should get out a green-green flare and fire it. There should be a pistol in a clip-rack next to the canister. He could fire it out of Butcher's slot.

"Roger," he said, and there was that old ironical lilt in his voice; doubtless he was delighted to have something to do.

"Wait a sec," I said. "Do you remember what time we were supposed to get fighter support?"

"Sixteen sixteen hours," Clint said, "same time as course change at fifty degrees thirty-eight minutes north dash oh six degrees oh three minutes east." That number-dogged mind of his was clicking; he could have told me the number of Jenny in Minneapolis or of Peggylou in Biloxi, if I had asked, I'm sure.

249

Then Prien came on and said, "What's green-green, Lieu-tenant?"

I said, "It means, 'My ass is dragging, friendly fighters take note.'"

Next it was Bragnani; brave, bully-boy Bragnani. "We going to make it, sir?"

There is a mimic that lives in all of us, whose job is to hide our true selves from the world by pushing masks out onto our faces and sneaking others' gestures into our hands, and I was on the point of saying, "Listen, son, you fire your gun," but I paused a second, over the thought that the boys in the back didn't know what was going on, not a thing, and I said, instead. "The nose is opened up. Two and three are feathered. We're losing altitude, about seventy-five a minute now, but we're holding one-thirty i.a.s. . . . They got Lieutenant Brindt." I thought I might as well tell them that.

Then, clear and strong, almost like a vivid memory, we all heard Marrow's voice, "Lamb? You awake? Give me a fix, kid."

"Yes, sir," Butcher said.

There was a silence, a long one, and then Marrow, "Come on, come on, come on."

Lamb must have been trying to get cross bearings on the radio compass.

A floodgate of abuse broke open. That monotonous, whin-ing voice which made you cringe. In the middle of it, on CALL, there was an unintelligible phrase in Farr's voice. More of Mar-row's cursing. Then Farr, "Aw, f— this, I'm through with this crap." Farr clicked out and Marrow was still going. Lamb tried to cut in with the fix, but Buzz didn't want it any more. Marrow was flying now with really dangerous want of co-ordination—washing all over the sky, careening, flirting with death and shouting at it. That is surely what some deep part of him was doing. Not only with his own but with ours.

Farr pushed his button and rasped, "For Christ's sake, do

something, even if it's wrong. . . . Ah, s—! I can fly till I'm sixty. I'll do five hundred missions. They can't hit me no more than . . . I'm telling you, you son of a bitch, I'm no rookie. I'll outlast every mother f—er of you. You can't knock me off. They tried! The bastards plugged the s— out of me, but they . . . This is so *dumb*. I could've told those God-damn toidy-seat generals. . . . How dumb can you get? . . . Don't you put a finger on me, you bastards. . . ."

I saw Marrow, across the way, unbuckle his seat belt.

I said, as sharply as I could, on CALL myself, "Farr!"

He paused, and I said, "Bragnani, get that brandy away from him."

Marrow reached under his seat, pulled his parachute out (I remembered with a start that I had left mine below), and half stood up. As he did so the plane slowly climbed till it was on the edge of a stall. I pushed the column forward, and *The Body* fell off to one side and after a long, swooping plunge picked up buoyancy again.

Marrow settled back in his seat. He seemed puzzled, undecided, old.

I said, "I'll fly her awhile, Buzz."

Marrow grabbed the wheel and tensely held it.

"Give her to me," I said. "Let me fly some."

No answer. Marrow was leaning forward toward the column.

Prien said, "Four fighters coming in, six o'clock level."

I stood up in the aisle, just in back of the trapdoor, and I tapped Marrow on the shoulder, and when he turned his head I jerked my right thumb toward my seat. For what seemed to me a long time nothing happened, then slowly Marrow unplugged his suit-heater cord and his headset jack, and he put his hands on the sides of his seat, pushed himself up, slid out from under his wheel, straightened up in the aisle, and then in the overcautious way of a senile man sat down in my place. I moved into the pilot's seat, and that was all there was to it.

THE MILK RUN
FROM *TALES OF THE SOUTH PACIFIC*

---

by JAMES A. MICHENER

Tales of the South Pacific is a cultural icon of the generation that fought World War II. First published in 1946, it was Michener's first novel and launched a literary career that made him one of the most widely read, popular writers on earth for the next four decades.

The book is a huge, sprawling collection of loosely-related short stories set in the South Pacific during the first two years of World War II. There is no conventional plot and zero suspense. Some of the stories are related in the first person, some in third; sometimes the storyteller is omniscient, sometimes not. All that said, the book is extraordinary, a triumphant tour de force by a literary genius.

One of the short stories contained in the book, the romance of nurse Nellie Forbush from Arkansas and French planter Emile De Becque, was the basis for the fabulously successful Rogers and Hammerstein musical *South Pacific*, which in turn became a hit movie.

Over the years, millions of people who were enchanted by the musical and movie never read the novel, which was their loss. Easily Michener's best work, *Tales of the South Pacific* is also one of the best American novels ever written, a literary masterpiece on par with *The Adventures of Huckleberry Finn, For Whom the Bell Tolls,* and *The Old Man and the Sea.*

The excerpt that follows is a flying story entitled "The Milk Run" and it is vintage Michener, which is as good as literature gets.

It must make somebody feel good. I guess that's why they do it.—The speaker was Lieut. Bus Adams, SBD pilot. He was nursing a bottle of whiskey in the Hotel De Gink on Guadal. He was sitting on an improvised chair and had his feet cocked up on a coconut stump the pilots used for a foot rest. He was handsome, blond, cocky. He came from nowhere in particular and wasn't sure where he would settle when the war was over. He was just another hot pilot shooting off between missions.

But why they do it—Bus went on—I don't rightfully know. I once figured it out this way: Say tomorrow we start to work over a new island, well, like Kuralei. Some day we will. On the first mission long-range bombers go over. Sixty-seven Japs come up to meet you. You lose four, maybe the bombers. Everybody is damn gloomy, I can tell you. But you also knock down some Nips.

Four days later you send over your next bombers. Again you take a pasting. "The suicide run!" the pilots call it. It's sure death! But you keep on knocking down Nips. Down they go, burning like the Fourth of July. And all this time you're pocking up their strips, plenty.

Finally the day comes when you send over twenty-seven bombers and they all come back. Four Zekes rise to get at you, but they are shot to hell. You bomb the strip and the installations until you are dizzy from flying in circles over the place.

The next eight missions are without incident. You just plow in, drop your stuff, and sail on home.

Right then somebody names that mission, "The Milk Run!" And everybody feels pretty good about it. They even tell you about your assignments in an offhand manner: "Eighteen or twenty of you go over tomorrow and pepper Kuralei." They don't even brief you on it, and before long there's a gang around take-off time wanting to know if they can sort of hitch-hike a ride. They'd like to see Kuralei get it. So first thing you know, it's a real milk run, and you're in the tourist business!

Of course, I don't know who ever thought up that name for such missions. The Milk Run? Well, maybe it is like a milk run. For example, you fill up a milk truck with TNT and some special detonating caps that go off if anybody sneezes real loud. You tank up the truck with 120 octane gasoline that burns Pouf! Then instead of a steering wheel, you have three wheels, one for going sideways and one for up and down. You carry eight tons of your special milk when you know you should carry only five. At intersections other milk trucks like yours barge out at you, and you've got to watch them every minute. When you try to deliver this precious milk, little kids are all around you with .22's, popping at you. If one of the slugs gets you, bang! There you go, milk and all! And if you add to that the fact that you aren't really driving over land at all, but over the ocean, where if the slightest thing goes wrong, you take a drink . . . Well, maybe that's a milk run, but if it is, cows are sure raising hell these days!

Now get this right, I'm not bitching. Not at all. I'm damned glad to be the guy that draws the milk runs. Because in comparison with a real mission, jaunts like that really *are* milk runs. But if you get bumped off on one of them, why you're just as dead as if you were over Tokyo in a kite. It wasn't no milk run for you. Not that day.

You take my trip up to Munda two days ago. Now there was

a real milk run. Our boys had worked that strip over until it looked like a guy with chicken pox, beriberi and the galloping jumps. Sixteen SBD's went up to hammer it again. Guess we must be about to land somewhere near there. Four of us stopped off to work over the Jap guns at Segi Point. We strafed them plenty. Then we went on to Munda.

Brother, it was a far cry from the old days. This wasn't The Slot any more. Remember when you used to bomb Kieta or Kahili or Vella or Munda? Opposition all the way. Japs coming at you from every angle. Three hundred miles of hell, with ugly islands on every side and Japs on every island. When I first went up there it was the toughest water fighting in the world, bar none. You were lucky to limp home.

Two days ago it was like a pleasure trip. I never saw the water so beautiful. Santa Ysabel looked like a summer resort somewhere off Maine. In the distance you could see Choiseul and right ahead was New Georgia. Everything was blue and green, and there weren't too many white ack-ack puffs. I tell you, I could make that trip every day with pleasure.

Segi Point was something to see. The Nips had a few anti-aircraft there, but we came in low, zoomed up over the hills, peppered the devil out of them. Do you know Segi Passage? It's something to remember. A narrow passage with maybe four hundred small pinpoint islands in it. It's the only place out here I know that looks like the South Pacific. Watch! When we take Segi, I'm putting in for duty there. It's going to be cool there, and it looks like they got fruit around, too.

Well, after we dusted Segi off we flew low across New Georgia. Natives, and I guess some Jap spotters, watched us roar by. We were about fifty feet off the trees, and we rose and fell with the contours of the land. We broke radio silence, because the Japs knew we were coming. The other twelve were already over target. One buddy called out to me and showed me the waterfall on the north side of the island. It looked cool in the early morning sunlight. Soon we were over Munda. The milk run was half over.

I guess you heard what happened next. I was the unlucky guy. One lousy Jap hit all day, on that whole strike, and it had to be me that got it. It ripped through the rear gunner's seat and killed Louie on the spot. Never knew what hit him. I had only eighty feet elevation at the time, but kept her nose straight on. Glided into the water between Wanawana and Munda. The plane sank, of course, in about fifteen seconds. All shot to hell. Never even got a life raft out.

So there I was, at seven-thirty in the morning, with no raft, no nothing but a life belt, down in the middle of a Japanese channel with shore installations all around me. A couple of guys later on figured that eight thousand Japs must have been within ten miles of me, and I guess that not less than three thousand of them could see me. I was sure a dead duck.

My buddies saw me go in, and they set up a traffic circle around me. One Jap barge tried to come out for me, but you know Eddie Callstrom? My God! He shot that barge up until it splintered so high that even I could see it bust into pieces. My gang was over me for an hour and a half. By this time a radio message had gone back and about twenty New Zealanders in P-40's took over. I could see them coming a long way off. At first I thought they might be Jap planes. I never was too good at recognition.

Well, these New Zealanders are wild men. Holy hell! What they did! They would weave back and forth over me for a little while, then somebody would see something on Rendova or Kolombangara. Zoom! Off he would go like a madman, and pretty soon you'd see smoke going up. And if they didn't see anything that looked like a good target, they would leave the circle every few minutes anyway and raise hell among the coconut trees near Munda, just on chance there might be some Japs there. One group of Japs managed to swing a shore battery around to where they could pepper me. They sent out about seven fragmentation shells, and scared me half to death. I had to stay there in the water and take it.

That was the Japs' mistake. They undoubtedly planed to get my range and put me down, but on the first shot the New Zealanders went crazy. You would have thought I was a ninety million dollar battleship they were out to protect. They peeled off and dove that installation until even the trees around it fell down. They must have made the coral hot. Salt water had almost blinded me, but I saw one P-40 burst into flame and plunge deeply into the water off Rendova. No more Jap shore batteries opened up on me that morning.

Even so, I was having a pretty tough time. Currents kept shoving me on toward Munda. Japs were hidden there with rifles, and kept popping at me. I did my damnedest, but slowly I kept getting closer. I don't know, but I guess I swam twenty miles that day, all in the same place. Sometimes I would be so tired I'd just have to stop, but whenever I did, bingo! There I was, heading for the shore and the Japs. I must say, though, that Jap rifles are a damned fine spur to a man's ambitions.

When the New Zealanders saw my plight, they dove for that shore line like the hounds of hell. They chopped it up plenty. Jap shots kept coming after they left, but lots fewer than before.

I understand that it was about this time that the New Zealanders' radio message reached Admiral Kester. He is supposed to have studied the map a minute and then said, "Get that pilot out there. Use anything you need. We'll send a destroyer in, if necessary. But get him out. Our pilots are not expendable."

Of course, I didn't know about it then, but that was mighty fine doctrine. So far as I was concerned. And you know? When I watched those Marine F4U's coming in to take over the circle, I kind of thought maybe something like that was in the wind at headquarters. The New Zealanders pulled out. Before they went, each one in turn buzzed me. Scared me half to death! Then they zoomed Munda once more, shot it up some, and shoved off home.

The first thing the F4U's did was drop me a life raft. The first attempt was too far to leeward, and it drafted toward the shore. An energetic Jap tried to retrieve it, but one of our planes cut him to pieces. The next raft landed above me, and drifted toward me. Gosh, they're remarkable things. I pulled it out of the bag, pumped the handle of the CO_2 container, and the lovely yellow devil puffed right out.

But my troubles were only starting. The wind and currents shoved that raft toward the shore, but fast. I did everything I could to hold it back, and paddled until I could hardly raise my right arm. Then some F4U pilot with an IQ of about 420—boy, how I would like to meet that guy—dropped me his parachute. It was his only parachute and from then on he was upstairs on his own. But it made me a swell sea anchor. Drifting far behind in the water, it slowed me down. That Marine was a plenty smart cookie.

It was now about noon, and even though I was plenty scared, I was hungry. I broke out some emergency rations from the raft and had a pretty fine meal. The Jap snipers were falling short, but a long-range mortar started to get close. It fired about twenty shots. I didn't care. I had a full belly and a bunch of F4U's upstairs. Oh, those lovely planes! They went after that mortar like a bunch of bumblebees after a tramp. There was a couple of loud garummmphs, and we had no more trouble with that mortar. It must have been infuriating to the Japs to see me out there.

I judge it was about 1400 when thirty new F4U's took over. I wondered why they sent so many. This gang made even the New Zealanders look cautious. They just shot up everything that moved or looked as if it might once have wanted to move. Then I saw why.

A huge PBY, painted black, came gracefully up The Slot. I learned later that it was Squadron Leader Grant of the RNZAF detachment at Halavo. He had told headquarters that he'd land the Cat anywhere there was water. By damn, he did, too. He reconnoitered the bay twice, saw he would have to make his run right over Munda airfield, relayed that information to the F4U's and started down. His course took him over the heart of the Jap installations. He was low and big and a sure target. But he kept coming in. Before him, above him, and behind him a merciless swarm of thirty F4U's blazed away. Like tiny, cruel insects protecting a lumbering butterfly, the F4U's scoured the earth.

Beautifully the PBY landed. The F4U's probed the shoreline, Grant taxied his huge plane toward my small raft. The F4U's zoomed overhead at impossibly low altitudes. The PBY came alongside. The F4U's protected us. I climbed aboard and set the raft loose. Quickly the turret top was closed. The New Zealand gunner swung his agile gun about. There were quiet congratulations.

The next moment hell broke loose! From the shore one canny Jap let go with the gun he had been saving all day for such a moment. There was a ripping sound, and the port wing of the PBY was gone! The Jap had time to fire three more shells before the F4U's reduced him and his gun to rubble. The first two Jap shells missed, but the last one blew off the tail assembly. We were sinking.

Rapidly we threw out the rafts and as much gear as we could. I thought to save six parachutes, and soon nine of us were in Munda harbor, setting our sea anchors and looking mighty damned glum. Squadron leader Grant was particularly doused by the affair. "Second PBY I've lost since I've been out here," he said mournfully.

Now a circle of Navy F6F's took over. I thought they were more conservative than the New Zealanders and the last Marine gang. That was until a Jap battery threw a couple of close ones. I had never seen an F6F in action before. Five of them hit that battery like Jack Dempsey hitting Willard. The New Zealanders, who had not seen the F6F's either, were amazed. It looked more like a medium bomber than a fighter. Extreme though our predicament was, I remember that we carefully appraised the new F6F.

"The Japs won't be able to stop that one!" an officer said. "It's got too much."

"You mean they can fly that big fighter off a ship?" another inquired.

"They sure don't let the yellow bastards get many shots in, do they?"

We were glad of that. Unless the Jap hit us on first shot, he was done. He didn't get a second chance. We were therefore dismayed when half of the F6F's pulled away toward Rendova. We didn't see them any more. An hour later, however, we saw thirty new F4U's lolly-gagging through the sky Rendova way. Four sped on ahead to relieve the fine, battle-proven F6F's who headed down The Slot. We wondered what was up.

And then we saw! From some secret nest in Rendova, the F4U's were bringing out two PT Boats! They were going to come right in Munda harbor, and to hell with the Japs! Above them the lazy Marines darted and bobbed, like dolphins in an aerial ocean.

You know the rest. It was Lt. Comdr. Charlesworth and his PT's. Used to be on Tulagi. They hang out somewhere in the Russells now. Something big was on, and they had sneaked up to Rendova, specially for an attack somewheres. But Kester shouted, "To hell with the attack. We've gone this far. Get that pilot out of there." He said they'd have to figure out some other move for the big attack they had cooking. Maybe use destroyers instead of PT's.

I can't tell you much more. A couple of savvy Japs were waiting with field pieces, just like the earlier one. But they didn't get hits. My God, did the Marines in their F4U's crucify those Japs! That was the last thing I saw before the PT's pulled me aboard. Twelve F4U's diving at one hillside.

Pass me that bottle, Tony. Well, as you know, we figured it all out last night. We lost a P-40 and a PBY. We broke up Admiral Kester's plan for the PT Boats. We wasted the flying time of P-40's, F4U's, and F6F's like it was dirt. We figured the entire mission cost not less than $600,000. Just to save one guy in the water off Munda. I wonder what the Japs left to rot on Munda thought of that? $600,000 for one pilot.—Bus Adams took a healthy swig of whiskey. He lolled back in the tail-killing chair of the Hotel De Gink.—But it's sure worth every cent of the money. If you happen to be that pilot.

CHIEF WHITE HALFOAT

FROM *CATCH-22*

---

by JOSEPH HELLER

The decision to include an excerpt from *Catch-22* in this anthology can be questioned—some will argue that regardless of whatever else *Catch-22* might be, it is not a flying story: very little of the action takes place in the air, the few flying scenes do little to advance the plot—such as it is—and the characters are anti-warriors, the beat generation's version of heroes.

Joseph Heller's first novel, published in 1961 with a certified war hero living in the White House, was an anti-establishment romp from first page to last. The main character is Yossarian, a B-25 bombardier whose mission in life is to survive the war. Yossarian's existence is desperate not because of the Germans, who go about their task of killing Allied fliers in a logical, predictable, sane manner, but because of the insane ministrations of his own military machine, as embodied in the person of his nemesis, Colonel Cathcart, who keeps raising the number of missions that the air crewmen must fly before they can be rotated home.

Like all good humor, Heller's over-the-top tale is an exaggeration of the truth. At some level, war *is* an insane activity (at the most basic level, so is life).

The survival of his troops is not the number one priority of any military leader—if it were, his troops would never fight. The system is indeed designed to force the unwilling into combat, and does so with ruthless efficiency. Yossarian and his friends tell us these truths and many others; our humanity begs us to listen.

Doc Daneeka lived in a splotched gray tent with Chief White Halfoat, whom he feared and despised.

"I can just picture his liver," Doc Daneeka grumbled.

"Picture my liver," Yossarian advised him.

"There's nothing wrong with your liver."

"That shows how much you don't know," Yossarian bluffed, and told Doc Daneeka about the troublesome pain in his liver that had troubled Nurse Duckett and Nurse Cramer and all the doctors in the hospital because it wouldn't become jaundice and wouldn't go away.

Doc Daneeka wasn't interested. "You think you've got troubles?" he wanted to know. "What about me? You should've been in my office the day those newlyweds walked in."

"What newlyweds?"

"Those newlyweds that walked into my office one day. Didn't I ever tell you about them? She was lovely."

So was Doc Daneeka's office. He had decorated his waiting room with goldfish and one of the finest suites of cheap furniture. Whatever he could he bought on credit, even the goldfish. For the rest, he obtained money from greedy relatives in exchange for shares of the profits. His office was in Staten Island in a two-family firetrap just four blocks away from the ferry stop and only one block south of a supermarket, three beauty parlors, and two corrupt druggists. It was a corner location, but nothing helped. Population turnover was small, and people clung through habit to the same physicians they had been doing business with for years. Bills piled up rapidly, and he was soon faced with the loss of his most precious medical instruments: his adding machine was repossessed, and then his typewriter. The goldfish died. Fortunately, just when things were blackest, the war broke out.

"It was a godsend," Doc Daneeka confessed solemnly. "Most of the other doctors were soon in the service, and things picked up overnight. The corner location really started paying off, and I soon found myself handling more patients than I could handle competently. I upped my kickback fee with those two drugstores. The beauty parlors were good for two, three abortions a week. Things couldn't have been better, and then look what happened. They had to send a guy from the draft board around to look me over. I was Four-F. I had examined myself pretty thoroughly and discovered that I was unfit for military service. You'd think my word would be enough, wouldn't you, since I was a doctor in good standing with my county medical society and with my local Better Business Bureau. But no, it wasn't, and they sent this guy around just to make sure I really did have one leg amputated at the hip and was helplessly bedridden with incurable rheumatoid arthritis. Yossarian, we live in an age of distrust and deteriorating spiritual values. It's a terrible thing," Doc Daneeka protested in a voice quavering with strong emotion. "It's a terrible thing when even the word of a licensed physician is suspected by the country he loves."

Doc Daneeka had been drafted and shipped to Pianosa as a flight surgeon, even though he was terrified of flying.

"I don't have to go looking for trouble in an airplane," he noted, blinking his beady, brown, offended eyes myopically. "It comes looking for me. Like that virgin I'm telling you about that couldn't have a baby."

"What virgin?" Yossarian asked. "I thought you were telling me about some newlyweds."

"That's the virgin I'm telling you about. They were just a couple of young kids, and they'd been married, oh, a little over a year when they came walking into my office without an appointment. You should have seen her. She was so sweet and young and pretty. She even blushed when I asked about her periods. I don't think I'll ever stop loving that girl. She was built like a dream and wore a chain around her neck with a medal of Saint Anthony hanging down inside the most beautiful bosom I never saw. 'It must be a terrible temptation for Saint Anthony,' I joked—just to put her at ease, you know. 'Saint Anthony?' her husband said. 'Who's Saint Anthony?' 'Ask your wife,' I told him. 'She can tell you who Saint Anthony is.' 'Who is Saint Anthony?' he asked her. 'Who?' she wanted to know. 'Saint Anthony,' he told her. 'Saint Anthony?' she said. 'Who's Saint Anthony?' When I got a good look at her inside my examination room I found she was still a virgin. I spoke to her husband alone while she was pulling her girdle back on and hooking it onto her stockings. 'Every night,' he boasted. A real wise guy, you know. 'I never miss a night,' he boasted. He meant it, too. 'I even been puttin' it to her mornings before the breakfasts she makes me before we go to work,' he boasted. There was only one explanation. When I had them both together again I gave them a demonstration of intercourse with the rubber models I've got in my office. I've got these rubber models in my office with all the reproductive organs of both sexes that I keep locked up in separate cabinets to avoid a scandal. I mean I used to have them. I don't have anything any more, not even a practice. The only thing I have now is this low temperature that I'm really starting to worry about. Those two kids I've got working for me in the medical tent aren't worth a damn as diagnosticians. All they know how to do is complain. They think they've got troubles? What about me? They should have been in my office that day with those two newlyweds looking at me as though I were telling them something nobody'd ever heard of before. You never saw anybody so interested. 'You mean like this?' he asked me, and worked the models for himself awhile. You know, I can see where a certain type of person might get a big kick out of doing just that. 'That's it,' I told him. 'Now, you go home and try it my way for a few months and see what happens. Okay?' 'Okay,' they said, and paid me in cash without any argument. 'Have a good time,' I told them, and they thanked me and walked out together. He had his arm around her waist as though he couldn't wait to get her home and put it to her again. A few days later he came back all by himself and told my nurse he had to see me right away. As soon as we were alone, he punched me in the nose."

"He did what?"

"He called me a wise guy and punched me in the nose. 'What are you, a wise guy?' he said, and knocked me flat on my ass. Pow! Just like that. I'm not kidding."

"I know you're not kidding," Yossarian said. "But why did he do it?"

"How should I know why he did it?" Doc Daneeka retorted with annoyance.

"Maybe it had something to do with Saint Anthony?"

Doc Daneeka looked at Yossarian blankly. "Saint Anthony?" he asked with astonishment. "Who's Saint Anthony?"

"How should I know?" answered Chief White Halfoat, staggering inside the tent just then with a bottle of whiskey cradled in his arm and sitting himself down pugnaciously between the two of them.

Doc Daneeka rose without a word and moved his chair outside the tent, his back bowed by the compact kit of injustices that was his perpetual burden. He could not bear the company of his roommate.

Chief White Halfoat thought he was crazy. "I don't know

what's the matter with that guy," he observed reproachfully. "He's got no brains, that's what's the matter with him. If he had any brains he'd grab a shovel and start digging. Right here in the tent, he'd start digging, right under my cot. He'd strike oil in no time. Don't he know how that enlisted man struck oil with a shovel back in the States? Didn't he ever hear what happened to that kid—what was the name of that rotten rat bastard pimp of a snotnose back in Colorado?"

"Wintergreen."

"Wintergreen."

"He's afraid," Yossarian explained.

"Oh, no. Not Wintergreen." Chief White Halfoat shook his head with undisguised admiration. "That stinking little punk wise-guy son of a bitch ain't afraid of nobody."

"Doc Daneeka's afraid. That's what's the matter with him."

"What's he afraid of?"

"He's afraid of you," Yossarian said. "He's afraid you're going to die of pneumonia."

"He'd *better* be afraid," Chief White Halfoat said. A deep, low laugh rumbled through his massive chest. "I will, too, the first chance I get. You just wait and see."

Chief White Halfoat was a handsome, swarthy Indian from Oklahoma with a heavy, hard-boned face and tousled black hair, a half-blooded Creek from Enid who, for occult reasons of his own, had made up his mind to die of pneumonia. He was a glowering, vengeful, disillusioned Indian who hated foreigners with names like Cathcart, Korn, Black and Havermeyer and wished they'd all go back to where their lousy ancestors had come from.

"You wouldn't believe it, Yossarian," he ruminated, raising his voice deliberately to bait Doc Daneeka, "but this used to be a pretty good country to live in before they loused it up with their goddam piety."

Chief White Halfoat was out to revenge himself upon the

white man. He could barely read or write and had been assigned to Captain Black as assistant intelligence officer.

"How could I learn to read or write?" Chief White Halfoat demanded with simulated belligerence, raising his voice again so that Doc Daneeka would hear. "Every place we pitched our tent, they sank an oil well. Every time they sank a well, they hit oil. And every time they hit oil, they made us pack up our tent and go someplace else. We were human divining rods. Our whole family had a natural affinity for petroleum deposits, and soon every oil company in the world had technicians chasing us around. We were always on the move. It was one hell of a way to bring a child up, I can tell you. I don't think I ever spent more than a week in one place."

His earliest memory was of a geologist.

"Every time another White Halfoat was born," he continued, "the stock market turned bullish. Soon whole drilling crews were following us around with all their equipment just to get the jump on each other. Companies began to merge just so they could cut down on the number of people they had to assign to us. But the crowd in back of us kept growing. We never got a good night's sleep. When we stopped, they stopped. When we moved, they moved, chuckwagons, bulldozers, derricks, generators. We were a walking business boom, and we began to receive invitations from some of the best hotels just for the amount of business we would drag into town with us. Some of those invitations were mighty generous, but we couldn't accept any because we were Indians and all the best hotels that were inviting us wouldn't accept Indians as guests. Racial prejudice is a terrible thing, Yossarian. It really is. It's a terrible thing to treat a decent, loyal Indian like a nigger, kike, wop or spic." Chief White Halfoat nodded slowly with conviction.

"Then, Yossarian, it finally happened—the beginning of the end. They began to follow us around from in front. They would try to guess where we were going to stop next and would begin drilling before we even got there, so we couldn't even stop. As soon as we'd begin to unroll our blankets, they would kick us off. They had confidence in us. They wouldn't even wait to strike oil before they kicked us off. We were so tired we almost didn't care the day our time ran out. One morning we found ourselves completely surrounded by oilmen waiting for us to come their way so they could kick us off. Everywhere you looked there was an oilman on a ridge, waiting there like Indians getting ready to attack. It was the end. We couldn't stay where we were because we had just been kicked off. And there was no place left for us to go. Only the Army saved me. Luckily, the war broke out just in the nick of time, and a draft board picked me right up out of the middle and put me down safely in Lowery Field, Colorado. I was the only survivor."

Yossarian knew he was lying, but did not interrupt as Chief White Halfoat went on to claim that he had never heard from his parents again. That didn't bother him too much, though, for he had only their word for it that they were his parents, and since they had lied to him about so many other things, they could just as well have been lying to him about that too. He was much better acquainted with the fate of a tribe of first cousins who had wandered away north in a diversionary movement and pushed inadvertently into Canada. When they tried to return, they were stopped at the border by American immigration authorities who would not let them back into the country. They could not come back in because they were red.

It was a horrible joke, but Doc Daneeka didn't laugh until Yossarian came to him one mission later and pleaded again, without any real expectation of success, to be grounded. Doc Daneeka snickered once and was soon immersed in problems of his own, which included Chief White Halfoat, who had been challenging him all that morning to Indian wrestle, and Yossarian, who decided right then and there to go crazy.

"You're wasting your time," Doc Daneeka was forced to tell him.

"Can't you ground someone who's crazy?"

"Oh, sure. I have to. There's a rule saying I have to ground anyone who's crazy."

"Then why don't you ground me? I'm crazy. Ask Clevinger."

"Clevinger? Where *is* Clevinger? You find Clevinger and I'll ask him."

"Then ask any of the others. They'll tell you how crazy I am."

"They're crazy."

"Then why don't you ground them?"

"Why don't they ask me to ground them?"

"Because they're crazy, that's why."

"Of course they're crazy," Doc Daneeka replied. "I just told you they're crazy, didn't I? And you can't let crazy people decide whether you're crazy or not, can you?"

Yossarian looked at him soberly and tried another approach. "Is Orr crazy?"

"He sure is," Doc Daneeka said.

"Can you ground him?"

"I sure can. But first he has to ask me to. That's part of the rule."

"Then why doesn't he ask you to?"

"Because he's crazy," Doc Daneeka said. "He has to be crazy to keep flying combat missions after all the close calls he's had. Sure, I can ground Orr. But first he has to ask me to."

"That's all he has to do to be grounded?"

"That's all. Let him ask me."

"And then you can ground him?" Yossarian asked.

"No. Then I can't ground him."

"You mean there's a catch?"

"Sure there's a catch," Doc Daneeka replied. "Catch-22. Anyone who wants to get out of combat duty isn't really crazy."

There was only one catch and that was Catch-22, which specified that a concern for one's own safety in the face of dangers that were real and immediate was the process of a rational mind. Orr was crazy and could be grounded. All he had to do was ask; and as soon as he did, he would no longer be crazy and would have to fly more missions. Orr would be crazy to fly more missions and sane if he didn't, but if he was sane he had to fly them. If he flew them he was crazy and didn't have to; but if he didn't want to he was sane and had to. Yossarian was moved very deeply by the absolute simplicity of this clause of Catch-22 and let out a respectful whistle.

"That's some catch, that Catch-22," he observed.

"It's the best there is," Doc Daneeka agreed.

Yossarian saw it clearly in all its spinning reasonableness. There was an elliptical precision about its perfect pairs of parts that was graceful and shocking, like good modern art, and at times Yossarian wasn't quite sure that he saw it all, just the way he was never quite sure about good modern art or about the flies Orr saw in Appleby's eyes. He had Orr's word to take for the flies in Appleby's eyes.

"Oh, they're there, all right," Orr had assured him about the flies in Appleby's eyes after Yossarian's fist fight with Appleby in the officers' club, "although he probably doesn't even know it. That's why he can't see things as they really are."

"How come he doesn't know it?" inquired Yossarian.

"Because he's got flies in his eyes," Orr explained with exaggerated patience. "How can he see he's got flies in his eyes if he's got flies in his eyes?"

It made as much sense as anything else, and Yossarian was willing to give Orr the benefit of the doubt because Orr was from the wilderness outside New York City and knew so much more about wildlife than Yossarian did, and because Orr, unlike Yossarian's mother, father, sister, brother, aunt, uncle, in-law, teacher, spiritual leader, legislator, neighbor and newspaper, had never lied to him about anything crucial before. Yossarian had mulled his newfound knowledge about Appleby over in private for a day or two and then decided, as a good deed, to pass the word along to Appleby himself.

"Appleby, you've got flies in your eyes," he whispered helpfully as they passed by each other in the doorway of the parachute tent on the day of the weekly milk run to Parma.

"What?" Appleby responded sharply, thrown into confusion by the fact that Yossarian had spoken to him at all.

"You've got flies in your eyes," Yossarian repeated. "That's probably why you can't see them."

Appleby retreated from Yossarian with a look of loathing bewilderment and sulked in silence until he was in the jeep with Havermeyer riding down the long, straight road to the briefing room, where Major Danby, the fidgeting group operations officer, was waiting to conduct the preliminary briefing with all the lead pilots, bombardiers and navigators. Appleby spoke in a soft voice so that he would not be heard by the driver or by Captain Black, who was stretched out with his eyes closed in the front seat of the jeep.

"Havermeyer," he asked hesitantly. "Have I got flies in my eyes?"

Havermeyer blinked quizzically. "Sties?" he asked.

"No, flies," he was told.

Havermeyer blinked again. "Flies?"

"In my eyes."

"You must be crazy," Havermeyer said.

"No, I'm not crazy. Yossarian's crazy. Just tell me if I've got flies in my eyes or not. Go ahead. I can take it."

Havermeyer popped another piece of peanut brittle into his mouth and peered very closely into Appleby's eyes.

"I don't see any," he announced.

Appleby heaved an immense sigh of relief. Havermeyer had tiny bits of peanut brittle adhering to his lips, chin and cheeks.

"You've got peanut brittle crumbs on your face," Appleby remarked to him.

"I'd rather have peanut brittle crumbs on my face than flies in my eyes," Havermeyer retorted.

The officers of the other five planes in each flight arrived in trucks for the general briefing that took place thirty minutes later. The three enlisted men in each crew were not briefed at all, but were carried directly out on the airfield to the separate planes in which they were scheduled to fly that day, where they waited around with the ground crew until the officers with whom they had been scheduled to fly swung off the rattling tailgates of the trucks delivering them and it was time to climb aboard and start up. Engines rolled over disgruntledly on lollipop-shaped hardstands, resisting first, then idling smoothly awhile, and then the planes lumbered around and nosed forward lamely over the pebbled ground like sightless, stupid, crippled things until they taxied into the line at the foot of the landing strip and took off swiftly, one behind the other, in a zooming, rising roar, banking slowly into formation over mottled treetops, and circling the field at even speed until all the flights of six had been formed and then setting course over cerulean water on the first leg of the journey to the target in northern Italy or France. The planes gained altitude steadily and were above nine thousand feet by the time they crossed into enemy territory. One of the surprising things always was the sense of calm and utter silence, broken only by the test rounds fired from the machine guns, by an occasional toneless, terse remark over the intercom, and, at last, by the sobering pronouncement of the bombardier in each plane that they were at the I.P. and about to turn toward the target. There was always sunshine, always a tiny sticking in the throat from the rarefied air.

The B-25s they flew in were stable, dependable, dull-green ships with twin rudders and engines and wide wings. Their single fault, from where Yossarian sat as a bombardier, was the tight crawlway separating the bombardier's compartment in the Plexiglas nose from the nearest escape hatch. The crawlway was a narrow, square, cold tunnel hollowed out beneath the flight controls, and a large man like Yossarian could squeeze through only with difficulty. A chubby, moon-faced navigator with little reptilian eyes and a pipe like Aarfy's had trouble, too, and Yossarian used to chase him back from the nose as they turned toward the target, now minutes away. There was a time of tension then, a time of waiting with nothing to hear and nothing to see and nothing to do but wait as the antiaircraft guns below took aim and made ready to knock them all sprawling into infinite sleep if they could.

The crawlway was Yossarian's lifeline to outside from a plane about to fall, but Yossarian swore at it with seething antagonism, reviled it as an obstacle put there by providence as part of the plot that would destroy him. There was room for an additional escape hatch right there in the nose of a B-25, but there was no escape hatch. Instead there was the crawlway, and since the mess on the mission over Avignon he had learned to detest every mammoth inch of it, for it slung him seconds and seconds away from his parachute, which was too bulky to be taken up front with him, and seconds and seconds more after that away from the escape hatch on the floor between the rear of the elevated flight deck and the feet of the faceless top turret gunner mounted high above. Yossarian longed to be where Aarfy could be once Yossarian had chased him back from the nose; Yossarian longed to sit on the floor in a huddled ball right on top of the escape hatch inside a sheltering igloo of extra flak suits that he would have been happy to carry along with him, his parachute already hooked to his harness where it belonged, one fist clenching the red-handled rip cord, one fist gripping the emergency hatch release that would spill him earthward into air at the first dreadful squeal of destruction. That was where he wanted to be if he had to be there at all, instead of hung out there in front like some goddam cantilevered goldfish in some goddam cantilevered goldfish bowl while the goddam foul black tiers of flak were bursting and booming and billowing all around and above and below him in a climbing, cracking, staggered, banging, phantasmagorical, cosmological wickedness that jarred and tossed and shivered, clattered and pierced, and threatened to annihilate them all in one splinter of a second in one vast flash of fire.

Aarfy had been no use to Yossarian as a navigator or as anything else, and Yossarian drove him back from the nose vehemently each time so that they would not clutter up each other's way if they had to scramble suddenly for safety. Once Yossarian had driven him back from the nose, Aarfy was free to cower on the floor where Yossarian longed to cower, but he stood bolt upright instead with his stumpy arms resting comfortably on the backs of the pilot's and co-pilot's seats, pipe in hand, making affable small talk to McWatt and whoever happened to be co-pilot and pointing out amusing trivia in the sky to the two men, who were too busy to be interested. McWatt was too busy responding at the controls to Yossarian's strident instructions as Yossarian slipped the plane in on the bomb run and then whipped them all away violently around the ravenous pillars of exploding shells with curt, shrill, obscene commands to McWatt that were much like the anguished, entreating nightmare yelpings of Hungry Joe in the dark. Aarfy would puff reflectively on his pipe throughout the whole chaotic clash, gazing with unruffled curiosity at the war through McWatt's window as though it were a remote disturbance that could not affect him. Aarfy was a dedicated fraternity man who loved cheerleading and class reunions and did not have brains enough to be afraid. Yossarian did have brains enough and was, and the only thing that stopped him from abandoning his post under fire and scurrying back through the crawlway like a yellow-bellied rat was his unwillingness to entrust the evasive action out of the target area to anybody else. There was nobody else in the world he would honor with so great a responsibility. There was nobody else he knew who was as big a coward. Yossarian was the best man in the group at evasive action, but had no idea why.

There was no established procedure for evasive action. All you needed was fear, and Yossarian had plenty of that, more fear than Orr or Hungry Joe, more fear even than Dunbar, who had resigned himself submissively to the idea that he must die someday. Yossarian had not resigned himself to that idea, and he bolted for his life wildly on each mission the instant his bombs were away, hollering, *"Hard, hard, hard, hard, you bastard, hard!"* at McWatt and hating McWatt viciously all the time as though McWatt were to blame for their being up there at all to be rubbed out by strangers, and everybody else in the plane kept off the intercom, except for the pitiful time of the mess on the mission to Avignon when Dobbs went crazy in mid-air and began weeping pathetically for help.

"Help him, help him," Dobbs sobbed. "Help him, help him."

"Help who? Help who?" called back Yossarian, once he had plugged his headset back into the intercom system, after it had been jerked out when Dobbs wrested the controls away from Huple and hurled them all down suddenly into the deafening, paralyzing, horrifying dive which had plastered Yossarian helplessly to the ceiling of the plane by the top of his head and from which Huple had rescued them just in time by seizing the controls back from Dobbs and leveling the ship out almost as suddenly right back in the middle of the buffeting layer of cacophonous flak from which they had escaped successfully only a moment before. *Oh, God! Oh, God, Oh, God*, Yossarian had been pleading wordlessly as he dangled from the ceiling of the nose of the ship by the top of his head, unable to move.

"The bombardier, the bombardier," Dobbs answered in a cry when Yossarian spoke. "He doesn't answer, he doesn't answer. Help the bombardier, help the bombardier."

"I'm the bombardier," Yossarian cried back at him. "I'm the bombardier. I'm all right. I'm all right."

"Then help him, help him," Dobbs begged. "Help him, help him."

And Snowden lay dying in back.

HELL OVER GERMANY

FROM *BOMBER*

————

by LEN DEIGHTON

When a master of characterization, action, and suspense tries his hand at a flying story, the result can be astounding. Len Deighton usually writes spy thrillers. He has written over two dozen books, including *The Ipcress File*, *Funeral in Berlin*, and *An Expensive Place to Die*. Two of his books are superb flying novels, *Goodbye Mickey Mouse*, a story of American World War II P-51 pilots, and *Bomber*, which is a tale of a British night raid on an industrial city in the Ruhr valley gone awry. The RAF marks the wrong town. The bombers pulverize an inoffensive rural village, Altgarden, and slaughter most of the inhabitants.

Bomber is often cited as a powerful anti-war book. Every honest depiction of war is a voice against it, a despairing, futile one. Writers have been accurately describing wars since Thucydides gave it a go and have not yet made a detectable dent. One doubts they ever will. Describing cancer doesn't cure it.

Bomber is my favorite Deighton book, which is saying a lot. All of his books are terrific; *Bomber* is in a class by itself. But enough . . . it is time to fly.

Night has fallen over Europe on the 30th day of June, 1943. Bomber crews in Lancasters and Stirlings and pathfinders in Mosquitos are on their way to Germany. They are dodging flak, searching for their target, and they are being stalked by merciless killers in invisible night fighters. . . .

"*Levator labii superioris aloequae nasi.*" For no reason at all Pilot Officer Fleming, at the controls of *The Volkswagen*, intoned the words like grace. He had in fact once said it as grace in the Officers' Mess and had got by unchallenged, but he'd taken care not to do it when the Medical Officer was at table.

"What's that, sir?" said Bertie, the flight engineer, who thought it might be a technical matter he'd neglected.

Fleming closed his eyes and tilted his head. "It's the longest name of any muscle in the human body."

"What's the name of the shortest one?" said the mid-upper gunner and was promptly answered insultingly, accusingly and unscientifically by the wireless operator.

"O.K., chaps," said Fleming. "Let's have a bit of hush."

Four of the Leiden searchlights had been on for some time but now another six were switched on. "Look at that," said Fleming.

"Searchlights," said the flight engineer. In every group of lights there was one that remained vertical. That one was controlled by a Würzburg radar; it was called the master searchlight.

"I'm going to steer a bit to the north, Mac," Fleming told his navigator. "No sense in heading straight toward that muck."

"Don't let's even head for the fringe of it," said the flight engineer.

Fleming laughed; perhaps the boy wasn't such an idiot after

all. It was a bad system, training an engineer apart from the crew. Fleming had known the rest of them for weeks, but he'd flown only a few hours with this child, his assistant pilot. Fleming wondered if the boy could handle the controls sufficiently well for him to go back to the lavatory. Next trip he would take that tin can he'd been offered and be grateful for it. Was it fear that did it? He'd noticed that the engineer and the bomb aimer had already been back there. It was easy for them, but he was strapped into the pilot's seat and getting out of it was a struggle.

Fear should tighten the rectum and bladder, not loosen them, or so his medical training told him. In the Briefing Room he had watched his fellowmen grow pale as fear diverted their newly thinned blood from the skin and the viscera to the brain. That's why so many had been unable to eat their supper. He'd felt his own heart begin to beat faster as his blood—now red-corpuscle dominated, sugar-rich and laden with adrenalin—rose in pressure. He handled the heavy controls with newly found strength and knew that fear had supplied blood to his muscles and his liver had released carbohydrate into his veins. His lungs benefited too, taking more oxygen in breaths that were both deeper and faster.

The first sight of the searchlights had provided him with further physiological evidence of his fear: loss of peristalsis and gastric juice had turned his supper into a hard knot and his saliva had gone, so that his tongue was rough against his mouth. Lastly, his scrotum had constricted tight against his body. Resulting from these changes Fleming believed he could detect a rise in body temperature as a result of the increased basal metabolic rate. To confirm his theory a trickle of sweat rolled down his spine. His father—a truly dedicated physician—would be interested to hear of these observations.

"Keep this course, Skip," said the navigator. "We'll turn five miles inland instead of over Noordwijk. That should keep us well clear of Leiden."

"Okey dokey," said Fleming and for the first time felt truly like a skipper.

Robin, fellow officer and bomb aimer, had been sitting at the navigator's table filling in his log. He collected up his parachute, target map, log and Thermos flask, disconnected his oxygen supply and came forward. He pushed the flight engineer gently to one side and, waving a greeting to Fleming at the controls, bent double to put his foot downward until it reached the step formed by the glycol tank. Carefully he ducked his head under the traversing ring of the front gun turret with its twin Browning guns. This was his world. It was quieter here. He spread the map out and lay full length, with his belly on the exit hatch and his head in the clear-view bowl that formed the nose of the airplane. Outside, the night was growing lighter; the moon was coming out. He looked round with interest but not surprise; he had always known it would be like this.

To the right, one of the searchlight beams was shorter than the others and instead of tapering, its beam ended in a blunt hammerhead. "Look," said Robin, "they've got someone in the searchlights."

"Poor swine," said Fleming as he watched more searchlights affix their beams to the airplane.

The trapped plane was tilting and twisting like a tormented animal, but although it broke clear of some of the beams, always at least one of them hung on to it. The flak had started now; some of the bursts were so close to it that the smoke obscured their view for a second or two but still the plane flew on.

"We have him on our set now," said Löwenherz.

"Where do you want him?"

"Just starboard and level."

"Let me put him a trifle high, Herr Oberleutnant."

"Very well."

"We're closing too fast again."

In the searchlights everything was white. Two more had him now and they were fixing him to the sky like gleaming hatpins holding a fluttering white moth in a black velvet box. There was a brief flicker under the plane and it shivered slightly.

"He's hit."

"It's *B Beer*, the Navigation Leader."

"The immortal Lud."

The navigator couldn't see. "Are they getting out?"

"No, he's jettisoning his bombs."

As they watched it the bomber seemed to swell up very gently with a soft *whoomp* that was audible far across the sky. It became a ball of burning petrol, oil and pyrotechnic compounds. The yellow datum marker, which should have marked the approach to Krefeld, burned brightly as it fell away, leaving thin trails of sparks. The fireball changed from red to light pink as its rising temperature enabled it to devour new substances from hydraulic fluid and human fat to engine components of manganese, vanadium, and copper. Finally even the airframe burned. Ten tons of magnesium alloy flared with a strange greenish blue light. It lit up the countryside beneath it like a slow flash of lightning and was gone. For a moment a cloud of dust illuminated by the searchlights floated in the sky and then even that disappeared.

"Jee—sus!" exclaimed Pilot Officer Cornelius Fleming in horror.

"No parachutes," pronounced Robin from the nose. The searchlights began moving again.

"Flak did it," said the mid-upper gunner, who had the best view of all.

Far away near Utrecht, Fleming saw another master searchlight tilt from the vertical position at which it rested. The top of its beam seemed to explode as it moved across cloud patches.

Between the patches it reached seven miles into the sky. Unfalteringly it found a victim.

"The stream isn't routed over Leiden," said Fleming to his crew. "All of those aircraft are off course." It sounded not only prim but callous, but before he could modify the sentiment the mid-upper gunner said, "I don't give a bugger who they are; it takes the heat off us and for that I am truly grateful. Amen."

"Kettledrums, kettledrums," said Löwenherz.

"Lancaster," said the observer, putting away his field glasses.

Löwenherz hardly increased speed at all; he inched underneath the huge airplane very very slowly. He looked up through the tip of his cabin and he could see every detail of it. He let its red-hot exhaust pipes pass back overhead until he was exactly underneath the bomber. The two planes roared through the sky in close formation until, in the classic maneuver of the night fighter, Löwenherz pulled the control column back with all his strength. His nose went up closer and closer to the great bomber. The fighter shuddered as it neared stalling point, hanging on its propellers, thrashing like a drowning man but suspended and stationary for a moment. Over him came the bomber. "Horrido," said Löwenherz to tell Bach what he was about to do, and he pressed his gun buttons and raked its belly from nose to tail. The gunfire lit both aircraft with a gentle greenish light. Löwenherz squinted to preserve his night vision as much as possible. These Richards were nothing but highpowered gun platforms and the demented hammering of the big cannons deafened the fliers even through their closely fitting helmets—just as the smell of cordite got into their nostrils in spite of their oxygen masks. Working exactly by the instruction book, Löwenherz kept his guns going even after the nose of the Junkers began to fall back toward earth. Suddenly the gunfire ended. The drums were empty.

Three 20-mm. M.G. F.F. cannons were fitted in the nose of

Löwenherz's Junkers 88R. In sequence of threes there was a thin-cased shell containing 19.5 grams of Hexogen Al. high explosive filling, an explosive armor-piercing shell with a reinforced point and an incendiary that burned at a temperature between 2,000 and 3,000 degrees centigrade for nearly one second. Each cannon was firing at the rate of 520 rounds per minute and was fed by a drum containing 60 rounds. So in seven seconds all of the cannon drums were empty and 180 shells had been fired at *The Volkswagen.* The target measured 300 square feet, and 38 struck the airplane. Theoretically 20 shells would have constituted an average lethal blow.

"My legs," screamed Fleming. "God! Help me, Mother Mother Mother!"

The first shell that penetrated the aircraft came through the forward hatch. Missing the bomb aimer by only an inch, it exploded on contact with the front turret mounting ring. It dislocated the turret, severed the throttle and rudder controls, burst the compressed air tank and broke open the window-spray glycol container. In the airstream the coolant atomized into a cloud of white mist. One-twenty-sixth of a second later the second shell came through the bomb compartment and exploded under the floor of the navigator's position. In the mysterious manner of explosions, it sucked the navigator downward, while blowing the astrodome, and the wireless operator standing under it, out into the night unharmed. Although without his parachute.

Three shells—one H.E., one A.P. and one incendiary— exploded in glancing contact with the starboard fuselage exterior immediately to the rear of the mid-upper turret. Apart from mortally harming the gunner, the explosion of the H.E. shell fractured the metal formers at a place where, after manufacture, the rear part of the fuselage is bolted on. The incendiary shell completed the severance. A structural bisection of *The Volkswagen* occurred one and a half minutes later and two thousand feet lower. Long before this, another H.E. shell passed through the elevator hinge bracket on the tail and blew part of the servo trim tab assembly into the rear turret with such force that it decapitated the rear gunner. Those six hits were the most telling ones, but there were thirty-two others. Some ricocheted off the engines and wings and penetrated the fuselage almost horizontally.

He couldn't hold her, he couldn't. Oh dear God, his arms and legs! Dropping through the night like the paper airplane. "I'm sorry, chaps," he shouted, for he felt a terrible sense of guilt. Involuntarily his bowels and bladder relaxed and he felt himself befouled. "I'm sorry."

It was no use for Fleming to scream apologies; there was no one aboard to hear him. He outlived any of his crew, for from 16,000 feet the wireless operator falling at 120 m.p.h. (the terminal velocity for his weight) reached the ground ninety seconds later. He made an indentation 12 inches deep. This represented a deceleration equivalent to 450 times the force of gravity. He split open like a slaughtered animal and died instantly. Fleming, still strapped into the pilot's seat and aghast at his incontinence, hit the earth (along with the front of the fuselage, two Rolls-Royce engines and most of the main spar) some four minutes after that. To him it seemed like four hours.

The air-conditioning in Ermine's plotting room wasn't intended to cope with so many off-duty personnel standing round as spectators. In addition, the tension seemed to raise a man's body temperature, as does a meal. August mopped his brow and heard Löwenherz give the traditional victory cry: *"Sieg Heil!"*

"Sieg Heil!" said August. Willi came to attention and gave August a formal salute of congratulation in a situation where most men would have shaken him by the hand. There were shuffles and coughs from the onlookers and murmurs of congratulation. The loudspeaker crackled.

"He's breaking up," said Löwenherz. "The main spar has snapped and the fuselage is doubling back like a hairpin."

Willi wiped the wax marks off the table.

"Order: Go to Heinz Gustav One," said August.

"Please: Via Noordwijk?"

"Announcement: Yes, *Katze One*." To Willi August said, "He might get a visual contact if they are still putting flares down but I can't call the flak to a stop just because he is overflying them."

"He won't hang around," said Willi. "He's a bright fellow."

"We're all smart fellows," said August. Willi smiled at August, his ruddy battered face twisted like a freshly squeezed orange.

Löwenherz let the Junkers fall from its vertical position and after gaining speed he eased the antlers back and began climbing to fly back through the stream. Mrosek took off his seat straps, lit his torch and crawled down into the nose to change the 60-round cannon magazines on the Oerlikons. Löwenherz held the same shallow climb, but a patch of turbulent air caused Mrosek to blister his hand upon the breech. Changing the drums was an awkward job even on the ground in daytime, but Mrosek never complained. They flew on past Noordwijk without spotting any bombers, although there was lots of flak, including even some brightly colored 3.7-cm. stuff from Valkenburg aerodrome. The Junkers continued right out to the extreme western end of Ermine's range. Those two interceptions had been quick and easy, but next time he might need to traverse the whole sector under August's guidance before he made a contact.

In *Joe for King*, Roland Pembroke, the young Scots navigator, had overcompensated for the wind error. His Gee was unusable owing to German jamming. Now his mistake had brought *Joe for King* to the Dutch coast five miles south of the turning point. Ahead of him, flying through flak and searchlights, there were others who had made the same error of reckoning.

"We'll go south of it," said Tommy Carter.

"South of Leiden?" said Roland, who had worked out his plot carefully and rather objected to abandoning the flight plan.

"South of that muck," said Tommy, waving toward the flak and lights ahead of them.

"O.K., boss," said Roland.

The brand-new airplane had a strong smell of fresh paint and varnish. The controls were hard and stiff under Tommy Carter's hands and as he turned the wheel it made brittle cracking sounds. On the other hand, everything worked properly. On his previous airplane two or three of the instruments were suspect and would stick and lag behind the others. In some ways he liked having this nice new airplane. He wondered whether they'd be allowed to keep it.

Tommy knew it as a bad idea as soon as he changed onto the new heading. It wasn't only Leiden that was alive with flak, it was this whole coast; The Hague under the starboard wing was damn nearly as bad as Leiden. There were Grossbatterien of dozens of guns and searchlights working under radar control. The whole land was asparkle with gunfire. Tommy fixed his eyes upon a black region of countryside beyond the gunfire and pushed the throttles forward.

"Close your eyes and swallow," said Tommy. "It will soon be gone." The motors screamed loudly.

There was an explosion rather nearer than the previous ones. It rocked the wings and made an acrid smell.

"There's light stuff too," said Tapper Collins, the bomb aimer. He was in the nose watching ropes of red and yellow tracer curve toward them and fall away at what he knew to be thousands of feet below but which looked close enough to touch. "Lots of light stuff now, from directly below us."

"That must be the aerodrome at Valkenburg," said Roland Pembroke.

"Jesus," said Tommy. "Leiden to the left of us, Hague to the right of us and now we are doing a straight and level over a bloody Hun aerodrome. What do you think you're on, charge of the flipping Light Brigade?"

"Sorry, Tommy," said Roland politely. He didn't point out that the change of route was Tommy's idea.

Tommy Carter didn't answer, for at that moment all of his attention was taken with a searchlight that, having remained vertical and immobile for some time, had tilted and now moved toward them.

"It's coming at us," shouted Collins from his position at the bombsight.

"You berk, Tommy!" shouted Ben Gallacher, and Tommy Carter was outraged that he should be blamed for something so obviously beyond his control and not of his liking.

"Sideslip down the beam," said Collins. He was a veteran and Tommy respected his experience. This new airplane required extra strength to move its controls. He heaved at them and banked until the light was blinding bright. It had them. The cockpit was so brightly lit that it made his eyes ache and he could see only by almost closing them.

The theory was that if you sideslipped down the beam the seachlight would (by continuing to move along) lose you. This searchlight crew seemed to have seen the trick before, although in fact Tommy Carter's sideslip was not nearly violent enough to test the theory.

"Fire into the light," Tommy shouted.

"Turn more, I can't reach, I'm full traverse and I can't reach," called the gunner.

Suddenly the light went out. Tommy and Ben tugged at the controls and the bomber eased out of its steep bank. The flak and searchlight had gone and the night was agreeably dark and silent. He began to climb again. It was more than a minute before anyone spoke and then everyone spoke, chattering hysterically and trying to make jokes.

"Everyone shut up," said Tommy Carter in the tone he used when he didn't want an argument—what his crew called his copper's voice.

"Navigator," said Tommy with unusual formality of address, "give me a course so that we'll join the stream beyond Leiden."

"O-eight-five," said Roland in his prime public school accent.

They flew on in a silence broken only by the drone of the motors. "Sorry, boys," said Tommy finally, intimidated by the silence of his crew. "Bloody stupid of me to go south of Leiden."

"That was a master searchlight," said Collins, the expert. "The blue ones are always radar controlled." Because arc lamps seem more blue when angled toward the viewer, R.A.F. crews believed that the ones pointing at them (the bluish ones) were the most accurate, i.e. radar contolled. Luftwaffe crews over Britain believed the same thing, but there were no blue searchlights.

"Then why did the flaming thing go off?" said Ben Gallacher.

"We were a bit small," said Tommy. "They decided to throw us back and wait for a Stirling."

"I'd like to know why," said Ben.

"It's a secret new weapon that some of our planes carry," theorized Collins.

"We'll never know for certain," said Tommy, "so belt up and be grateful."

At that moment on the ground near Valkenburg a young Indian Feldwebel was shouting abuse in Hindustani, which is well suited for that purpose. He watched three phlegmatic signals regiment mechanics remove the front of his searchlight. In the British army, before capture, they had been separated by caste. The Wehrmacht, however, had mixed their new volunteers together, with only these brightly colored turbans—lilac, ocher, green, and even pink and white with blue spots—to show the difference between himself and the lowest of the pariahs. Again he swore an ancient oath at the mechanics. One of the fools proclaimed it to be an ill omen. It was difficult to contradict him, for today they had been told that the local Dutch civilians had protested at the presence of *kaffers* and they were to be moved to France with all their new flak equipment.

This was one of the first of the new high-performance 200-cm. lights to be delivered. A beauty—2.7 million candlepower. Damn! He kicked the cable angrily. It was just his luck that, after a first-class contact on the Würzburg and a *Tommi* in the beam, just then the carbons should go. Sometimes he wished he were back home in Delhi.

In the potato fields a few miles to the west of Ahaus the young Leutnant who had spoken to August and Max during their delay on the road surveyed his Grossbatterie. The two Hitler Jugend guns were manned and ready; those boys were always the keenest. Some of the other guns were not completely jacked up and some were not even uncoupled from their prime movers. It had been a long hard day, with many delays on the road and his Oberst complaining every step of the journey.

The young Leutnant sniffed the air and detected a faint smell of soot and smoke. Whenever the wind was from the south it brought the aroma of the Ruhr with it. During last month's raids the air had also carried the smell of fouled earth, brick dust, cordite and burning buildings.

The sound of aircraft engines came suddenly. He phoned to his control room and when the phone was in his hands he looked up and saw the glint of moonlight upon a wing. He saw it for only a moment and it was too high to be more than a speck of light but it was leaving a condensation trail that glowed in the moonlight. Even had his 8.8-cm. guns been ready to fire they couldn't reach that height.

The information was passed to Deelen but already it was superfluous. Other reports showed that the aircraft were two Mosquitoes at 32,000 feet.

"They are turning at Ahaus," said the Plot Officer.

The Operations Officer moved his hand to make an arc southward from Ahaus, pivoting upon the Oboe transmitter at Dover. His thumb swiveled across the open country until it encountered the shaded pattern of a large town in the Ruhr. He looked then at the bomber stream's reported position. The heading of the bombers would bring them over the same place.

"Krefeld," he said. "I'll bet a week's pay on it."

The other officer nodded. He didn't take up the wager.

The plan was now clear. On their present heading the bomber stream would pass over Krefeld at half past midnight. Moving a hundred miles an hour faster and turning to approach from the north, the Mosquitoes—with their secret Oboe device—would pass over Krefeld three minutes earlier. That would be exactly enough time for the colored indicator bombs to mark the target for the heavy bombers.

The routes were converging like the rays of light through a burning glass and tonight attention was focusing on one town. The leaflet raids over northern France, the lone Mosquito that was causing the alarms to sound all the way to Berlin, and the dog-leg course that had taken the stream to Noordwijk before turning were all clearly seen for the ruses they were; the target for tonight was Krefeld. Deelen Control and Duisburg FLUKO began to arrange the defenses of the Reich accordingly.

In peacetime a complicated electronic device like Oboe would have spent six months more on the test bench and four or five in prototype, and anything up to a year would have passed before they were sold, installed and in use. But this was war and Oboe was in production. It needed nursing all the way to the target and even then it was no surprise to Flying Officer Mac-

Intosh when the set went dead twenty-five miles short of Krefeld.

"Not a sausage. What a nuisance; the signals were clear as a bell—then it went dead."

"We'll turn back then."

"Might as well. We're on a curve but we'll never find the target with a dud set."

"Bloody thing. I canceled a date tonight."

"You shouldn't have joined."

The Mosquito turned abruptly until it faced west to England. There was no sense in going a yard nearer to the Ruhr than was absolutely essential.

"Let's get out of here, Mac."

There were two radio transmitting stations in England from which the signals went to activate Oboe. The stations could handle only two Mosquitoes every ten minutes. The two planes that should mark the target for the very first bombers to arrive were now reduced to one plane. That one was piloted by Pilot Officer Alan Hill; his observer was Peter Hutchinson.

They had done everything according to the book. They had flown at 32,000 feet, for only at this height were the signals able to reach over the radar horizon. At a point fifty miles north of Krefeld they had turned southward. Keeping the steady beat of the signals in his ears, the pilot had banked his wing to fly a gentle curve that would—at the moment the signal from the second transmitter reached him—bring him at the right distance from Krefeld to allow for the forward movement through the air of the 250-pound target indicator bombs.

They did not know that the accompanying Mosquito had turned away with its Oboe device out of action. Nor did they know that they were accompanied by a German airplane up in this region of the sky that was almost the stratosphere. It was a specially equipped Ju88S in which the GM1 system injected nitrous oxide into the superchargers and thus provided oxygen that boosted its performance by nearly twenty percent. Its endurance was measured in minutes and a few nights previously it had used up its Ha-ha device just as it caught sight of the Mosquito. Tonight there had been no miscalculation. Tonight the moonlight had made the upper reaches of the sky into a floodlit arena.

"Bombs armed," reported the observer. At the speed they were going, Krefeld was only two minutes away. There was suddenly a thumping sound and the controls were wrenched from the pilot's grasp. The panel was bent and torn and the glass from its instruments flew in all directions. Two Perspex panels had suddenly gone white and the sky was no longer to be seen through them. Even when the bangs stopped, the engines were screaming an octave above their normal tone. The Mosquito performed a flick roll, steadied itself for a moment and then put its nose up and stalled. As he dived the aircraft to regain control they saw the Ju88 far away on the port beam. Its wings shone in the moonlight as it turned to find them for a second attack.

"Fire!" shouted Peter Hutchinson.

"What with?" shouted Alan Hill angrily, until he noticed that the port engine was coughing blue flame and spitting orange sparks and his few remaining instrument needles were collapsing. He wrenched at the tiny jettison box by his side and tore a nail as he broke the safety wires. There was a lurch as two 250-pound target indicator bombs—each almost as big as a man—fell out of the bomb bay, and then he struggled with the box for what seemed like hours until the other two went. Relieved of the weight of its bomb load, the airplane responded more readily to its controls. He kept the nose down and headed desperately for the cloud bank, but it was still 2000 feet below him as the Ju88 came in again. More pieces of wing disappeared as the cannon shells punched holes through the wood.

"To hear you two young fellows talk you'd think the Germans had no fighter planes."

"They don't as far as we're concerned, Dad. We're too high for them."

"Well, I didn't say this in front of your mother, Alan, but mark my words, your Jerry is a damn good engineer and if he wants to get up to you, one of these nights he'll do it."

"Drink up, Dad, we've two more days of leave yet."

"And change the subject, I know. Your job's too hush-hush to talk to your father about."

"Peter, Peter, jump! She's coming to pieces." Peter didn't move. That last attack must have done it. Please God, don't let that Junkers come round again!

In the Junkers the fuel warning lights were on. He'd had his forty-five minutes' fun and now the nitrous oxide was used. He turned away from the Mosquito. It was done for, he could see that. He wondered if Luftwaffe High Command would let him claim it; they were so keen to keep the Ha-ha secret.

Alan Hill held the stick with one hand and shook Peter frantically with the other. There was no sign of life. He grabbed at the flying helmet and turned the head to look into his friend's glassy eyes. As he shook him the oxygen mask fell aside and he had difficulty in refixing it. Peter's face was covered with fresh blood.

Down where the bomber stream was flying it was cold—colder than the coldest of domestic freezers—but up here it was much colder. Sixty degrees below zero and the air was rarefied and its pressure fatally low for a human lung. Alan undid his safety belt and Peter's too before he put the stick over. When the Mosquito was upside down he fell out of his seat. He tried to pull his observer with him but Peter's leg was caught under the bent instrument panel. He tugged at Peter's arm but that too became bloody even as he watched.

Alan took one last gulp of oxygen and then, holding his breath, he let himself fall. He dropped a long, long way before pulling the rip cord but even so he had slight frostbite and lost the joint of an index finger that stuck to the metal handle. Perfectly, the canopy bloomed above him. He landed in a plowed field two miles from the Dutch border. His only other injury was a bad cut on his right hand that must have happened during the first attack. He realized then that the blood on Peter's face and arm was from this cut. He asked himself if he could have saved Peter's life. Alan was interned together with other bomber crews and was thus not interrogated in the way he would have been had they guessed him to be an Oboe pilot. He spent the rest of the war in a prison camp and died aged forty-nine in a motorcar accident in Liverpool, and yet there was not a day when he did not ask himself that same question.

A layer of cold air lay closed upon the great district of the Ruhr, untroubled by any wind. This cold still air trapped smoke from the furnaces and factories and held it like a gray woolen blanket. Water droplets had built up against this layer and formed a roof as dense and flat and smooth as a sheet of gray aspic: what today we call smog. One target indicator jettisoned by the Oboe Mosquito went into this layer near the Rhine at Duisburg. The second went into the Rhine. One and half minutes and nine miles later the second two landed on the southeast edge of Altgarten.

Detonated by barometric pressure at 1,000 feet, each marker bomb spewed benzol, rubber and phosphorus for a hundred yards in all directions, so that there were two pools of red-colored fire easily seen by the bomber stream four miles above the earth. It was Altgarten's fate to be on the track of the bombers as they flew from the coast toward Krefeld. Had the bombers passed a few more miles to one side or the other then the stream might not have seen the burning T.I.'s waiting to be bombed. It was an extra misfortune for the town that the markers dropped on its far side, for the creepback would start to bring the bombing right across the town toward the approaching stream. Each crew would bomb as early as they could do so without shame. Then they would turn away before the concentration of guns and searchlights that guarded the Ruhr on Altgarten's far side. Perhaps some of the more experienced crews would not have been deceived by the markers into bombing the little town, except that to the H2S radar the acres of green houses that were Altgarten's special pride appeared on the green radar screen like enormous factories.

The first Finder circled twice before putting flares down to the southeast of the markers, trying to get a visual confirmation. Then a Supporter—on his first trip—put a string of high explosives between the flares and the red T.I.s and a second Supporter did the same. The last of these bombs hit the Venlo road and set fire to a gas main.

Tommy Carter in *Joe for King* the Second was a Backer Up. He arrived five minutes early and put his four green markers onto the reds. One thousand feet above Altgarten sixty pyrotechnic candles were ejected from each marker. Each was suspended under a tiny parachute. Falling in close proximity and according to wind and weight they assumed the shape of a bunch of fiery grapes, or, if bottom-heavy, a Christmas tree.

Within ten minutes dozens of Supporters and Finders had dumped their flares and H.E. upon Altgarten and inevitably the release points were creeping back northwest across the town.

Meanwhile, at zero plus three minutes, an Oboe Mosquito arrived exactly on time over Krefeld and marked the real target with four perfectly placed reds. They burned unseen by the bombing force. By now attention had been centered upon Altgarten and the plan had begun to go terribly wrong.

AN HOUR TO SAN FRANCISCO

FROM *THE HIGH AND THE MIGHTY*

BY ERNEST K. GANN

Ernest Gann is widely regarded as the dean of aviation writers. Some folks just say he was the best that ever did it, period, and let it go at that. He was a rarity, a professional aviator who turned out to be a great writer.

Gann learned to fly in the barnstorming era and went to work for American Airlines flying DC-2s. During World War II he flew all over the world for the military airlift command. After the war he left American and flew the Hawaii–California route for a steamship company that created a short-lived subsidiary airline. This experience was the basis for *The High and the Mighty*, a 1953 out-of-the-ballpark home run that catapulted Gann into the top echelon of popular novelists.

The book is the story of one flight, from Honolulu to San Francisco, set just after World War II. When an engine throws a prop in mid-ocean and twists partially off its mount, it becomes doubtful if the piston-engined airliner can reach land. The lives of the twenty people aboard come to a crisis together.

In this era of Boeing-747s hopping oceans filled with hundreds of people, a lumbering four-engine prop-job will strike some readers as quaint. Still, it was a perfect vehicle for Gann's story: it was small enough that Gann could introduce to you all the passengers and all the crew; and it flew at a speed that allowed the story to ripen naturally, allowing the suspense to grow until it shrieked.

Gann's strength as a writer was his ability to get the technical and emotional aspects of flight absolutely perfect. He puts you in the pilot's seat and takes you flying, gives you the emotions and sensations of flight without ever leaving the comfort and safety of your armchair. Before Gann, the actual mechanical manipulations required to fly the airplane were considered trivial details that would slow the pace of the story, if the writer even knew them. Usually he didn't. Gann was the first to use the mechanics of flying as integral parts of the story, devices to give the reader the feel of flying, the actual sensation of being there. Many writers have tried to emulate him; no one has ever written flying better.

The High and the Mighty was made into a movie starring Robert Stack as Sullivan and John Wayne as the gray eagle, Dan Roman. We'll join them now as Flight 420 nears the coast of California. Dawn is still hours away. As usual, the Golden Gate is shrouded in fog and cloud; huge swells roil the cold Pacific. The three remaining engines of Flight 420 are devouring the last drops of gasoline as Sullivan and Dan Roman nurse the dying plane toward San Francisco airport, and safety.

In the cockpit of the Coast Guard B-17, Lieutenant Mowbray kept the lights turned up brightly because there was nothing to see, anyway. The rain had ceased very suddenly, but it would certainly come on again and the heavy overcast still obliterated everything outside the windows.

It was now certain that Lieutenant Mowbray would be forced to rely entirely on mechanical contrivances to complete his interception of Four-two-zero. While his own ship transmitted the letters *M* and *O* in alternate groups so that Sullivan could maintain a series of bearings, Mowbray switched on a high-frequency homing adapter and for a time isolated himself from all other signals. He could not hear Hobie Wheeler's voice when he transmitted at three-minute intervals; Keim could repeat anything important Hobie might have to say. Instead Mowbray heard only a steady hum in his earphones when the nose of his ship was pointed directly at Four-two-zero. If he veered off the tight course to the left he heard the letter *D* transmitted, and if he went off to the right the letter *U* was repeated. Thus he flew a nearly exact course toward Four-two-zero, feeling his way as a blind man might touch the walls of a narrow corridor.

The radarman first-class, just behind Mowbray, was already intent on his screen. It was empty.

"Radar? Anything yet?"

"No target, sir."

"Roger."

They flew on in silence for several minutes. It became more difficult for Mowbray to straddle the narrowing flight path. He called to Ensign Pump.

"Navigator? How's our position relative to interception?"

"Right on. I just got a loran fix. We should be right with them if their navigator was anywhere near right."

"Radar?"

"No target yet, sir."

"Navigator? You're sure?"

"Positive." A few minutes passed. They twisted in their seats—waiting.

"Radar?"

"No target."

"Dammit . . . somebody's wrong!"

Keim leaned across to Lieutenant Mowbray. He was all business now and his eyes were worried.

"Four-two-zero says their needle is fluctuating rapidly."

"What's their altitude?"

"Still twenty-five hundred."

"Radar?"

"No target, sir."

"There's *got* to be. We're right on top of him."

"The screen is blank, sir."

"Keim. Ask Four-two-zero to transmit at thirty-second intervals. We can easily miss this guy."

"Roger."

Keim spoke into his microphone and the minutes passed. They were invaluable minutes, for if they failed to ascertain Four-two-zero's exact position in time to turn with them, the two ships would sweep past each other bound in opposite directions, and their combined speed would separate them a considerable distance in a very few minutes. To turn then, and attempt to overtake them, would add immeasurably to the difficulties of interception.

"Radar?"

"No target."

"I think that navigator was a lot farther west than he thought he was. We're seven minutes overdue."

"Radar?"

"No target." To rest his straining eyes the radarman looked down at his bare arm. He was fond of looking at his arm for it was muscular and well molded. Two years before he had submitted to a tattooing—the only one he would tolerate on such a fine arm. It was, he thought, a unique design—a curvaceous blonde wearing pink diapers. Below the blonde was the name "Booboo."

"Radar?"

His attention returned quickly to the screen.

"Roger, Skipper! Target! Strong blip four degrees left. Eight miles! Looks like he's about five hundred feet below us!"

A slow smile crept across Lieutenant Mowbray's lean face.

"Sparks! Get on the horn! Advise Sea Frontier . . . interception Four-two-zero completed at fifty-six!"

The B-17 banked through the murk, and soon the two ships flew as partners within a half-mile of each other—invisible yet together.

Leonard Wilby had begun to shake again and he found himself staring at the glistening surface of the hardwood tray for long moments, as if it might provide some measure of calm. Yet the tray was unrewarding. There was no answer written on it, no set of figures neatly spaced to rebuke him and show where he had made any mistake.

He went back over his flight log once more, searching for a lost eleven minutes. He tugged at his second chin and tried to concentrate on the simple arithmetic involved in his last two wind computations. The difference between his own recorded position in the sky and the position established by the navigator of the Coast Guard plane was preposterous. Eleven minutes to the west ... eleven minutes farther from the Coast, eleven minutes which could mean the difference between crawling gratefully into bed beside Susie, or perhaps never seeing Susie again. She would smell of liquor, probably, she always did, and she might refuse to wake up, but she would be there, warm and smooth and so like a little girl napping after the exhaustion of play. But those eleven minutes? Sullivan was calling for them—insistantly, as he had every right to do. He must know whether the Coast Guard navigator was right, or if Leonard Wilby, in whom he had placed so much trust, was right.

"Leonard! Come on, fellow! What about it?
Time's wasting!"

"In a minute, Skipper. I'm still checking."

Time was wasting? Time was running out altogether. The cushion of eleven whole minutes was gone somewhere, evaporated into the atmosphere while the man who must find them and fit them carefully back into the thin fabric of the next little time space shook like an epileptic. If you can find those minutes, the shaking will cease. Your confidence will return, old boy, so discover them quickly. Stop the shaking with the minutes. Find the minutes and find Susie. Minutes, minutes ... who's got the minutes? Susie has the minutes and she has them speared on the end of a toothpick in her Martini glass. Susie, give me the minutes ... I need them instantly.

"Come on, Lennie! What's holding things up?"

"I'll be right with you."

"Hurry."

Hurry thoughts that were already speeding through the brain so fast it was almost impossible to do anything but sit back and watch them go by? You are going mad, Captain. The pressure is too much for you. Navigation is a precise and methodical business and it cannot be hurried. You must remember that I have found my way unerringly over the seas and among the stars for many years and therefore I could not be mistaken—not now, when the matter of eleven minutes means so much to all of us. It is the Coast Guard navigator who is mistaken. He is probably a very young man of little experience. He has probably been careless in his computations, because what is it to him if a mere eleven minutes vanish? He would just be eleven minutes older without suffering the passage of time. Eleven minutes to him would not seem like eleven years. He would not care about them in the slightest, because for one thing he would not have Susie to return to.

"Oh God! Sweet, merciful God!"

Leonard closed his eyes and pushed the words through his tight lips in a groaning whisper. For he had found his mistake and the enormity of it stunned him. He had done something which was past explanation—incredible. The shaking was to blame for it. It must have severed the audible senses of his brain, disconnecting them so completely they had failed to translate a most elementary message. It was easy now to read back and see exactly how and when the folly had been committed. Only a terrified man could be guilty of such absolute rejection of habit. Only a man who was frightened to his bones and blindly clinging to another man for his salvation could make such a mistake.

The sight of the fire, the engine burning against the night, must have started the fear and it had leaped upon his brain. And watching the pilots, listening to them worry about the way the ship was flying, had completed the debacle. Leonard Wilby, experienced navigator, designated by the government and the airline as capable of finding himself without the aid of a crystal ball, had made a most rudimentary error in neglecting to transpose miles-per-hour into knots!

For years he had obtained the ship's speed from the indicator above his work table. It recorded in nautical miles, or knots, to correspond with all the world's charts. But a pilot's air-speed recorded in miles per hour, as it should, since a pilot's chief concern was with approaches and stalling speeds, and miles per hour was the traditional way of marking them, as dollars and cents represented profit and loss to a business man. Pilots thought in miles-per-hour, navigators in knots. There was an important difference. A knot was approximately one and one-fifth miles. In this case the difference had become eleven priceless minutes. Leonard could remember it very clearly now. He had verbally asked Sullivan for their speed instead of taking it from his own instrument. Sullivan, watching the flight panel, had simply called off numbers—one thirty-two, and one thirty-six. He was speaking in miles per hour and Leonard was listening in knots. And without thinking he had written the figures down as knots on his log. Later, matched against his last position fix, the projected combination gave promise that they would reach the Coast more quickly—eleven minutes sooner than they actually would.

"Skipper?" The shaking had stopped very suddenly and now Leonard was perfectly calm. His mind was clear and he was surprised to discover that he was no longer afraid. He stood up and hitched his pants over his potbelly. "Skipper, can you come here a minute?" He knew what he had to say and somehow it would be a relief to confess his felony.

Sullivan came quickly to bend over his navigation table. "Well?"

"I got bad news." Leonard swallowed and watched the concern set more firmly into Sullivan's eyes. "The Coast Guard is right. I made a dumb kid's mistake. You can add eleven minutes on to our coast estimate."

"Eleven minutes . . . ?" Sullivan shook his head unbelievingly. "You sure?"

"I am now. I must have been out of my head. I'm sorry, Skipper. I guess I was just scared. . . ."

Sullivan did not look up from the chart. The knobs on his jawbones moved slowly back and forth, and for a moment Leonard wondered if he understood what he had said. He appeared to shrink in physical stature as Leonard had seen him do earlier. He became a bent man, more aged suddenly than Dan or Leonard himself, and it was easy to pity him. As Leonard stood waiting, the idea of pitying Sullivan fascinated him until he could think of nothing else. Sullivan, too, would be thinking of the Coast, of the lights there, and of dear people waiting. Then gradually Sullivan's face became firm again and the knobs were still. Leonard knew instinctively that he had reached the only decision left to him, really the one he had favored all along. He lit a cigarette and it must have been his last because he crumpled the package slowly and tossed it onto the chart. He reached across the table and took up the hardwood tray. He examined it thoughtfully for a moment and passed his strong fingers across its polished surface. Then he handed the tray to Leonard and looked at him not accusingly, but rather as a man determined to blame himself.

"I hope this will float," he said quietly.

There was now a gigantic cleavage in the sky-space which held the two airplanes. The ships broke out very suddenly from the clouds' captivity, and temporarily without hindrance, they swam across an immense womblike cavern. All about them the clouds formed high, vaporous ramparts. Straight down, the black sea served as a foundation for these walls and the only illumination came faintly from the stars.

The path of the ships across this chasm was marked only by their navigation lights. Those on Four-two-zero blinked alternately red, white, and green, in the special manner of airliners. Those on the Coast Guard plane were steady. They emerged almost simultaneously from the western embankment of cloud and continued toward the east as if supported on invisible wires.

For several minutes they moved smoothly together across this space, signaling to each other with their landing lights like fireflies parading. As the ships neared the eastern side of the opening, their minute stature in the scheme of things was emphasized by their slow approach to the clouds. In spite of the actual speed, they appeared to crawl toward the east, and when at last they were once more swallowed in cloud, their passage was ignored by the sky.

The men who controlled the limping progress of Four-two-zero were long since disenchanted with the sky. Yet the break in the cloud deck gave them a little respite, in which visually observing a like creation, they were able to believe again that their own world had not abandoned them. The actual sight of the B-17, her graceful lines barely outlined in the starlight, was of greater morale value than all of the radio conversations with impersonal voices sunk beyond the horizon. Though they were well aware that the men on the B-17 were helpless to lend immediate aid—they could not trail a tow rope and pull the lame hulk homeward—still the sense of existing at the wrong end of a telescope was gone. With this and the temporary smoothness of the air and the cessation of rain, their spirits rose until they were once more inspired to act as if they could control their futures. And so they peered out of the left window eagerly, leaning across each other and shading their eyes, staring at the B-17, absorbing the sweet fact of its presence slowly.

Sullivan broke their spellbound observation just before they plunged into the eastern wall of cloud and his voice had regained much of its authority.

"Hobie," he said firmly. "You go back now. Dan will take your place. Take the Gibson Girl along and get the passengers set for ditching. You'll have plenty of time . . . so use it. I'll turn on the seat belt sign ten minutes before we start for the water. Have everything set by then. When I turn on the no smoking sign, you and Spalding take your own brace and hang on."

"How about the rear door?" Hobie took off his earphones and hung them carefully on a hook at his side. He smoothed his hair automatically and stood up. His young face was covered with perspiration and his eyes were puffy, as if he had just awakened. He looked even younger than his twenty-two years, in the way that a young man who is really tired and suddenly dependent on bravado, can seem physically to recapture his childhood. "When shall I let the rear door go?"

"As soon as you're sure we've stopped. Don't hurry . . . remember. Get your people in the raft and wait as long as you can for us. If we can get together . . . it will be just that much better."

"Okay." He moved around the control pedestal and stepped down beside Sullivan. He looked thoughtfully at Leonard and then at Dan. This was a separation, a division of effort which he obviously viewed with distaste. Now he would be forced to make innumerable decisions on his own, and however small they might be, he knew they would have to be right.

"Good luck to you guys," he said sheepishly.

He tried a smile and then walked reluctantly aft toward the passenger cabin. As he passed through the crew compartment he pulled down the Gibson Girl from the receptacle over the bunk which held it. This was a small, wonderfully compact radio transmitter, so-called because of the fashion in which its waterproof case was curved. Hobie, who was not at all sure about the derivation of the name since he could not remember ever having seen any girl named Gibson in the movies, was preoccupied with the technicalities of the machine. He mentally reviewed its remarkable operational ability and remembered that although it fitted under his arm quite easily, it had been the savior of many distressed persons. By simply turning a crank, its signaled SOS could be heard for more than a hundred miles and any surface or air ship could take a bearing on it. This was, he knew, one of the latest types and was equipped with a device for automatically tripping emergency alarm bells on ships scattered over a wide area. A kite for carrying the antenna aloft was provided if there was wind on the surface, and a hydrogen balloon was available if there was calm. It was a very wonderful little machine, capable of withstanding the most rugged treatment—yet Hobie held it tenderly against his side as he passed through the cabin door.

"All right, Dan," Sullivan said. "I'll take her now." He leaned forward and held the control wheel while Dan slipped out of the left seat. Their eyes met as they exchanged places, but they said nothing. The flight deck bounced as the ship re-entered the overcast and the rain came hissing angrily once more.

Dan did not reoccupy Hobie's seat immediately. Sullivan had put on his headphones and if any further communication was necessary during the next few minutes he could handle the message himself.

Dan studied the fuel gauges, forcing himself to read them pessimistically. Then he did some simple arithmetic. The total in all of the tanks was now two hundred and twenty gallons! Two hundred and twenty gallons in an airplane that was consuming very close to two hundred gallons each hour, became a very simple equation. Too simple. Something would have to give very soon.

Leonard was bent over his electric altimeter and stopwatch, unhappily seeking confirmation of the wind he already marked as a traitor. Dan stepped back until he stood beside him.

"Anything new with the wind, Lennie?"

"No."

"We're not very fat then?"

"No. I wish . . . Oh Christ, I wish we had another ten minutes of fuel! Just another ten minutes. . . ."

"You're sure that would do it, Lennie? You're *sure* now?" Dan's manner was merely curious and the tone of his questioning was as easy as it might have been on a routine flight. He could have been asking Leonard if he knew the league status of a baseball team. As he stood there, slowly passing the end of his finger down the long crease in his cheek, some of his calm was caught up by Leonard and he laughed bitterly.

"As they say in the books . . . I have now positively established our exact whereabouts. Ten more minutes of fuel would see us through this thing."

"How much would the wind have to increase in velocity to accomplish that little thing?"

"Twenty knots in the next hour."

"That's asking for a lot."

"It couldn't happen so I'm not even asking. But if it swung around a little more on our tail, and it seems to be doing that . . . well, it just could be." With a forlorn gesture Leonard placed his hands on his knees. He looked up at Dan and shook his grey head. "Ah well . . . I guess they'll pick us up before we get too damp. But it sure will worry Susie. She'll lay down the law. Probably insist I quit flying."

"Will you?"

Leonard squinted his eyes as if the question was a complete surprise to him and finding the answer brought him acute pain. He took his hands from his knees to massage his belly and then returned them decisively to his knees again.

"*No*, by God!"

"In other words, you're not going to get gypped out of your pension?"

"Something like that."

"You'll get it, Lennie. I've got a feeling you'll collect."

Dan walked back to the crew compartment. It was noisier here, with the engines pounding only a few feet beyond the thin aluminum skin. But he wanted to be alone for a few minutes and have a last try at solving the problem which had troubled him ever since the first radio contact with the Coast Guard plane.

In the darkness he passed beneath the overhead ventilator. A fine stream of rain water leaked through the ventilator and splashed down his face and the back of his neck. Swearing softly, he stepped away from the ventilator and switched on the light. He yanked the black curtain across the passageway leading to the flight deck and switched on the compartment light. He leaned against the bulkhead, lit a cigarette, and thoughtfully watched the water pour down from the ventilator. Below it, there was now a large pool on the deck.

If Sullivan had his way, Dan thought, the water in this compartment would very soon be far above anyone's neck.

He drew hard at his cigarette. This was hardly the sort of thing he had expected when he asked Garfield to let him fly again. He had foreseen that uncomfortable situations of a minor nature might come to pass and had deliberately prepared himself to face such embarrassment, but this . . . ? On any flight he was likely to be the oldest crew member and as such, he had told himself, he should know enough to keep his mouth shut no matter what the temptation to draw on thirty-five years of flying experience. This was different—or was it? There were so many factors to confuse the situation. It was time, almost past time, to do some swift and very clear thinking.

Commandwise, the laws of the sky were almost exactly like the laws of the sea. The captain of an airplane was held solely responsible for the performance and safety of his ship; he automatically assumed the blame for any accident no matter whose fault it actually might be. His power, too, was absolute, and the cases of mutiny on aircraft were so rare they could not be worth considering. Once in ten thousand flights a crew member might openly question a captain's judgment, but such arguments, if the captain permitted any discussion to develop, were inevitably settled on the ground. It was not that most captains closed their minds to suggestion the moment their wives sewed four stripes on their uniform sleeves—rather that any large aircraft was a very fast-moving, highly complicated beast—and the crew members themselves were the first to realize someone aboard must be in supreme command. At two or three hundred miles-per-hour, arguments could consume priceless minutes. No captain had ever been known to try deliberate suicide and so for all practical purposes arguments just didn't happen.

And now Sullivan intended to ditch. He proposed to put his plane and all the souls on board into the wild sea at night when the safety of land was only ten minutes further. Was he doing the right thing—the *only* thing that could be done?

It was a question Dan had asked himself innumerable times during the past hour. If he could be sure that Sullivan was right, then he wouldn't care so much what happened—since Alice and Tony were killed nothing seemed to matter very much—but *was* Sullivan right? Of course he would want to ditch while he still had enough fuel to give him power of maneuver. And he was wise in flying as long as he could so that the nearly empty tanks would give the ship greater buoyancy on the water. As captain it was not his duty to gamble. Gambling was for people who could afford to lose. But there were only those ten minutes—and fuel gauges were not exact to the gallon, any more than Leonard Wilby's navigation was exact to the mile. So there *could* be a chance of making San Francisco airport, and if a part of that chance was luck, then luck must also play a part in how Sullivan managed finally to hit the water. The balance, it seemed, was almost exactly equal.

It was Sullivan's choice. Apparently he had already made his final decision, and persuading him otherwise now could be both difficult and dangerous—particularly, Dan reminded himself, when the persuader occupied a subordinate position. Much would depend on how thoroughly Sullivan had been able to retake command of himself. For a while, he had been perilously near the breaking point. The signs were unmistakable; yet now he seemed again forceful and sure of his way.

Dan tried to whistle but the tune that came to his lips was mournful and he soon stopped.

Would Sullivan listen to an old man he had every right to classify as obsolete? How secret was his pity for Dan Roman— a beat-up has-been? It was the custom these days for the younger men, highly trained in prescribed schools, to politely tolerate the old timers. They respected them, not for what they could do, because often as not they were past the keen edge of top flying, but rather the respect came from an appreciation of what they *had* done. They had built a new world, and it had passed them by very swiftly, on the very speed which gave it life. Old timers, which included any pilot who had flown before 1935 or so, were like antique furniture—admired and even loved, perhaps, but often suspected of functional instability. And in recent years, the science of aerial flight was progressing so rapidly even the younger men were having difficulty keeping pace with it. Yet dammit . . . this situation was not science. It was luck.

Dan forced himself to remember Garfield's words. "You'll find out you've had it, Dan. This is a kid's game now . . . young, bright guys with a cap full of education and minds that work like high-pressure pumps. Hang up your helmet and goggles and forget it." So?

Sullivan, except for his temporary lapse, was exactly the kind of younger man Garfield was talking about. He was even more. He already had a great deal of over-ocean experience behind him, and he would have every reason to discount the opinions of a man he knew had principally confined himself to

318

flying smaller airplanes over dry land. And he could be right, Dan—both in his refusal to accept your ideas and in the decision he had already made. You really haven't admitted that.

He held out his cigarette so that it was directly beneath the ventilator and let the dripping stream of rainwater extinguish it. Am I wrong in believing that Sullivan should carry on until the tanks are dry? Am I wrong in believing that, by pressing luck, we can make it? Am I committing another crime in trying to change his decision . . . and maybe succeeding?

He rose and crossed the compartment to the bunk. Reaching over it, he pulled three life vests from their storage place. He removed the rubberized protective cover from one and placed the life vest over his head. He tied the straps around his legs and chest, then he set deliberately to the task of unfastening the life raft from the heavy straps which held it over the bunk.

In its disinflated state the raft resembled an overlarge bedroll. It was very heavy and awkward to handle. Later, when the ship had come to rest on the sea, they would pull the emergency release on the astrodome and presumably have strength remaining to push the raft straight up through the small opening.

He moved the raft to the ready position by the flight-deck passageway and, picking up the two remaining vests, walked forward. He handed one of the vests to Leonard.

"The color may not become you, Lennie . . . but they're in fashion."

"Thanks for nothing." Leonard stared solemnly at the yellow vest. "I never thought I'd really have to put one of these things on."

"Better check the cartridges and make sure they're okay."

"Yeah. . . ."

As Leonard pulled the cover from his vest, Dan moved forward to Sullivan. He placed the last vest on his lap. Sullivan said thanks, but he kept his eyes on the instruments.

319

Dan sat down in the right seat. Taking his time, moving with elaborate slowness, he loosened his tie, buckled his safety belt, and put on his headphones. Then he leaned across the control pedestal to Sullivan.

"Our air speed looks a little better."

"A bit."

"Lennie says if we can pick up ten minutes we can make it."

"If you didn't know ... Lennie has always been an optimist." Still Sullivan kept his eyes grimly on the instruments. The amber-red light from the panel cast deep shadows upward on his face as if a sculptor had worked at his features only from below; his strong chin and his mouth were unnaturally chiseled and his eyes appeared half-wild in their concentration.

"Lennie might be right," Dan said, without seeming to care.

"If he's wrong we've had it ... maybe wipe out a few bridges or apartment houses. I can't risk it."

"It's going to be a risk ditching. It will be rough down there."

"I know it."

"If we hit wrong, we've had it, too."

"I know that, dammit!" A new sharpness came to Sullivan's voice.

Dan waited for his mouth to relax. "Maybe now ... we might try easing off a little on the power?"

"A message came from Garfield while you were back there. He suggested a lower rpm."

"Why not try it?"

"I thought about it a long time ago. It won't work. She's barely flying now."

"Any objection if I try?"

For the first time Sullivan looked directly at Dan. It was only for the space of a second, yet Dan saw that there was neither hostility nor friendliness in his eyes. He was dead—frozen hard in his decision.

When he looked away Dan reached for the three operating propeller controls. He gradually pulled them back until the engines were only turning over sixteen hundred revolutions per minute. The sound of the engines fell to a low murmur, almost as if they had ceased to work at all. Dan ignored the placard which boldly stated that the engines should not be operated at such a low rpm. At a time like this it was a law to be broken. He told himself that nothing would break; not for a while, anyway. He watched the air-speed. It, too, was falling off. One hundred and thirty . . . one hundred and twenty-five . . . one hundred and twenty . . . one hundred and fifteen. But the fuel flow meters also dropped. She was burning thirty pounds per hour less for each engine. Enough, *maybe* enough to make San Francisco!

Sullivan squirmed uneasily in his seat. His hands gripped the control wheel so tightly it became a rigid part of his hands and his arms.

"It won't work! She's going to stall on me!"

Dan pushed forward on the throttles until they were wide open. The combination of very low rpm and full manifold pressure, he knew, was terrifically hard on the engines. The fuel flow increased only slightly, but the air-speed returned to one hundred and twenty.

"This is no good," Sullivan said. "We'll blow a jug."

"What's the difference? We'll blow 'em all if we ditch. Hang on. We'll make it."

"You're crazy. We've tried it and it won't do. Put those props back up where they belong!" The sweat was beginning to varnish Sullivan's face again. It broke out very suddenly as if welling up from a thousand springs. Fighting for a hundred feet of altitude that he had lost, he pulled back angrily on the control column and suddenly a quiver passed through the ship— the first warning of a stall. Sullivan quickly pushed the nose down again.

"Put those goddamned props back where they were!"

"Nothing doin', skipper."

"That's an order!"

Dan kept his hands on his knees. Sullivan looked at him in astonished anger and then reached for the controls himself. Dan caught his arm and held it firmly.

"Hang on, chum! We'll make it this way! You can do it, man! Just hang on. Fly, and let me pray!"

"Are you tired of living? If we try an instrument approach at San Francisco we'll run out of gas right in the middle of it!"

"Maybe yes, maybe no. Nothing is for sure yet. Try it this way for thirty minutes, will you? Don't be so goddamned anxious to go for a swim!"

"It's crazy! She's starting to shake again!" The air-speed had indeed fallen off to one hundred and ten—and Sullivan had lost another valuable hundred feet of altitude.

"Let her shake! The hell with it as long as she don't fall off on a wing. Let her mush down a little if you have to. Look at our gas consumption . . . only one-fifty per hour! Hang on and *fly*, man!"

Sullivan glanced at the fuel flow meters. His eyes that had been so empty of hope now brightened a little. He pulled his hand slowly away from the propeller controls.

"If it doesn't work," Dan said, "you won't have to get me fired. I'll quit."

Sullivan took a deep breath and sighed heavily.

"If it doesn't work . . . it won't make any difference what you do."

Then, like a man preparing to jump across an abyss he knew was impossibly wide, Sullivan set himself to the intricate, nerve-scraping struggle of flying an airplane that was not really flying.

ALONE
FROM
THE SHEPHERD

———

by FREDERICK FORSYTH

Frederick Forsyth is one of the premier thriller writers of all time. His master-piece was *Day of the Jackal*, which receives my nomination as the best thriller ever written. Among his monster international bestsellers are *The Odessa File, No Comebacks, The Dogs of War*, and *The Fourth Protocol*. Yet before he was a writer Forsyth was a pilot; at the age of nineteen he was the youngest fighter pi-lot in the Royal Air Force.

In the following excerpt from *The Shepherd* the narrator is flying a single-seat Vampire jet from a base in southern Germany home to England on Christ-mas Eve. One of the first jet fighters, the Vampire had fuel for just eighty minutes of flight and lacked an ejection seat. Alone, over the North Sea on a cold winter's night . . . here is how Forsyth told it.

The problem started ten minutes out over the North Sea, and it started so quietly that it was several minutes before I realized I had one at all. For some time I had been unaware that the low hum coming through my headphones into my ears had ceased, to be replaced by the strange nothingness of total silence. I must have been failing to concentrate, my thoughts being of home and my waiting family. The first time I knew was when I flicked a glance downward to check my course on the compass. Instead of being rock-steady on 265 degrees, the needle was drifting lazily round the clock, passing through east, west, south, and north with total impartiality.

I swore a most unseasonal sentiment against the compass and the instrument fitter who should have checked it for 100-percent reliability. Compass failure at night, even a brilliant moonlit night such as the one beyond the cockpit Perspex, was no fun. Still, it was not too serious: there was a standby compass—the alcohol kind. But, when I glanced at it, that one seemed to be in trouble, too. The needle was swinging wildly. Apparently something had jarred the case—which isn't uncommon. In any event, I could call up Lakenheath in a few minutes and they would give me a GCA—Ground Controlled Approach—the second-by-second instructions that a well-equipped airfield can give a pilot to bring him home in the worst of weathers, following his progress on ultraprecise radar screens, watching him descend all the way to the tarmac, tracing his position in the sky yard by yard and second by second. I glanced at my watch: thirty-four minutes airborne. I could try to raise Lakenheath now, at the outside limit of my radio range.

Before trying Lakenheath, the correct procedure would be to inform Channel D, to which I was tuned, of my little problem, so they could advise Lakenheath that I was on my way without a compass. I pressed the TRANSMIT button and called:

"Celle, Charlie Delta, Celle, Charlie Delta, calling North Beveland Control. . . ."

I stopped. There was no point in going on. Instead of the lively crackle of static and the sharp sound of my own voice coming back into my own ears, there was a muffled murmur inside my oxygen mask. My own voice speaking . . . and going nowhere. I tried again. Same result. Far back across the wastes of the black and bitter North Sea, in the warm, cheery concrete complex of North Beveland Control, men sat back from their control panel, chatting and sipping their steaming coffee and cocoa. And they could not hear me. The radio was dead.

Fighting down the rising sense of panic that can kill a pilot faster than anything else, I swallowed and slowly counted to ten. Then I switched to Channel F and tried to raise Lakenheath, ahead of me amid the Suffolk countryside, lying in its forest of pine trees south of Thetford, beautifully equipped with its GCA system for bringing home lost aircraft. On Channel F the radio was as dead as ever. My own muttering into the oxygen mask was smothered by the surrounding rubber. The steady whistle of my own jet engine behind me was my only answer.

It's a very lonely place, the sky, and even more so the sky on a winter's night. And a single-seater jet fighter is a lonely home, a tiny steel box held aloft on stubby wings, hurled through the freezing emptiness by a blazing tube throwing out the strength of six thousand horses every second. But the loneliness is offset, canceled out, by the knowledge that at the touch of a button on the throttle, the pilot can talk to other human beings, people who care about him, men and women who staff a network of stations around the world; just one touch of that button, the TRANSMIT button, and scores of them in control towers across the land that are tuned to his channel can hear him call for help. When the pilot transmits, on every one of those screens a line of light streaks from the center of the screen to the outside rim, which is marked with figures, from one to three hundred and sixty. Where the streak of light hits the ring, that is where the aircraft lies in relation to the control tower listening to him. The control towers are linked, so with two cross bearings they can locate his position to within a few hundred yards. He is not lost any more. People begin working to bring him down.

The radar operators pick up the little dot he makes on their screens from all the other dots; they call him up and give him instructions. "Begin your descent now, Charlie Delta. We have you now. . . ." Warm, experienced voices, voices which control an array of electronic devices that can reach out across the winter sky, through the ice and rain, above the snow and cloud, to pluck the lost one from his deadly infinity and bring him down to the flare-lit runway that means home and life itself.

When the pilot transmits. But for that he must have a radio. Before I had finished testing Channel J, the international emergency channel, and obtained the same negative result, I knew my ten-channel radio set was as dead as the dodo.

It had taken the RAF two years to train me to fly their fighters for them, and most of that time had been spent in training precisely for emergency procedures. The important thing, they used to say in flying school, is not to know how to fly in perfect conditions; it is to fly through an emergency and stay alive. Now the training was beginning to take effect.

While I was vainly testing my radio channels, my eyes scanned the instrument panel in front of me. The instruments told their own message. It was no coincidence the compass and the radio had failed together; both worked off the aircraft's electrical circuits. Somewhere beneath my feet, amid the miles of brightly colored wiring that make up the circuits, there had been a main fuse blowout. I reminded myself, idiotically, to forgive the instrument fitter and blame the electrician. Then I took stock of the nature of my disaster.

The first thing to do in such a case, I remembered old Flight Sergeant Norris telling us, is to reduce throttle setting from cruise speed to a slower setting, to give maximum flight endurance.

"We don't want to waste valuable fuel, do we, gentlemen? We might need it later. So we reduce the power setting from 10,000 revolutions per minute to 7,200. That way we will fly a little slower, but we will stay in the air rather longer, won't we, gentlemen?" He always referred to us all being in the same emergency at the same time, did Sergeant Norris. I eased the throttle back and watched the rev counter. It operates on its own generator and so I hadn't lost that, at least. I waited until the Goblin was turning over at about 7,200 rpm, and felt the aircraft slow down. The nose rose fractionally, so I adjusted the flight trim to keep her straight and level.

The main instruments in front of a pilot's eyes are six, including the compass. The five others are the air-speed indicator, the altimeter, the vertical-speed indicator, the bank indicator (which tells him if he's banking, i.e., turning, to left or right), and the slip indicator (which tells him if he's skidding crabwise across the sky). Two of these are electrically operated, and they had gone the same way as my compass. That left me with the three pressure-operated instruments—air-speed indicator, altimeter and vertical-speed indicator. In other words, I knew how fast I was going, how high I was and if I were diving or climbing.

It is perfectly possible to land an aircraft with only these three instruments, judging the rest by those old navigational aids, the human eyes. Possible, that is, in conditions of brilliant weather, by daylight and with no cloud in the sky. It is possible, just possible, though not advisable, to try to navigate a fast-moving jet by dead reckoning, using the eyes, looking down and identifying the curve of the coast where it makes an easily recognizable pattern, spotting a strange-shaped reservoir, the glint of a river that the map strapped to the thigh says can only be the Ouse, or the Trent, or the Thames. From lower down it is possible to differentiate Norwich Cathedral tower from Lincoln Cathedral tower, if you know the countryside intimately. By night it is not possible.

The only things that show up at night, even on a bright moonlit night, are the lights. These have patterns when seen from the sky. Manchester looks different from Birmingham; Southampton can be recognized from the shape of its massive harbor and Solent, cut out in black (the sea shows up black) against the carpet of the city's lights. I knew Norwich very well, and if I could identify the great curving bulge of the Norfolk coast line from Lowestoft, round through Yarmouth to Cromer, I could find Norwich, the only major sprawl of lights set twenty miles inland from all points on the coast. Five miles north of Norwich, I knew, was the fighter airfield of Merriam St. George, whose red indicator beacon would be blipping out its Morse identification signal into the night. There, if they only had the sense to switch on the airfield lights when they heard me screaming at low level up and down the airfield, I could land safely.

I began to let the Vampire down slowly toward the oncoming coast, my mind feverishly working out how far behind schedule I was through the reduced speed. My watch told me forty-three minutes airborne. The coast of Norfolk had to be somewhere ahead of my nose, five miles below. I glanced up at the full moon, like a searchlight in the glittering sky, and thanked her for her presence.

As the fighter slipped toward Norfolk the sense of loneliness gripped me tighter and tighter. All those things that had seemed so beautiful as I climbed away from the airfield in Lower Saxony now seemed my worst enemies. The stars were no longer impressive in their brilliance; I thought of their hostility, sparkling away there in the timeless, lost infinities of endless space. The night sky, its stratospheric temperature fixed, night and day alike, at an unchanging fifty-six degrees below zero, became in my mind a limitless prison creaking with the cold. Below me lay the worst of them all, the heavy brutality of the North Sea, waiting to swallow up me and my plane and bury us for endless eternity in a liquid black crypt where nothing moved nor would ever move again. And no one would ever know.

At 15,000 feet and still diving, I began to realize that a fresh, and for me the last, enemy had entered the field. There was no ink-black sea three miles below me, no necklace of twinkling seaside lights somewhere up ahead. Far away, to right and left, ahead and no doubt behind me, the light of the moon reflected on a flat and endless sea of white. Perhaps only a hundred, two hundred feet thick, but enough. Enough to blot out all vision, enough to kill me. The East Anglian fog had moved in.

LZ AMBUSH
FROM *THE DELTA*

———

by MARSHALL HARRISON

The blood and insanity of the low-and-slow war over South Vietnam was the subject for this fine novel by Marshall Harrison, who, like the hero of the tale, Sam Brooks, served a tour as a Forward Air Controller. The mark of a good writer is his ability to make the characters live in our imagination; Harrison's leap off the page.

So here we go, into combat in a Cessna O–1 Bird Dog with some smoke rockets on the wing and a sack of smoke grenades in the back seat. The men who flew this war had big *cojones*, a fact which will become readily apparent.

"OK, Blade Flight, this is Blackjack One One. I'll want your bombs in pairs. We're going to spread 'em on both sides of the LZ. I'm in for the mark now."

Sam brought the nose of his aircraft high above the horizon and stared at the wooded tree lines stretching along both sides of the bare red earth that would shortly receive the helicopters. The trees were a dull green, muted by the dust at the end of the dry season. He picked his spot and coordinated left aileron and rudder pressure to roll the aircraft onto its wing, then shoved the nose down toward the ground.

The tree line quickly filled his windscreen and he risked a quick glance at the altimeter—eighteen hundred feet. He let the speed build up until the slipstream whistled loudly through the opened window. He pressed the firing button on the stick at fifteen hundred feet and heard, then saw, the rocket leave the wing, trailing a thin wisp of smoke from the ignited motor. At twelve hundred feet he began the dive recovery, ending with the aircraft in a hard, climbing turn. Sam glanced over his shoulder to find the white smoke ball billowing up from the trees. "There's your first target, Blade Lead. Hit my smoke."

"Roger, Lead is in from the north, FAC and target in sight. I'll be off target to the east."

Sam twisted his aircraft into a tight, level turn until he saw the sun glinting from the wings of the diving F-100 jet fighter-bomber. He quickly checked its run-in line, staying in the turn to keep the fighter on his nose. "You're cleared in hot, Blade Lead," Sam said.

The two five-hundred-pound bombs fell cleanly from the wings of the attacking jet as it passed Sam. Twin condensation trails burbled from each wing tip as the fighter began its pull-out. The bombs, with drogue slabs extended to slow their flight, disappeared into the tree line, and near-simultaneous explosions cleared twin circular areas in the forest. The instantaneous fusing had caused the weapons to leave only shallow craters, but they did create havoc with the foliage.

"Lead's off to the east," the pilot grunted, fighting hard against the heavy g forces of the pullout.

"Good bombs, Lead," said Sam, already switching his attention to the other aircraft. "Blade Two, put yours about a hundred meters south of Lead's craters."

"Rog. Blade Two is in hot from the west. FAC and target in sight."

Sam eyed the roll-in of the sleek jet before he responded. "You're cleared in hot, Blade Two."

Two more explosions killed another hundred years of tree growth. Sam had shoved the nose of the Bird Dog down toward the smoldering jungle before Blade Two began his recovery. He leveled at five hundred feet, alternately kicking the rudders and moving the stick back and forth to prevent becoming a stable target for any potential gunners as he searched for movement beneath the trees. He didn't see a thing. He shoved the throttle full forward to begin a maximum climb back to a safer altitude. Just because he didn't see them didn't mean they weren't there.

Methodically, he worked the ordnance of the fighters along the dense growth surrounding the landing zone. Blade Flight was the second set of attack aircraft he'd used prepping the area for the helicopter assault, now already airborne. Smoke from the bombs and dust was beginning to obscure the clearing. Sam was satisfied with the bomb pattern he had laid around the LZ. He glanced at each wing to confirm he'd used all four of his marking rockets to put in the two flights of fighters, then lowered the aircraft's nose for a last assessment run.

The trees had been tumbled aside like giant matchsticks and he saw nothing moving among them. The area was far from pristine, however. The last pair of bombs had uncovered several irregularly spaced rectangular holes that he instantly recognized as reinforced bunkers. Sam hadn't a clue as to whether they were or had been occupied, for he could see no casualties. It was something for the helicopter gunships to check out before the main force went in.

"Blade Lead, this is Blackjack One One. Your BDA will have to be incomplete until we get some troops on the ground, but I'm going to give you a hundred percent of your ordnance in the target area. Looks like Blade Two uncovered some bunkers with his last bombs. I'll forward anything the crunchies turn up. You're cleared out of the area. See ya later."

"Roger, Blackjack. Thanks, and take care of yourself. Blade Two, let's go to company frequency."

"Two. Rog."

As soon as the two F-100s left Sam's radio frequency he heard another pilot calling him. This voice had the curious, vibrating quality readily identifiable as coming from a helicopter. "Blackjack One One," it warbled, "this is Red Lead."

"Go, Red Lead. Blackjack One One here."

"Rog. First stick is about five minutes out. What's the situation?"

"Red Lead, Blackjack. I've put in two sets of fighters along either side of the LZ. Negative movement seen. However, the last bombs uncovered bunkers on the eastern approach to the LZ. I can see five of them but they extend back under the trees. There's no confirmation as to whether they're occupied. You might want to send your gunnies on ahead to check 'em out before you come in."

"Roger that, Blackjack. That's what we'll do. Pink Lead, you want to take your gun elements on in and do like the man says while we do a slow three-sixty turn out here?"

"Roger that," a new voice said over the radio. "Let's go, Pinks."

Sam picked up the flight of four gunships as they approached from the south, then slammed into a tight turn in front of them and aimed for the bunker area. He'd been watching the bunkers from altitude and had almost convinced himself that they were old and no longer used. He descended to five hundred feet and flew directly at the bunkers visible in the blast-cleared area. He reached behind him and unhooked a smoke grenade from the wire behind his seat, pulling the pin but keeping the tongue depressed. When he was in the proper position, he straightened his arm out the window and released it. Leaning outside he watched the purple smoke trail to the ground and land squarely on the target area. "Pink Lead, this is Blackjack. Smoke's away."

"Rog. Pink Lead has Goofy Grape."

"That's it."

"We're on our way toward it."

Sam climbed up to two thousand feet to be sure he was out of everyone's way. The four gunships fell into a line astern, split into two elements as they approached the smoke, then began a counterclockwise wheel above the exposed bunkers. The leader dipped his nose and unleashed a high-explosive rocket toward the bunkers. There was no return fire or movement.

"Red Lead, this is Pink Lead," the gunship leader called the troop-carrying slicks' commander. "We've found the bunkers but it looks like nobody's home. I think it ought to be OK to bring 'em on in."

"Red Lead. Roger that."

Sam sat high and watched the first stick of slicks approach the barren LZ. They carried the elements of two companies of the 45th Ranger Battalion, one of the better fighting forces in the delta. Another stick of Hueys would be a couple of minutes behind the leader. A third would follow the second element. After they disgorged their initial loads, the birds would return to Soc Trang for the remainder of the troops. Things looked routine to Sam as the first stick approached the LZ. He opened his canteen and took a long drink of tepid water, shuddering at its chemical afterbite, then rescrewed the top and placed the canteen on the floor. Slightly bored now that his part in the operation was presumably completed, he rested his chin in his hand, arm propped on the window's ledge, and watched the show.

The four helicopters began to slow for their approach. A germ of uneasiness crept into Sam's mind as the leader disappeared into a red dust cloud kicked up by its own rotor. With true formation integrity the remainder of the slick flight followed their leader into the red murk.

"Red Flight, this is Red Lead! Abort! Abort! I'm instruments in the dust! Go around! Go arou—" His transmission was cut abruptly as the second Huey crashed down through his canopy, its skid breaking the air commander's neck and nearly severing the copilot's head from his body. Vietnamese Rangers tumbled from the opened doors, falling to their deaths beneath the flailing metal carcasses of the helicopters. Red Three and Four added to the carnage when they delayed an instant too long in responding to their flight commander's order to abort the landing. They unknowingly revenged his death by slamming unseen into Red Two. Sam watched in horrified silence as shards of blade, metal, and human body parts were tossed high above the red dust. He pressed the transmit button for the radio but found he couldn't speak, so he released it.

"Jesus Christ! Green and Purple Leaders, this is Pink Lead. Abort! I say again! Abort the approach!"

The next two sticks of troop carriers had arrived over the LZ but now broke away to circle aimlessly, their landing aborted by the gunship commander.

As the dust slowly cleared, the pattern of events became sickeningly clear. Red Two had landed squarely atop his leader's ship, and Three and Four had smashed onto it in turn. Two of the helicopters burned brightly, and Rangers were scattered about in the red dust as if sown by a giant hand. Some scrubbed angel wings into the loose dust; others lay very still.

The gunship commander took control. "Green Leader and Purple Leader, this is Pink Lead. All of Red Flight has dinged on the LZ, but I think it was because of the viz and not because the LZ's hot. Come on in but stay well clear of the center where Red Flight is down. It's a damned dust bowl there. You should be all right if Green takes the far right side and Purple the left. I say again, it's a cold LZ and Green Flight takes the extreme right, Purple the left."

The two sticks of helicopters touched down almost simultaneously at opposite sides of the wide LZ. The dust was still thick but nothing like Red Flight had tried to penetrate. The pilots gave each other more help by separating their individual touchdown points by a considerable distance. As they disgorged their troops another voice began to yell over the tactical net.

"Pink Lead! Pink Lead! This is Jolly Six! We're taking fire from the bunkers east of the LZ, back up into the tree line. We're taking fire from the bunkers to the east of the LZ."

"Jolly Six, Pink Lead. I heard you the first time" came the voice of the gunship leader. He sounded as though there could be few surprises left for him anywhere. A routine insertion had turned into tragedy right in front of him, and now this.

"Where's the heaviest source of fire, Jolly Six?" the gun team leader asked the American adviser on the ground with the Rangers.

"All along the eastern tree line, well back into the trees. There's also some from the northeast that's pretty heavy as well."

"I've got you, Jolly Six. Pinks, we're going to work out in the eastern tree line, starting where those bunkers are. Ah, Blackjack, do you think you could scare up some more TACAIR if we need it?"

"Rog, Pink Lead. I'll get some cranking," said Sam, watching the horror show unfold beneath him. Some of the small figures flung about by the helicopters' crash had gotten to their feet and were wandering aimlessly in circles; then they began to fall over again. Then Sam saw the bright sparkle of automatic weapons beneath the gloom of the tree line. The addled and injured ARVN Rangers were an easy target.

Sam switched his radio selector to his control room and placed an immediate request for additional fighters. He should be able to draw on the air assets of any preplanned strike in the delta, if the system operated properly. Should no fighters be immediately available, the Direct Air Support Center would forward the request to the Tactical Operations Center in Saigon, which would authorize birds from the alert pads at Tan Son Nhut and Bien Hoa. Unfortunately, that could take half an hour, and Sam didn't think the friendlies had that long. More and more of them were playing dead.

The helicopter gunships went right for the Viet Cong's throat and paid for it. Pink Two went in for the attack; it burst into a large ball of orange flame and fell into the trees, severing large branches all the way to the ground. The remnant burned for a while, then exploded, sending a greasy plume of black smoke drifting over the tree line, obscuring the target area for the remaining gunships. Where *had* all those dinks come from? Sam wondered.

"Blackjack One One, this is Blackjack Control."

"Go ahead."

"Roger. You've got a pair of A-1s coming up. ETA in zero five. Load is snake and nape."

"Thank you," said Sam. Nape was napalm, the soapy gaseous mixture that ignited on contact with the ground to spew along the flight direction of the aircraft, searing everything in its path. It also deprived any air breathers in its vicinity of oxygen. Bombs and nape were a lethal mixture.

"Control, this is One One. What's their call sign?"

"One One, call sign of the A-1 flight is Ramrod."

Sam stayed at altitude above the carnage and watched the three remaining gunships attack the tree line. Green tracer fire from the trees met each pass. The enemy troops had obviously rushed forward after the last of the bomb explosions to engage the infantry and helicopters they'd known would be coming. It was not the first LZ prep that this VC commander had seen. He obviously knew the pattern well, and Sam was forced to admire his ingenuity. The man had kept his troops well back until the most significant danger had passed, then pressed in close to his adversary for protection against air and artillery attacks while he inflicted maximum damage. Sam suspected that the enemy commander was prepared for a quick disengagement as well. He'd have to remember that when the fighters arrived.

Another gunship limped out of the fight to the south, a victim of the concentrated fire they were receiving on each pass. The fourth and last stick of troop-carrying slicks approached the LZ as far to the west as they could get from the ground fire. The door gunners raked the trees, their red tracers licking into the gloom in search of the enemy gunners.

Doubt was creeping unbidden into Sam's thoughts. Could he have prevented this? Should he have placed the bombs differently? He shook his head to clear his thoughts. No, he'd done it right. He'd put the ordnance where logic said to put it and if he'd missed the enemy it had been because they'd been lucky or better at this business than he.

The Rangers scrambled into a defensive perimeter around the mangled remains of Red Flight. The fire had spread to all of the broken helicopters and the troops worked hurriedly to pull the bodies from them. The two remaining gunships were still doggedly making firing passes against the tree line. Sam hoped the gunship leader was still there. He had to quickly find the most productive area in which to expend the approaching fighters.

"Pink Lead, this is Blackjack. I've got a pair of A-1s inbound. ETA in about two. Can you use them?"

"Hell, yes! We're getting the shit shot out of us. If you see where we're working, you can put them in anyplace in the trees. I don't know what we've got ahold of, but it sure ain't no VC local force platoon, like they briefed. You'd best tell your Spad drivers that there's a pair of fifties down there that are real good."

"Rog. I'll do that."

Sam continued a slow orbit over the fight. The Rangers were having a difficult time moving off the LZ toward the trees. A small group leapt to their feet and charged the wood line only to lose half their number to the withering fire. The survivors flopped prone and began inching back to the comparative safety of the defensive perimeter. Sam was concentrating so intently on the carnage below that he was startled when a new voice cut into the radio.

"Blackjack One One, this is Ramrod Lead. How do you read?"

Sam switched to his UHF radio. "Ramrod Lead, this is Blackjack One One. I've got you five by five. We don't have a lot of time for briefing so listen up. The situation is this: We've got friendlies pinned on an LZ. They're taking heavy fire from the trees to their east and northeast. There are five choppers down and one other has been shot out of the fight. There are at least two .50 calibers and numerous automatic weapons in the area. You'll have to make your run-in along a north-south line to keep from overflying the friendlies. You'll need an east break-off target. Elevation here is about fifty feet and the best bailout area is as far to the west of the LZ as you can get. Go ahead with your lineup and your ETA."

"Sounds absolutely charming. OK, Ramrod is a flight of two A-1s. We're wall-to-wall with Mark-82s and a full load of .50s. If you're working where all that smoke is off our nose we ought to be with you in a couple of minutes. We're coming in from the east at five thou."

"I'm sure that's us. We're the only smoke in the area," said Sam, trying to match the languorous tones of the Spad pilot. "Incidentally, I'm out of marking rockets so we'll have to do with smoke grenades. Stand by one and I'll get the gunships cleared off."

Without waiting for a reply he quickly switched back to his VHF radio. "Pink Lead, Blackjack. If you folks can clear to the west and stay below a thousand feet I'm about ready to bring the A-1s in and go to work."

"Roger that. Pink Flight, if any of you are still left out there, let's clear to the west at five hundred feet. Get some, Blackjack!"

Sam was already switching back to the fighter frequency as he watched the remaining gunnies wheel abruptly away from the tree line and head west. He peered through the dust and rising smoke and picked up the blocky frames of the approaching A-1 flight. They looked to be a couple of thousand feet higher than his orbit. "Ramrod, this is Blackjack. Got you in sight. I should be at your two o'clock low."

The lead aircraft tilted up on one wing. "Got you, Blackjack. Is the target that big batch of woods east of where the choppers are burning?"

"Affirm. I'm heading that way now. I've got all sorts of colored smoke in here so don't be surprised if it changes on you."

"Roger. Two, let's arm 'em up and take position."

"Two. Roger."

Sam turned until he was east of the tree line, well back over the heavily forested area, figuring that there would be less opportunity for a gunner to track him through the thick foliage. He shoved the throttle forward to the stop and dropped the Bird Dog's nose below the horizon. All 213 horses of the Continental engine screamed in protest at such ham-handed treatment. He watched the airspeed indicator nudge the red line—115 miles per hour! Jesus! This was ridiculous! He'd had automobiles that could go faster than this.

He leveled at a thousand feet and reached behind the seat, groping for a smoke grenade. He picked one from the cluster. There was the clash of metal against metal as something struck the fuselage hard. He forced his eyes toward the trees and saw that he was almost to the bunker complex. He pulled the pin from the grenade, keeping the handle depressed. He altered course slightly, waited, and finally threw the grenade toward the ground. Simultaneously, he tromped heavily on the rudder, shoved the stick to the side to stand the Bird Dog on its wing, then sucked back hard on the stick. The aircraft responded with an unbelievably quick change in direction before the excessive forces caused the air flowing over the top of the wings to burble and the wings stalled. The aircraft pitched down nearly three hundred feet before Sam could release enough back pressure on the stick to let it regain flying speed.

Once out of the immediate danger area he climbed back to his perch at fifteen hundred feet and looked at the red smoke just beginning to boil through the tree canopy. "OK, Ramrod. That's your first target. Lead, hit my smoke."

"Rog. Hit the smoke. Lead is in hot from the north. FAC and target in sight."

Sam eyeballed the lead attack ship's run-in line before he spoke. "Cleared hot, Lead."

The Skyraider rolled nearly inverted, then plummeted toward the ground in a sixty-degree dive angle. Its speed brakes jutted into the wind to prevent excess speed from building during the dive. Sam imagined that he could hear the roar of the big radial engine as it wound up tightly. Two shapes fell from the wings and sped toward the jungle as the A-1 pulled agonizingly into its recovery. Streams of tracers followed as its nose slowly crept above the horizon.

"Lead's off east," the pilot grunted.

"Ramrod Two is in from the south. FAC and target in sight. Where do you want it, Blackjack?"

The southern accent told Sam that this was also an American pilot. Unusual. Normally there would be only one to a flight. "Put yours about thirty long on Lead's smoke."

"Rog. Thirty long."

"Cleared hot, Two."

Sam watched the new explosions with a critical eye. He'd requested them to be dropped thirty meters north of the lead ship's craters; they were. "Good bombs, Ramrod Flight. I'll re-mark and we'll do it some more. How are you two fixed on fuel?"

"Enough to take out homestead papers," Ramrod Lead said laconically.

Sam shoved the power up again and aimed toward the LZ, hoping that it was the last time he'd need mark for the flight. He steered toward an unsullied section of the woods and reached for another grenade. Resting his left elbow on the window ledge, forearm sticking into the slipstream, he waited to drop the grenade.

Sam never saw the .50-caliber stream of high-explosive shells. The little aircraft never had a chance. Sam watched with stunned eyes as the engine disintegrated, chewed apart by the shells. Before he had fully comprehended his situation, the aircraft was thrown on its side and engine components began to rain back through the Plexiglas of the windscreen. Several smaller metal pieces grooved Sam's face on their way to their final resting place in the rear cockpit bulkhead. Something large and solid caromed across the top of his helmet, momentarily dazing him. A smaller piece cracked the sun visor of his helmet, breaking off the bottom half over his left eye and cracking the remainder so badly that it was useless. He slowly became aware that he was taking deep rasping breaths, but doing nothing. He pulled his head up with a jerk as he gained rational thought. Sight was impossible through the mutilated sun visor, so he viciously slammed it up with the heel of his hand.

Odd. He still couldn't see. His immediate fear was that his eyes were injured, for a thick red haze constituted his entire forward field of vision. Suddenly, he realized that the smoke grenade had been jarred from his hand and had rolled somewhere beneath his seat when the aircraft went on its side. Red stinging smoke billowed through the cockpit, so dense that Sam had trouble seeing even his instrument panel. In truth, he realized as the smoke cleared momentarily, there was little to be seen, for the .50 caliber exploding shells had left holes the size of a large coffee can all through the panel.

Sam could hear the hissing of the smoke canister as it purged itself of its pressurized contents. He realized with a start that the only reason he could hear it through the cocoon of his helmet was a complete absence of engine noise. OK, he thought, trying to steady himself, let's just see if we can't get all of this into perspective. The engine is definitely out because he'd seen it go. Besides, pieces of its innards were lying in his lap. No chance of restarting that sucker. He didn't know whether he was right side up or inverted because some asshole had rolled a smoke grenade under the seat. Since he could hardly see the instrument panel, much less outside the cockpit, it was just possible he was coming down right on Charley's head. Besides that, all that fucking red smoke was making him sick to his stomach and he was sure he was going to puke.

Sam tried to get his head out the window but his fastidiousness only got him a lap full of vomit as the slipstream hurled it back into the cockpit. This is really not my day, he thought. And worst of all, he was embarrassed. He could imagine the spectacle he was making of himself to both the friendlies and the Viet Cong. A powerless airplane that couldn't hit 120 knots when it was well, floating down in a whimsical fashion, belching red smoke like an aerial circus entertainer.

He found that if he used cross-control pressures he could slip the aircraft and draw some of the smoke out of the cockpit through the open window. Unfortunately, that maneuver cleared only the portion of the windscreen that was scarred. It did show him to be approximately right side up, however.

In addition to his other problems, some fool was trying to talk to him over the radio. "Blackjack! Blackjack! This is Ramrod Lead."

"What?" he answered querulously.

"What's your status?"

Sam choked back a bitter laugh. "I'm going to crash, that's what my status is. What else do you want to know?"

There was a long moment of silence before the A-1 leader answered. "Well, if you've decided that's what you want to do, do you mind if we slide in and take some pictures? It's really quite a show."

Sam gave a tight little grin and shook his head at the mordant humor of the attack pilot. "Yeah, you can take your pictures, but it might be a little more helpful if you'd tell me where I'm heading. I can't see a thing."

"OK, come right about twenty and get your nose up a little if you can. You just might be able to stretch your glide to some rice paddies. That's it. Just a little more. Perfect. OK, you're by the tallest trees. Too bad. That would have made a hell of a shot if you'd have straddled one of those babies. Well, not to worry. There's lots more chances to screw up before you crawl out of that thing. Crap! I think your smoke is going out. That *is* too bad. Now the scene won't be nearly as interesting. Can you see forward at all now?"

"Yeah, I can." What he saw was not encouraging. He estimated he was only two or three hundred feet above the ground. The attack pilot had been right. There were several large paddies just off the nose; with just a little luck . . .

He almost made it. The little aircraft stalled while he was still six or seven feet in the air, trying to milk it for distance. It fell to the earth like a rock only feet short of the rice paddy, then bounced back into the air only to crash down again, this time on its side, one wing folded under it.

Sam hung from the harness, dazed and unclear as to what had happened. When he smelled the gas dripping from the crumpled wing, he panicked and released his safety belts, only to fall through what had been a closed door. He lay beneath the aircraft on the door he'd taken with him and rubbed his shoulder, which had absorbed most of the fall. The smell of fuel was stronger and he struggled to his feet, realizing he must get away from the broken aircraft. He leaned back inside to turn off the ignition and battery and saw the stock of his shotgun in the rack in the rear cockpit. He grabbed it and a bandolier of shells and hurriedly crawled outside, then darted in again to pick up two of the smoke grenades now rolling loose on the inside of the cockpit. He slung the bandolier, put the grenades in the leg pocket of his flight suit, and began to survey the area.

The Skyraiders roared over his head, one in trail behind the other. He waved his shotgun at them before taking off in a stumbling lope for the nearest wood line. He gained the trees and belly flopped beneath some low bushes. His heart was racing; he could feel his pulse hammering away insanely in his ears. Several klicks away—to the south, he thought—he could hear the staccato of automatic weapons. He lay motionless, waiting. Waiting for what? He wasn't sure. Sweat began to sting the open gashes on his face. He found a dirty handkerchief in a breast pocket and tenderly wiped his face, then stared in horror at the bloody rag. Tentative fingers told him that the wounds were superficial. Hah! Superficial is when it happens to somebody else. He went back to waiting.

The earth suddenly shook beneath him as the double crump of detonating bombs showed that the A-1s had gone back to work by the LZ. What the hell did that mean? Were they just going to forget about him? Logic told him that the attack aircraft had gone where they were needed most; still, it disturbed him to be left alone. Warily, he stretched his neck up as far as he could and peered through the leaves of his bush. The fuel from the leaking tank must have seeped onto the hot exhaust stacks, for small flames had ignited and were building around the wrecked aircraft. Sam was torn between getting away from the flaming wreckage, knowing it would attract every unfriendly in the area, and staying close by, knowing it was also his sole source of contact with a rescue effort. He decided to stay, for the moment.

Sam's scrutiny had picked up a well-traveled trail that led into the darker recesses of the forest. That concerned him, since it lay roughly in the direction of the Viet Cong bunkers by the LZ some kilometers away to the southwest. If that were the case and the VC retreated, as inevitably they must when more and more firepower was deployed against them, odds were that Sam could soon find himself in the middle of a very cranky group of enemy soldiers.

He squatted and duck-walked out of the bushes, pausing often to listen for any unusual jungle noise. Hell! All the noises sounded unusual. He rose carefully to a crouch and slowly crept deeper into the gloom beneath the trees. Within fifty meters he found a small depression that was probably a jungle pool during the wet season. New growth crowded the edge, which was nearly thirty meters from the trail.

Sam crawled into the depression, wedging himself beneath

the low bushes, and waited. His tongue stuck to the roof of his cottony mouth, seeking moisture. He cursed himself for not having the foresight to grab the canteen from his aircraft. He searched the pockets of his flight suit until he came up with half a pack of very old chewing gum. He tried a piece and, after overcoming an initial failure to work up enough saliva to keep it from sticking to his teeth, found that it helped a little. He chewed noisily and surveyed himself. The cuts on his face were still stinging but had stopped bleeding. Gently, he dabbed the arm of his flight suit against his face, trying to blot the moisture. He noticed the entire sleeve, no, the entire flight suit, was completely darkened with sweat. He'd have to get water somewhere if his wait was too long.

The roar of the huge radial engines of the Skyraiders almost caused him to go into cardiac arrest as they buzzed the tree line where his Bird Dog burned. Sam took a long look around, then got to his feet. There were more explosions from the area of the LZ. Other aircraft must have joined the fight.

Sam stealthily retraced his route to the edge of the jungle. The A-1s had departed after one pass, the sound of their engines fading into the distance. In their place came another sound—a familiar one. It could only be another Bird Dog. On his belly, Sam slid away from the comforting haven of trees, peering suspiciously over his shoulder. The engine noise was getting louder. The last pass by Ramrod Flight must have been to show his location to the pilot of the approaching aircraft. Then he saw it, heading directly for the smoke rising from the wrecked aircraft. The new aircraft was flying low, damned low.

After peering carefully back into the forest once more, Sam got to his knees and waved the shotgun. The aircraft was close enough that Sam could see its pilot, who had his head turned away from him, watching the fire consume the wrecked O-1. The new aircraft wore the olive-drab paint scheme of the army rather than air force gray.

It overflew the wreckage and turned toward the trees. Sam waved lustily and knew immediately he'd been sighted when the pilot enthusiastically rocked the wings of his aircraft before passing over just high enough to clear the tall trees. Sam could follow his turning flight path by listening to the engine noise. OK, he'd been spotted. But now what? Was the army pilot directing a rescue helicopter? Sam shook his head and tried to mentally quiet himself. For all practical purposes he was out of the loop on anything that was to happen. He'd just have to take what came and try to use his common sense. But, damnit! He really thought they ought to be in more of a hurry to get him out of here before the dinks came back.

Sam watched the aircraft reappear and begin a puzzling maneuver. It crisscrossed the field at fifty feet as though the pilot had lost something and was looking for it. At the edge of the paddy clearing the pilot pulled up sharply and reversed course. Sam watched the large flaps on the aircraft come down in a partial setting and heard the increased pitch as the pilot pushed on more RPMs. It came to him. No! The idiot was going to try a landing! Forgetting about any Viet Cong in the area, Sam jumped to his feet and began waving both shotgun and his free arm back and forth desperately. The surface in the clearing around the paddies probably looked smooth from the air, but erosion had created deep trenches where the ground declined toward the trees. The ditches were concealed by matted grasses. The paddies were relatively smooth but were completely inadequate for a takeoff or a landing by anything other than a helicopter.

But a landing it was to be. Either the pilot had not seen Sam's frantic arm movements, had misinterpreted them, or had chosen to ignore them. Sam watched in dismay as the aircraft turned onto its final approach, flaps coming down full. The pilot sideslipped to lose altitude, then righted the aircraft just before it settled into a gentle, perfect, three-point landing.

There was a landing roll of a hundred feet or so before the inevitable disaster. The O-1's main gear dropped completely out of sight into a rain-carved gully, and the aircraft stood abruptly on its nose. It paused there, as if for dramatic effect, then slowly fell forward onto its back. It was enveloped in a cloud of dust.

Sam wasn't conscious of starting to run and was rather startled to find himself in full flight toward the stricken aircraft. The adrenaline pumping through his system seemed to allow him to float over obstacles, shotgun held in front at port arms to knock aside small bushes. He felt light as a feather and would not have been surprised to find that if he flapped his arms he could fly. He could see movement inside the inverted cockpit as the dust began to settle. Except for the bent prop and the crushed vertical stabilizer, the aircraft looked as though it could be righted and flown away.

He skidded to a halt, panting, beside the entry door in the fuselage. Wrenching it open, he stooped to help the plane's single occupant. The feet came first, and they were huge. Sam had never seen a pair of boots like those sticking into his face just now. The man's frame unfolded and as it eased through the opening Sam saw that the man matched the feet. Eventually, all of him was outside and standing upright.

Sam was not a little man. The helmeted figure now standing next to him had to be at least six feet seven inches tall. The visor of his helmet obscured the features from the nose up, but Sam could see a wide, goofy grin pasted onto the bottom of his face.

Sam couldn't believe it. This character stuck out his hand as if they were meeting socially. Even worse, Sam automatically accepted and shook it, all the time thinking of the incongruity of it all. An entire main force battalion may have them within their gunsights and here they were, shaking hands and smiling as though they were at a bridge party.

"How do you do? Name's Chief Warrant Officer Donald

Lyle. Friends call me Stretch for obvious reasons." He removed his helmet and surveyed the dinged aircraft with sad blue eyes. "Really fucked that up, didn't I? Thought they'd probably give me a DFC if I pulled you out by myself," he said with amazing candor. "Well, easy come, easy go. What's your name, Major?"

With his mouth hanging open, Sam stared at the good-natured face. It was long and the ears protruded slightly. A straight, narrow nose and firm chin were balanced by a broad forehead. There was a full head of rusty brown hair. A good-looking kid. But, didn't CWO Donald Lyle realize there was a firefight going on two klicks away and that they were both now standing dehorsed in Charley's backyard?

"Later," Sam responded shortly to the request for his name. "Let's get anything outta the bird we can use and get the hell out of this clearing."

Without waiting for the warrant officer's agreement, Sam knelt and began rummaging in the cockpit. He passed out the pilot's M16 and a bandolier of ammunition, two more smoke grenades, a canteen of water, a six-pack of Pepsi, a bag of Cheetos, three C rations, a large Hershey bar soggy from the heat, and a small cluster of finger bananas. He decided to leave the box of crackers, the peanut butter—Skippy's Smooth—the bag of Oreos, more C rations, the paperback books, and the small watermelon. After a moment's consideration he went back for the melon.

Chief Warrant Officer Lyle methodically stowed the material Sam passed to him in the voluminous pockets of his jungle fatigues and in his helmet storage bag. He'd retrieved a baseball cap from a side pocket. Sam scrambled out of the aircraft and looked queerly at the lanky man; then he grabbed the six-pack of soft drinks and, without turning to see if he was being followed, started for the trees at a slow trot. Most of the adrenaline that had coursed through his body was beginning to wear off. His legs felt heavy and it was with a great deal of relief that he reached the shadows once more. Cautiously, he led the lanky aviator to his depression and crawled into it. Donald Lyle looked around at his new surroundings with interest, as though he might want to put in a bid on this piece of real estate.

Sam lay back with the shotgun over his chest and tried to get his breathing under control. His face felt hot and flushed, and somewhere in the chain of events he'd swallowed his gum and his mouth had dried out once again. He caught Lyle's eye and nodded at the canteen in the helmet bag. The army pilot smiled with delight as though he was the host of a dinner party and a guest had asked for seconds on the roast beef. He passed the canteen and Sam was hard-pressed not to empty it. Instead, he allowed himself a couple of quick gulps, then hastily screwed on the top and passed it back before he lost his willpower. His eyes inventoried CWO2c. Donald "Stretch" Lyle. The army pilot stared back with a good-natured smile.

"What the hell were you doing with a watermelon in your airplane?" It seemed to be the most important question Sam could come up with at the moment.

All seventy-nine or eighty inches of Stretch Lyle wriggled with delight. "Well, you see, I'm the army sector pilot over in Kien Long sector; that's in Chuong Thien province, you know."

Sam nodded that he understood the geography and whispered, "Better try to keep your voice down."

The warrant officer nodded and smiled, happy to participate in such a fun game. "Anyway, there's this one dink over there who likes to take a shot at me every time I take off. He's about a mile off the end of the strip and he's there every day, rain or shine. He takes just that one shot, that's all."

"Why don't you drop some arty on him if you know where he is?" asked Sam.

Lyle looked horrified. "Oh, no! I wouldn't do that! You see, this guy has got to be the worst shot in the world. I mean, he's been taking a crack at me every day for at least four months and he's never once scored a hit. If I were to zap him they might replace him with somebody who is a very good shot."

"So what has that got to do with the watermelon?"

"You see, I don't want to get rid of my dink but I can't just ignore him blasting away at me all the time either. So, I came up with the idea of chucking these melons at him. I don't really try to hit him and I think he knows that. But I don't think he really tries to hit me either. So, 'bout once a week I buy a dozen or so of these, about the size of a bowling ball. I stow 'em in the Bird Dog to use during the week. They don't cost hardly anything at the market in Kien Long."

"How about the rest of this chow?" Sam swept his hand at the pile of snacks.

"I sometimes get a little hungry between meals," Lyle confessed.

Sam let his eyes linger on the amiable face for a moment, then let them drift over the lanky frame. The man was a walking arsenal. He carried the standard army .45-caliber automatic on his web belt along with a K-BAR knife. There was an additional handgun—it looked to be a .38 Special—in a shoulder rig. Taped upside down on the rig's main strap was a double-edged fighting knife.

"How old are you?" Sam whispered.

"Durned near twenty-one," Lyle answered. He peered at Sam's face. "Want me to dress those cuts?"

"Later, maybe." Sam shut his eyes and sighed. He opened them and they focused on the melon. Saliva began flowing freely in his month as he began to think of what it would taste like. If they ate it, there would be less to carry if they had to move. Besides, he really wanted it. Sam eased back from the lip of the depression to sit closer to Lyle.

"Listen," he said, "why don't we cut that melon? I need to get some moisture back into my system, but we'll do it only if you want to. After all, it's your melon."

Lyle looked pained. "Shoot, Major, this ain't my stuff. It's *our* stuff. Let's cut that sucker right now."

It took all of Sam's determination not to jerk the melon from the warrant's hands as he measured, then remeasured, the point where he would make the slice. Then he inserted the tip of the K-BAR, made a neat circular slice, and popped it into two halves.

Sam swallowed the first mouthful of red flesh, seeds and all. The juice seemed to fill in the cracks and crevices in the lining of his mouth. He looked at Lyle methodically munching his portion and gazing at the treetops while his jaws worked. Sam wolfed down the rest of his portion, even chewing into the paleness just inside the tough skin. He wiped his mouth with the sweaty sleeve of his flight suit. He saw Donald Lyle cock his head like an inquisitive puppy.

"Somebody's coming," he announced in a normal speaking voice.

Sam froze, head pointing toward the gloomy forest to the southwest. He heard it too. Someone *was* coming. A lot of someones. He could distinctly hear the sound of rubber sandals slapping the earth. Then he could make out the muted voices. There *were* a lot of them!

RAID ON THUD RIDGE

FROM *ROLLING THUNDER*

———

by MARK BERENT

No one ever wrote about the fighter pilots' war over Vietnam better than Mark Berent, a career Air Force officer who lived the life he wrote about during three tours in Vietnam. He is that rarest of rarities, a pilot who can write.

In the excerpt from his first novel, *Rolling Thunder,* that follows, Captain Court Bannister is flying in the back seat of a two-seat F-105. As usual, the war is being fought with one hand, the other being firmly tied by the politicians in Washington, who are using the American military to send "messages" to the Vietnamese communists. One prays LBJ is now shoveling coal in hell and Robert S. McNamara will wind up roasting beside him, but . . .

The year is 1966, it is three in the morning in Thailand, and you are going up north in an F-105. . . .

He awoke with a start when his alarm sounded a discreet bell. His mouth felt like an ashtray and his eyes were grainy and sore. He rooted around in his bag for his shaving kit and a fresh T-shirt. Twenty minutes later he walked into the wing briefing room, blinking in the harsh light. His legs were soaked with dew from the knees down because he had cut across the unmowed athletic field separating Wing from the barracks instead of taking the long way around on the sidewalks. It was two minutes to three.

He found Frederick and sat next to him. The force commander, an older lieutenant colonel with squint lines fanning from his eyes, told the assembled pilots that today's force of sixteen Thuds, four flights of four, was going against the rail yards outside of the Thai Nguyen steel mill. Secondary and tertiary targets were farther south in Pack 1. The Wild Weasel pilots, who flew the two-seater F-105F's loaded with electronic gear controlled by the Bear in the backseat, and exotic weapons to suppress flak and SAM's, looked as unconcerned as subway riders. The renowned Weasels were known for having the biggest balls in the SEA. Few survived 100 missions. Court recognized Westcott and Robinson among several others selected by Colonel Gary Willard to be the first Weasel pilots.

The lieutenant colonel was leading the four-ship Pintail F-105D flight, the other twelve airplanes were in Harpoon,

Crab, and Waco flights. His briefing covered the TOT, routes, tanker call signs, off-load fuel, and attack headings, and he gave a rundown on the butterfly, the formation he wanted to use rolling in on the target. Using chalk on the board, he described how the four flights, each flying as a corner in a flat, one-dimensional box pattern 2,000 feet on a side, would split, with two flights rolling in on the rail yards from opposite headings. He stressed detailed memorization of the target area to pre-clude any confusion on target identification and roll-in points. He answered a few questions about radio frequencies, then returned to his seat in the front row and turned the stage over to the weather briefer, a heavyset master sergeant in fatigues.

Using a pointer on the large four-by-eight pull-out aerial map of Thailand, Laos, and North Vietnam, the sergeant began his litany. "Weather in the refueling area will be broken layers between thirty and thirty-three thousand. Over the fence those layers will stay the same, but you will encounter early-morning buildups imbedded in the scattered to broken cumulus ranging from eight to ten thousand. You will reach the target area just after first light, where your visibility will be five plus miles, opening up to ten as the sun burns off the haze. Winds at release altitude will be from 250 at ten, altimeter 29.66."

Court heard a muttered "Yeah, sure" from several of the pi-lots. He knew winds over a target area were as predictable as the Army-Navy football score. The altimeter was reasonably valid because actual measurements were sent from a weather recce F-4 and unnamed assets on the ground. The master ser-geant concluded his briefing with the weather at the primary recovery base, Tahkli, and the other Thailand alternates of Korat, Udorn, and Ubon. He stepped down.

A dark and vivid major from the intelligence section briefed with quick motions and fast words. From the side oppo-site the weather maps he pulled out a sliding map board with Communist defenses neatly drawn on an acetate overlay. As he pointed to the locations he listed the amount and types of guns and SAM's along the ingress route, around the target, and covering the egress route. He said today's codename for MiG's was Steakhouse.

Everybody laughed, because when enemy planes were spotted, the cry was "MIGS! MIGS!" Why fool around trying to remember a word to classify an event the enemy already knew about?

He said the base altitude was 13,000 feet. He wrapped up his briefing with a reiteration of the safe bailout areas and the Rules of Engagement: "Don't fly within thirty miles of the Chinese border, thirty miles of Haiphong Harbor, thirty miles from Hanoi, and of course, you can't hit the MiG bases at Phuc Yen, Gia Lam, Kep or Hoa Loc." He stopped and looked about apologetically. "Lastly, gentlemen, you are forbidden to hit the Thai Nguyen steel mill itself. You may only bomb the rail yard servicing the mill."

"Isn't that the shits," a pilot muttered. "I hope somebody is writing all this down," said a second.

The force commander wrapped up the briefing with a final word. He stood, hands on hips, facing his audience. "This is a JCS target today, gents. Let's take it out, but let's get everyone home. No pressing. No radio chatter, No MiG calls, unless you're positive. Always, I mean always, use call signs." He gave a half salute and said, "Go get 'em."

Frederick turned in his seat to stare at Court.

"Listen, movie pilot," he said, "I didn't ask for you, I don't want you, but I'm stuck with you. Somebody even sent over a two-seater from Itazuki to fly you in, otherwise you'd never get off the ground. We'd never put you in our own two-seaters. They're Weasel birds configured with enough electronic crap for the Bear, the guy in back, to light up Times Square for a year. They go along to take out SAM's. It's damn near a kamikaze mission. Damn few Weasel pilots have made it to a hundred missions yet." He shook his head. "So if the Itazuki bird wasn't here, you wouldn't fly." Without another word, Frederick got up and walked out of the briefing room. The other pilots grouped together to head toward their individual squadron briefing rooms. The darkness concealed the faces of those who were apprehensive.

Court fell in step with Frederick, who continued the conversation as if it had never been interrupted.

"I sniveled us the Number Three slot with Pintail, the force commander's flight, today. We'll get off. You watch, though, some coward will find an excuse not to go. But I'll get you up there. I'll get you up where the big boys fly." He punched the night air with his free hand.

Each flight had a fifth man, a spare, who was briefed with the rest, with an airplane loaded for the strike. The pilot would start the airplane, check in, arm, and taxi to the runway in the event someone had to abort at the last minute. In an extreme case, the man even took off to fly just short of the tankers as an airborne spare.

Frederick and Court joined the members of Pintail flight to listen to the final briefing in the squadron building. When it was over, Frederick pulled Court aside for an individual brief about what he expected of his backseater. They both carried coffee mugs.

"We may be going on a real double-pump mission; that's when your heart has to double pump to keep up with your adrenaline flow. You'll see a bunch of flak when we roll in. That's normal, so don't pay any attention. Start staring at it and you'll scare yourself to death. Cinch up your seat belts. We might get a few negative g's when I maneuver and certainly a lot of positive g's when I pull off target. A lot of g's." He took a long swallow of coffee, gone cold, and continued.

"If we take a hit, don't arbitrarily punch out. We'll talk it over. The Thud takes a lot of punishment. I'm familiar with this airplane, you're not. I'll tell you when to punch. If we're north-east of the Red River, we've got to either get back west almost to Laos, or east out over the water to be picked up. The rescue helicopters can't make it into the Hanoi area. There's too much flak."

Frederick led Court to the PE room, where they started gathering their gear. He handed Court two baby bottles. "Fill these. Use them on the ground if we punch out. In the airplane, you've got a bottle and a hose to suck on in flight. If the crew chief is a nice guy, he'll have them filled with ice tea or lemonade. Don't let your canopy close on the hose or you'll dry out in an hour."

Court put on his G-suit and survival vest, slipped into his parachute, which, like on the F-100, was not built into the ejection seat. He picked up his helmet bag and his purse, a flat kit made in the parachute shop to hold maps, and followed Frederick out the door. They stood with the other pilots waiting for the van to take them to the flight line. No one spoke. The humid cool air reminded Court of an icehouse. Muted humming from APU's firing up for the KC-135 tankers sounded from down the flight line. They made blowtorch hisses as they spat out compressed air for the tankers to start their engines.

B-66's loaded with electronic warfare equipment had taken off earlier to get set up on station over eastern Laos, where they would help flood enemy radar with false signals to mask the inbound Thuds.

The van drove up to the pilots, the headlights illuminating them like deer in a field as it stopped. Each man automatically squinted and looked away to preserve his night vision. Equipment clanging and thumping as they moved, they climbed in and arranged themselves on the benches along each side.

Court noticed the other pilots didn't have much to say to Frederick. Whether it was from dislike or inarticulateness brought on by being around a living legend, Court couldn't tell. One pilot, Pintail Four, a lieutenant, chattered inanely about the low prices at Jimmie's Jeweler. His voice was thin and edged with nervousness. Court knew it was his eleventh mission, but his first in the Pack 6 area. All new pilots usually flew their first ten missions in the relative safety of Pack 1 before being admitted into the fraternity of the men who flew beyond the Red River into the Hanoi and Haiphong areas. The lieutenant's jumpiness is catching, Court thought, as he caught himself in a jaw-cracking nervous yawn.

The van stopped at each of the four planes to let off the members of Pintail flight. There were no protected revetments at Tahkli. Rows of F-105's lined up like soldiers on flight-line parade. Outside of minor and highly unsuccessful sapper attacks, no Communists rocketed or mortared the Thud bases of Tahkli and Korat.

Court felt mounting apprehension as he followed Frederick to their camouflaged two-seat F-105F. The crew chief, in fatigue pants and T-shirt, took Frederick's helmet up the long ladder to the cockpit. Frederick pulled the rolled-up Form One from behind the ladder, found no previous maintenance write-ups, then began to preflight, using his olive-drab Boy Scout flashlight to illuminate dark crevices of the massive airplane. The 25-ton plane stood so tall they could walk under the wings to shake the fuel tanks and inspect the electronic jamming pods. They looked for hydraulic leaks in the aft section. They crouched under the belly of the giant fighter-bomber to check the fuses on the six 750-pound bombs strapped into their ejection racks.

"See heeyah," Frederick said, holding his flash on the wires that extended from the rack into each bomb's fuse, "this ahming wiyah. I found them using the wrong size. Bombs hung. Fixed naow." They checked the pitot tube, engine inlets, and various other items, until Frederick pronounced the plane safe to fly.

Both men stood still, their attention drawn to the runway where KC-135 tankers, each weighing a quarter of a million pounds, took off one by one, sounding like runaway freight trains as they used every inch of the runway to get airborne. The noise of their shrieking engines seemed to vibrate the very ground. Ninety tons of their weight consisted of fuel for the strike force.

"By God, I couldn't do that," Frederick said. Court nodded, unseen, in the darkness. They turned back to their fighter.

It was a long climb, about ten feet, Court judged, from the flight line to the rear seat of the F-105. He settled down as the crew chief helped him strap in. He put on a sweatband, wondering why Hun jocks hadn't discovered that valuable idea yet, and pulled on his helmet. Frederick made an intercom check, got clearance from his crew chief, then punched the starter button to fire the oversized shotgun cartridge that turned the engine over with a roar, venting acrid smoke into night air. Court looked down into his cockpit and saw the throttle move to idle at 8 percent. The big J75 engine rumbled and whined into life as the gauges moved like tiny semaphores. Court went through the checks Frederick had told him to make. He paid particular attention to the Doppler radar, so vital for navigation in the target area away from fixed Tacan stations.

"Pintail check," the force commander transmitted, calling for check-in. His flight and all the rest answered at machine-gun speed.

"Two."

"Three."

"Four."

"Spare."

"Harpoon."

"Two."

"Three."

"Four."

"Spare."

And so on with Crab and Waco. Twenty airplanes had checked with their leader in under ten seconds. Any pilot who broke the sequence would buy a lot of beer that night.

The twenty airplanes taxied to the arming area one after the other, twenty engines blowing gas that could tumble a man at 100 feet, struts chattering and walking back and forth under twenty-five tons of bombs and fuel and airplane. On reaching the arming area, each plane cocked left forty-five degrees and braked to a stop. They formed a long symmetrical row in the harsh glare of the floods. Court saw the armorers and crew chiefs scurry from airplane to airplane, checking, arming, pulling red streamers, and taking a last look. It was here a lowly two-striper airman could signal a full colonel he was not going on this mission in that airplane.

Two men in khaki 1505's walked together past the airplanes. They waved at each one, made blessing signs with their hands, and gave each a thumbs-up sign. "Chaplains," Frederick said, "Baptist and Roman Catholic. They always come by when they know we're going on double-pumpers. I don't much go for that. Why ask God's help to go kill people?"

"Maybe they're only asking for help to get us back safely," Court said. Frederick blew a puff of air into his mike.

When the checks were completed, the F-105's taxied to the runway, lined up, and took off at eight-second intervals. Court had no forward visibility from the rear cockpit, but he could see the glow of the blue-and-yellow afterburner flames on the grass along the sides of the concrete runway. Their airplane shook and shuddered in the buffeting jet exhausts of the 105's in front of them.

When his turn came, Frederick ran it up, told Court the fluctuating oil pressure was normal for a Thud, and released the brakes. Court saw the throttle move outboard, but there were three seconds of waddling along the runway until the burner lit.

When it did, he felt as if they had been rear-ended by a Mack truck. At the same time, Frederick flipped the switch to inject water into the flame tubes, allowing more heat and 1,000 pounds more thrust. At 185 knots on the vertical tape speed indicator, Frederick raised the nose, at 195 they were airborne as the 7,000-foot marker flashed by. In seconds, the water burned out; Frederick had the plane cleaned up, unplugged the burner at 350 knots, and told Court to take control and fly 018 degrees for a rendezvous with the tanker on Green anchor.

Four minutes later they slid into formation with the other Pintail Thuds. Lead kept his navigation lights at "bright-steady" as as they flew in a loose five-man fingertip formation, Pintail Lead being the middle finger.

Twenty-five minutes and 140 miles later, Pintail Lead, Two, and Three, Frederick, had taken 1,000 pounds of fuel each from Green tanker as an initial tap to test their systems. Owing to a foul-up in his fuel system plumbing, Four couldn't receive and was directed to RTB by Pintail Lead. RTB meant Return to Base. He put his lights on "bright flash" and peeled away from the flight to disappear quickly in the night air. They heard him contact radar site Dora, which everyone called Dora Dora, to get a steer for Tahkli. "Good luck, Pintail," he transmitted before he changed his radio channel. His voice sounded relieved, yet disappointed he was not logging another counter after getting all psyched up and coming so far on this one. "Pintail Spare, you are now Pintail Four." "Rodge," the spare transmitted and slid into position.

When it was his turn, Frederick dropped into position under the tanker for his full load of fuel.

"Depressurizing," he told Court over the intercom.

Frederick opened a valve to the outside, equalizing the cockpit pressure from 8,000 feet to 13,000, the refueling altitude. One of the intakes for the air conditioning system was just aft of the receptacle and would suck in the fuel invariably spilled at disengage. When that happened, eyestinging fuel vapor was drawn into the cockpit, so the pilots shut the system down during refueling.

The boomer, lying prone in the aft fuselage under the tail of the giant tanker, looked out at the F-105 flying formation a few feet under and behind the giant tanker. He manipulated the controls that extended the telescopic boom, held it steady as Frederick eased his airplane up to the tip, then moved the control handle that operated vanes on the probe to fly the boom to the port in front of the cockpit. He found it, plugged in and started pumping JP-4 fuel into the tanks of Pintail Three.

Court relinquished the controls to Frederick and felt the plane grow sluggish from the added weight. The pilot had to ease back on the stick, which tilted the airplane to an even higher angle to keep flying as the already heavy F-105 filled up with thousands of pounds of fuel. As he did, he added more power to overcome the increased drag caused by the high angle of attack. The four tanker engines could not propel the converted Boeing 707 through the air at a speed much higher than the stall speed of a fully loaded Thud, resulting in some very delicate flying. Behind Pintail flight were four other tankers refueling their fighters.

After they topped off, Pintail led his force to Channel 97, known as North Station. Passing the North Station, he signaled the sixteen ships to form into the giant box pattern and headed them 045 degrees toward North Vietnam.

The glow to the east grew brighter. Below, karst mountains punctuated the green velvet like torn gray boxes. Their shadows pointed west like jagged sharp spears of black.

0620 HOURS LOCAL, 29 SEPTEMBER 1966
F-105'S EN ROUTE TO THE THAI NGUYEN STEEL MILL,
DEMOCRATIC REPUBLIC OF VIETNAM

"Music on," Pintail Lead said as they approached the border, which they called the fence, between Laos and North Vietnam. All sixteen F-105 pilots flipped the switch that activated electronic countermeasure devices that radiated energy from the pods (the pilots called them "whizzies") that hung from their wings. They spread out in formation to maximize the combined ECM to confuse gun-laying and SAM search radars.

The radiated energy blossomed and bloomed on enemy gun-laying and SAM radar scopes like liquid phosphorus poured down a TV screen. Some of the enemy sites would try to burn through the energy glow by increasing the strength of their own pulses. Others would fire their guns barrage-style into what they judged to be the core of the electronic emanations.

Then they were over North Vietnam. "Green 'em up," Pintail Lead transmitted. Sixteen gloved hands reached to the left side of the instrument panel to flip up the red plastic guard and move the MASTER ARM switch on. Now the pickle button on the control stick was electrically hot to drop the bombs in whatever order the pilot had set on his armament panel: single, pairs, or ripple. The Weasels went on ahead to blast the defenses in the target area. On their way in they called the launch of a SAM heading up to Pintail's place in the sky.

"SAM, one o'clock, Pintail," Lead huffed. "Hold it in, let the pods work." He pushed over slightly to vary the altitude from 15,000 down to 12,000, then back up again in undulations that would never give radar trackers a permanent altitude fix. It wasn't much of a defensive move, but it was better than holding steady at an altitude that maybe a trailing MiG could radio back to the Hanoi Air Defense Sector. "Another one right behind it," Frederick transmitted in a ho-hum manner. Court felt his pulse race as SAM's arced up to them, then seemed to push over. He looked at the airspeed. It registered 540 knots as each pilot had slowly inched his throttle up to stay with the force commander. It was daylight now.

They flew straight into the fierce glow of the morning sun rising from the South China Sea. At eleven o'clock low, Court saw the high narrow hill called Thud Ridge rise up in razorback menace, perfectly oriented northwest and southeast. He saw two more SAM's, shining in the morning sun, rise up like smoking javelins thrown by twin hurlers, then three more. They picked up speed as they aligned themselves into a spread pattern. Pintail Lead steadily arced the flight up a few thousand feet. They were close to the rail yards, and he needed the altitude to perform a successful butterfly attack.

Below, the rail lines shone in the early sun to the left of the formation. The Weasels had dashed about attacking the SAM sites like angry hornets. It was a game of diminishing returns; too many sites, too few Weasels.

Pintail Lead held the flight steady for a few seconds. The giant box he controlled was a half mile on a side. He had positioned his own flight of four in the left front corner. He turned northerly, toward the yard, causing the giant box to rotate on the same flat plane as his wings. He rolled them out. The target was starting to disappear under the nose of his airplane. He put his thumb on the mike button and pressed.

"Ready, r-e-eady, SPLIT," Pintail Lead shouted into his transmitter.

The eastern eight ships broke left as the western eight broke right, splitting the box down the middle, with each half racing away from the other at a separation speed of 1,200 miles per hour. At the sixty-degree point in each section's turn, they reversed, pulled up, and rolled in to the rail yards from 14,000 feet on headings exactly opposite from each other.

Two explosions, so loud and close Court felt the concussion in his stomach, blew his feet up from the rudder pedals. Then flak began to bang and boom around their airplane like pop-corn. On each side of them, Court saw the big black-and-brown puffs with fiery red-and-orange centers of the 37's and 57's and 85's as they made multiple layers of steel fragments at stag-gered altitudes among and below the diving airplanes. Muzzle flashes on the ground made the target area look like New York at night.

"I'm hit. Waco Two is hit," a voice shouted over the radio. Court looked back at seven o'clock to see a 105 going down trailing a long plume of black smoke and bright-red flame.

"Waco, SAM, SAM. SAM at seven o'clock. SAM coming up," someone shrieked. There was a sudden pause on the radio.

"Naw, that's Two going down," Waco Lead said in a laconic voice.

After some initial fast stick pumps and rolls, Frederick held the F-105 steady as Court watched the altimeter tape unwind. To improve his bombing accuracy, Frederick had slowed the big craft to 450 knots. Court knew Frederick had his eyes swiftly cross-checking his gunsight pipper drifting up to the target, his airspeed, and his dive angle, which Court saw was pinned at a perfect sixty degrees.

He had set his command marker at 4,500 feet, the absolute minimum pickle altitude for a Thud in a 60-degree dive over downtown Hanoi. The white altitude tape numbers slid down the dial in a blur. The command marker came and went as the ships on each side released their bombs and pulled sharply up and away from Frederick's airplane to start their hard-jinking climb back up to altitude. As they shot through 4,000 feet, Court began to wonder if Ted Frederick was alive and if he was, did he have in mind a suicide dive right into the heart of the Thai Nguyen rail yards? Then he realized Frederick was hum-ming the same tune and repeating the same word, "Down-town," over and over like a broken record.

At 3,500 feet Court felt the ejector cartridges go off, then almost blacked out as Frederick overstressed Republic's best airplane since the P-47 by pulling 8½ g's to escape Russia's best air defense system outside of the Moscow ring. Then he felt the plane leap as Frederick engaged the afterburner for a few seconds to accelerate his jinking maneuvers back up to altitude. Suddenly the radio came alive with calls.

"Four's hit."

"MiG's! MiG's!"

"Four WHO is hit?"

"Christ, look at them."

"Damn it, where are the MiG's? Who called 'em?" a voice that sounded like Pintail Lead's called out in a testy rasp.

Fighting the g-load and the rapidly rotating cockpit as Frederick jinked left and right, Court looked back over each shoulder for their wingman, Pintail Four. Suddenly, on his left at seven o'clock, he saw an F-105 trailing a long sheet of flame. In the same instant it disappeared in a ball of fire and black smoke, from which the cockpit section somersaulted and small parts arced in all directions, then fell rapidly back. There was no chute.

"I think Pintail Four just blew up back off our left wing," Court told Frederick over the intercom.

"Ay yup, saw it. There's Lead and Two at our two o'clock. And, ahhh, let's see, yup, there's a MiG dropping in on them." Court looked high and to the right to see what looked like a MiG 19 swooping down from a position high behind the lead F-105.

"Pintail Lead," Frederick transmitted, "that was Pintail Four that just blew up. You got a MiG on your ass, and I'm pulling up into him." Frederick's voice sounded almost gleeful, Court thought. He looked more closely at the MiG and the airspace behind it. Higher up was a second MiG in position to shoot at anybody who went after the MiG attacking Pintail Lead. He told this to Frederick on the intercom.

"I don't have him," Frederick said. "You keep your eye on him. I'm going to get this first one. With a violent pull he racked the F-105 into a tight climbing right turn to get a quartering head shot at the attacking MiG. Without forward visibility, Court couldn't see the MiG Frederick was after, although he had a good contact on the other enemy fighter higher in the sky.

Berrrrrump. He heard and felt Frederick fire a burst. Then another. Suddenly, Frederick slammed the plane into a left bank so hard that Court's feet flew off the rudder pedals and his helmet cracked the canopy. Only by snapping his head back and to the right could he keep his eye on the high enemy MiG. Frederick fired again.

"Hah, got him," he hollered into the intercom. Court felt the plane jolt as they flew through the debris of the exploded MiG. "Where's that second one?" Frederick asked,

"He's at four o'clock. He pulled up high, off to one side in a modified chandelle, then rolled on his back. I think he's coming in on us." Court could just barely make out the enemy fighter.

"I don't have him."

"He's rolling in now."

"Damn, I don't have him."

"Gimme the airplane," Court yelled. He had his head bent way back over his right shoulder and didn't dare look in the cockpit, knowing he'd lose the tiny speck. By feel, he reached down and grabbed the stick.

"You got it," Frederick said.

"Gimme a few seconds of burner while I unload," Court demanded. He eased off the heavy G-load on the airplane as Frederick plugged in the afterburner long enough to increase the airspeed another 100 knots. "I still don't have him," he said. Their airspeed climbed to 525 knots.

"I'm going to pull around, and put him at your eleven o'clock position, then you take it." Court knew that when he rolled out with the MiG in front, he would lose sight of him from the rear seat, but by then Frederick should have him pinpointed. Without taking his eyes from the MiG, Court pulled the big fighter almost straight up, quickly using up the speed they had gained from the afterburner. Although he had never flown the Thud, he had the pilot's innate feel for how far to take a plane before it would stall. He didn't have to look at the airspeed indicator to know that in a few seconds that point would be reached.

"How the hell will he be at my eleven if he's on my right side now? Don't you mean one o'clock? And look out you don't stall us." Frederick grunted out against the G-load. Court didn't answer. He'd taken enough crap from one each Major Theodore Frederick. Court eased off the G-load as the F-105 pointed straight up. He held the stick with a delicate grip as he babied it through the nibbles of a stall waiting for the right second to swing it in the direction he wanted. He still had the MiG in sight, but now had the eastern sun at his back so that the MiG pilot, if he were trying to track him, would lose him in the glare.

The MiG pilot held his steady-state bank angle, seemingly waiting for Frederick's airplane to stall and start falling, when he would pounce. He's good, Court thought. I'll bet he's got blond hair and blue eyes and is a lead jock in the Soviet *Frontovaya Aviatsiya*.

Just when it would look to an outsider like the Thud had stalled and was going to spin or slide into oblivion, Court started to pull the nose down to the horizon as if coming through the top side of a loop. As the nose fell to a position just above the horizon, still inverted, he quickly rotated his head from over his right shoulder to look forward and down through the top of the canopy at the MiG. Though still upside down, the maneuver placed him up-sun and in the MiG's six o'clock position.

"What the hell?" Frederick said, hanging from his straps.

"Start pulling the trigger, Frederick, he's all yours," Court cracked out as he ruddered the inverted airplane a few more degrees, nose low and to the right. He lost sight of the MiG as it slid behind the instrument shroud in front of him, but directly at Frederick's eleven o'clock position as seen from their inverted position. If Frederick had to roll out to complete the kill, the MiG would be at his one o'clock position.

"You got the airplane," Court said, light-headed from the negative g's. "He's at your eleven o'clock."

Frederick wiggled the stick slightly to show he had control of the airplane and pressed the trigger on the B-8 stick grip. He placed forty-two rounds from the 20mm M-61 Vulcan gatling gun in the left wing root area of the MiG 19. Still firing, he let the pipper of his gunsight slide back to the center of the fuselage to the engine bay. Sparkling impact points lit the path. The MiG gracefully arced over as a great tongue of flame belched from the tailpipe and then the wing root. Frederick rolled to a wing low position, and quit firing as the left wing of the MiG separated in a blinding flash and the fuselage started violent snap rolls to the left. The side-load G-forces were so heavy the pilot would never be able to grab the handles and eject. He'd have to ride it down the remaining two miles contemplating his Marxist belief in no life after death. Frederick and Court watched for about one second, then Frederick stuck the nose down to gain speed and rolled to a westerly heading.

"See any more?" he asked Court.

"As a matter of fact, I do," Court said, as calm as he could, considering his heart was jack-hammering his chest. He had spotted a MiG very low to the east of Thud Ridge. So low, in fact, it looked about to belly in or land on a grass strip.

"Youuuuu got it," Frederick said. "Let's see what you can

do for a second act." As cool as both men were trying to sound to each other, they were both panting and sweating and jerking their heads around constantly to keep track of who was where in the swirling air battle. Since their wingman, Pintail Four, had blown up, they had to keep scanning their six o'clock in addition to all the other sectors of the sky.

Court rolled inverted, pulled the throttle back to 80 percent, and pulled the nose through until he was aiming at the eastern edge of Thud Ridge. Unlike with the second MiG, he had to dive straight at this one to get into position, but to do so would hide the MiG behind the instrument shroud in front of Court. The F-105F simply wasn't made to be piloted in combat from the backseat. He had to turn it back to Frederick.

"You got him?" he asked.

"Yeah, I got him. Gimme the airplane."

"You got it," Court said.

"I got it," Frederick said and wriggled the stick.

Frederick held the dive while rolling left and right in a modified diving jink. As he swung back, Court could get a glimpse of the MiG. It was another MiG 19 and its gear and flaps were down. It was trailing a thin wisp of smoke.

"Heh, heh," Frederick said, "I'm not even going to pull the trigger. He's got a little engine fire and has to land. Watch this."

He lowered the nose even more, pushed the throttle up to 100 percent, and held steady until it seemed they would dive into the ground at the side of the hapless MiG. Then he pulled a 5-G level-off to recover at 200 feet above the ground. The airspeed indicator read 762 knots. They were splitting the air faster than the speed of sound. The supersonic F-105 trailed two conical shock waves, one from the nose and one from the tail. Had there been any windows or crockery under the airplane, which there were not, they would have shattered from the overpressure and vibration caused by the successive shock waves.

The MiG was at 400 feet, nose high at 135 knots, gear and flaps down, trying to land. Frederick flashed under it and started an immediate pull to the right as he headed west to fly up and over Thud Ridge. Both pilots looked back over their right shoulders. The MiG, caught in the two shock waves and the violent vortex of the supersonic Thud, was pitched into a position where its nose pointed straight up, and then it made a partial roll, as if the pilot were trying to recover. Out of control, the plane tumbled and fell and slammed into the ground, where it exploded into a ball of red-and-orange fire and black, greasy smoke.

"We got him," Court yelled. "We got him."

In the midst of his elation, Court's flyer's four-dimensional sense of space and time made him look forward just in time to see Thud Ridge begin to fill the side panel of his windscreen. Without time to blink, or shout a warning, his hand shot to the stick and eased it back a fraction. They were so close the speeding plane clipped the top of a tree when they swept over the Ridge. Frederick didn't say anything as he regained control and started a climb to the west. A moment later he put out a call on the outbound frequency.

"Pintail Three's on the way out. Lead, what's your position?" No answer. "Anybody read Pintail Three?" No answer.

"Probably too low," Court said. Frederick grunted. He held the climb headed west toward Laos and Thailand. He leveled at 32,000 feet and switched to tanker frequency. There were no other airplanes, friendly or enemy, in the sky.

"White, you up?"

"Calling White say your call sign."

"White, Pintail Three. I need gas. Gimme a steer."

"Roger, Pintail Three, hold down for a steer."

Frederick pressed the mike button for five seconds, allowing White tanker's direction-finding equipment to home in on his signal. Court had noticed earlier that the fuel gauge registered lower than their scheduled Bingo, the fuel level at which a pilot had either to head home or go for a tanker.

"Gotcha, Pintail. Steer 232. You copy?"

"Roger, 232."

Thirty minutes later Frederick slid the F-105 under the tail of the White tanker. "Balls," he said over the intercom, the first word he had spoken since they had nailed the three MiG's. Court, who had been damn near biting through his oxygen mask to keep from shouting victory yells, had made up his mind he wasn't going to say one bloody word until he absolutely had to. He had long ago emptied his water bottle of lemonade, but his mouth was so dry from the adrenaline surges that he figured he probably couldn't talk anyhow. He wondered what Frederick had seen about the tanker that had made him say, "Balls."

"White, are you a papa?" Frederick asked.

"Roger that, Pintail. Thought you knew. Our frag order shows Pintails on Green today, not White. You must be a tad skosh on fuel to come to us." White was the closest tanker to Frederick and Court's egress point from North Vietnam. Had they come back directly with Pintail flight as briefed, they would have had enough fuel to go to the scheduled poststrike tanker.

Frederick cleared his throat. As they eased up to the tanker, Court saw there was a long hose with a basket on the end dangling back from under the tail, instead of the boom with the flyable vanes that the boomer would plug into the Thud's receiving bay. To get fuel from the basket meant the receiving airplane had to have a probe, a long metal pole to stick into the basket to make connection with the female receptacle at the center. Once plugged in, fuel would flow back through the pole into the receiver's main fuel tank. The system was called probe-and-drogue. It was the method used by the F-100 and all the Navy and Marine airplanes in the air. Only the USAF had airplanes that needed a flying boom to plug into its innards and transfer fuel. The F-4 was rigged that way as well as the F-105, and all SAC bombers.

The boom method required someone to lie down in the rear end of the tanker facing aft and fly the boom tip into the gizzard of the receiver. There could be only one on a KC-135, or any other tanker. The probe-and-drogue method didn't need a boomer, just a big pod from which to reel out the hose with the basket on the end. A tanker could carry three pods, one under each wing tip in addition to the one under the tail. The call sign of any tank with a basket always had the letter P as in "papa" affixed to it. Many times Court had refueled with two other F-100's at the same time on the same tank. Now here they were, Court thought to himself, too low on gas to go any place while flying next to a truck full of it, but from which they couldn't tap.

Then he felt a hydraulic system activate, followed by a roaring sound to the left side of the front cockpit. It was a probe hydraulically moving out from its stowed position. Court hadn't known the Thud had both systems installed. He wondered briefly why no one referred to it as bisexual. He heard Frederick clear his throat again.

"Ah, Bannister," he said in a voice like a rich man required to ask a beggar for a dime to place a phone call, "you do this probe-and-drogue business all the time in the F-100. Get us a little gas, will you?" Court leaned his head against the left side of the canopy and saw the probe extended into the breeze. He took the controls. By kicking right rudder he could see the basket. He slid up to it, straightened out at the last minute and stuck the probe into the basket without rippling the hose. He was extremely gratified to hear the boomer, who had nothing else to do except monitor the situation, say, "Nice hookup, Pintail. You're receiving."

"Run that by me again," the wing commander said, "about the one you claim to have spun in." The crowd had gathered in the intelligence room when Ted Frederick and Court Bannister started their debriefing. No one else from Tahkli had gotten any MiG's that day. The wing had, in fact, lost two of their own, Pintail Four and Waco Two, and had had one so badly shot up the pilot barely made it to a safe recovery at Udorn, a base close to Laos. Now a pilot was claiming three MiG's shot down.

MiG shootdowns were a great occasion, since only twenty-two had been shot down so far for a loss of sixteen USAF and Navy aircraft to MiG's. The ratio was not good. In Korea, it had been 12 to 1; twelve MiGs shot down for the loss of each friendly airplane.

Current Pentagon policy makers were beginning to dimly perceive what fighter pilots had been trying to tell them for years: To run an aggressive fighter program that turns out top-level fighter pilots, the air combat maneuvering (ACM) portion must be realistic. To be realistic meant procuring airplanes that looked and flew like MiG's, and accepting the peacetime crashes that invariably are a part of realistic ACM training. So far the USAF had done neither, despite the reports from pilots like Boyd, Suter, and Kirk, top jocks from the fighter school at Nellis Air Force Base by Las Vegas who didn't have enough horsepower to change the system, but who had the skill and guts to push for change.

The U.S. Navy had already received Captain Frank Ault's report detailing the needs and was starting to act on his recommendations for more realistic fighter training at its fighter school at Miramar near San Diego.

Frederick again told of the low-level pass at the landing MiG again. Court corroborated the story.

"Your gun camera film will confirm your first two shootdowns," the wing commander said, "but we need another source to confirm your third. Two crew members from the same plane can only file the claim; to corroborate it, film or an independent party must provide confirmation. As it stands, when your film comes back, Frederick will get credit for one and a half, Bannister for one half." He turned to Court. "You're not doing so bad, considering you are only supposed to be flying with us for flak and SAM experience."

His expression became stern. "But that's it. No more chasing MiG's." He looked at Frederick and shook a finger in his face. "You are forbidden to fly Bannister anyplace but where the orders call for. He is here to learn our tactics, not chase MiG's, and you damn well will teach them to him, or I'll bust you back to flying Blue Four for the rest of your tour. You understand, Frederick?" Major Ted Frederick informed his full-colonel wing commander that he understood. He had had his turn as Blue Four, the position flown by brand-new pilots, as a second lieutenant.

COREY FORD BUYS THE FARM

FROM *FLIGHT OF THE INTRUDER*

by STEPHEN COONTS

During the Vietnam War while I was flying A-6 Intruders from USS *Enterprise*, the thought occurred to me that the world of modern, high-tech naval aviation in the jet age would make a good novel. After a divorce in 1984, I got serious about writing the flying tale, as I called it. By that time I had thought up a tiny plot about a pilot who tried too hard to house my little collection of flying stories.

Here is one of those stories, designed to take you, the reader, flying on a low-level day attack mission against a heavily defended target. A friend of mine flew a mission similar to this; I fictionalized his experience in an attempt to capture the human truths of that time and place. Regardless of the politics of the Vietnam War, the men who fought there in American uniforms were Americans serving their country, doing the best they could under difficult circumstances. I am proud that I was one of them.

Jake Grafton was strapping himself into the cockpit one cloud-less morning when Cowboy Parker ran across the flight deck toward the aircraft. Grafton and Tiger Cole had briefed a strike on a suspected fuel dump with Little Augie and Big Augie, who were manning the machine next to Grafton's. They planned to set this target afire with the sixteen Rockeyes each plane car-ried. Boxman and his pilot, Corey Ford, were manning the spare, armed with sixteen Mark 82 500-pounders, which would go only if one of the other bombers had a mechanical problem before launch. Grafton watched Parker with a sinking feeling. Not a hurry-up target!

Cowboy climbed the boarding ladder. "You got a new tar-get, Jake. Forget the fuel dump." Holding up a piece of a chart, he pointed to a crude triangle drawn in pencil. Jake saw it was a North Vietnamese airfield.

"What's there?"

"MiGs," Parker said. "One or two, maybe three. They landed less than two hours ago and the decision's been made to try to bag them before they sortie again. You have the lead. We're going to launch the spare so there'll be three of you. Brief on squadron tactical after you rendezvous." Cowboy handed him the strip of chart and several aerial recon photos of the airfield. He took one step down the ladder, paused, and looked back at Grafton. "This'll be a tough one. It's heavily defended."

"Tell the other guys to meet me at ten grand overhead."

Cowboy nodded and disappeared down the ladder.

Jake examined the chart with Tiger. "Shit," Cole muttered. "The son-of-a-bitch is in Laos." The target airfield lay five or six miles across the Laotian border on the far side of Barthelemy Pass, which the chart showed at 3937 feet above sea level. Jake remembered from the weather brief that low clouds covered the mountains.

How should they approach? If they flew all the way to Hue, then west to Laos and north to the airfield—what was the name?—Nong Het, the trip would be long and the bad guys would have a lot of warning. Fuel would run low only if they elected to return by the same route. If they flew straight in, across North Vietnam, they'd attract flak en route, but there would be less time for the North Vietnamese to prepare a reception at the airfield. If the MiGs were bait to lure the lion, the less warning the better.

Jake Grafton rubbed his chin and stared at the swells on the sea. He thought about the flak and the airfield in the bottom of a valley. Maybe they should go straight in. "What do you think, Tiger? Straight in?"

"Yep."

The plane captain signaled for a start. Jake gave the chart and pictures to the bombardier and busied himself with the starting procedure. He was too preoccupied to enjoy the cat shot when it came.

They rendezvoused over the ship at 10,000 feet. When all three planes had joined, Jake took the lead, and Corey Ford flanked him on the left with Little Augie on the right. Jake then used his hand to signal the switch to the squadron tactical frequency and began a gentle climb to altitude.

"Two's up." Little's voice.

"Three's up." That was Corey.

"Let's go covered voice." All three turned on their scramblers, which encrypted the voice transmissions. To a listener without a scrambler with the daily code properly set, the conversation would be merely an incomprehensible buzz. "Okay, guys. We're going straight at it. Coast in north of Vinh, find the right valley, get under the clouds, go through the pass, and drop down on that airfield like the angel of doom. Any gripes?"

When all he heard was silence, Jake continued. "This field will no doubt be oriented east and west, up and down the valley." Cole was looking at the photos and concurred with a thumbs up. "Little, you take the right side of the field, and Corey and I'll take the left. Put the ordnance just inside the tree lines. They'll park those MiGs under cover. I'm willing to bet they'll be in the trees. But if you see them out on the airfield, you'll know what to do. Okay so far?"

Mikes clicked in response. "As I read this chart, the target will be in a valley that curves around to the left. High mountains on both sides. The mountains on the right peak at more than sixty-two hundred feet. After we drop, Little, you're on your own. Just to be safe, I want you to make a right turn off target and get out the best way you can. Corey, you stick with me and we'll turn left off target. They may try to put a SAM up somebody's ass as we leave. Everybody's to avoid flying into one of those granite clouds. Any questions?"

There were none. The flight switched back to the Strike frequency.

"Think we'll surprise them?" Jake asked Tiger.

The bombardier shook his head.

"Me neither," Jake grunted. "I have a sneaking suspicion we're trying to steal the cheese out of a mousetrap."

They had only two practical choices on the method of attack: go in high above the mountains and the cloud tops, or go in low on the deck below the clouds. If Rockeyes were released too high, the clamshell opened too soon and the bomblets would disperse so widely that the pattern density was unacceptably low. So they really had no choice at all. Jake thought about these matters as he followed the computer steering for the coast-in point Cole had chosen twenty miles north of Vinh. They would approach the coast from the southeast. He leveled at 20,000 feet and scanned the distant horizon. He could see the land obliquely on his left and the clouds on the mountains that rose beyond the coastal plain.

Jake instructed the other crews to reengage the scramblers. "Devil Three, since you have GP bombs, you may have to pop up high enough for the fuses to arm." Corey Ford clicked his mike. "Just don't get so wrapped up in the attack that you hit a ridge."

"Roger that."

"After you drop your load, climb over the ridges and beat feet. No rendezvous."

"I gotcha."

"Boxman, how's your radar?" Since Grafton was the leader, he let his concerns show.

"It's fine, Jake. A sweet system."

"You may have to S-turn or slow down a little to let me move ahead a bit before you drop." Corey clicked his mike. Jake wanted to make sure that Corey would delay his release so that Jake, down low, would not be struck by his bombs or caught in their blast. A second or two delay would be enough.

Jake thought of one more point. "This hole's probably heavily defended. So if anyone takes a hit and goes down, he's on his own. Don't stay and watch for chutes or any of that crap. Everybody else haul ass out of there." Mike clicks were his reply.

They flew on in silence. Jake's mouth was so dry he took a swig from his water bottle. He offered the bottle to Cole, who took his mask off, tilted the bottle, then passed it back.

Jake eased the nose over and trimmed for a descent. Each crew worked through the combat checklist. Passing 10,000 feet, fifteen miles from the coast, Jake reported to the airborne controller that he was strangling the parrot and secured the IFF. They were on their own. He checked his wingmen and told them to spread out some more. When each plane was about one hundred feet away he turned his attention to the land ahead. Rice paddies reflected the afternoon sun.

Frank Camparelli and Cowboy Parker huddled over a chart in Mission Planning. The skipper had three aircraft on their way to a well-defended target, in daytime, without adequate planning, and the possibilities for disaster ate at him.

"How do you think Grafton will go in?"

"Jake'll go straight at 'em, Skipper. He thinks feints and deceptions in a theatre this small just give the enemy more time to alert their defenses."

"That's true." Camparelli went to the flak chart on the wall. Pins bristled around the airfield. "I think they're waiting for us in that valley."

"Maybe so, but they've baited the trap with real MiGs." Parker joined Camparelli at the wall chart. "The MiGs are there," he said, thinking of the electronic intelligence report that described MiG-19 radar signals as emanating from the Nong Het airfield for the last two hours. "The hard fact is we can afford to trade plane for plane."

Camparelli turned slowly and looked over Cowboy from head to toe. "You'll make a good admiral someday, Parker."

Cowboy reddened. "Skipper, I didn't mean—"

"I know, I know." Camparelli cut him off with a gesture and scanned the charts and tables as he ran his hand over his hair. Six men, three airplanes. Six lives and eighteen million dollars worth of hardware at risk for one or two fifteen-year-old single-seat day fighters that in the air would be mincemeat for Phantoms. "Why don't you go to Combat and listen in on the Strike frequency."

"Aye, aye, sir." Parker left immediately.

The skipper wandered from chart to chart. He stopped at the SAM-threat display and examined it with interest. From the Nong Het airfield his gaze meandered north toward Hanoi. Because Grafton was on his mind he looked at the area around the power plant at Bac Giang.

"Steiger!" The commander strode to the door of the photorecon space: "Steiger! Where's Steiger?"

Thirty seconds later a flushed Abe Steiger stood before the SAM-threat chart staring through his glasses at Camparelli's finger, which tapped imperiously on the black dot on the railroad labeled Bac Giang. "Why aren't there SAM sites here? Where are those sites that shot at Grafton the other night?"

The air intelligence officer opened and closed his mouth several times.

"I told you I wanted those sites that shot at Grafton spotted on these charts. I told you specifically to make sure they were in the intelligence report." The finger pointed. "Get me that report. Mister Steiger. Now, I want to see it."

"The sites aren't in the reports, sir." Abe couldn't lift his eyes. The hand on the table was absolutely still.

"I think you had better come down to my stateroom, Mister Steiger, and we'll have a little chat."

The Intruders crossed the coast at 480 knots at 6000 feet, still descending. "Devil flight, feet dry," Jake told the Hawkeye circling somewhere in the Gulf of Tonkin.

He received the usual reply. "Good hunting."

The cloud base seemed to be at about 2500 feet, but Jake kept descending. If they were going in low in the daytime, they had better skim the trees to give the gunners the toughest shots. And the lower they were, the fewer the people who could see them.

They passed directly over a crossroads village at 1000 feet descending. Flashes in the air revealed flak, so all three planes jinked slightly while holding their formation. When they leveled at 50 feet, just above the trees, there was no room left for jinking. All they had was speed. Jake advanced the throttles to the stops, expecting to be told if someone could not keep up. In less than a minute, Corey's voice came over the radio: "Gimme a couple, Jake."

Grafton pulled two percent RPM off the engines and tightened the friction lock that would prevent him from inadvertently advancing the throttles. He concentrated on the task of threading the machine over the occasional tree lines. The warplanes rushed over acres of rice paddies, a road, shacks, more rice paddies, another road, a tree line, and more paddies. The sensation of speed was sublime.

"We're in the valley," Cole told him.

He saw the powerline almost as he crossed over it, missing by inches.

A flock of birds burst from a tree right under his nose. Jake saw them flash beneath and knew the birds would be slammed back into the trees by the downwash from his machine.

Guns on the road ahead. Muzzle flashes. A row of them, like flash bulbs popping. The Intruders rocketed toward the road and in an instant it lay behind.

The valley floor was rising. There were more trees now. The sensation of speed was lessening. Unconsciously he pushed the throttles, then remembered the friction lock and checked that he still had the proper power setting. I'll die of old age before we get there, he thought.

Within half a minute the walls began closing in and the planes picked their way up the valley. Thick tropical foliage covered the flanks of the hills, whose ridges reached higher and higher until they touched the clouds. Jake checked the altimeter. They were 1700 feet above sea level.

Back in the States, Jake Grafton had taken great pleasure in flights like this along training routes over stretches of wilderness where the legal altitude was a minimum of 500 feet above the ground. Being young and full of himself, he often flew as low as his nerves allowed just for the sheer hell of it. In those days, when military planes were still permitted to fly under visual flight rules, he would occasionally return to NAS Whidbey Island over the Cascade Range at 200 or 300 feet above the floor of the craggy valleys, shoot through the passes at full throttle and snake his way down between the cliffs, following the streams until they emptied into rivers that flowed into Puget Sound. He had wondered what the hikers had thought of the man-made eagle that split the solitude with a roar, then disappeared as quickly as it had come. Higher authority had finally stopped the illegal flights. Now he was glad he had had the experience.

The valley became serpentine. The altimeter revealed they were climbing rapidly. Not much farther now. "Master arm," he said over the radio. Cole flipped the switch with his left hand, then fingered the other armament switches to satisfy himself that they were in the correct positions.

Jake saw the end of the valley ahead, a gentle upslope to a ridge not quite touching the clouds. The green forest seemed to caress the undersides of the planes as they shot up the slope.

Through the bombsight glass, Grafton saw the ridge and the flashing guns that lined the treeless summit. Streaks of white-hot artillery shells veined the air.

They can't miss. They can't. We're too close. Jake sensed the white bolts racing straight for the cockpit, then, at the last possible instant, veer away and flash to the right or left or over.

They can't miss. They can't. We're too close.

He looked down as he crossed the naked summit. Impressed on his brain for as long as he had yet to live was the confused image of flashing guns, men in black loading and firing the weapons, and rising dust clouds.

He glanced across at Corey Ford and the Boxman and saw that their plane was almost abreast about a hundred feet away. A streak of fire ripped aft from its belly. Then the machine exploded.

The fireball was yellow with a white core. It slowed as it expanded and disappeared behind.

Jake and Little Augie swept down into the valley.

"They got Ford." Little said over the radio.

"There's the runway," Cole told him. The narrow valley was filled with the rising streaks from automatic weapons. The dust devils created by the hammering guns lined the sides of the runway like sentries from a netherworld. Knowing that Little would take the right. Jake aimed his plane down the trees on the left side of the runway. He held the plane level and let the ground fall away.

Whump!

The Intruder took a sledgehammer blow. The pilot's eyes flicked to the instrument panel—right RPM unwinding, right exhaust gas temperature climbing. He chopped the throttle on the dying engine to cutoff and began a hard turn to the left to climb the ridge.

Panic and revulsion welled up in him and he thought, Got to get the hell out of here before they get the other engine!

Then from the middle of the tree line halfway down the runway a glint of light on silver caught his eye. A MiG!

What the hell! We're dead anyway!

Jake flung the plane toward the MiG. As the target reached the bottom of the sight glass, he brought his thumb down on the bomb-release pickle. He felt the small, slow thumps as the Rockeyes kicked off the racks, a pair each third of a second.

A stream of white streaks licked across the top of the canopy and smashed into the Intruder's tail. The needle on the airspeed indicator flipped to zero.

On the west end of the airfield only two lone artillery pieces blasted into the sky.

With the last of the bombs gone, he pulled the plane left and up. He would climb the ridge. One last look over his shoulder at the airfield. A fireball was rising from the trees. "Got one," he whispered.

The clouds enveloped them. "We should have come in from the west," he told Cole.

Back over the ocean Jake reported on covered Strike frequency the loss of his wingman to the ship. He told them that if they sent another strike it should come in from the west and get up into the clouds off target. Then he called Little to arrange a rendezvous.

The other A-6 appeared as a white seed floating in a sun-bleached sky. The seed sprouted wings and a tail. Soon Jake could distinguish the men in the cockpit. Little Augie brought his plane in alongside until Jake could see each rivet, each streak of oil, each smudge of dirt.

"You have four or five nice holes in the tail, Jake." Augie slid under and lingered there, then surfaced on the right side. "No holes around the right intake. Can't see anything. Maybe something went down the intake?" Something sure as hell had, something launched from a gun barrel. "You have two small holes in the right flap, Jake. And some bad dings in the armor plate over the right engine. Other than that. . . ."

Jake and Cole examined the other A-6 inch by inch and found only a small hole in the left horizontal stabilizer.

When Jake had the lead again, he dropped his hook, then raised it. He tested the gear and flaps. The plane tended to slew right or left as he added or subtracted power, but this was normal for single-engine flight and easily corrected with rudder. "You look pretty good to me," Little informed him. Jake raised the gear and dropped the nose to get enough airspeed to raise the flaps. The extent of the damage was reported to the ship, and in a few moments the Strike controller ordered Jake to land aboard rather than divert to Da Nang.

The damaged Intruder was the last jet aboard the ship. Jake flew a straight-in approach without speed brakes. He knew that the most common error of single-engine approaches was a pilot's reluctance to reduce power on the good engine for fear of entering a descent that the one engine could not break, so he concentrated on reducing power when necessary and on doubling his power additions. He caught the three wire, and Cole said, "Not bad for a single-engine approach."

The wings folded slowly because only one hydraulic pump supplied the pressure. He was directed to the number-two elevator and was immediately lowered to the hangar deck. After taxiing off the elevator into the cavernous bay and waiting for the blue-shirted men of the tie-down crew to install chocks and chains, he opened the canopy and chopped the engine.

A crowd of somber men waited at the foot of the boarding ladder. Grafton took refuge in the familiar tasks—lifting the safety latches on the ejection seat handles, securing the proper switches, and unfastening the lapbelt and parachute riser fittings. When he could put the moment off no longer, he climbed from the cockpit and lowered himself down the ladder.

Cowboy met him. "I'm sorry, shipmate."

Jake Grafton began to weep. He had not cried since his grandmother had died when he was sixteen. Cowboy and Sammy Lundeen led him to a stairwell off the hangar deck where he sat on the ladder.

Cowboy closed the hatch leading to the hangar bay and lit a cigarette that he passed to Jake. "Have his hands been like that very long?" Jake heard Cowboy ask Sammy.

The raw smoke after two hours on oxygen scoured his lungs. The cigarette burned out when the fire reached the filter. Carefully he put the butt in his left sleeve pocket. "I'm all right now," Jake said. He stood up and looked his roommate in the eye. "I made the wrong choice. I should've come in from the west."

"You couldn't have known that." Sammy put his hand on Jake's shoulder. "Hang in there, Jake. Hang in."

Jake nodded. He would try. But it was becoming more and more difficult, and he was getting so damned tired.

POWDER RIVER MOA

FROM *SKY MASTERS*

———

by DALE BROWN

For five or six years prior to the 1991 Gulf War, military-political thrillers chock full of high tech—the so-called "techno-thrillers"—were the hottest thing in publishing. After the world watched the newest generation of smart weapons in action during Desert Storm, the public lost its awe of the technocrats' magic and the thirst for techno-thrillers cooled. They became just another genre, more or less.

One of the guys who really knew what to put in the techno was ex-Air Force pilot Dale Brown. Published in 1991, *Sky Masters* was the techno-thriller in full flower. In the excerpt that follows, notice how the details of the B-2 stealth bomber's cockpit and systems—then under development and highly classified— seem so plausible, then pause and consider: If Brown had access to classified information on these systems, it would have been a felony for him to reveal those secrets . . . and he didn't go to jail. The F-23 Wildcat fighters that appear in this excerpt are fiction in its purest form—the F-23 never existed outside of Dale Brown's imagination. And yet . . . while we read, it's almost as if we're sitting in the cockpit.

Come on, let's go flying with Dale. When we land, you tell me—is there really an EB-52, or did he make it up?

They called it Powder River. It was a pleasant-enough sounding name, almost relaxing—completely out of place for a high-tech bombing, navigation, and gunnery range.

The Powder River weapons complex encompassed the southeast corner of Montana, a bit of the northeast corner of Wyoming, and an even smaller part of northwestern South Dakota. It was almost perfectly flat, with only a few windswept rolling hills and gulleys to break up the awful monotony of the terrain. In nearly eight thousand square miles of territory, there were only six towns of any size, mostly along route 212 that ran between Belle Fourche, South Dakota, and Crow Agency, Montana. The northern edge of Powder River A contained parts of Custer National Forest, while the very southern tip of Powder River B claimed an even greater landmark—Devil's Tower, the unusual cylindrical rock spire made famous in the movie *Close Encounters of the Third Kind.* Other than Devil's Tower, however, there was almost nothing of interest—this was truly the "badlands," as depicted by writers of the Old West.

It was truly the badlands this day. Sixteen men had already been "killed" in Powder River in one day.

Men were "dying" because the Happy Hooligans from Fargo, North Dakota, were having an exceptionally good day.

The 119th Fighter Interceptor Group was out in force, with four F-16 ADF Fighting Falcon air-defense fighters and two F-23 Wildcat advanced tactical fighters rotating shifts, plus two KC-10 aerial refueling tankers, and they were running rampant through the wide-open expanse of sky under Powder River MOA (Military Operating Areas) A and B.

The training sorties, which they had been running for the past several weeks, were all a part of General Calvin Jarrel's Strategic Warfare Center program designed to train the aircrews that made up the newly integrated First Air Battle Wing.

Late on this particular afternoon, two F-23 Wildcat fighters were patrolling the Powder River MOA. In the lead was Colonel Joseph Mirisch, the deputy commander of operations of the 119th Fighter Interceptor Squadron from Fargo; his wingman was a relatively low-time Wildcat fighter named Ed Milo. After checking his wingman in, Mirisch took him over to the tactical intercept frequency and keyed his mike: "TOPPER, this is raider Two-Zero flight of two, bogey-dope."

No reply.

"TOPPER, how copy?" Still no response. They were within range—what was going on here?

On interplane frequency, Mirisch said, "I've got negative contact with the GCI controllers. Looks like we might be on our own."

"Two," was Milo's response.

Mirisch tried a few more times to raise TOPPER, the call sign of their ground radar intercept team in the Strategic Range Training Complex, at the same time steering the formation toward the entry point of the military operating area. When they were at the right spot, Mirisch called out on an interplane, "Raider flight, still negative contact with GCI. Go to CAP orbit . . . now."

"Two," Milo said. On Mirisch's order, Milo made a hard left bank and executed a full 180-degree turn until he was heading southeast toward the center of the MOA, while Mirisch continued heading toward the entry point of the MOA. They would continue to orbit the area in counter-rotating ovals, offset about twenty miles apart, so that their radars would scan a greater section of sky at one time. When radar or visual contact was made, the other plane would rendezvous and press the attack.

There was only one more training sortie scheduled that day, call-sign Whisper One-Seven, that was not identified by type of aircraft. That didn't matter, of course—it was a "bad guy," it was invading the territory of the Happy Hooligans, and it was going to go down in flames.

That is, as soon as they could find it.

For some reason, both the VIPVO GCI radar sites at Lemmon and Belle Fourche had failed to report the position of any attackers—and now the sites were off the air, which in General Calvin Jarrel's make-believe world on the Strategic Training Complex meant that the sites had been "destroyed." But someone was out there, and the Happy Hooligans were going to find them. . . .

ABOARD WHISPER ONE-SEVEN

"Twenty minutes to first launch point, Henry," Patrick McLanahan announced. "Awaiting final range clearance."

The B-2 Black Knight stealth bomber pilot, Major Henry Cobb, replied with a simple "Rog" on the interphone.

Patrick McLanahan looked over at his pilot. Cobb was not young—he had spent nearly seventeen years in the Air Force, most of it as a B-52 or B-1 aircraft commander—and had been with the HAWC at Dreamland for only a year, specifically to fly HAWC's B-2 bomber test article. Cobb was a most talented but, to McLanahan's way of thinking, unusual pilot. Except to push a mode button on the main multi-function display, Cobb sat silently, unmoving, with one hand on the side-stick controller and the other on the throttles, from takeoff to landing. He flew the B-2 as if he, the human, were just another "black box," as integral a part of the massive four-engine bomber as the wings. If he hadn't been in a military aircraft with the threat of an "enemy" attack so imminent, Cobb seemed so calm and relaxed that it would have looked natural for him to cross his legs or recline in his seat and put his feet up.

In contrast to Cobb, Patrick McLanahan's hands and body seemed in an almost constant state of motion, due mostly to the high-tech cockpit layout in the right-seat mission commander's area. Dominating the entire right instrument panel was a single four-color multi-function display, called an SMFD, or Super Multi Function Display, measuring three feet across and eighteen inches wide, surrounded by function switchlights. The massive monitor had adjustable shades that could block out most of the light in the cockpit and reduce glare, but the big screen was so bright and had such sharp high-resolution images that glare shields were generally unnecessary—McLanahan kept them retracted so Cobb could easily see the big screen. The right-side cockpit had several metal bars around the SMFD that acted as handholds or arm-steadying devices so the screen could still be accurately manipulated even during radical flight maneuvers.

The main display on the huge SMFD was a three-dimensional view of the terrain surrounding the Black Knight, along with an undulating ribbon that depicted the bomber's planned course. The B-2 was depicted riding the flight-path ribbon like a car on a roller coaster. The ribbon had "walls" on it, depicting the minimum and maximum suggested altitudes they should fly to avoid terrain or enemy threats—as long as they stayed within the confines of the computer-generated track, they could be on course, safe from all known or radar-detected obstructions and avoiding all known threats. Messages flashed on the screen in various places, several timers were running in a couple of corners of the screen, and "signposts" along the undulating flight-plan route ribbon flashed to warn McLanahan of upcoming events. The "landscape" in the God's-eye view display was checkered with colored boxes, each depicting one square nautical mile, and small diamonds occasionally flashed on the screen to highlight radar aimpoints or visual navigation checkpoints.

To General John Ormack, the deputy commander of the High Technology Aerospace Weapons Center, seated in the instructor pilot's seat between the two cockpit crew members, it seemed like a completely incomprehensible jumble of information flitting across the big screen. Ormack was along to observe this very important test of the Sky Masters NIRTSat reconnaissance system interface on an Air Battle Force bombing exercise, but for most of this incredible mission he had been hard-pressed to keep up with the flurry of data. Patrick McLanahan, the B-2's mission commander, seemed to drink it all in with ease.

McLanahan was using three different methods to change the display or call up information. The two primary methods were eye-pointing and voice-recognition commands. Tiny sensors in McLanahan's helmet tracked his eye movements and could tell a computer exactly where his eyes were focused. When his eyes were on the SMFD, McLanahan could call up information simply by looking at something and speaking a command—the computer would correlate the position of his eyes, the image on the screen, a set of commands associated with that image, then compare the digitized spoken command with the preprogrammed set of allowable commands and execute the proper one. All this would occur in less than a second. McLanahan could also point to the SMFD and touch a symbol or image to get more information or move the image where he wanted it.

It was actually funny for Ormack to watch and listen to McLanahan as he worked—his interphone sounded like a series of unintelligible grunts and incomplete sentences. Ormack would see a cursor zip across the big screen, and he would hear a guttural "Pick." A submenu would appear, and Patrick would read the information, then utter a quick "Close" to erase the display and return it to the main God's-eye display. Every second was like that. McLanahan would be manipulating several different windows on the SMFD at once, zooming around each window, calling up streams of data that would be visible for only seconds at a time, and all while letting fly with a stream of seemingly random words: "Radar . . . pick . . . close . . . zoom . . . zoom . . . close . . . one . . . five . . . close . . . pick . . . pick one . . . close . . . track . . . one . . . left . . . close . . ."

Weapon-status information was arranged along the bottom of the display so both crew members could check their weapon status instantly. McLanahan could resize any display, move displays around the SMFD, and even program certain displays to appear or disappear when a timer expired or when he switched in or out of certain modes. He was getting very adept at using his left index finger to move or change displays while his right hand worked a keyboard or hit the voice-command button mounted on the control stick on the side instrument panel.

To Ormack, it was like watching a kid play six different video games at once. McLanahan was flashing the different screens around the SMFD at an astounding rate. He was calling up radar images, scanning for fighters, setting up his bombing systems, talking on the radio, monitoring terrain, and sending messages on SATCOM, all with incredible speed and without missing one bit of information. "Wait a minute, Patrick, wait a minute," Ormack said over the interphone in absolute frustration. "You had the radar screen up for just a few seconds and then you took it down. Why?"

McLanahan put the radar image back on the left side of the

SMFD so Ormack could see it clearly and explained, "Because all I need to check on that screen is whether or not the crosshairs fell close to the offset aimpoint—here . . ." He pointed to the screen.

"I don't see anything."

McLanahan touched the circular crosshairs on the radar display and a menu appeared. He slid his finger down to a legend that read, 1/10 MRES. The screen instantly changed to show a tiny white dot near a cluster of buildings. A circular cursor was superimposed over the dot, with a set of thin crosshairs lying right on it. "Here's the offset, a grain storage bin." He motioned to a set of numbers in a corner of the enlarged display. "Crosshairs are within a hundred feet of the offset, so I know the system is good. I also check for terrain, but since we're VFR and heads out of the cockpit, and it's so flat around here anyway, I don't have to spend too much time worrying about the terrain—the nearest high terrain is Devil's Tower, over fifty miles away."

"I get it," Ormack said. "You also don't want to be transmitting that long either, right? The fighters can pick up your radar emissions . . ."

"I was transmitting for about three seconds," McLanahan explained. "I was in 'Radiate' on the radar long enough to get this image, then shut down. But the bombing computer digitizes the radar image and stores it in screen memory until I release it. I can complete the rest of the bomb run with a radar image that's over two minutes old, and aim on it right up to release. When we get closer to the target I'll start fine-aiming on the release offsets, which are much more precise, but right now I'm trying to find those fighters."

"How does that compare with the satellite data you received?"

"There is no comparison," McLanahan said with true enthusiasm in his voice. "The NIRTSat stuff is incredible—and

I thought, sitting here in the most incredible machine I've ever seen, that I'd seen it all. I can't wait to see the data from the Philippines that we're supposed to be collecting as well."

He punched instructions into a keyboard, and the graphic display of the terrain and symbols on the SMFD changed—it was as if he had switched from a fuzzy turn-of-the-century snapshot to a high-resolution color laser photo. The image was slightly different from the main SMFD display, but it still showed the ribbon "highway" of the pre-planned route, the timing and mileage icons, and target markers throughout the area. "The strike computer has already redrawn the route to real-time data—our route of flight goes farther west, and the launch point for the SLAM missile is earlier than before."

McLanahan zoomed in on the target area and switched from a bird's-eye view to a God's-eye view, which showed the target area from directly above but enhanced to show objects in three dimensions. "There's a whole row of simulated mobile-missile launchers out here . . . ?" McLanahan touched the screen and zoomed in closer to rows of cylinders on flatbed trailers. "They all look the same, but I think we can break out the real ones on the next NIRTSat pass. We should be receiving the new data in a few minutes.

"Watch this, John—with the NIRTSat data, I've already seen what the bomb run and missile launch will look like." McLanahan changed the screen again to show a photograph-quality view of the same cylinders. "Here's what the computer thinks the SLAM missile will see a few seconds before impact—the computer doesn't know which one is the real one, so it's aiming for the middle one in the group." He changed screens again, this time to a more conventional-looking green and white high-res radar image. "Here's the computer's predictions for the target-area radar-release offsets, based on the NIRTSat data. Here's the mountain peak and grain-storage bins I was just using . . . here are the two release offsets. I can start aiming on these offsets and not touch anything until release."

"Amazing," Ormack said. "Friggin' amazing. The NIRTSat system does away with shadow graphs, year-old intelligence data, hand-drawn predictions, even charts—you have everything you need to do a bomb run right here . . ."

"And I received it only thirty minutes ago," McLanahan added. "You can launch NIRTSat-equipped bombers on a mission with no pre-planned targets whatsoever. You no longer need to build a sortie package, brief crews, schedule simulator missions, or get intelligence briefings. You just load up a bomber with gas and bombs and send it off. One NIRTSat pass later, the crew gets all its charts, all its intelligence, all its weapon-release aimpoints, all its terrain data, and all its threat data in one instant—and the computer will plot out a strike route based on the new data, build a flight plan, then fly the flight plan with the autopilot plugged into the strike computers. The crew can replay the satellite data from the point of view of the flight plan and can even dry-run the bomb run hours before the real bomb run begins."

McLanahan then switched the SMFD screen back to the original tactical display, but this time with NIRTSat data inserted into it. "Unfortunately, you can't search for fighters with the NIRTSat data," he said, "and it takes a few seconds of radar time to update the screen . . ."

Suddenly several symbols popped onto the right side of the big screen, resembling bat's wings, far to the west of the B-2's position. Each bat-wing symbol had a small column of numerals near it, along with a two-colored wedge-shaped symbol on the front. The wider edge of the outer yellow-colored portion of the wedge seemed to be aimed right for the symbol of the B-2 in the center of the SMFD, while the red inner portion of the wedge seemed to be undulating in and out as if trying to decide whether to touch the B-2 icon.

"And there they are," McLanahan announced. "Fighters at two o'clock. Two F-23s. Doppler frequency shift processing estimates they're twenty miles out and above us. Signal strength is increasing—their search radar might pick us up any second. I don't think they got a radar lock on us yet, Henry . . . their flight path is taking them behind us, but that could be a feint."

Cobb seemed not to have heard McLanahan—he remained as motionless as ever, as if frozen in place with his hands on the throttles and control stick and his eyes riveted forward—but he asked, "Got jammers set up?"

"Not yet," McLanahan said, double-checking the SMFD display of the fighter's radar signal. The colored portions of the fighter's radar wedges, which represented the sweep area, detection range, and estimated kill range of the fighters, was still not solidly covering the B-2's icon, which meant that the stealth characteristics of the B-2 were allowing it to continue toward the target without using active transmitting jammers. He selected the ECM display and put it on the right side of the SMFD, ready to activate the electronic jammers at the proper time. "PRF is still in search range, and power level is too weak. If we buzz them too early, they can get a bearing on us."

"If you buzz them too late, they'll get a visual on us."

"Maybe, maybe not," McLanahan said. "In any case, they're too late." He brought the communications screen forward and activated a pre-programmed SATCOM message, then transmitted it. "Sending range-clearance request in now," he said. Sent by SATCOM and coded like normal SAC message traffic, the message or its response would not alert the fighters searching for them.

The reply came thirty seconds later: "Range clearance received, all targets clear," McLanahan reported. "Less than fifteen minutes to first launch point."

He enlarged the weapons screen and brought it higher up on the large SMFD screen so Cobb could check it as well. The

B-2 carried one AGM-84E SLAM conventional standoff missile in the left bomb bay and a three-thousand-pound concrete shape, which simulated a second SLAM missile but was not intended to be released. With its turbojet engine, the AGM-84E SLAM, the acronym for the Standoff Land Attack Missile, could carry a one-thousand-pound warhead over sixty miles. It had an imaging infrared camera in the nose that transmitted pictures back to its carrier aircraft, and it could be flown and locked on target with pinpoint precision. It was designed to give SAC's bombers a precision, high-powered, long-range conventional bombing capability without exposing the bomber to stiff target-area defenses. The right bomb bay carried two AGM-130 Striker rocket-powered glide bombs, which had a range of only fifteen miles but carried a two-thousand-pound bomb with the same precision as the SLAM. Striker worked in conjunction with SLAM to destroy area defenses and strike hardened targets with one bomber—and with the B-2 stealth bomber, which could penetrate closer to heavily defended targets than any other bomber in the world, it was a lethal combination.

McLanahan glanced at the weapons arranged along the SMFD, then spoke, "Unsafe . . . ready," to ready all weapons. Each weapon icon changed from red to green, indicating all were ready for release. "Weapon status verified, full connectivity."

Cobb turned to look, then nodded his agreement. "Checks."

McLanahan relocked all weapons, then unlocked the SLAM rocket bomb only. "Left bay SLAM selected," he told Cobb.

Another quick glance from Cobb, then he resumed his seemingly petrified position. "Checks. Left bay weapon unlocked. All others locked." McLanahan thought Cobb looked a little like the Lincoln Memorial, sitting erect and unmoving in his seat, hands on either side of him, staring straight ahead.

McLanahan selected a special symbol in the upper-right corner of the SMFD with his head-pointing system. He spoke

"Active" and it began to blink, indicating that it was active and preparing to send data. "I'm calling up satellite-targeting data from the latest NIRTSat surveillance scan," he told Ormack. "In a few minutes I should have an updated radar image of the target area, and with the composite infrared and visual data, I should be able to program the SLAM missile for a direct hit. We got this bomb run wired."

ABOARD THE F-23 WILDCAT FIGHTERS

The F-23 pilots, Lieutenant Colonel Mirisch and Captain Ed Milo, felt as if they were chasing a ghost ship—there was an attacker out there, but he barely registered on any of their sensors. If they didn't find him within the next five minutes or less, they would lose max points for any intercepts done outside the MOA.

Well, Mirisch thought, this mystery plane couldn't escape the Mark One attack sensor system—their eyeballs. Jarrel's Air Battle Force had B-1 and B-2 bombers in it now, so just maybe this attacker was one of those stealthy beasts. Mirisch noted the direction of the shadows on the ground and began to search not for the airplanes themselves; but for big, dark shadows—a bomber's shadow was always many times larger than the plane itself, and there was no camouflaging a shadow . . .

Got it!

"Tally ho!" Mirisch shouted. He was so excited that he forgot his radio discipline: "Jesus Christ, I got a B-2 bomber, one o'clock low! It's a fucking B-2 bomber!" That's why their attack radars wouldn't lock on or the infrared scanners wouldn't work—the B-2 was supposed to have the radar cross-section of a bird, and birds don't paint too well on radar. Mirisch was expecting a black aircraft, but this bat-winged monstrosity was painted tan and green camouflage, blending in perfectly with the surrounding terrain. It was flying very low, but the late afternoon's shadows were long and it was a dead giveaway. At night, Mirisch thought, it would be next to impossible to find this bastard. "Raider flight, this is Raider Two-Zero flight, we got a Bravo Two bomber, repeat, Bravo Two, at low altitude. Closing to . . ."

Suddenly there was the worst squealing and chirping on the UHF radio frequency that Mirisch had ever heard. It completely blotted out not only the UHF channel, but the scrambled FM HAVE QUICK channel as well. Except for the Godawful screeching, the jamming was no big deal—they had a visual on the bomber, and no B-2 was going to outrun, outmaneuver, or outgun an F-23. This guy is toast. The newcomer, whoever he was, was too far out to matter now. He would deal with the B-2, then go back and take care of the newcomer with the big jammer.

Mirisch had a solid visual on the B-2, so he took the lead back from Milo and began his run. The B-2 had begun a series of S-turns, flying lower and lower until his shadow really *did* seem to disappear, trying to break Mirisch's visual contact. In fact it did take a lot of concentration to stay focused on the bomber as it slid around low hills and gullys, but the closer the F-23 got, the easier it was to stay on him. Now, with the B-2 noticeably closer, the attack radar finally locked on at four miles. The heavy jamming from the bomber occasionally managed to break the range gate lock and spoil his firing solution, but the F-23's attack radar was frequency-agile enough to escape the jamming long enough for the lead-computing sight to operate. No sweat . . .

ABOARD WHISPER ONE-SEVEN

The throttles were at full military thrust, and Cobb had the three-hundred-thousand-pound bomber right at three hundred feet above the ground, and occasionally he cheated and nudged it even lower. He knew the wild S-turns ate up speed and allowed the fighters to move closer, but one advantage of the water-based custom camouflage job on the B-2 that had been applied specifically for this mission was that it degraded the one attack option that no B-2 bomber could defend against—a visual gun attack.

With the fighter's attack radars in standby or in intermittent use, the B-2's most powerful sensor was the ALQ-158 digital tail-warning radar, a pulse-Doppler radar that scanned the skies behind the bomber and presented a picture of the positions of the fighters as they prosecuted their attack. Each time the fighters began to maneuver close enough for a gun shot, McLanahan called out a warning and Cobb jinked away, never in a predictable pattern, always mixing sudden altitude changes in with subtle speed changes. Without their attack radar, the F-23 pilots had to rely on visual cues to decide when to open fire. If nothing else, they were losing points or wasting ammunition—at best, the B-2 might escape out of the MOA before the fighters closed within lethal range.

Plus, they had one more ace in the hole, but they were running out of time. "Guardian must be around here close to be blotting out the radios like this," McLanahan told Cobb and Ormack, "but I have no way of knowing where he is. He might be only a few minutes away. . . ."

ABOARD THE F-23 WILDCAT FIGHTERS

"Fox three, Fox three, Raider Two-Zero, guns firing," Mirisch cried out on the primary radio. The B-2 had finally remained steady for the first time in this entire chase, long enough for Milo to safely join on his wing and for Mirisch to get his first clean "shots" off at the big bomber's tail. The B-2 had accelerated, *really* accelerated—it was traveling close to six hundred nautical miles per hour, much faster than he ever expected such a huge plane to travel.

Suddenly the threat scope lit up like a gaudy Christmas wreath. There was a powerful fighter radar somewhere up ahead, *dead* ahead, not a search radar, but a solid missile lock on. A "Missile Launch" warning soon followed. It wasn't coming from Milo—there was another fighter out there, and it was attacking *them!* His RHAWS was indicating several different threats in several different directions—surface-to-air missiles, fighters, search radars, at least a dozen of them. It was as if six VPVO sites and six "enemy" fighters had appeared all at once.

Mirisch had no choice. He couldn't see his attackers, he had no radio contact or data link with GCI to tell him what was out there, he was less than two thousand feet above ground, and the loud, incessant noise of the jamming on all channels, bleeding through the radios into the interphone, was beginning to cause disorientation. He checked to be sure where Milo was— the kid had managed to stay in formation with him, thank God, and had not yet moved into the lead position—then called out on the emergency Guard channel, "Powder River players, this is a Raider flight, knock it off, knock it off, knock it off!"

Whoever was jamming him obviously heard the call, because the noise jamming stopped immediately. Mirisch leveled off at two thousand feet, waited until Milo was back safely in position on his wing, then scanned the skies for the unknown attacker.

He spotted it that instant. He couldn't believe his eyes.

It was a damned B-52 bomber. But it was like no B-52 he had ever seen before.

As it banked right, toward the center of the Powder River MOA, Mirisch saw a long pointed nose, a rounded, swept-back V-tail, eight huge turbofan engines, and twin fuel tanks on each wingtip. But the strange bomber also sported a long wedge-shaped fairing on its upper fuselage resembling a specialized radar compartment, and . . . he saw pylons between the fuse-lage and the inboard engine nacelles, with what looked like AIM-120 air-to-air missiles installed!

"Lead, I've got a tally on an aircraft at our eleven o'clock high, five miles . . ."

"I see it, Two, I see it," Mirisch replied. Dammit, Mirisch cursed to himself, why didn't you pick that sucker up two minutes ago? But it was too late to blame anyone else. Whatever that plane was out there, it had "killed" them both. "I don't know *what* the hell it is, but I see it."

ABOARD WHISPER ONE-SEVEN, OVER POWDER RIVER MOA, MONTANA

General Ormack strained against his shoulder harness to look out the B-2 bomber's cockpit windscreens just in time to see the huge EB-52 Megafortress do a "wing wag" and then bank away to the north. "Jesus, what a beautiful plane. We could use a hundred of those."

McLanahan laughed. "Well, it just sent those F-23s running, didn't it? That thing is tailor-made for the Air Battle Force. You give every heavy bomber going in a Megafortress to provide jamming and air-defense support, you've got an awesome force."

McLanahan and the other participants at the Strategic Warfare Center had been hearing about the EB-52 for weeks. Nobody had expected it to show up during the exercises. But it had, and McLanahan was right, it was awesome. It had a radome on its spine that had been taken off an NC-135 "Big Crow." The radome could probably shut down all communications in and out of Rapid City. It certainly jammed everything the F-23s who'd been on McLanahan's tail had on them. The plane also had capability of carrying twenty-two AMRAAMS—twelve on the wings, up to ten internally on a rotary launcher, including rear-fighting capability. Plus HARM missiles, TACIT RAINBOW antiradar missiles, rear-firing Stingers, Harpoon antiship missiles, conventional cruise missiles, SLAM and Maverick

TV–guided missiles, Striker and Hammer glide-bombs, Durandal antirunway bombs . . .

General Brad Elliott had six such planes. One was under repair and two more were authorized.

They would revolutionize SAC and SWC.

RETALIATION
FROM *THE WAR IN 2020*

---

by RALPH PETERS

Besides being one of the best military thriller writers today, former U.S. Army Lieutenant Colonel Ralph Peters is an outspoken commentator on world events and the current state of the United States military, with his essays and interviews appearing in the *Wall Street Journal, Washington Monthly*, and on the PBS television show *Frontline*. Author of the nonfiction book *Fighting for the Future: Will America Triumph?*, he has seen first hand the good and the bad in the military, and is not afraid to speak his mind.

In the following excerpt from his novel *The War in 2020*, Peters takes us to the front line in a vicious future, where top-of-the-line high-tech Japanese equipment combines with the groundpounding savagery of Iranian soldiers to create a new, lethal threat to American interests and world peace. Against this enemy the U.S. military unleashes the M-100, an aircraft with advanced tactical imaging systems and the biggest anti-armor gun out there. And on this night raid, bigger is definitely better. So saddle up with the high-tech, hard-hitting cavalry soldiers of the future and their armored, fire-breathing flying machines of 2020.

"Ruby minus ten minutes," the copilot said.

"Roger," Heifetz responded. "Combat systems check." He glanced down at the control panel. "Weapons suite?"

"Green."

"Target acquisition suite?"

"Green."

"Active countermeasures suite?"

"Green."

"Go to environments check."

"Roger," the copilot said.

Throughout the regiment, Heifetz knew, other combat crews were running through the same drill. Making sure. One last time.

The environments check took them through the range of visual "environments" in which they could choose to fight. The forward windscreens also served as monitors. The first test simply allowed the crew to look out through the transparent composite material the way a man looked through a window. Outside, the night raced with snow, the big flakes hurrying toward the aircraft at a dizzying speed.

"Better and better," the copilot remarked. The storm meant that even old-fashioned visually aimed systems on the ground would have added difficulty spotting their attackers.

"Go to radar digital," Heifetz said.

The copilot touched his panel, and the night and the rushing snow disappeared. The big windscreens filled with a sharp image of the terrain over which they were flying, as though it were the middle of a perfectly clear day.

"Ruby minus eight minutes," the copilot said.

Heifetz briefly admired the perfection of the radar image before him. The view had the hyperreality of an especially good photograph, except that this picture moved with the aircraft, following the barren plains gone white under the snow and the sudden gashes and hills of waste that marked the open pit mines scarring the landscape. Then he said:

"Go to enhanced thermal."

The copilot obliged. The windows refilled, this time with heat sources highlighted over a backdrop of radar imagery.

"Target sort," Heifetz directed.

Immediately, each of the heat sources that the on-board computer had identified as a military target showed red. Hundreds of targets, near and far, filled the screen, as though the display had developed a case of measles. Below each target, numbers showed in shifting colors selected by the computer to contrast with the landscape. These were the attack priorities assigned by the computer. As the M-100 moved across the landscape, the numbers shifted, as new potential targets were acquired and others fell behind.

"Jesus," the copilot said. "Just look at that."

Heifetz grunted. It was as close as he would allow himself to come to admitting that he was impressed.

"Makes you just want to cut loose," the copilot said. "Blow the hell out of them."

"At Ruby."

"Ruby minus seven," the copilot reported.

"Go to composite," Heifetz said.

The next image to fill the screen resembled the "daytime" digital image with targets added as points of light. This was a computer-built image exploiting all on-board systems plus input from space systems and a programmed memory base. In an environment soaked with electronic interference, or where radar countermeasures buffeted a single system, the computer reasoned around the interference, filling in any gaps in real-time information from other sources. The result was a constantly clear pure-light image of the battlefield. Further, if a particular target held special interest for the crew, they had only to point at it with a flight glove and the magnified image and all pertinent information appeared on a monitor mounted just below the windscreen.

"Ruby minus six," the copilot said. "Initial targets on radar horizon."

"Roger," Heifetz said. Then he entered the command net, calling Lieutenant Colonel Tercus, the First Squadron's commander, with whom he was tagging along.

"Whisky five-five, this is Sierra one-three. Over."

"Whisky five-five, over," Tercus responded. Even over the comms net the squadron commander managed to sound dashing, flamboyant. Tercus stretched the regulations when it came to the length of his hair, and he wore a heavy cavalryman's moustache that would have been permitted on no other officer. Tercus was simply one of those unusual men in the Army who managed to make their own rules with baffling ease. Tercus seemed to be the eternal cavalryman, and he was always ready for a fight. In the past his valor had always outdistanced his occasional foolishness, but Taylor was taking no chances today—and so he had sent Heifetz along to make sure Tercus did not gallop out of control. "Superb officer," Taylor had remarked to Heifetz, "as long as you keep him in his sandbox."

"This is Sierra one-three. I've been off your internal. Status report. Over."

"Roger," Tercus responded. "All green, all go. Ruby minus five. Going to active countermeasures at minus three. Jeez, Dave. You been watching the target array? Unbelievable."

"Roger. Active countermeasures at minus three. Weapons free at minus one."

"Lima Charlie. And another great day for killing Indians. Over."

"One-three out," Heifetz said. He turned to his copilot. "Maintain composite."

"Composite lock. Alpha Troop diverging from main body."

"Roger. Stay with them." Alpha Troop had been assigned the mission of striking the Japanese-Iranian repair and marshaling yards at Karaganda, while the remainder of the squadron went after the headquarters and assembly areas of the III Iranian Corps. Heifetz had elected to maneuver along with Alpha Troop, since the squadron commander would remain with the main body of his unit. Heifetz could assist in controlling the action—and he could add additional firepower for Alpha Troop's big task.

"Ruby minus three."

"Activate jammers." For all his self-discipline, Heifetz could not help raising his voice. He felt the old familiar excitement taking possession of him.

"Jammers hot," the copilot said. "Full active countermeasures to auto-control."

There was no change in the sharp image that filled the M-100's windscreen. But Heifetz imagined that he could feel the electronic flood coursing out over the landscape. The simple stealth capabilities and passive spoofers had hidden the systems on their approach to the objective area. Now the attack electronics would overwhelm any known radar or acquisition systems. Enemy operators might see nothing but fuzz on their monitors, or they might register thousands of mock images amid which the First Squadron's birds would be hidden. The jammers even had the capability to overload and physically destroy certain types of enemy collectors. The latest technology allowed powerful jamming signals to "embrace" enemy communications, piggybacking on them until they arrived at and burned out the receiving-end electronics. It was a war of invisible fires; waged in microseconds.

"Ruby minus two," the copilot said. "That's Karaganda up ahead, on the far horizon."

"Sierra five-five, this is Sierra one-three, over," Heifetz called Taylor.

The old man had been off the radio set for a few minutes, but now his voice responded immediately.

"This is Five-five. Go ahead, One-three. Over."

"Objective area visual now. All systems green. Jammers active. No friendly losses en route."

"Good job, One-three. Give 'em hell."

Heifetz almost terminated the communication. Taylor's voice had seemed to carry a tone of finality and haste, of no more time to spend on words. Spread over a breadth of a thousand nautical miles, the regiment was moving to battle, shifting its support base, entering the unknown. Taylor had a thousand worries.

But the colonel was not quite finished speaking to Heifetz. Just before the operations officer could acknowledge and sign off, Taylor's voice returned:

"Good luck, Dave."

The tone of the small mechanical voice in his headset somehow managed to convey a depth of unashamed, honest emotion of which Heifetz would not have been capable. The three syllables reached into him, making human contact, telling Heifetz that he mattered, that he should have a future, not merely a past. That at least one man in the world cared for him. That he, too, mattered on a personal level.

Damn him, Heifetz said to himself, meaning just the opposite, as he fought down a wave of emotion.

"And good luck to you," Heifetz said. His voice sounded stilted and insufficient to him. Suddenly, he wished that he had made the effort to sit down and speak honestly to Taylor at least once, to explain everything, about Mira, about his son, about the loss of beauty, the loss of the best part of himself along with his family and his country. Just once, they should have spoken of such things. Taylor would have understood. Why had he been so proud? Why couldn't men reach out to one another?

"Ruby minus one minute," the copilot said.

"Unlock weapons suite."

"Shooters to full green."

No sooner had the copilot touched the forward controls than Heifetz felt a slight pulsing in the M-100. The high-velocity gun had already found its priority targets. The feel under Heifetz's rump was of blood pulsing from an artery. The stabilization system on the M-100 was superb, but the force of the supergun was such that it could not all be absorbed. Slowly, after hundreds of shots, it would lose accuracy and need to be recalibrated.

But that was in the future. Right now, the gun was automatically attacking distant targets that remained well beyond the reach of the human eye.

The visual display blinked here and there where targets had already been stricken. Dozens of successful strikes registered simply from the fires of the company with which Heifetz was riding.

"Ruby now, Ruby now," the copilot cried. *"Look at that. The sonofabitching thing works."*

Heifetz glanced down at the master kill tally that registered how many effective strikes the squadron had managed. Barely a minute into the action, the number—constantly increasing—was approaching two hundred kills. His own system had taken out fourteen, no, fifteen—*sixteen* enemy systems.

Lieutenant Colonel Tercus's voice came ringing over the command net, rallying all the members of his squadron, yelling down the centuries:

"Charge, you bastards, charge!"

One of his subordinates answered with a Rebel yell.

The elation was unmistakable. Almost uncontrollable. Even Heifetz wanted to leap from his seat.

He recalled something an Israeli general officer had told him many years before. When he had been young. And invincible.

"Only the soldier who has fought his way back from defeat," General Lan had confided, "really understands the joy of victory."

The counter showed that the brilliant machine in which Heifetz was galloping through the sky had already destroyed thirty-seven high-priority enemy combat systems.

Make that thirty-eight.

For the first time in years, David Heifetz found himself grinning like a child.

Senior Technical Sergeant Ali Toorani was very disappointed in the machine the Japanese had given him. They had fooled him, and the thought of his gullibility filled him with anger. The Japanese had been alternately falsely polite and unforgivably superior at the training school on the outskirts of Teheran, but he had been told that they would give the Faithful infallible weapons, weapons far more perfect than those of the devils in the north and to the west. He had believed, and he had struggled to learn, while the Japanese had been inhuman in their expectations of how much a man could study.

He had been proud of his mastery of the radar system, and

he had possessed great faith in his abilities and in the machine. He had learned how to read all of the data, to comprehend what the displays foretold. He had acquired great skill. And he had even attempted to perform the maintenance tasks the Japanese demanded, although such menial labors were far below the station of a senior technical sergeant. Usually, he performed the maintenance when no one was around to see him. And the methods seemed to work. Even when the other machines broke down, his continued to function. He had done great things with his radar machine in this war.

But, in the end, the Japanese devils had lied like all of the other devils before them. Even when you humbled yourself to work like the lowest of laborers to care for the machine, it failed you.

Ali looked at the screen in despair and rising anger. The night had been quiet. There were no Russian airplanes or helicopters in the sky. There had been fewer and fewer of them over the past weeks, and now the skies belonged entirely to his own kind.

But, without warning, the screen set into his console had washed with light. According to the Japanese instructors, such an aberration was impossible. Now the treacherous screen registered thousands of elusive images, each one of which purported to be an enemy aircraft of some sort. Such a thing was impossible. No sky could ever be so crowded. Anyway, the Russians had few aircraft left. The machine was simply lying.

Ali stood up in disgust and turned away from the useless piece of devilry. He stepped through the gangway into the next cell, where his friends Hassan and Nafik were also working the late shift.

"God is great," Ali said, greeting his friends. "My machine doesn't work tonight."

"Truly, God is great," Hassan responded. "You can see that

our Japanese machines do not work properly, either. The head-phones merely make a painful noise."

"The Japanese are devils," Nafik muttered.

Captain Murawa's day was long and bitter, and his sleep was deep and hard. Until now his life had given him no cause to question the wisdom of his superiors. To be Japanese was to feel oneself part of the dominant political and economic power on earth, and to be a Japanese officer was to be part of a military whose abilities—if not actual forces—whose technological might, had humbled the great powers of the previous century. First, the United States, a flabby, self-indulgent giant, had received its lesson in Africa, where Japanese technology had savaged the ignorant Americans. And now it was the turn of the Russians, who had yet to put up any resistance worthy of the name. Yes, to be a Japanese officer, especially one of the new elite of electronic engineering officers, was a very fine thing. The entire world respected you.

It was a terrible feeling for Murawa to suddenly discover doubt in himself.

He hated the Iranians. He hated their indolence and filth, their inability to deal with reality as he knew it and their assumption that all things were theirs by due. Their criminal neglect of expensive military equipment was bad enough, what with their passive resistance to the accomplishment of basic maintenance chores, the neglect of a desert people to perform a task as fundamental as changing sand and dust filters, and their reluctance even to check fluid levels. But their social behavior was far worse. Murawa's image of the Iranians was of spoiled, bloodthirsty children. When their expensive toys broke— invariably through their own fault—the children threw temper tantrums, blaming the toymaker's deceit and bad faith—or lack of skill, an accusation Murawa found especially cutting and unjustified. The Japanese equipment that had been provided to the Iranians was the best in the world—the most effective and most reliable. Easy to operate and maintain, it required willful misuse to degrade its performance. It was, in fact, so simple to operate most of the combat systems that even the Iranians had been able to employ them effectively in combat.

The colossal repair effort had long since overrun its estimated costs. For want of a bit of lubrication or simple cleaning, major automotive and electronic assemblies were destroyed. Outrageously expensive components required complete replacement rather than the anticipated repairs. And the Iranians merely jeered: *You have sold us goods of poor quality. You have broken your promise. You have broken faith.* Murawa was sick of hearing it, and he did not know how much longer he would be able to control his temper. His military and civilian-contract repair crews were exhausted. And the effect of seeing their hard work result only in less and less care on the part of the Iranians and ever greater numbers of fine Japanese systems showing up ruined in the Karaganda repair yard—some for the second or third time—well, it was very bad for morale. Instead of being rewarded, their labor only turned them into fools.

Today, a barbarous crew of Iranians had turned in a kinetic-energy tank whose prime mechanisms had been hopelessly fouled by dirt. The vehicle would have been merely one out of hundreds—but the savages had played a trick. Struggling to contain their laughter, they had loitered in the reception and diagnostic motor pool. No one paid much attention, assuming they were simply typical badly disciplined Iranian troops, loath to return to duty. But, when a Japanese technician began climbing into their tank, they stopped laughing and watched with rapt attention. Only when the technician clambered madly out of the vehicle, screaming at a volume that tore the throat, did the Iranians resume their gaiety. They laughed like delighted children.

The Iranians had released a poisonous snake inside the

crew compartment. Now a critical member of Murawa's team lay in the sickbay, delirious and possibly dying. And all the Iranians had offered in leaving was the comment that:

"God is great."

Murawa had wanted to shout at them, "If your god is so great, let *him* fix your damned tank." But it would have been unacceptable. Un-Japanese.

The incident had released a torrent of doubts that he had long been suppressing. He doubted that the wise, high men who led Japan truly understood all of this. He doubted that the Iranians would ever be faithful allies to anyone. Hadn't the Americans learned the hard way, almost half a century before? The Iranians were all too convinced of their own bizarre superiority. The world owed them everything. They understood neither contractual relations nor civilized friendship. What elusive concept of honor they had was little more than vanity soaked in blood. They could not even tell the truth about simple matters, as though honest speech were biologically impossible for them. Why on earth had Tokyo backed them? What would happen when the Iranians and the rest of the Islamic world turned again? Murawa could not believe that he was the only person to see the truth.

He wished he were home in Kyoto. At least for one night. Murawa felt lucky to have been born in that most precious, most Japanese of cities, so unlike Tokyo with its compromises with Western degeneracy. There was nothing more beautiful than the gardens of Kyoto in the autumn. Unless it was the Kyoto girls, with their peculiar, disarming combination of delicacy and young strength. Certainly, they were unlike the gruesome women of Central Asia in their dirty, eerie costumes, with their gibbering voices. Those with plague scars—obviously untreated in this primitive environment—were only grimmer than the rest by a matter of degree. There was no romance in Central Asia for Murawa. Only ugly deserts interrupted with excavation scars and cities erected madly in the middle of nowhere, choking with half-dead industries whose principal product seemed to be bad air. It was like taking an unpleasant journey back through a number of bygone centuries, collecting the worst features of each as you went along. Central Asia made Murawa feel sick in spirit, and he was grateful for each new day that his body did not sicken, as well.

Apparently, it was not only the Iranians who were a problem. At the maintenance councils back at headquarters, Murawa had spoken with fellow officers who served with the Arab Islamic Union forces. Their tales made it plain that there was little to choose between their charges and Murawa's.

Despite unprecedented successes, the front was beginning to bog down. There was no military reason not to press on now. The Russians were clearly beaten. But each new local breakthrough proved harder to support and sustain logistically. The Iranians and the Arabs had gone through so many combat systems that they had too little left for the final blow. Their leaders barked that Japan was obliged to replace their losses. But even Murawa, a mere captain, knew that the additional systems did not exist. Japanese industry had gone all out to provide the vast forces already deployed. And, even if additional systems had been available, it would have been impossible to transport them all from Japan to the depths of Central Asia overnight. The prewar buildup had taken years.

The Iranians refused to understand. Murawa worked his crews until the men literally could no longer function without sleep. He sought desperately to do his duty, to return enough combat systems to the fighting forces to flesh out the skeletal units pointed northward. And all he heard were complaints that had increasingly begun to sound like threats.

Now all he wanted to do was sleep. It had been a hard day, a bad day. Sleep was his only respite and reward.

The explosions woke him.

Murawa had been dreaming of red leaves and old temple bells. Until suddenly the bells began to ring with a ferocity that hurled him out of his repose. He spent a long moment sitting with his hands clapped over his ears in a state of thorough disorientation.

The noise was of bells loud as thunder. Louder than thunder. The walls and floor wobbled, as though the earth had gotten drunk. *Earthquake*, he thought. Then a nearby explosion shattered all of the glass remaining in the window of his room and an orange-rose light illuminated the spartar quarters.

My God, he realized, *we're under attack.*

He grabbed wildly for his trousers. He was accustomed to seeing the mechanical results of combat. But he had never felt its immediate effects before. Once, he had seen an old Russian jet knocked out of the sky at some distance. But nothing like this.

The huge noise of the bells would not stop. It hurt his ears badly, making his head throb. The noise was so great that it had physical force. The big sound of explosions made sense to him. But not the bells.

The sound of human shouting was puny, barely audible, amid the crazy concert of the bells.

He pulled on his boots over bare feet and ran out of his room, stumbling down the dark corridor toward the entrance of the barracks building. The Iranian military policeman on guard duty huddled in the corner of the foyer, chanting out loud.

"What's going on?" Murawa demanded in Japanese. But he was not really addressing the cowering Iranian. He hurried out past the blown-in door, tramping over glass and grit.

Outside, heavy snowflakes sailed down from the dark heavens. The white carpet on the ground lay in total incongruity with the array of bonfires spread across the near horizon.

The motor park. His repair yards.

He watched, stunned, as a heavy tank flashed silver-white-gold as if it had been electrified, then jerked backward like a kicked dog. Nearby, another vehicle seemed to crouch into the earth, a beaten animal—until it jumped up and began to blaze.

With each new flash, the enormous bell sound rolled across the landscape.

The bells. His tanks. His precious vehicles. His treasures.

What in-the-name-of-God was going on? What kind of weapons were the Russians using? Where had they come from?

Another huge tolling noise throbbed through his skull, and he briefly considered that the Iranians might have turned on them. But that was impossible. It was premature. And the Iranians could never have managed anything like this.

He pointed himself toward the communications center, feet unsure in the snow. He brushed against an Iranian soldier whose eyes were mad with fear, and it occurred to Murawa belatedly that he had come out unarmed. The realization made him feel even more helpless, although a sidearm was unlikely to be very effective against whatever was out there playing God in the darkness.

He ran along the accustomed route—the shortest way—without thinking about the need for cover. The air around him hissed. At the periphery of his field of vision, dark figures moved through the shadows or silhouetted briefly against a local inferno. He was still far too excited to seriously analyze the situation. His immediate ambition was limited to reaching the communications center. Someone there might have answers. And there were communications means. Other Japanese officers and NCOs. The comms center called him both as a place of duty and of refuge.

He almost made it. He was running the last gauntlet, slipping across the open space between the devastated motor parks and the administration area, when a force like a hot ocean wave lifted him from the earth and hurled him back down. The action happened with irresistible speed, yet, within it, there was time to sense his complete loss of orientation as the shock wave rolled him over in the air exactly as a child tumbles when caught unexpectedly by the sea. For an instant gravity disappeared, and time stretched out long enough for him to feel astonishment then elemental fear before the sky slammed him back against the earth. In the last bad sliver of time, he thrust out a hand to protect himself. It hit the ground ahead of his body, at a bad angle, and his arm snapped like a dry biscuit.

He lay on the earth, sucking for air. He felt wetness under his shoulder blades. He raised his head like a crippled horse attempting to rise. He felt impossibly heavy.

He tried to right himself, but it simply did not work. He almost rolled up onto one knee, but he found that his right arm would not cooperate. When he realized that the dangling object at the end of his limb was his own hand, a wave of nausea passed over him. There was blood all over his uniform, all over his flesh. He could not decide where it had originated. The world seemed extraordinarily intense, yet unclear at the same time.

He dropped the broken limb, hiding it from himself. The snow turned to rain.

He collapsed, falling flat on his back. Cold rain struck his face. He could see that it was still snowing up in the heavens. A white, swirling storm. The stars were falling out of the sky. He felt the cold wetness creeping in through his clothing, chilling his spine, his legs, even as the exposed front portion of his body caught the warmth of the spreading fires. He lay between waking and dreaming, admiring the gales above his head and blinking as the snow turned to rain in its descent and struck him about the eyes.

He waited for the pain, wondering why it would not come.

"I'm all right," he told himself. "I'm all right."

The sound of the bells had stopped. In fact, the world was utterly silent. Yet the flashes continued. The pink wall of firelight climbed so high into the heavens that it seemed to arch over the spot where Murawa lay.

What was wrong? Why couldn't he get up? Why was everything so quiet?

The sky's on fire, he thought.

What was happening?

The fuel dump, he decided lucidly. They've hit the fuel dump. The Iranians had been allowed to manage it themselves, and expecting no further threats from the Russians, they had been careless, neglecting to build earthen revetments or even to disperse the stocks.

It's all burning, he thought resignedly. But why couldn't he get up? It seemed to him that he had almost made it to his feet at his first attempt. But now his muscles would not pay attention to him.

It crossed his mind that they would have to send him home now. Back to Kyoto.

Where was the pain?

Gathering all of his will and physical strength, Murawa hoisted himself up on his good elbow.

Everything was on fire. It was the end of the world. There should have been snow. Or mud. But dust had come up from somewhere. Clouds and cyclones of dust, flamboyantly beautiful. The burning world softened and changed colors through the silken clouds.

He began to choke.

The world had slowed down, as if it were giving him time to catch up. As he watched, a tracked troop carrier near the perimeter of the repair yard rose into the sky, shaking itself apart. He could feel the earth trembling beneath his buttocks.

Ever so slowly, dark metal segments fell back to earth, rebounding slightly before coming to rest.

He was choking. Coughing. But he could not hear himself coughing, and it frightened him.

Yet, it was all very beautiful in the silence. With the universe on fire.

Where was the pain?

He saw a dark figure running, chased by fire. The man was running and dancing ecstatically at the same time, flailing his arms, turning about, dropping to his knees. Then Murawa's eyes focused, and he saw that the man was burning, and that there was no dance.

Murawa collapsed back into the mud created by his own wastes. He wished he had not forgotten his pistol, because he wanted to be dead before the fire reached him.

ZERO-G DOGFIGHT

FROM *STORMING INTREPID*

by PAYNE HARRISON

To close this anthology of flying fiction we have chosen an excerpt from *Storming Intrepid* by Payne Harrison. Published in 1989, before the collapse of communism, this tale mixes high-tech warplanes and space fighters as the United States attempts to prevent a Soviet spy from stealing a space shuttle, the *Intrepid*, with its cargo of Star Wars components.

Once upon a time any tale with a spaceship in it was science fiction, but not anymore. As everyone on earth is well aware, the flying adventure that began at Kitty Hawk in 1903 has gone into space, so it is only fitting that fiction follows.

We join this tale immediately after the Americans have launched a top secret space fighter, the *Kestrel*, to pursue the *Intrepid* and destroy it. Meanwhile the Americans have launched an assault force of stealth bombers against the Soviet's Baikonur Cosmodrome, *Intrepid*'s intended point of landing.

As I read Harrison's tale, the thought occurred to me that Jules Verne and H. G. Wells would have enjoyed it, too.

Mad Dog felt a vibration as he checked the control panel. "Liquid booster has separated," he radioed. "We're clear. Lining up orbit insertion burn now." The Kestrel was completely free of its Titan booster and would now rely on its own orbital maneuvering system (OMS) engines.

"Roger, Kestrel," said the Cap Com from CSOC. "You are go for insertion burn."

Monaghan checked his attitude direction indicator to confirm it was in the inertial mode and that the digital autopilot was engaged. The NavComputer was wired into the autopilot and would execute the firing of the OMS engine to insert them into orbit. Mad Dog kept his hand off the pitch and yaw controller and let the computers take over. "Here we go, Hot Rod."

"I'm with you," replied Lamborghini.

The flight plan called for the Kestrel to be inserted into the same orbital vector as the Soyuz and *Intrepid*, but the space fighter's initial position would be two hundred miles behind and fifteen miles below its target. The strategy was to initially keep some distance, in order to guard against any ASAT weapons the Soyuz might have brought along. From two hundred miles away, Lamborghini would scan the *Intrepid* with the long-range radar and engage it with the Phoenix missiles. Then the space fighter would close the gap to inspect the damaged shuttle, or finish it off with the Sidewinders.

Because the Kestrel was traveling in a lower orbital plane, it could catch up to the *Intrepid* like a sprinter who had the inside track around a curve.

No attempt would be made to disable or board the *Intrepid*. Monaghan and Lamborghini were to simply blast it out of the sky.

DAY 5, 1253 HOURS ZULU

THE SOYUZ-*INTREPID* RENDEZVOUS

"They what?" cried Iceberg.

"Just as I told you, *Intrepid*," explained Lubinin patiently. "We have received word from our Flite Centre that the Americans have launched a vehicle from your Vandenberg cosmodrome. It is approaching our position on this same axis of advance. Flite Centre wants to know if you have any idea what it could be."

Iceberg began sweating as his mind raced. What could it be? Not an ASAT missile. Those had been destroyed under the treaty. Besides, they were launched from an airborne F-15 fighter, not from a launch facility like Vandenberg. Another shuttle? No way. They couldn't possibly have prepped another shuttle in just a few days. And it couldn't be a manned vehicle. The shuttle was the only manned launch vehicle in the U.S. inventory. What could it be, then? Some ASAT improvisation? Or a photorecon bird? Yeah. Recon. Now that made more sense.

"Tell your Flite Centre I don't know for sure, but it's my guess it's some kind of reconnaissance satellite coming up to take close-up pictures of what's going on."

Lubinin wasn't convinced, but said, "Very well," and informed Kaliningrad.

Iceberg was impatient. "How much time until we try your retro engine again?"

"Eleven minutes," replied Yemitov.

"Good," said Iceberg. "I'll be out of here before they can do anything with that Vandenberg vehicle, whatever it might be."

"Yes," observed Lubinin. "*You* will be."

DAY 5, 1258 HOURS ZULU

THE KESTREL

After the OMS engines shut down, Monaghan jettisoned the launch shrouds covering the Phoenix missiles on the topside wing pylons. Then he activated the reaction control thrusters so he could maneuver the space fighter.

The three spacecraft were now orbiting on a roughly common ground track in single file, heading south above the South Pacific. The *Intrepid* was in the lead, followed closely by the Soyuz. The Kestrel was 217 miles behind.

"Take a look, Hot Rod. See what you can find."

"Roger," said Lamborghini, and he turned on the powerful AWG-14 Doppler-pulse radar. Using the hand controller, he rotated the slotted planar antenna in the nose cone to search for the rogue spacecraft. Around and around he went, peppering the target space with electromagnetic pulses from the LTV radar, but his tactical information display (TID) screen remained blank. "I'm not getting anything, Mad Dog."

Monaghan's earphones crackled. "Kestrel, this is CSOC. Please advise on your status."

"Nothing yet," replied Monaghan. "We're still scanning with the radar. Anything you can tell us?"

"Wait one," ordered the Cap Com. "The *Intrepid* is already being scanned by the NASA tracking ship. We're waiting for you to come into range. Yeah. Okay they've got you! We mark you two-one-seven miles behind the *Intrepid* and one-seven miles below. Also, your ground track is slightly west of the target. You copy that?"

"Roger, CSOC," said Monaghan, and he yawed the space fighter a bit to the right. "Try it now, Hot Rod."

Again, Lamborghini swept the ether with his planar antenna. "I've got something!"

Mad Dog whooped. "That's gotta be them. CSOC, we got 'em in our sights."

"We copy, Kestrel," replied the Cap Com in Colorado. "Eagle One says take the shot as soon as you can."

"Roger," said Lamborghini as he began powering up the electronics in the Phoenixes. "It's hard to say for sure at this range, Mad Dog, but the TID screen says we're picking up two signatures."

"You probably are," said Monaghan. "A big one and a smaller one, I bet."

"Yeah. Very little separation between them, though."

"I figure the big one is Iceberg," speculated Monaghan, "and the small blip is that Russian Soyuz. Better take 'em both out to be sure."

"Roger," said Lamborghini. "Seems a shame to blast the Soyuz, too. Those Russian cosmonauts are probably just following orders."

"Yeah. That's a shame," agreed Monaghan. "Now nail the fuckers."

Lamborghini flipped on the Phoenix AWG-14 fire-control system, then punched in some keystrokes on the armament panel, which assigned a target, and a target priority, to each missile. He set both Phoenixes for dependent guidance, so they would be guided by the Kestrel's radar for most of their death journey. Lastly, he popped open the safety cover on the red arming switch and flipped it to ENGAGE. The two blips on his TID screen started blinking, indicating the missiles were locked onto their targets in the priority sequence he had assigned. All

Lamborghini had to do now was press the red button on the hand controller. "We've got lock-on, Mad Dog."

"Take 'em!" ordered Monaghan.

There was a white flash as the first Phoenix leapt off the left pylon. Monaghan instinctively blinked, and the Kestrel wobbled slightly from the missile's release. But the fire-control computer quickly readjusted the spaceplane's attitude so it would regain its stability for the next shot. A few moments elapsed, and with a second flash, the final Phoenix raced into the night sky.

As Monaghan watched the two white dots streak off in the distance, he said, "God, Hot Rod, that was weird. I didn't hear a thing."

Lamborghini watched his screen. "The TID's readout says five minutes, thirty seconds to impact."

DAY 5, 1300 HOURS ZULU
THE SOYUZ-*INTREPID* RENDEZVOUS

"Five minutes to retrofire," radioed Lubinin. He and Yemitov were a mere sixty feet from the tail of the *Intrepid*, and as close to the Progress retro engine as they dared be. They could only hope their backup trigger transmitter would function properly. "If the device works this time, *Intrepid*, the American spacecraft will be too late to prevent your escape."

"Just make sure it does work this time," replied Iceberg. "I don't want to have to ride down with you guys in that Soyuz capsule."

Lubinin didn't tell the American that if they failed, they'd all be better off just staying in orbit.

As the seconds dragged by inside the *Intrepid*, Iceberg found himself perspiring again, and the little droplets of sweat remained suspended around his face. It had to work this time. The success of his lifetime mission now rested on a silicon chip inside a hand-held device. Would it work or wouldn't it? He cursed, but whispered no prayer. If an atheist could be devout, then Iceberg was devout. His god had become the mission—the final, complete obedience to his mother.

DAY 5, 1305 HOURS ZULU
THE KESTREL

Lamborghini was glued to his TID screen now. The range to target was rapidly shrinking as the Phoenix missiles homed in on their targets at 2,500 miles per hour. "Sixty seconds to impact," he said in a tight voice. "Switching to independent guidance now." He punched the appropriate button on the armament panel, and the missiles' on-board planar antennae became active. From this point, the Phoenixes would guide themselves in for the terminal kill phase.

"Forty seconds," announced Lamborghini.

DAY 5, 1305 HOURS ZULU
THE SOYUZ-*INTREPID* RENDEZVOUS

"Seven . . . six . . . five . . ." Lubinin read off the countdown one last time. ". . . Four . . . three . . . two . . . one . . . fire!"

Yemitov mashed the red button, and the Progress engine erupted before them, silently belching out a tower of yellow flame.

"We have ignition!" shouted Lubinin as the *Intrepid* started moving away.

For Iceberg, the vibration from the jerry-rigged engine imparted an almost sexual feeling of release. At last—at long last—he was on his way. Yet instinctively, he peered out the window—as if he might be able to see the American bogie that had been sent up from Vandenberg.

DAY 5, 1306 HOURS ZULU
THE KESTREL

Lamborghini had become mesmerized by the TID screen.

"How's it lookin'?" asked Mad Dog.

"Thirty seconds," came the clipped response, then, "Hold on a minute—what is this?"

"What is what?" demanded Monaghan.

Lamborghini blinked a few times to make sure he was seeing it correctly. "Mad Dog, I'm picking up a third radar signature."

"What? A *third* signature?"

"Yeah, a third image," replied Lamborghini. "It's moving away from the other two and becoming more distinct. Its range is increasing . . . and it's *descending*."

"What about the other two?" asked Monaghan.

Lamborghini was flustered now. "Still stationary. The first Phoenix will impact in five seconds."

DAY 5, 1306 HOURS ZULU
THE SOYUZ-*INTREPID* RENDEZVOUS

Yemitov's blue eyes watched the *Intrepid* grow smaller and smaller in the distance. "We did it, Vasili! We did it!" cried the cosmonaut in exultation.

Lubinin was about to echo his compatriot's excitement when, over Yemitov's shoulder, he noticed a white flash in the distance. Puzzled, he pointed with his gloved hand. "Sergei . . . I saw something over there."

Yemitov was turning to look behind him when the nearby Soyuz silently exploded in a burst of light, sending fragments spinning in all directions.

DAY 5, 1306 HOURS ZULU

THE KESTREL

"We have impact on one!" shouted Lamborghini. "And two!"

"What about the third one?" demanded Monaghan.

Lamborghini watched the screen. "It's still there . . . range still increasing . . . and descending. I don't understand. Where could it have come from?"

The answer was painfully simple. One of Lamborghini's targets—which the $128 million Phoenix-VII prototype had destroyed—was the spent launch shroud that had covered the Progress engine and mating collar while they were transported on the Russian cargo booster. After being jettisoned, the launch shroud had drifted a mile from the other two spacecraft—reflecting a lovely radar signature.

At the same time, the Soyuz was poised directly between the Kestrel and the *Intrepid,* where the butterfly solar panels of the Soviet spacecraft blocked Lamborghini's radar sweeps before they could strike the American shuttle. When the *Intrepid* retrofired and moved out from behind the "mask" of the Soyuz, the Kestrel's AWG-14 radar picked it up—too late to assign it as a target for the Phoenix missiles.

"Range still increasing." Lamborghini was reluctant to admit what was coming into focus as the bitter truth. "Mad Dog . . . I think that's Iceberg getting away."

Monaghan didn't even take time to think. With his four thousand hours in jet fighter aircraft and his Irish chromosomes, nothing but distilled instinct governed him now. He spat, "My ass!" then disengaged the autopilot from the fire-control computer and quickly flipped the Kestrel so it was traveling upside down and backward. He checked the attitude direction indicator to make sure his alignment was correct, then without hesitation he mashed the trigger button to fire the OMS engines.

As the spacecraft vibrated, Lamborghini shouted, "Mad Dog! What the hell are you doing?"

Monaghan felt himself sink into his seat as the braking action of the OMS engine took effect. "I'm going after that son of a bitch!"

DAY 5, 1300 HOURS ZULU, 5:00 P.M. LOCAL
A MIG-29 FULCRUM OVER THE KAZAKHSTAN STEPPES

Oh, joy! *This* was flying!

Lt. Fyodor Tupelov put his MiG-29 into a double snap roll and howled in absolute delight.

The young aviator had been a top graduate from the Frunze military academy, as well as the number-one graduate in his flite school class. His proficiency, his Party activism, and the fact that his father was a high-level Party *apparatchik* had enabled Tupelov to land a plum assignment—flying the highly sophisticated MiG-29 Fulcrum fighter with the 77th Interceptor Regiment at Tbilisi. It was a rare honor for such a young man, and he was one of only two lieutenant pilots in the entire regiment. Such expensive and sophisticated aircraft were usually entrusted to older, more experienced aviators.

And what an aircraft this Fulcrum was! The athletic, blond Tupelov often boasted that with a Fulcrum he'd gladly go to the newly reoccupied Afghanistan for a chance to tangle with one of those vaunted Pakistani F-16s. Yet because he was a young officer, Tupelov rarely got the opportunity to push his sophisticated MiG-29 to the edge of its performance "envelope." The Fulcrum was an expensive plane, and despite his flite school credentials, Tupelov was young. Therefore, tight controls were consistently imposed on his flying. Always, from the moment he took off until he landed, his every movement was monitored by senior commanders and ground controllers. On any given training mission, Tupelov was told when to take off, when to join the formation, when to peel off from the formation, what training maneuver to execute, when to execute it, when to stop, and when to rejoin the formation. Everything was done within strict parameters. He never had a chance to truly let loose and bore holes in the sky— no opportunity to become one with the aircraft.

Until now.

Tupelov had just picked up a brand-spanking-new Fulcrum from the air-maintenance depot at Tselinograd and was en route to join his regiment at Tbilisi near the Black Sea. His new Fulcrum had been outfitted with its complement of AA-10 and Aphid missiles, along with external tanks to carry the aircraft through the 3,000-kilometer journey. Tupelov was alone with his aircraft, flying over the Kazakhstan steppes, which were covered with a patchwork quilt of giant cumulonimbus clouds. The young pilot was having the time of his life, snaking through the canyons created by the giant white thunderheads—rolling, climbing, and playing tag with the airborne pillows to his heart's content. He'd always dreamed flying could be like this, and now his dreams were fulfilled.

But Tupelov wasn't one to let his headiness carry him too far. In zipping over and around the clouds, the last thing he needed was a midair collision. He checked his map and saw that he was crossing into another air traffic control division— Sector 23-R. He set his radio for the proper frequency and keyed his mike. "Air control division, two-three-Romeo, this is MiG seven-seven-echo, do you read? Over."

"Roger, seven-seven-echo," came a detached voice over the radio, "we read you, over."

Tupelov said, "I am flying on air defense flite plan number niner-seven-whiskey-foxtrot, from Tselinograd to Tbilisi, on vector two-three-two at eight thousand meters altitude. I am on visual flite rules. Is there any traffic in my area? Over."

"Stand by," came the robotic voice. A few seconds elapsed, then, "Negative, seven-seven-echo. You have no traffic in your sector except for an Aeroflot jetliner. It is seventy kilometers east of you at eleven thousand meters altitude en route to New Delhi on vector one-five-seven."

Seventy kilometers east, and Tupelov was traveling west. The path ahead of him was clear as could be. "Roger, air control two-three-Romeo. Thank you. MiG seven-seven-echo, out."

But the ground controller wasn't finished yet. "We have noticed your course has been somewhat erratic, MiG seven-seven-echo. Are you having any difficulty with your aircraft?" The question was asked in a quasi-threatening tone, and this caused Tupelov to be wary. Ground controllers were always snoopy—and arrogant. They acted as if they owned the airspace. Tupelov wanted to give a response that was plausible, yet not offensive. Something that would not stir up any trouble, but allow him to keep having a good time. He keyed his mike and tried to sound authoritative. "There is no problem, air control. I am checking out the performance on a new aircraft." Which was true. "Request clearance for discretionary climb and descent between seven thousand and twelve thousand meters on my present vector."

"Very well, seven-seven-echo. Proceed at your discretion, but you are advised not to deviate from your flite plan."

That meant no loops or backtracking, but as long as he kept heading for Tbilisi, he could play as much as he wanted to—until he came within range of his regimental radar control centre. Then he would have to play it by the book. "Thank you, air control two-three-Romeo. MiG seven-seven-echo will comply with your instructions. Out." The young pilot smiled. Evidently he'd sounded authoritative enough. Now he could have some more fun.

Tupelov was cruising along the top of a puffy field of clouds at eight thousand meters altitude, but ahead of him the clouds billowed up into two Goliath thunderheads, extending to fifteen thousand meters in height and creating a giant canyon between them. Tupelov hooted, then shoved his throttles in and climbed up the middle of the canyon. At eleven thousand meters he leveled off and wove back and forth between the canyon walls—brushing up against one fluffy side, then the other. Ahhhhhh! Complete delight! He was deep into the canyon gorge now, and he brought his aircraft midway between the white towers to put the Fulcrum into a slow, lazy barrel roll. Tupelov was halfway through his aerobatic maneuver—poised in the heads-down inverted position—when two giant black batwings roared out of the cloud bank, sandwiched his Fulcrum between them, and then plunged into the far canyon wall—vanishing as quickly as they had appeared.

DAY 5, 1305 HOURS ZULU, 5:05 P.M. LOCAL
THE STEALTH BOMBERS

Had Ghost Leader not been held firm by his shoulder harness, he would have leapt out of his seat as he screamed, *"Shit!"*—and yelped at his companion, "Did you see that!?"

Whizzo's bug eyes were transfixed on the nose-camera video screen. "Yeah!" he replied in a quaking voice. "And I think I saw some missiles under the wing!"

Ghost Leader uttered another high-pitched "Shit!" Then he gulped and asked, "Is the laser channel open?"

Whizzo nervously fiddled with his hand controller before saying, "Open, Skipper."

The pilot keyed his mike. "Ghost Two, this is Lead. Did you see that?"

"See it?" came the excited reply. "I nearly took his fucking tail section off!"

Lead's stomach started knotting up. "Oh, great, just what we need. Did you catch what it was?"

"I dunno," said Ghost Two anxiously. "It was too fast. A Fulcrum? Maybe a Flanker? Can't say. Whatever it was, it had a double tail—I can tell you *that* for sure. It didn't clear my windshield by more than ten feet. You think they got us spotted?"

"I don't know. Hold on." Leader was sweating as he turned to the major and asked, "You picking up anything?"

The Whizzo scanned his instruments. "Nothing, Skipper. Threat board shows only normal search radars working. Nothing in the X-ray or India bands."

"My Whizzo says we're not picking up any SAM search, air-to-air search, or lock-on," said Leader to Ghost Two. "Only normal navigational search."

"My Whizzo says the same thing," replied Two. "But how did they know where to look for us?"

"Damned if I know," said Leader through his teeth. "Listen, we better split up and take evasive action. If Omaha transmits the go signal, you take the alternate southern approach to the target and I'll come in from the north. Stay in the clouds as much as you can. They may be looking for us, but I bet we're still blind on their radar."

"Roger, Lead. We'll see you back in Muskrat"—slang for Muscat. "If we get the go, put your load where it counts."

"You got it, Ghost Two. Good luck. Lead out." After cutting the transmission, Leader said through the intercom, "All right, Whizzo, I don't know how they found us, but it looks like we've been spotted. Even so, we're sticking with the game plan. I think we'll be okay as long as we stay in the clouds. If we get the go, Ghost Two will approach from the south and we'll come in from the north. Keep an eye on that threat board."

"Roger, Skipper."

Leader pushed his control stick forward and turned the wheel. The batwing responded and began a lumbering, diving turn to the northeast.

DAY 5, 1306 HOURS ZULU, 5:06 P.M. LOCAL
THE FULCRUM

Fyodor Tupelov tried to hold the Fulcrum steady in level flight, but he was shaking so violently from fright that it was difficult. And when his shaking turned into sobs, it became almost impossible. God in heaven! What had he seen? Those big, black, sinister creatures had come out of nowhere and almost swallowed his Fulcrum. They did not look of this world. Tupelov clutched the control stick with two hands. He'd never known such panic. He forced himself to take long, even breaths. Good. That helped . . . deeper breaths now. Better. He kept the oxygen going in and out, and slowly the terror subsided. Tupelov was regaining control of himself and his aircraft. As the clouds whipped by his cockpit, he told himself to go back to flite school basics. Identify the problem, then correct it.

First, what *were* they? They were unlike anything Tupelov had ever seen. The concept of a UFO was foreign to him, so it didn't even enter his mind. He knew that however bizarre, those flying black batwings were of this earth. And if they were in Russian airspace, that meant the ground air traffic controllers *had* to know about them; for in the Soviet Union, no one *ever* left the ground without filing a laborious flite plan. And if that was the case, the air controller in Sector 23-Romeo had been grossly negligent, incredibly stupid, or had deliberately lied to him. When this thought took hold in Tupelov's mind, his fear was quickly supplanted by anger—a deep, searing, blinding fury—and he keyed his mike. "Air control division, Sector two-three-Romeo, this is MiG seven-seven-echo. Do you read? Over."

There was a pause until a bored voice came on the air. "Roger, seven-seven-echo, we read you, over."

Tupelov recognized the voice as the one that had given him his original clearance. "Air control, on our last transmission I thought you said there was no air traffic in my area!"

There were some moments of silence before the controller came back: "Affirmative, seven-seven-echo. I have you on my screen at one-one-zero-seven-eight meters altitude, bearing two-two-niner degrees. There is no traffic in your area except for the Aeroflot flite you were advised of earlier."

Tupelov's face turned scarlet. "You listen to me, you stupid ass! I just avoided a midair collision by no more than three meters with two unidentified aircraft! Why did you not advise me of them?"

The controller responded in a puzzled voice, "You say you almost had a midair collision?"

"Yes, you ass! How many times do I have to repeat myself? Your negligence could have gotten me killed!"

There was a pause before the controller said, "You are mistaken, seven-seven-echo. I see nothing on my screen in your area but your aircraft."

"*Mistaken!* I could have touched those bogies if I had wanted to! Are you asleep down there? Or just stupid? Or both?"

There was another pause, longer this time, and a different voice came on the radio. "MiG seven-seven-echo, this is the commander of Sector two-three-Romeo air traffic division. You claim you had a near miss?"

The fact that the ground control commander was on the radio stole some of Tupelov's thunder, but nevertheless, he pressed his case. "Yes, Commander, that is correct."

"Describe the aircraft to me," ordered the commander.

"There were two aircraft," said Tupelov precisely. "Delta shaped. Black in color. No markings that I could see. Very large. Bigger than a Backfire bomber. Perhaps as big as a Blackjack."

A moment of silence. "Big as a Blackjack bomber?"

"Yes, Commander," replied Tupelov.

It was a biting voice that came over the radio now. "You listen to me, MiG seven-seven-echo. If we can see your tiny aircraft on our screen, do you not think we would be able to see two huge Blackjack-sized airplanes?"

Tupelov was careful. "Yes, Commander, I would think so. Are you saying you are not tracking them?"

"That is exactly what I am saying, seven-seven-echo," replied the commander. "We are tracking no aircraft of any kind near your location, except for the Aeroflot jetliner that is far from you. How do you explain that?"

Puzzled, Tupelov said, "I cannot explain it, Commander. I only know what I saw. The two aircraft were very large, and I almost collided with one."

A grunt came over the air. "Would you be suffering from hypoxia, seven-seven-echo?"

Tupelov was startled at this suggestion. "Absolutely not, Commander. My oxygen is working fine."

Another grunt. "Your flite plan shows you are assigned to the 77th Interceptor Regiment at Tbilisi. Is that correct?"

"That is correct, Commander."

The ground control commander's voice was hard now. "You are hereby ordered to continue on your flite plan. I am preparing a report about your hallucinations that will be on your commanding officer's desk when you arrive. In the future, I suggest you stay away from the vodka before piloting one of the Motherland's aircraft."

"But Comrade Commander," protested Tupelov, "I saw—"

"Our radar can *see* better than your vodka-filled, bloodshot eyes, MiG seven-seven-echo. In fact, I can *see* you now on my screen, but I do not *see* these two Blackjack-sized aircraft you claim to have nearly collided with. Now quit hallucinating, get off this channel, and report to your commanding officer in Tbilisi at once! Preferably sober. Sector two-three-Romeo, out."

Now another kind of fear gripped Tupelov. If such a report made it to his commanding officer's desk, his military career would be finished before it even began. Now he wished he'd kept his mouth shut. . . . But no. He'd seen those two—whatever they were—with his own eyes. That meant they were still out there somewhere. Why in the world couldn't the damn fool controllers see them? Tupelov was a bright young man, and he made a quick decision, for he knew it was his only chance. In order to avoid being hauled up on the carpet, branded a drunkard, and busted out of the service, he had to find those mystery aircraft and report their location. He scanned his instruments, and rapidly computed time and distance back to where the near collision had taken place. His external fuel tanks were almost empty now, but the fighter's organic tanks were full. To do what he was about to do was a violation of a ground control order. A court-martial offense. But what did he have to lose? Could jail be any worse than a humiliating dismissal from the Air Defense Force? Tupelov figured one fate was just as distasteful as the other. He gulped, jettisoned his external tanks, and whipped the Fulcrum around in a 180-degree turn to begin his hunt for the flying black batwings.

DAY 5, 1308 HOURS ZULU

THE *INTREPID*

Iceberg felt the vibrations of the Progress engine cease, causing him to experience relief like nothing before in his life. Whatever the Americans had sent up from Vandenberg, it was too little, too late, to stop the *Intrepid* now. In about fifty-five minutes he would be touching down on the Baikonur runway, and he was home free. He engaged the reaction control thrusters and rotated the spacecraft into the correct attitude for atmospheric reentry. The explosive bolts holding the Progress engine in place would fire shortly.

DAY 5, 1308 HOURS ZULU
THE KESTREL

"Monaghan!" Maj. Gen. Chester McCormack's voice reverberated in Mad Dog's earphones. "What kind of crazy stunt are you trying to pull now?"

"We missed the *Intrepid*, Eagle One," said Mad Dog in a flat voice, "and now we're going after it. Give me the coordinates for the Baikonur Cosmodrome."

"You weren't authorized for—"

Monaghan's voice turned mean. "Save it, Eagle! I don't have time for your bureaucratic bullshit. You want to put me in jail after we get back home, then that's just Jake by me. But if we're going to catch that son of a bitch Iceberg, I need those coordinates—now!"

"Now you listen to me, *Commander*—"

"Beg pardon, sir," cut in Lamborghini, "but Mad Dog is right. We've already gone through de-orbit burn, and there's no way to reverse it. If we're going to have a chance at catching the *Intrepid* we need the coordinates at once."

There was a pause. "All right, hang on." Another few moments passed before McCormack returned. "Okay. . . . the coordinates for the Baikonur Cosmodrome are forty-seven degrees forty-one minutes north, sixty-six degrees eleven minutes east."

Monaghan rapidly punched the numbers into the NavComputer and engaged the digital autopilot. The two astronauts immediately felt a change in the Kestrel's attitude and a quick eight-second burn of the OMS engine. Monaghan had executed a "seat of the pants" retro burn, and now the autopilot was correcting the spacecraft's course alignment for its descent to Baikonur.

"So what's your game plan?" asked Eagle One.

"We'll try and reacquire *Intrepid* by radar," replied Monaghan, "then see if we can close it up enough to fire the Sidewinders before we start heating up on reentry. If not, then we'll try to pick him up after we exit the blackout."

Another few moments passed, until McCormack asked in a resigned voice, "Do you go along with this, Pete?"

Lamborghini sighed. "Call me a late convert, but yes, sir. I think we have no choice but to try to nail the *Intrepid*. Whatever the risks."

Now it was McCormack's turn to sigh. "Since you'll be coming down in Russia, make sure you find some way to destroy the Kestrel when you land. I would say the odds of our extracting you out of there are just about zero."

"Aye, aye, sir," replied Monaghan. "Now if you don't mind, we've got some hunting to do. Okay, Hot Rod, fire up your radar."

DAY 5, 1310 HOURS ZULU, 6:10 A.M. LOCAL
CHEYENNE MOUNTAIN

Whittenberg, Fairchild, Dowd, and Lydia Strand stood in open-mouthed shock as they monitored the transmission between McCormack and the Kestrel. It was inconceivable that Lamborghini and that loco Navy pilot were going straight into Soviet airspace to chase down the *Intrepid*. It was insane. But there wasn't a blessed thing any of them could do about it.

If Whittenberg had had thirty seconds' warning that Monaghan was going to try something so stupid, he could have warned the lunatic off and told him about the stealth bombers. But it was too late now. And Whittenberg wasn't going to put out word about the stealth bombers over the radio without good reason. Maybe the Russians could descramble their transmissions, too. It seemed there was nothing they couldn't do these days—and now the Kestrel was flying into their midst.

The CinC felt a load of depression sink into him. He figured Lamborghini was as good as dead.

"Mad Dog," muttered Strand softly.

Whittenberg turned. "What was that, Major?"

Strand shrugged. "I understand Commander Monaghan's call sign is Mad Dog . . . I guess that says it all."

Whittenberg nodded. "I guess it does." He was silent for a few moments before saying, "I shouldn't have let Pete go."

DAY 5, 1311 HOURS ZULU, 5:11 P.M. LOCAL
THE FULCRUM

Fyodor Tupelov was back in the vicinity of his encounter with the flying black batwings. The ground radar station had detected his course reversal, and the controller was now issuing shrill orders and vile threats over the radio. But Tupelov had made his decision, and he turned off his radio receiver to keep the ground chatter from distracting him.

Now then, what to do? He could chase off in the same direction he'd last seen the mystery aircraft, but that didn't feel like the right move. He remembered a holiday trip he and his father had once taken into Siberia to hunt for caribou. They'd found some tracks of a small caribou herd in the snow, and the impetuous young Tupelov had started off after them. But their Yakut guide had quickly admonished the boy. "You do not want to be where they have *been*," he explained. "You want to be where they are *going*." The old trapper had taken Tupelov and his father off on a course that was at a right angle to the path of the animal tracks, and sure enough, they'd caught the caribou as they circled around on a feeding circuit.

Tupelov figured that was as good a strategy as any, and banked his aircraft sharply to the right. He'd travel due south for a hundred kilometers, then make a search pattern to the southeast until his fuel ran low and he had to put down somewhere. He was scared. But there was no turning back now.

He cut in the Fulcrum's afterburners.

DAY 5, 1317 HOURS ZULU, 3:17 P.M. LOCAL
KALININGRAD FLITE CONTROL CENTRE

"The explosive bolts on the engine clamps have fired," squawked the speaker box, "and I maneuvered the orbiter around so I could see if the docking collar pulled free. It did. So there should be no problem on reentry."

In a relieved voice, Mission Commander Malyshev said, "Excellent, *Intrepid*. Stay in contact until you reach the transmission blackout."

"Roger, Flite Centre," replied Iceberg.

The Mission Commander looked at Popov, who nodded. Malyshev keyed his mike, and asked, "*Intrepid*, can you tell us anything about our Soyuz crew? They went off the air shortly after your retrofire."

"I have no idea, Flite Centre," said the flat voice. "Maybe that American spacecraft out of Vandenberg had something to do with it."

"Yes . . . perhaps so, *Intrepid*," said Malyshev bitterly.

Popov covered his eyes with his hands. "Vasili . . . Sergei," he whispered mournfully. Somehow he knew they were dead. More blood on his hands.

DAY 5, 1320 HOURS ZULU
THE KESTREL

The OMS engine died as the fuel ran out.

"Dammit!" Mad Dog was pissed. Without more fuel, the

Kestrel couldn't close the gap to the *Intrepid*. "Can you take him now, Hot Rod?"

Lamborghini scanned his TID screen. "He's right on the edge of Sidewinder range at one hundred twenty-five miles. I'd hate to waste another shot. How close can we get to him on the backside of the blackout?"

"Probably pretty close," replied Monaghan. "I can put the Kestrel into a little bit steeper descent gradient than the shuttle. The NavComputer says we can make it to Baikonur as is. So we may have a chance."

"Then I vote we hold off and pick him up on the backside. I think we're just wasting a missile if we try it now."

"Okay, you got it," said Mad Dog.

There was a period of silence, but Lamborghini could hear his own heart thumping. He still couldn't believe they were going down into the Soviet Union. The typical emotions of air combat—which combined the gut-wrenching fear of dying with the exhilaration of being alive—washed over him. "Say, Leroy?" he said, in a jabbing use of Monaghan's Christian name.

"Yes, Peter?" replied Monaghan in an equally mocking voice.

"You really are mad as a hatter, aren't you?"

Monaghan chuckled nervously. "You betcha. A regular U.S. Government certified Section Eight." Then in a more somber tone he added, "Guess I should've asked you if you were game for this action before I hit the retro switch."

Lamborghini emitted a high-strung laugh. "Guess it's a bit late now, but no sense in having second thoughts. I pull on the blue suit every morning, and I know what that means."

"Yeah," agreed Monaghan. "But still, if you'd like to get out now, it's all right with me."

Lamborghini emitted another high-pitched laugh. "Thanks, but I think I'll tag along, if you don't mind."

DAY 5, 1320 HOURS ZULU
THE *INTREPID*

Iceberg was over Antarctica now, making preparations for atmospheric reentry. Like the machine he was, he ran through the procedures from memory.

First, he dumped the unused fuel from the orbital maneuvering engines, which Rodriquez had crippled. Since the engines had not been used much, there was a considerable amount to jettison, and it was necessary to get rid of the excess liquid so the orbiter would be properly balanced for reentry. Luckily, Rodriquez had not damaged the purge, vent, and drain circuitry.

He then flipped a series of switches into their proper position: Antiskid to ON. Nose Wheel Steering to OFF. Air Data to NAV. ADI Error to MED. ADI Rate to MED. Hydrazine Main Pump to NORM.

Finally, he corrected the orbiter's attitude until its nose was pitched up 32 degrees. This ensured that the silica tiles on the underbelly were properly positioned to absorb the horrendous atmospheric friction during the black hole of reentry.

DAY 5, 1323 HOURS ZULU, 5:23 P.M. LOCAL
THE FULCRUM

Desperation was starting to cloud Lt. Fyodor Tupelov's thoughts, which were already punctuated by images of a dismal prison cell. He'd traveled a hundred kilometers south after a quick spurt from his afterburners, and was now flying a slow, sawtooth search pattern on a southeasterly course. There was no sign of the mystery planes as his Fulcrum flew in and out of the clouds. He wished he'd held his temper with the radar controller, but it was too late to worry about that now. Besides, the near miss had frightened him to his core, and there was no way he could have capped his anger.

He kept searching. Whenever the Fulcrum flew into a gap between the clouds, his eyes would dart back and forth, looking for some sign of the black batwings. But there was none. He activated his on-board radar and swept the airspace in front of him, but his screen showed no return. The image of the jail cell was becoming all too intrusive on his thoughts. . . . Then suddenly—there it was! At ten o'clock low! Over two thousand meters beneath him!

Tupelov's Fulcrum flew into the clouds again for a few moments, and when the fighter broke into the clear, the mystery aircraft was gone. He threw the fighter into a diving left turn and headed for the spot where he thought he'd seen the black batwing. Was his mind really playing tricks on him? Maybe he was suffering from hypoxia? No. He rejected both scenarios. His eyesight was excellent, and his oxygen system was working perfectly. He'd seen the . . . whatever it was.

Again he illuminated his on-board radar, and again there were no returns. Dammit. Where had the infernal thing gone? The young pilot's lip was starting to quiver when the black batwing popped out of a small thunderhead above him at two o'clock high, traveling on the same vector. Tupelov howled in relief and brought his fighter up to about three hundred meters behind and a hundred meters above the mystery machine.

Inside his oxygen mask, Tupleov's jaw dropped as he studied the bizarre vision before him. What on earth was it? The aircraft was unlike anything he'd ever seen. It had no vertical tail stabilizer, and no engine pods, as far as he could see. He squinted to look for markings, but he was too far back to discern the subdued black-on-black USAF lettering on the wings. And where was the second batwing? No matter. He had this one in his sights, and that was enough. He turned his radio back on. "Air control division, Sector two-three-Romeo, this is MiG seven-seven-echo. Do you read? Over."

The response was not long in coming. "Seven-seven-echo! This is the commander of Sector two-three-Romeo. You are to consider yourself under arrest! I order you to put down at the nearest airfield immediately! Is that clear?"

"I must disregard that order, Comrade Commander," replied Tupelov. "I have located one of the mystery aircraft that I almost collided with. I am on its tail at this very moment."

"I have had enough of your hallucinations, seven-seven-echo! I have you on my screen and there are no other aircraft in your vicinity! Do you understand me?"

Tupelov was incredulous. How could it not be on radar? It was right there, in front of him. And this was no hallucination. "I do not understand, Comrade Commander. I have the 'bogie' in sight not three hundred meters ahead of me. As I said before, it is approximately the size of a Blackjack bomber."

"Enough of this lunacy!" screamed the radar commander. "You listen to me, seven-seven-echo—"

"No!" shot back Tupelov. *"You* listen, Commander! I think you are the one who is drinking the vodka. I have in my sights, at this moment, a large unidentified aircraft. I demand you connect me with your superior so I may report this sighting. You are obviously incompetent and unfit to execute your duties."

"You are a dead man, seven-seven-echo! I will personally see to it that you are court-martialed and shot! There is *no* unidentified aircraft!"

Tupelov heard desperation in the commander's voice, so he played his trump card. "Very well, Comrade Commander. You give me no choice. If you do not patch me through to your superior, I am going to shoot this nonexistent aircraft down. Do you understand me? Shoot it down—that is my mission as an interceptor pilot, after all. Then when an investigation team finds the debris of this nonexistent aircraft, you will have to explain why you could not locate such a large airborne object on your radar. Then we will see which one of us hangs. . . . Now patch me through to your superior. At once!"

There was a long pause before a chastened voice responded: "Wait one . . . I am patching you through to the Aerospace Defense Warning Centre."

DAY 5, 1330 HOURS ZULU
THE *INTREPID*

Iceberg watched the external temperature gauge start to inch up. His altitude was 400,000 feet above the earth, traveling at 16,500 mph, and the external tiles were beginning to warm up. He jettisoned the remaining fuel in the forward reaction control tanks to further improve the spacecraft's balance, then inflated his anti-g pressure suit and switched the pitch, yaw, and roll controls to AUTO. In five minutes he would be in the grip of the blackout, and until he took back manual control, the guidance of the spacecraft rested in the hands of the NavComputer and digital autopilot.

DAY 5, 1330 HOURS ZULU
THE KESTREL

Monaghan hit the switch, and the pylons which had held the Phoenix missiles in place on top of the wings were released. Lamborghini watched them drift up and away from the spacecraft, and felt the pressure inside his spacesuit increase.

"The outside is heating up," said Monaghan. "On the way down I'm gonna make the S-turns a little tighter than programmed so we can reel in Iceberg on the flip side of the blackout. We're not gonna have that much time to find him before we have to put down somewhere, so let's keep the radar warmed up."

"I'm with you, Mad Dog."